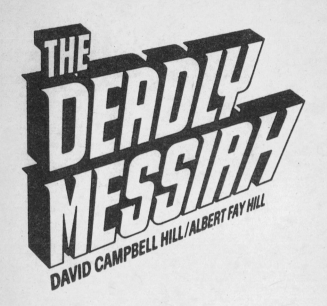

THE DEADLY MESSIAH

DAVID CAMPBELL HILL / ALBERT FAY HILL

 AVON
PUBLISHERS OF BARD, CAMELOT AND DISCUS BOOKS

AVON BOOKS
A division of
The Hearst Corporation
959 Eighth Avenue
New York, New York 10019

First Avon Printing, April, 1977

AVON TRADEMARK REG. U.S. PAT. OFF. AND IN
OTHER COUNTRIES, MARCA REGISTRADA,
HECHO EN U.S.A.

Printed in the U.S.A.

To Raggedy Ann

And what rough beast, its hour come round at last,
Slouches towards Bethlehem to be born?

The Second Coming
WILLIAM BUTLER YEATS

Acknowledgments

We want to thank a number of friends who gave us help and encouragement. In the beginning, Judy Chumlea, Mike Shimkin, Herb Alexander and Bob Gleason were kind and supportive. Gleason's continued enthusiasm was particularly important to us. We are indebted to Knox Burger and Bob Krepps for their invaluable help in teaching us so much about writing. We want to thank Kristin Hill, sister, daughter and friend, for her ideas and sharp criticism. Cydney, Geoffrey and Jim Hill also helped by asking so many questions about the book that they made us rethink ideas. Marge McKee labored mightily over the manuscript.

We are specially grateful to Dr. Paul Hamilton for his assistance in reading the manuscript and making suggestions about the medical aspects of the story—sometimes with an eyebrow cocked quizzically and a whimsical smile. Bonnie Hildreth and Cathy Wilson gave us important information on Kentucky and Judy Cole not only taught us more than we were able to absorb about astrology, but also inspired the character of Vera. Of course, the authors take all responsibility for errors—and for the freedom taken with reality!

Lastly, without Nancy, wife, editor, supporter, we couldn't have finished this book.

THE
DEADLY
MESSIAH

1

"WHERE IS EVERYBODY?"

Jess Barrett glanced across the seat at his brother and said, "This place is almost deserted."

Dr. Bob Barrett stopped his station wagon on the gravel parking lot at the golf course. The two doctors in the back seat immediately clambered out and opened the tailgate to get their clubs.

Nyland looked around. "It *is* just about empty. Good!"

Jess got out of the car and reached for his golf bag.

"Where are all the Shiloh professors, Jess?" asked Ken Fisher. "This place is always full of them as soon as the kids are gone. Didn't you have graduation last Saturday?"

"Yes. There must be a faculty meeting," said Jess.

"Why aren't you there, then?" asked Bill Nyland. "Given up teaching?"

"Just about, Bill. I'm doing mostly consulting now." Jess walked to the front of the car and looked at his brother, who had not moved from behind the wheel. "Bob? You all right?"

Dr. Barrett sighed. "I can hardly move. That flu I had a couple of weeks ago must be coming back." He got out, stretched, sank back onto the seat, and began slowly to change to his golf shoes.

Fisher looked at him in concern. "Man, you've been working too hard. Every night the lights are on in your office; you ought to take it easy."

"Bob, you're pale as ashes. Want me to take you home? Maybe you need a day in bed instead of exercise."

1

"No, Jess, thanks; I just need some fresh air." He stood up. "Let's go."

They all shouldered their clubs and walked to the little pro shop to sign up.

It wasn't much of a country club by metropolitan standards. The doctors and businessmen of three little Kentucky towns had joined together to build it. The clubhouse was only a tiny headquarters for the staff and a lunchroom opening onto a patio. There were no locker rooms or showers, no elegant ballrooms for fiftieth-wedding anniversaries and coming-out parties. Still, the business and professional people could meet there and drain off their tensions playing golf or swimming in the little natural pond.

At this early hour on the second of June, the few men in sight were golfers; and because it was Wednesday, most of them were doctors, following their own advice to get some exercise and firm up sagging muscles.

Jess and Bob Barrett, Ken Fisher, and Bill Nyland headed from the pro shop to the first tee. The four tried to get together every Wednesday for a casual round of golf. Nyland and Fisher were there regularly, but it was a rare week when both Barretts were present. Bob often worked on his day off, and Jess traveled frequently on his consulting business; he was an internationally known electronics expert.

The three doctors watched as Jess teed up. He was ten years younger than they, deeply tanned, six feet four, 230 pounds of well-toned muscle.

Bob was a sharp contrast, wholly lacking the glamour of his younger brother. He had a narrow, heavily lined face with lusterless, thin brown hair drifting across the forehead. Bob was a friendly man, unselfishly dedicated to his work, but he was serious and had little sense of humor.

The other two, Ken Fisher and Bill Nyland, made an amusing pair: the slender, bald, nervous Fisher and the phlegmatic Nyland, whose paunch threatened momentarily to burst out of control. Both were good-natured, decent men, but Fisher had a trigger temper.

2

Two businessmen from Bensonville came up to the tee.

"It's Wednesday again, and all the doctors are at play. Nobody in town better get sick today." Al Pastore, who ran the liquor store, snickered. He considered himself a wit.

His golf partner, Ed Voight, said wearily, "Be nice to these guys, Al. The way I feel, I'll need 'em before I finish the front nine."

Jess had lined up for his drive, and the others fell silent. His swing was smooth and powerful, and the ball flew straight down the fairway.

Fisher bent over to tee up as Al asked, "When'd you get back, Jess? Heard you were over in France telling the president how to run his country."

Jess said with patience, "Got back last night. I wasn't talking to politicians, Al, just trying to help debug their new radio telescope."

Fisher hit a long drive and stepped back from the tee. "Ed, you all right? You're as pale as Bob. Not getting sick on us, are you?"

"Damned if I know, Ken," said Voight.

Al Pastore said scornfully, "Nobody ever gets sick in Bensonville. That's the reason all the doctors came here. Nothing to do but deliver babies." His eyes shifted slyly to Jess. "Why'd *you* come, Jess? You could've gone anywhere." Al's brand of humor was visibly annoying the others, but Jess was unruffled.

"I grew up here. I thought you knew."

Al grimaced. "That's just what I mean. You should know better. Hell! You could go anywhere, do anything—Heisman Trophy winner, All-American, Rhodes scholar, Ph.D.! If you'd stayed at NASA, you'd be boss by now. Why stick in this burg?"

Jess had answered similar questions a hundred times. "Well, Al, I like it. I play a little golf and a lot of tennis, and I teach some at Shiloh, and I travel as widely as I like to solve interesting puzzles for people. Can you describe a more satisfactory life?"

Nyland, testier than usual, said, "Al, if you're through with your guidance counseling, I'll hit." He sliced his ball into the woods and swore, glancing malevolently at the talkative man.

Bob Barrett moved up and hit a feeble drive. Jess looked at his brother closely but said nothing. The foursome started down the fairway.

But Al would not quit, and before they could move out of earshot, he called, "Hey, now, Jess, *really*. What are you doing here?"

"I can't think of a nicer place. If *you* don't like it, why don't you leave?"

"Hell, where'd I go?" Then Al muttered under his breath, "I'll bet it's still Ginny who keeps him here."

Ed Voight, wiping cold sweat from his face, didn't answer.

They had played three holes before the interruption. The skinny boy with the long neck, who swept floors and gardened for the manager, came running across the course. He was out of breath, and his excitement caught Ken Fisher's attention first.

Ken's eyes crinkled as he watched the boy coming. More than the others, he hated to be interrupted on the course. An emotional man, Fisher was just as quick with his sympathy as he was with his temper, but he habitually tried to cover his emotions with a veneer of cynicism. Now he said, "Well, here it comes. I suppose he'll tell us the whole town is dying, and we really ought to give up our game."

The boy stopped in front of Bill Nyland, panting. "Sir, I know we ain't supposed to bother doctors on their day off, but we been gettin' calls all morning from your offices and the hospital. Now it's your wife, says it's really urgent."

"Myrtle?" Nyland's round face tightened. "It must be important. She never interrupts me out here." Bag in hand, he rushed to the clubhouse.

But Fisher paused to question the boy. "Son, you say our offices called? We don't want to be disturbed for every damn head cold when we're playing, but if something serious happens, we are to be called *immediately*."

4

"Sorry, sir. The manager ain't here, and we didn't know what to do. There were so many calls, then Dr. Nyland's wife——" The boy's Adam's apple ran up and down his throat.

Bob Barrett came slowly over to them. "You did the right thing, son. I was going to quit anyway. I feel awful."

His voice was so weak that Jess turned in alarm. Bob was sick white, leaning on his driver. Fisher and the boy headed quickly toward the clubhouse as Jess followed slowly with his brother.

Inside the pro shop, Nyland took the phone and listened grimly to his wife. He was still there, and Fisher was fidgeting anxiously when Jess and Bob walked in.

Against one wall of the little shop were cold-drink and food-dispensing machines. There were two tables and a few chairs. Bob sank into one of the chairs. Jess watched him, deeply concerned, but his voice was casual as he said, "Bob, when did Myrtle Nyland and Alma get back from New York?"

After a silence to gather strength or memory, the older brother said, "Why, uh, just a couple of hours before you, Jess. God, I'm sick! I think I'm going to throw up!"

Bill Nyland cradled the phone. He said between his teeth, "Something *crazy* is happening in town! Myrtle said my nurse has called five times. Patients are jamming the office; the hospital's desperate to find us. Now my own two kids are pale, almost in shock from the sound of it. Bob, Alma called Myrtle. Your oldest boy's sick, too. We'd better go quickly."

Ken Fisher snapped, "What can it be? Flu?"

"Whatever it is, I've got it, and it sure makes a guy sick," said Bob. He was sopping with perspiration.

Jess put an arm around his brother's waist and helped him to the car. The others picked up the golf bags and followed. Bob handed the keys to Jess and weakly crawled in back with Nyland.

As Jess swung toward the road, Al Pastore came running, shouting. "Hey, you guys! Ed's passed out;

he looks like hell. Jack Concannon's throwing up all over the second green. Can you come and help?"

Fisher said grimly, "Al, get some of the men to help you; bring them both to the hospital. Bob's sick, and there's some kind of serious emergency in town. We'll meet you there. Pass the word to every physician on the course, will you?"

Jess shot the wagon out onto the highway and headed toward Bensonville.

Suddenly Ken Fisher turned from the front seat and shouted, "My God, what is it? Look at Bob!"

Barrett had collapsed and was lying on the floor vomiting convulsively, his stark-white face twisted with pain. Nyland was trying to pull him out of the mess when the sick physician lost consciousness. His bowels and bladder discharged, and the wagon was filled with the stench of diarrhea.

Jess pushed the accelerator to the floor as Fisher leaned back to help Nyland tug and drag Barrett onto the seat, where they loosened his collar and wiped his face ineffectually. Nyland rummaged through the golf equipment in the back, found Bob's black medical bag, took out a stethoscope. He pressed it against the sick man's chest and tried to listen.

As they passed the entrance to the furniture factory at the edge of town, Fisher looked out in disbelief. The lot was filled with people, some milling around, others leaving in their cars.

"The plant's letting out! There's at least two men lying on the pavement and another heaving his guts out. We've got a bitch of an epidemic on our hands, Bill!"

The little brick-and-glass hospital was just ahead. A small mob crowded around the double front doors. As Jess braked to enter the lot, a woman carrying a screaming child ran in front of them.

Nyland yelled from the back seat, "Bob's heart stopped! Jess, Ken, get in there for a cardiac kit!"

Jess slammed to a stop, and Nyland pulled Barrett out onto the paved lot and quickly began to search through the medical bag for adrenalin. Jess bolted for the door, Ken Fisher close behind, trying to push their way through the crowd. "Let us through, please! Let us through!"

But the people were sick and frantic and paid little attention, so Jess had to clear a path roughly, bulling in until they reached the nurses' station at the emergency room. A nurse was trying to help an old man who'd collapsed in a chair.

Fisher cried, "Nurse! Cardiac kit! Dr. Barrett's had an arrest!"

The nurse turned from the old man, her eyes feverish; she plainly had trouble focusing on the problem. "Dr. Thomas took it a minute ago for an arrest in Room eleven."

A woman in the corridor screamed, "Help me! Help me! He's dying!"

The urgent up-and-down welp of the town's ambulance added to a growing cacophony of groans, shouts, and pleas. Jess shoved his way violently back through the crowd and into the hall, jerking open the door to Room 11. Inside was a middle-aged man in overalls lying on the bed, staring sightlessly, toothless mouth open. A thin woman sat on the bed beside him, sobbing as she leaned against the dead man.

Jess said, "Where's Dr. Thomas?" The woman continued to sob, and Jess shook her by the shoulders. *"Where is Dr. Thomas?"*

Tears ran down her lined face. She whimpered, "He's dead, my husband's dead, an' he warn't even sick."

Jess rushed into the hall again, crying, "Dr. Thomas, Dr. Thomas!" But the hall was crammed with sick people overflowing from the emergency room, and he had to fight his way through more ruthlessly than before. He slipped on vomit and all but fell as he made his way down the hall.

Ken Fisher came out of a room at the end of the hall and shouted, "Jess! I have it; help me get outside."

Jess shoved and lifted people, clearing the way. Once he moved a corpulent teen-ager who shrieked when the big hands touched him. Jess saw that his whole shoulder was cherry red around an ulcerous center. Jess involuntarily paused in horror, and Ken shot out through the door and onto the lot, pulling the cart. Muttering a shamed apology to the frightened, weeping boy, Jess dashed after his friend.

He found Bill Nyland kneeling over Bob. Ken Fisher looked helplessly at the electrodes in his hands and then up at Jess and said, "He's gone. Bill says he never responded to adrenalin or massage. Bob's gone."

Jess scowled, for a moment uncomprehending. "He can't be dead. He was fine just last night when I called about our game today." His mouth worked soundlessly. The pain of slow awareness paralyzed him as he stared at the body of his brother.

Nyland was shaking his head; tears filled his eyes. "He was such a conscientious bastard. Couldn't stop working—goddamnit!"

Then a woman recognized Fisher, ran to him, clutched his arm, whined pathetically, "Doctor, help me! Marvin's dying. Look at him!"

Dr. Fisher shook his bald head and stared numbly at the woman, then at the little boy on the pavement. The child was unconscious, pallid, covered with sweat.

"Look at him! Oh, Doctor, please help me. He's dying."

Fisher came out of shock, picked up the boy, and fought his way through the crowd into the hospital, down the corridor to an empty room. At the door, one of his patients, Mrs. Eggert, clutched at him.

"Dokker, Dokker, heh me! An cahn bree!" Her face was beet red.

He pulled away. "I'll be right with you, but I've got to help this child."

As Fisher laid the little boy on the bed, the mother came in and stood hesitantly behind him. He saw that treatment was impossible. The child was coma-tose and within seconds would be gone. He put his hand on the mother's shoulder in helpless consolation and found her skin fiercely feverish. He glanced around for a thermometer. There was none.

He patted her again and murmured, "Mrs. Taves, your boy is gone. But you're sick, too, and I want you to rest here while I get some help. I'll be back as soon as I can."

She was sobbing as he slipped outside.

Immediately ten, twenty people crowded around him, with eyes burning and faint or hysterical voices asking for help. He searched for Mrs. Eggert, saw her sitting against the opposite wall, and pushed through the people around him. Her skirt was around her hips, and she had ripped open her blouse trying to get more air. Her fat face lolled to one side, and she was unconscious. She began to turn blue, and he tipped her head to look inside her throat. He had already seen her once that week for a mild case of tonsillitis, but he was not prepared for what he saw now. The tissue had swollen closed, and she was struggling vainly for breath.

He swore violently and cried out, "Nurse! Scapel! Tracheotomy here—"

Even as he called, he realized that it was useless, that nobody could possibly hear him above the screaming, wheezing, groaning, wailing racket. Frantic, he groped for a pocketknife, a fingernail file, anything sharp. Sick people were begging him to help or to feel the foreheads of their children.

A huge young farmer in overalls burst through the group roaring, "You a doctor, ain't you? Come look at Mildred. She's in terrible shape."

"I can't till I help this woman," Fisher yelled. "Help me find a knife."

"Her? Doctor, she's dead already. Mildred is still alive."

"Dead. She can't be. I just—"

He turned back to Mrs. Eggert, put his ear to her chest. Nothing. It wasn't possible, but the farmer was right—she was dead.

In a nightmare daze, he staggered after the young man, who cleared their way through the crowd. As they fought through and down the corridor, the farmer bellowed, "What the goddamn hell *is* this thing, Doc? Mildred and me come to town Wednesdays to get our supplies. When we left home this morning she was fine, but look at her now! Mildred!"

The man lunged forward and knelt beside an unconscious young woman lying on the floor, blood-streaked sputum dripping from her mouth. A thin woman dressed in pink slacks and a flowered blouse. Probably pretty. Like so many farm girls, she had left her hair up in curlers, intending to take them out just before entering the town. Now they made her look even more grotesque.

The big farmer held her in his arms, sobbing. "Oh, Mildred! What's happened to you?"

Fisher tore him away and quickly examined the woman, listening to her breathing as well as he could without a stethoscope.

"She ever have tuberculosis?"

"She had a spot on one lung a couple of years ago, but she's s'posed to be O.K. now, Doc."

"Well, she's got it back and is hemorrhaging. She's in shock. Let's get her to a bed."

The huge man lifted his wife, and together they pushed through the crowd. Fisher's bald head bobbed like a cork in the sea of people as he disappeared down the hall.

Bill Nyland was sick with concern for his own two boys. His eyes searched the milling crowd for his wife Myrtle as he looked up from Bob's body. He saw her nowhere. For a second he was tempted to go home; then the years of discipline made him turn back to the sick people around him.

Almost instantly he was swept away. They clutched at him and screamed in his face, pulling him back and forth till he fought them off and rammed through the outside entrance to the emergency room. A nurse, backed into a corner by a frantic knot of men and women, was valiantly trying to stay calm and move them out of the small room.

"Irma, what the hell is going on here? What *is* this thing?"

When the nurse saw him, she dropped her arms and burst into tears.

"Irma! Pull yourself together! What is this thing? Answer me!" Nyland knew that it was a desperately stupid question. He was really asking it of God.

"Doctor, I don't know *what* it is—I mean it's not any *one* thing. It's just crazy. It's acute ulcerations and infections and flu and—" Her voice, usually hard and penetrating as a star drill, was weak and quivering. She began gulping and sobbing. He realized that it was more than emotion causing her collapse; Irma was very ill herself. He put an arm around her, pulled her into one of the little examining rooms, and helped her gently onto the table. She was pale—everyone in town is pale, he thought—and sweat was soaking her uniform. He covered her with a sheet.

"Irma, stay here and rest while I try to get some order into the mess. Do you know where Dr. Thomas is? He's still on duty this morning, isn't he?"

She had closed her eyes. She whispered weakly, "Doctor, whatever this awful thing is, I've got it. I'm sorry but—" Her voice trailed off.

"Irma, please try to tell me where Dr. Thomas is."

She couldn't answer. He straightened up and stared for a moment at her, then returned to the boiling mass of people.

Two other nurses had fought their way into the emergency room and were trying to shove people back into the hall so they'd have room enough to work. Outside, a police car arrived with siren wailing, and from the downtown area, the ambulance could be heard on another run.

"Let me through! Please! Let me through! I've got to get into the emergency room if I'm to help you. Please! Let me through!"

This was Brad Thomas, the new young resident from Tennessee. Finally he managed to join Nyland. He was a tall, lanky man, too stooped for his age,

11

his face perpetually set in a mask that he thought expressive of concern but that others saw as one of smug self-satisfaction.

The older man shouted, "Where the hell have you been?"

"Don't you yell at me, Doctor. It's my first day back from vacation, and in the last three hours I had nine cardiac arrests and lost every one of them. I tried to do an emergency appendectomy and lost *him*. And I tried to reach you the entire damn morning."

A black nurse stepped between them. "Stop it, you two! The whole town's dying, and you fight. Cut it out!" She was close to hysteria herself. Nyland felt her forehead. It was burning with fever.

"Brad, help me. This girl's got the bug, too."

Dr. Thomas reached out, but she pushed him away. "I'm all right. We've got to do something for these people. They're panicking. Can't we get them lined up and treat them systematically? Can't we—"

Before she finished the sentence, she began to cry and staggered into their arms. They carried her into the examining room where Irma lay unconscious, gently helped her to lie on the floor. As she closed her eyes, Nyland said, "Now, Brad, let's get this place organized."

When Doctors Thomas and Nyland finally opened the doors to the shrieking, contaminated, terrified mob outside, they were as ready as they could be. A single nurse was still with them. Trays of medicines were laid out beside the examining tables, and so far as they could control the press, they let patients in only one at a time or in family groups.

One of the first was the wife of the town librarian. She was holding a crying infant and was staggering herself. She said what everyone was saying over and over. "Oh, Doctor, please do something." She was not only sick but hysterical with grief and fear. Brad's flesh crawled as he took the little body into his arms. The boy had had a mild case of conjunctivitis three days before; now the scarlet inflammation had spread over his entire face, and his eyes were swollen closed and oozing pus. Thomas laid the child down on the table and tried to examine him; but the moment his fingers touched the baby's face, a screech convinced him that an exam would not be useful or even possible. He had the nurse prepare a hypodermic with a massive dose of penicillin, and as she stuck it into the child's bottom, Thomas turned to the mother.

"This ought to help. But you're sick, too."

"Yes, Doctor! I'm *so* sick! What's happening to our town?"

He patted her on the shoulder. "Sometimes a bug will go around and cause an epidemic, but I'm sure we'll get this one under control." To himself he added, I hope to hell.

Ken Fisher pounded on the door of the emergency room until they recognized his voice and let him in. Soon he was caught up in their work, ordering ampicillin for a woman with a leg ulcer that had spread and deepened to expose the bone, giving a prescription to a patient with hemorrhagic cystitis, treating hepatitis, bladder infections, rubella.

They admitted a man whose lingering staph infection had gone berserk. The man was delirious and could only be induced to lie on the table after some rough handling. The nurse got a thermometer into his mouth, and they gaped in disbelief when the mercury hit an impossible 107°. A child died in convulsions in Dr. Fisher's arms as her father sobbed that a simple ear inflammation had been transformed overnight into the massive infection that had killed her.

Dr. Nyland treated old Mrs. Heath. For years Grandma Heath had confounded the doctors with her survival. She had been given up as a hopeless case many years before, but her cancer of the colon had not progressed, and she had lived on and on. She and the cancer had become adjusted to each other, had worked out a sort of truce. So he was shocked to see her that morning. Mrs. Heath was unconscious and as white as the dress of the nurse who cradled her old

13

head in her arms. There was really nothing Nyland could do.

Nor was that the only case of cancer. Little Ted Farney, who lived with a regressed case of leukemia, collapsed and was brought to the hospital unconscious. John Helfer had seemed to have recovered from his cancer of the prostate. But when Ken Fisher treated him that morning, or rather when he tried to treat him, he was suffering from an advanced case of metastatic cancer. Both he and Ted Farney died within an hour after being brought to the hospital.

It was the boy with acne who made Fisher finally realize that they had to have help. He was thirteen years old and the son of George Hinton, vice-president of the furniture factory. Dick Hinton had a horror of acne because of his father's scarred face. When the inevitable teen-age pimples began to appear, he became overwrought, almost paranoid, and spent hours inspecting himself in the mirror and washing his face with medicated soap. Whenever anyone looked at him for more than a second, Dick was sure they were staring at his slightly acned face. That morning when his father broke through the crowd at the door and staggered into the emergency room with Dick in his arms, Fisher not only gasped, he almost screamed in horror, a thing that as a physician he had never come close to doing before. The child's features were a mass of pus and blood. His lips were like balloons, and even his ears bled. His face and body were saturated with bulbous, infectious acne.

"Ken, look at him! Help me, for God's sake! I've been trying to get you ever since I woke up this morning and found him like this. Please *do* something!"

Fisher took the boy from his father and laid him on the table. Dick and his own son were best friends and spent hours together swimming in the pond at the club and searching among the cattails on the far bank for crawdads and frogs.

He unbuttoned the boy's jeans and pulled down his underwear. Even his lower body and upper legs were

14

covered with the hideous sores. He quickly gave the boy a shot of penicillin, not because he thought it would do much good, but because he had to do something.

Suddenly Fisher threw back his head and gave a terrible, obscene cry. He pounded his fists on the wall and cursed at the top of his voice. Over the babel, Nyland heard it and came running.

"Ken! Snap out of it!"

"Damn! Damn! What's happening here? Look at these people, not a goddamned thing we do makes any difference! They just die and die and die! We have to pull in help from somewhere. Why in God's name haven't we sent for somebody? We haven't saved *one single soul,* and we still stand here, sticking needles into moribund bodies. Why haven't we sent for"—he choked, and his speech began to garble as his thoughts floundered—"for the National Guard and the Mayo Clinic and the m-marines and some *doctors?*"

Nyland put an arm around his friend's shoulders and said, "You're right, Ken, this is a lot worse than we could've dreamed. We need help. We've got to call the hospital in Chalmers and have Jack Hughes bring medicine, ambulances, and men to help us. Why don't you make that call?"

"My God, what'll I tell him? That people are dying from chicken pox and ear infections and—and *acne?* What *is* this? Is the whole town rotting away? Have the plagues of the Middle Ages come back?"

"Looks like it. I'll do what I can, but you try to get some help for us."

"I'll get it. God, Bill," said Fisher pathetically, "I don't even know about my own wife and kids. They may be out there in that madhouse. I haven't had a chance to call home. And didn't Myrtle tell you that your boys were—"

Nyland turned away. He said, "She was going to bring them here. If you see them in that mob, will you—" and then his voice broke, and he moved blindly back to his patients.

The telephone switchboard was a wall of blinking

lights and sounding buzzers. Operator Lois DeVaux had worked until her own head swam with fever. When the sweat and the bad chills came, she had fainted and now lay on the floor unconscious.

Unable to do anything for her, Ken Fisher numbly groped his way back through the crowd in the corridor.

"Bill, I'll have to make it to an outside phone. Lois has been hit, too."

From the window he could see a constantly swelling mass of patients crying for treatment and hammering on the outside door of the emergency room. The ambulance came screaming, careering into the parking lot again, depositing patients on the lawn. He hesitated for a moment, then opened the window and climbed out.

He had barely landed on the grass when a woman screamed, "Dr. Fisher's running away. Stop him!"

Instantly he was surrounded by desperate people shrieking imprecations and begging for help. He couldn't move. The long-held tears began to run down his sweating face.

2

GINNY MASON LOWELL had hoped to sleep late that morning. Harvey was out of town on one of his long sales trips, and the two older boys were home from Bloom Military Academy. Two-year-old Dennis had been restless the night before, and she was sure he would sleep late. She needed some rest. Her neurodermatitis was so much worse when she was tense and anxious. It was the older boys who wakened her by pounding on the bedroom door.

"Mother, wake up. Dennis is being sick all over himself. Please wake up!"

She struggled out of sleep, feeling as if she were buried in a mass of cotton, swimming against the strands. Painfully she sat up, opened her eyes, tried to get her bearings, and muttered, "Come in, come in, John."

But she could hardly see the boys who entered her room. Her eyes were swollen almost shut. John only stood there looking at her in horror. It was the other boy who screamed.

"Mommy! Mommy! What's happened to you?"

"Tommy! What's the matter?"

Her voice was thick and her words almost unintelligible. She put her hands to her face, then jerked them away in horror. Instead of the familiar contours, she had touched some horrifying mass of irregular tissue. In disbelief she stared at her hands. They were covered with blood. Numbly she looked at her pillow; it was sticky and red. Again she felt her face, clasping it, trying to fathom what had happened to her. This time she screamed. Something had ravaged her

17

face, had swollen it out of proportion and peeled away the skin and dried it, letting it crack and bleed. As she screamed, her head exploded with agony, and her two boys began to cry in terror.

She threw back the bedclothes, staggered uncertainly to her feet and into the bedroom where her two-year-old lay in his crib. As she passed Tommy, she patted him reassuringly on the shoulder, muttering that she would be all right. Her hand left a bloody print on his pajamas.

Dennis was lying unconscious in a pool of vomit, his face crimson. When her hand touched his forehead, she recoiled. The child had a fever such as she had never known before. Quickly she gathered him into her arms and groped her way to the bathroom, reaching weakly for a cloth to soak in cool water. She passed the mirror, the blurred vision of her own face drained what strength she had left, and she fainted, sliding down the wall with the feverish child held tightly in her arms.

John and Tommy followed her, crying, terrified by the sight of their mother. Tommy flung himself on her, screaming, sobbing, begging her to waken. The other boy turned and dashed out the front door, heading for the hospital a mile and a half away, running blindly. When the sunlight hit his eyes, John blinked, shut them involuntarily, and stumbled into the path of an auto taking the corner on two wheels. He jumped back just in time to avoid being hit. Another car came toward him, and he waved frantically for help, but the distraught driver sped past. He went on toward the hospital. Soon his heart was pounding, and his breath came in agonizing gasps.

Again and again cars swept past the desperate child. Some were headed toward the hospital; others were filled with panicked families trying to get out of the stricken town. So urgent was their own need that they paid no attention to his frantic gestures. Then he met Jess Barrett.

Jess had helped the attendant carry his brother's

body to the hearse. He sat in the front seat with the chattering driver.

As the fat little man maneuvered the black Cadillac around cars stopped in the middle of the street and past groups of people standing frightened and bewildered on corners, he said, "What's goin' on? Sixth call I've had this morning. All those people at the hospital. Something wrong. I think it's some kind of epidemic, don't you? This job is dangerous enough as it is. I don't want to get involved if—".

He paused as a farm pickup shot past him, a wild-eyed woman at the wheel. "I knew a guy once got typhoid from handlin' corpses. Terrible. You got no idea what a dangerous job this is. If we are in some sort of epidemic, I'm gettin' out of town."

At the mortuary, Jess cursed himself for having left the station wagon at the hospital. Still shaken, he dreaded taking the news about Bob to Alma and their three children. It was almost two miles to his brother's new ranch-style home on the outskirts of town.

He phoned for a cab, but the dispatcher, Ruth Bianci, said, "Oh, *hell,* Jess! I've got three drivers home and the other two on calls. I go on vacation for a couple of weeks; when I get back I find the whole goddamn town sick. What the hell is it, anyway, Jess? Bill told me that some folks have even died."

Jess softly agreed that the outbreak of disease was serious and hung up. He was just leaving the mortuary to walk back for Bob's wagon when he met young John Lowell.

In high school Jess Barrett and Ginny Mason had been inseparable. She was a pretty, shy, and sensitive girl. Her father was the Baptist minister, and her mother was a tired schoolteacher working to supplement her husband's small income. Jess and Ginny went steady from the time they were freshmen until the end of their senior year.

Yet as his abilities developed, she seemed to with-

19

draw from him, frightened perhaps by the sheer magnitude of his future.

The entire town had been jolted when its All-State fullback and honor student saw his girl suddenly marry Harvey Lowell the summer following graduation. Harvey was another Bensonville native who had often tried and failed to date Ginny. He was a charming, wild young fellow whose parents sent him to a military academy to learn discipline. When Ginny had retreated from Jess in awe, she'd fallen straight into Harvey's arms.

By the time Jess had been voted All-American for the third time and received the Heisman Trophy, she had two children. That Christmas, when he came home to Bensonville from Northwestern for the holidays, Jess attended services at the Baptist church. Everyone there noted that he was alone and that he tried and failed to keep his eyes off Ginny Lowell. She was at the service, alone as usual, and afterward she and Jess stood talking for a long time.

The next day the little town buzzed with speculation that Ginny and Harvey would break up. And once more people wondered and shook their heads over what had made her turn down Bensonville's superstar for a man who clearly would never amount to anything, who was already drinking too much. Ginny seemed to grow more frail each year, but she remained a faithful wife.

When Jess met her son John the morning of the catastrophe the child was hysterical and sobbing, his thin legs pumping as though he were a baby again, trying to run. Jess caught him up in his arms, "John, what is it? What's the trouble?"

"Mommy, Mommy!"

Holding him, Jess raced to the Lowell house. As he opened the door, the stench of vomit made him blink, and his nostrils pinched together protectively.

"Ginny? Ginny? Where are you?"

The house was deathly quiet. He dropped John gently on the couch and looked into the kitchen, then

20

the bedroom, saw the bloody pillow, and turned down the hall to the bathroom. When he peered in he gave a ghastly, inarticulate cry. Ginny Lowell was half lying, half sitting on the floor, her face an unrecognizable pulp, her nightgown soaked in blood. She was barely breathing, and the two-year-old was dead in her arms. Tommy sat on the edge of the tub, his eyes staring in hypnotized terror.

Jess bent over and took Ginny's hand, spoke to her, tried to rouse her. She moved her head slightly, and one eye looked at him through puffed lids.

She whispered, "Jess! Oh, God! Jess!" And she was dead.

He stood up, his throat constricting. He looked at Tommy, now almost catatonic with fear, and at the pathetic woman and baby, and he smashed his fist into the plasterboard wall.

"Goddamnit! *Goddamnit!*"

He struck the wall again, and it crumpled, dust boiling out into the air. Then he got hold of himself and looked at Tommy, still mute. He bent and tenderly picked up the distorted corpse of the young mother, carried her into a bedroom and laid her on the bed. Then he brought in the body of Dennis, laid him beside her, and pulled the sheet up over both of them.

He carried Tommy from the bathroom into the hall, where he saw Ginny's purse. He searched through it until he found the keys to her station wagon. Then he grabbed John with his other hand and carried both boys outside to the car. Putting them in front with him, he drove to Bob and Alma's house.

As Jess came up the driveway, Alma opened the door and ran toward the car, then stopped when she saw that he was driving the Lowell wagon and had Ginny's boys beside him, her gray eyes widening in bewilderment and fear. Tommy was still mute with shock; John was limp and crying silently. Jess got them out of the car somehow, trying not to look at Alma.

All the way to her house, he had groped frantically for a way to tell her about Bob's death. Fury at the plague, grief at the loss of both Ginny and Bob, concern for Alma, anxiety over the Lowell boys were tangled in his mind.

By now he knew that he had to be softly but bluntly honest with her—and that he had to return to town as quickly as possible to help in whatever way he could.

He patted the boys on the shoulder and gently told them to go into the house and find E.J. and Susie. They walked through the open door, small, obedient robots.

Jess turned to the slender woman. He looked at her straight, saw the questions her direct, frightened eyes were asking. Her chin quivered for a moment and then tightened.

"Alma, I have some news. It's about Bob."

"Yes," she said.

"Bob was sick, very sick when we left the club, and on the way into town, he passed out. By the time we got to the hospital, he—damn it, Alma, his heart stopped. We did everything we could, but he's gone."

Alma stared at him and said nothing. Her eyes filled with tears. "Are there others who have died, Jess? You have Ginny's boys here."

"Yes, there must have been fifteen or twenty dead in the hospital when I was there. And the hearse driver told me he'd made six calls in other parts of town."

"And Ginny?"

"I was on my way here when I met John. I went home with him and found Tommy. Dennis was already dead. Ginny died while I was there." He took her hand. "We heard that Rob's sick?" He'd forgotten that till now.

"He's terribly ill, Jess. Myrtle told me her boys were, too, and that she'd call you men at the club. What about Bill and Ken?"

"The last time I saw them, they were O.K. Let me take Rob to the hospital."

"I'll go with you. I can't stand to stay here now."

"No! This thing is incredibly contagious."

"But I'm a nurse, Jess. I *must* go and help."

"How are Susie and E.J.?"

She said, distracted by the muddle of grievous news, "Rob woke up this morning with a headache, and now he's so sick that it—oh, Jess, I'm *scared!* But the two little ones seem all right."

"Then you've got to stay here with them. I'll take Rob; you stay with E.J. and Susie and Ginny's boys. If I find other kids that need care but aren't sick, I'll bring 'em here. This town needs you healthy. I'll call about Rob as soon as I can."

They went into the house to get the teen-ager. Jess picked him up and carried him out and down the walk. He put Rob in the front seat, and Alma patted the boy, who looked so like his father, stroked his forehead, and closed the wagon's door. Jess drove directly to the hospital.

Ken Fisher was surrounded by feverish and frightened people when Jess drove up with Rob. He gently laid the boy on the lawn next to Fisher.

The doctor looked at his friend with relief. "God, Jess, I'm glad to see you! Help me move these people inside. Then get to a phone. We can't call from here —Lois is dead—and we've got to have some help. Everything's getting worse. We're running out of antibiotics. We're on the verge of a riot."

"I'll do anything I can, Ken. There are sick and dead people all over town."

Ken briskly brought him up to date and instructed him to call Dr. Jack Hughes at Chalmers and tell him to send ambulances, every other doctor he could round up, antibiotics, bandages. They could set up emergency rooms in the schools. There was also Dr. Jim Andrews at the medical school in Louisville; he could ship in the same sort of aid.

"Ken, shouldn't you break away long enough to make those calls? I'm not a physician, and I don't know what to tell them."

Fisher exploded in frustration. "*You* don't know what to tell them? My God, neither do I! It's chicken pox and pneumonia and impetigo and colds—all gone wild and killing people! We shoot 'em full of antibiotics, and they die before we can turn around. Go make those calls, Jess. You have more influence than Bill or I, anyway."

Jess helped carry Rob and two others into the emergency room, again forcing a way through knot after knot of panicky people. Then he ran down the street to the phone booth outside the gas station. Quickly he looked up the number, dialed, asked to speak to Dr. Hughes immediately.

"Dr. Hughes is with a patient now. May I take your number, and I will have him call back. He should be free about five this afternoon." The nurse had been well trained.

"You tell Jack Hughes this is Jess Barrett, and that Bensonville is in the middle of a runaway epidemic. He's got to get off his butt and over here right away."

"Dr. Hughes does not like to be disturbed when he is with a patient. I'll call him to the phone as soon as he is free."

"Nurse, this is no joke. It's a disaster call!"

She put him on hold. Jess waited, fidgeting. Finally Hughes came on the line. "Jess! What's this about a disaster?"

"Jack, it's pure hell." Briefly he outlined the situation and what they needed.

Hughes said, his voice muted, "You have three of the best doctors in Kentucky right there in Bensonville."

"Only two now, Jack. Bob died this morning."

"My God, Jess! I'm sorry! This is unbelievable. I'll be there in an hour."

The next call Jess made was to Dr. Andrews, dean of the medical center in Louisville. It took minutes of shouting at a telephone operator before he came on the line.

"Dr. Andrews? This is Jess Barrett in Bensonville. I'm calling for Dr. Fisher and Dr. Nyland. We have an emergency here beyond belief. Hundreds of our people are sick; at least fifty or sixty have died

24

within the last three hours. I've called other doctors in the towns around us, but we've got to have more help than they can bring. Fisher told me to ask you for disaster help." Then as quickly as he could, he described the symptoms.

For a moment there was silence, and then Andrews asked, "Is this *the* Jess Barrett, the football player?"

Jess gritted his teeth. "It was fifteen years ago. Yes."

"Well, Barrett, you may be a fine fullback, but you're a lousy reporter. What you describe is absolutely impossible. If there's a real problem there, have Nyland or Fisher call me personally."

"I tell you they *can't* call; they can't get away from the hospital!"

"Have one of them call from the hospital, then."

"The switchboard operator is dead."

"Well, I'm not going to swallow a story like this one without corroboration from a physician. Frankly, I think you're drunk. Good-bye, Barrett."

The telephone went dead in Jess's hand. He swore violently and slammed it back on the cradle. Shoving in more coins, he redialed Andrews's number. When he'd penetrated the screen of secretaries and receptionists again and had Andrews on the line, he lifted his voice to a roar.

"Dr. Andrews, this is Jess Barrett. Either you listen to me and get off your ass and *act,* or by God I'll call Walter Cartwright and tell him his med school has refused to help in one of the worst disasters in the history of this country! I'll have your office crammed with the state police! What's *wrong* with you?"

There was a pause; then Andrews spoke cautiously. "Is this *really* Jess Barrett? I thought surely it was some drunk, a crank. Can you amplify the problem a little for me?"

Jess briefly repeated the incidents of the morning: the deaths, the illness, the people fleeing town, the ordinary diseases gone wild.

Andrews asked soberly, "Mr. Barrett, do you think it could be mass hysteria?"

It took iron restraint to stay calm, but Jess said, "Dr. Andrews, it wasn't mass hysteria that killed my brother. It didn't destroy Ginny Lowell's face and kill her son. Hysteria doesn't produce blood and pus and death in minutes; even I know that. Something's gone wrong with—with *nature* here. For God's sake get us some help right away."

Jess hung up and called Mayor James McDonald, who was away on vacation. The mayor was owner of the furniture factory and the radio station, and was one of the richest men in the Commonwealth of Kentucky. He spent most of the summer at his favorite resort, Cool Hills, 150 miles away. Jess got him there and told him what was happening.

"Dead?" McDonald gasped. "Dead, you say? That many? Listen, I'll be there soon's I can charter a plane or—hell, it'll take less time to drive my car. Be a couple of hours at least, but I'm on my way."

"Jim? Why don't you leave Marilu and the kids there? This thing has to be contagious."

"Jess, Marilu isn't here. She's been in Bensonville getting the kids ready for camp. I hope they're all right." He cleared his throat and went on huskily, "Don't you think I better call the governor, get him to send the National Guard to cordon off the town, stop people from leaving? They could be spreading the disease all over the state."

"Yes, do that, Jim. And have him notify the Red Cross."

"Right. Do what you can till I get there."

Jess dialed Bill Nyland's house. After a while he reluctantly hung up and called the Fishers'. Again there was no answer.

Jess went back to the little hospital to discover that the nightmare had grown worse. The stench was unbearable. Bodies were lying outside, on the lawn, and in parking lots, and many of the sick sat beside them, too weak to move. Jess found Fisher and Nyland in the emergency room, reported on his calls and his inability to contact their families. The two doctors looked at each other in bewildered sorrow.

"Ken—how's Rob?"

Fisher shook his head sadly.

"I'm useless here," said Jess. "I'll go call Alma and see if I can find Myrtle and the boys. I'll look for Pat and your kids, too, Ken."

He left the haggard men working furiously over their dying patients and fought his way back outside. Angrily he slammed the door of Ginny's car. Away from the hospital, he sucked down great lungfuls of clean air. Stopping at a phone booth, he dialed Alma's number and told her as gently as possible that Rob was gone, too. He could hear her throat catch, visualized her struggle to keep from breaking down. "Dammit, Alma, the world's gone crazy! How're the other kids?"

"They're all right so far. I'm watching them, but they seem to be O.K. Ginny's, too. But, Jess, don't they need me there?"

"You've got to stay where you are! Those children need you."

Reluctantly she agreed with him.

"Alma, any idea where I can find Myrtle Nyland or Pat Fisher?"

"Pat was going to take her kids on a picnic, but I don't know where. Myrtle should be at home. She told me—on the way back from New York she said—that she was going to spend the day cleaning house and baking, but now with her boys sick—"

"Thanks. I'll see if I can find them. I'll call or come by later. *Stay there.*"

He drove to Fisher's house but found no one. At the Nylands' he walked straight in, calling for Myrtle. When no one answered, he went through the house. In Dicky's bedroom was a pool of vomit, congealing on the pillow.

As he drove back through town, Jess saw frightened families fleeing to the country and sick people slouching or lying on curbs, park benches, front porches. Cars, stopped when their drivers became too nauseated to drive, were abandoned. Steve Ross's big

27

Buick was tilted up against a tree. Ross lay across the steering wheel, his face covered with blood, his eyes open. Jess saw that he was dead.

When he reached the hospital again, Jess met four ambulances just arriving from neighboring towns, red lights flashing and sirens wailing on a single tone or whooping in a welp. He flagged them down before they could enter the driveway, got out to talk to the doctors. Hughes was the first to reach him.

"God, I'm glad to see you, Jack."

Hughes's eyes were wide with shock and horror. "I've never seen anything like this. Dead and dying people everywhere."

"Jack, Ken suggests you set up one center at the elementary school and one at the junior high. I'll collect some guys, and we'll get patients to you as fast as we can. As soon as you've unloaded and set up, have your drivers go through the town to pick up anybody who's unconscious or too weak to move."

Hughes nodded, and the caravan of ambulances followed Jess to the elementary school. The doors were locked. Jess smashed a window, climbed in, and opened the doors. While three doctors set up rooms for treatment, Jess led the other two to the junior high. Within half an hour he was making trips from the hospital, carrying some of the sick who'd congregated there to the schools.

It was in the middle of the frantic throng at the hospital that he finally found Myrtle Nyland and her boys. Both of the children were ashen, covered with cold perspiration, and unconscious. Myrtle was frantic. She had tried to get inside the hospital but had been unable to jam a way through the crowd. Jess scooped the boys up in his arms and carried them to the station wagon. With Myrtle beside him, he drove quickly to the elementary school. Jess carried one boy in, then the other, knowing that the second was already dead. The first died even as the doctor examined him.

Jess never found Pat Fisher and her children. It was much later that her car was discovered in the woods. A hundred yards away were the bodies of the once-lovely young woman and her three children, huddled together as though they had been facing some tangible enemy.

At the junior high, Jess was helping an orderly lift a young woman out of an ambulance when he saw Mayor McDonald's Lincoln Continental speed into town, its siren screaming. The huge car rocked to a halt beside Jess. McDonald got out, looking disheveled and distraught, his hair like a tangled clump of thick black steel wool. His summer tan could not hide the lines of worry, and the crow's-feet around his eyes were deeper than usual.

He squinted at Jess. "What the hell *is* this goddamned blight, Jess? They find out yet? I stopped three times to call Marilu, but nobody answered. Have you seen her? Is she sick?"

Jess shook his head. "I haven't seen her, Jim. But I think almost everybody is sick. There's only one nurse left in the hospital who's healthy, and it's chaos over there."

For an instant, only a breath of time, the question flicked across Jess's mind: When do I catch it? When do *I* vomit and bleed and die? Then he shut out the thought. Can't waste energy worrying about that.

McDonald was staring around at the sick and the dead and shouting, "Why do you have them here? In God's name, is the hospital *that* crowded?"

"Afraid so," Jess answered. "Ambulances are working between here and the hospital, picking up people on the street, but I think you'd better get some men together and start searching homes."

"Yeah, I will, Jess, but first I've got to find Marilu. She might be sick, too. And I've got to call the camp and see if the children are O.K." Tucking his shirt around his paunch, the mayor returned to his Continental and drove off.

All that afternoon, Jess ferried people to the schools. Once, as he neared the downtown area, he saw an ambulance from the little hospital in Chalmers slowly driving up the street. The driver was peering out at the sick people he saw everywhere. Suddenly he made a swift U-turn in the middle of the street, tires screaming, accelerated, and drove off in the direction of Chalmers.

Jess swore and went after him. When he came abreast of the ambulance, he gave a wrench to the wheel of his wagon, forced the ambulance to the side of the road, jumped out, and jerked open the driver's door. They were just within the border of Stover's Woods.

"You coward! Aim this back to Bensonville, or I'll wring your neck."

The small driver stared at him with a curious expression: neither terror nor disgust, but some emotion that Jess could not read. "Leave me alone. I'm not going back there. The whole town is dying," he said levelly.

With one huge hand, Jess grabbed the little man, pulled him halfway out, slapped him hard, shoved him back into the driver's seat. "Drive to the hospital! You're not going to run out on all those people."

The young man shrank away, but his eyes flamed with cunning. Suddenly he flung open the opposite door, rolled out, and dashed away. He fled across an open space and into a clump of trees, where a light reflected briefly from something, a discarded piece of metal or glass, making Jess blink; then the boughs flailed back into place, and the fellow was gone. Jess was sorry that he'd hit him. The man must have gone mad with the grisly horror of the dead and dying multitudes.

Jess climbed into the ambulance, put it in gear, whipped it in a circle, and started back toward town. Soon he saw in the rearview mirror a convoy of army trucks coming into Bensonville. He stopped, flagged it down. The guardsmen were mostly very young and plainly terrified at the thought of entering the plague-ridden town. They had left their civilian pursuits so hastily that some of them were only half in uniform; one had his fatigue jacket pulled over a Hawaiian sport shirt. Jess found the captain in charge and suggested that they set up blocks on all roads leading into Bensonville so that the town could be quarantined.

"I don't think you'll find many people trying to get out; nearly everybody who could move has already left. But at least keep anyone from coming in; we don't want this disease spreading." Jess rubbed his face. "We'll need some of your men and trucks to pick up the sick and get them to the hospital and the schools."

The captain nodded grimly, and most of the trucks fanned out to set up the roadblocks. The others followed Jess's ambulance into Bensonville.

3

Jess was at the hospital when he heard the sharp, fast *whap-whap-whap* of helicopters. He squinted into the late-afternoon sunlight and saw three of them circling the town, looking for a place to land. One by one they descended onto a large empty field near the hospital. Jess went over there.

As the roar of the copters subsided and a huge cloud of dust and debris floated to the ground, Jess watched the doctors climb out of the cockpits and run across the field toward him. There were nine of them, each with a satchel full of medicine and instruments. Except for the leader and one old man, they looked remarkably alike: young, efficient, and with the smug self-importance that recent graduation from a medical school so often seems to confer with a degree. The first to reach Jess was a gray-haired, scholarly-looking man with a surprisingly youthful spring in his step. He said, "I'm Dr. Tull from Louisville. Where can I locate Jess Barrett?"

"I'm Jess Barrett. Glad you're here. You'll find our own doctors at the hospital, and the men from our neighboring towns have set up treatment centers in the schools."

Two army trucks arrived, and the doctors piled in for the short ride to the hospital. But one did not move. He was short, old, bent, and wore a drooping moustache that might have struck Jess at any other time as quaintly funny.

"Barrett, I heard you speak at the university once, and I liked your way of thinking. Can I go along with you? I want to hear what you have to tell me about this thing."

"Sure, be glad to have you." Jess walked to the driver's side of the ambulance.

"Gus? You coming?" Dr. Tull had turned in irritation.

"Nope, I want to pick this man's brain. You've got enough helpers. I'll join you later." As the others drove off, he got in the front seat of the ambulance, his knees cracking loudly, and extended a gnarled hand to Jess.

"I'm Bill Gustofson. Call me Gus. I'm supposed to know something about epidemiology, but what I've heard about this mess makes me doubt it. Tell me as much as you can while we drive."

The newsmen had arrived by scores, then hundreds, with truckloads of electronic equipment. Those who got there first made a show of insisting to the National Guard officers that they be permitted to enter Bensonville, but when denied access, they settled down at one of the army outposts to wait for what news they could garner from watching the town and from talking to the doctors who passed through the checkpoint. When television crews arrived, they trained their telescopic cameras and shotgun mikes on the little town and picked up the sight of the flashing red lights and the sound of the insistent sirens and welps of ambulances and other emergency vehicles scorching through the streets.

By late afternoon, Harold Stamler, a surgeon from Bloom, arrived and was passed into Bensonville. At the junior high he found Dr. Hughes. To the inevitable question, the latter growled, "It's hell. It's an epidemic of unprecedented virulence, but not an epidemic of any one thing. It's ordinary diseases expanding to unbelievable limits."

"I was on a fishing trip. I got here as soon as I could."

"Can you stay and help us, Hal?"

"Of course. I have a couple of suggestions. There are quite a few sick Bensonville people out on the road and probably in other towns. To keep this from

33

spreading, we've got to get them back. But every ambulance in the county is here."

"My God, Hal, I haven't heard of this. Why weren't we warned?" Hughes shook his head. "I didn't think anyone struck down by whatever-it-is could manage to get across the town limits without collapsing."

"I tried to call you, and so did others, but apparently the system is jammed. We couldn't get through."

"O.K., let's do this. Talk that captain into assigning some of his outfit to run the telephone office, relay messages to us. Then man a couple of ambulances, and go bring in the living victims. Have the guard drive some hearses, follow you around to pick up the dead. We want all the bodies back here immediately. Do you think we dare send some of the sick to the Chalmers hospital? We're so overloaded here; every bed's taken as fast as we set it up."

Before Stamler could speak, Hughes answered his own question. "No. We can't do that. It's more important to contain this thing than to make the patients comfortable. Bring them all back here. Lord knows, they're all dying anyway."

Stamler nodded grimly. As he started off, Hughes called to him. "Oh, Hal, will you do me a favor, and take Bill Nyland and Ken Fisher on one or two of your trips out? They're both half crazed with grief and fatigue, but they won't quit. Nyland's lost two sons; Fisher's whole family is missing. Getting out of this nightmare might save their sanity—maybe their lives."

"Will the med school guys object to our plan? Who's in charge here?"

"Nobody, really, but this has to be the right thing to do. You can check with Tull if you like, but get *going*, Hal!"

By evening Channing Powell was on the scene and stationed himself at one of the army checkpoints. It was indicative of the seriousness of the situation that CBS-TV sent him. He was one of the network's highest-paid men and handled only the very big stories.

His van and equipment added considerably to the confusion that already existed at the checkpoint. The army had parked two trucks so that they narrowed the road to a one-car-width passageway. This in turn was blocked by a movable wooden barrier and guarded by soldiers. They kept their rifles slung ready, and only for army or medical vehicles did they lug aside the barrier.

The checkpoint was crowded on one side with newsmen and their equipment and on the other with people clamoring to leave the area.

Powell had been prevented from interviewing the distraught residents and finally decided to catch doctors as they passed through the point.

It was he who stopped Bill Nyland. Nyland's eyes were red, and his round face was as tightly drawn as a bowstring. All his impassive good nature had seeped away. The vomit and blood of half a hundred patients had stained his clothes, and he stank like an abattoir.

"Doctor, I wonder if I might have a few words from you about this disaster. Just what is the sickness? Some say it is cholera. Speak right into the cameras, Doctor."

Nyland waved angrily at Powell to move. "We've got some mighty sick folks out there, but if we can get them back to the hospital, they may have a chance."

"But, Doctor, just a *word* to our viewers on Bensonville's tragedy?"

Nyland's eyes glittered with anger, but he wearily opened the door and stepped out of the ambulance. "What is there to say?" His voice was rasping as he ran dirty hands through his dirty hair. "Something I've never seen or heard of has slaughtered nearly the whole town."

"You mean you have no idea what's causing this catastrophe? That it's beyond the ken of modern medical science?"

Nyland glared at him for a moment and then said,

"It's beyond *my* modern medical science, anyway. Maybe the epidemiologists can make some sense out of it. All I know is that suddenly my town is dying, is nearly dead, and I can't stop it. I shoot gallons of antibiotics into them—and it doesn't do a damn thing."

"Doctor, we've received reports from around the country that residents of Bensonville who are away on vacation or business are suffering from the same kind of illness. In fact, we have even heard that some of the students from Shiloh College have died at their homes in other states."

"Well, I'm not surprised," said Nyland slowly. "With the exception of Jess Barrett, I've been told that the entire faculty is dead, and most of their families, too."

"Doctor, just how many fatalities have there been? Is it *really* as bad as you say?" Channing Powell was noted for his insulting manner with the people he interviewed.

Nyland eyed him carefully for a minute. "You stupid, pompous son of a bitch. I've lost my two sons and almost every friend I have, and you imply I'm exaggerating." Suddenly in a black rage he swung his fist and smashed Powell in the face. He got back in the car. "Come on, son, let's get going."

All that night the doctors worked with the stream of people who came to them vomiting, feverish, pallid with chills, swollen, shrunken, bleeding, sightless, in every condition of extreme illness. Beds were brought to the schools from neighboring houses, and patients were laid on them until they died, to be replaced with others. As the night wore on, the sirens never stopped screaming, the red lights never ceased flashing, and Jess Barrett thought he would go mad. At times he believed that he already had. He worked prodigiously: carrying people into examining rooms, setting up beds, trying to comfort the few survivors, driving ambulances.

Gustofson, the old doctor, was with Jess all night. At the elementary school they met Jim McDonald carrying his wife.

"I found her out in the woods, Jess. She'd gone for a walk and collapsed. She was so sick I didn't dare bring her in. She kept cryin' and cryin'. She must've thrown up a dozen times. And she had such a fever! Now she's so cold it scares me. Help, Jess."

Dr. Gustofson spoke gently. "She's dead, friend."

The mayor staggered at his words, and Jess and Gustofson took the woman out of his arms. McDonald leaned against the wall, uncomprehending. Then he put his hands over his face and began to sob.

Jess tried to comfort him, but he had long ago run out of words. McDonald's shoulders shook, and the gray of fatigue and sorrow had overwhelmed his tan. Suddenly he looked up in alarm. "You ain't heard anything about my children, Jess? I've been so busy taking care of Marilu that I haven't called the camp."

Jess stiffened. He had actually forgotten it. "Jim, the newsmen stopped me at the checkpoint and asked where to find you. They heard that your children— well, they caught this thing, too. They're gone, Jim. I'm sorry."

"Oh God! Oh *God!*" He turned away, sobbing, and disappeared into the night.

By midnight, nearly the entire population of the town had succumbed to the mysterious illness.

Jess and Gustofson were on their way to another section of town when they heard helicopters again. This time Gus urged Jess to go to the landing field, which by now was bright with army searchlights.

"That'll be Walter. He told me before I left that he was going to call the Center for Disease Control in Atlanta."

"You know the governor?"

"We've been friends since we were shirttail tads together in Dry Bottom Creek. Good thing for me, too. I'd have probably been fired long ago if it weren't for Walter. That consarned Tull started over here today without me—the only legitimate epidemiologist on the whole faculty. Walter was in Louisville today,

37

and we were having lunch together when he had the call from Andrews. Walter insisted I come."

At the edge of the field, military emergency vehicles were waiting, headlights on, red signals flashing. As the first helicopter descended, its blast of wind sent up huge clouds of dust, and the two men retreated a few steps. The bubble copter set down, the rotors flapped to a stop, the door opened, and out stepped Walter Cartwright.

He had been governor of Kentucky for so long that nobody could remember when there'd been another. His age surprised Jess. The television cameras always showed his best side, and it had been years since Jess had seen him face to face. He had grown very old, but it made no difference to the people of Kentucky. With regularity they returned him to office. His opponents sneered at the "father figure" of Kentucky, but he kept on smiling and giving good government and being reelected.

He shook hands with Dr. Gustofson. "Hi, Gus. I came as soon as the team from the Center for Disease Control got off the jet. How're things going?"

Gustofson introduced Jess and then briefly described the epidemic that had overwhelmed Bensonville. The governor shook his white head, appalled. "What about Jim McDonald? Is he here?"

For years McDonald had been one of the governor's staunchest supporters and had made huge contributions to his campaigns. Many reporters had speculated that the mayor might run for governor himself when Cartwright retired. Jess told him about McDonald's dead wife and children. Again the old man shook his head, speechless, horrified.

The air filled with the gusty wind and *whap-whap-whap* of a larger helicopter. It touched down, and four men wearing dark suits and carrying attaché cases got out and ran across the field to join them.

Governor Cartwright stepped forward, in command of himself now. "Gentlemen, introduce yourselves to my old friend Dr. William Gustofson, who is something of an epidemiologist himself."

One by one they did so: Dr. Mandelbaum, chairman of the team, a specialist in microbiology and virology, impressive in height and girth, with black hair slicked down and a very thin moustache, said, "I've heard of you, Gustofson; the work you did for the State Department in Bolivia was superb."

Dr. Fornier was a specialist in industrial and agricultural pollutants; Dr. Ogden, in public health and sanitation. The fourth member of the team was also the oldest. His face, wrinkled from much laughter, was solemn now. "I'm Jordan Brown," he said. "I'll be in charge of the autopsies."

They climbed into the army jeeps and were driven to the junior high. As they walked through the halls, seeing the patients, the classrooms cleared of desks and chairs and stacked with the bodies of the dead, the doctors could not speak. At last Mandelbaum whispered, "In my entire career, I have never seen such virulence."

Ken Fisher and Bill Nyland met them in the library, where they sat down at a big oval table. Gustofson began. "I'm going to ask Nyland and Fisher to tell you how this hell started. I sent for Dr. Tull of our medical school, too. He's at the hospital, but I'm sure he'll join us. Dr. Nyland?"

Nyland was beyond exhaustion. Shock and sheer physical fatigue had left him numb. He spoke in a voice so soft that the others had to strain to hear him. Quickly he outlined the events of the day, making no reference to his own loss.

When he'd finished, Mandelbaum asked, "Do you have any ideas about the cause?"

Ken Fisher answered. "Hard to say. Certainly we're seeing some kind of massive septicemia or bacteremia. But what's causing it? And furthermore, sometimes it's not that, but a normal minor infection. A woman came in this morning with a cold sore that had expanded to cover her whole face. Malignancies are showing explosive growth.

"And kids we inoculated with polio virus two weeks ago have all developed bulbar polio of the fulminate type. We've treated ulcers, colds, infections, flu, mumps, syphilis, and infected acne; ringworm, arthritis, phlebitis, infected hemorrhoids, hepatitis, ear infections—everything. All their conditions have collapsed, and they're dying.

"We've even had some cases of smallpox. A family planning to go to Africa had inoculations a week ago, and every one of them died of the pox today.

"If that isn't enough to baffle you, think about this: We've had no success with standard modes of therapy. A few of the least serious cases are still hanging on, but so far not one patient has been saved. We have given massive doses of every antibiotic we have, and you'd think it was a placebo."

"I'll tell you what it is! It's germ warfare!" Mayor McDonald stood in the doorway, disheveled, filled with his fury and grief. "It's true! I've been everywhere, and I tell you it's some kind of attack, poison gas or bacteria bombs or something. Even the animals are all dead. I found dogs, cats, squirrels, and even birds dead. Those sons of bitches have killed my whole town and my whole family." He clutched at his wiry hair. "It's the Reds," he said, and turned and left them staring at one another.

"Animals, too?" Mandelbaum frowned. "But what would an attacker use? There's no artificial agent that produces effects like this. Animals? That sounds like a trauma or poison. Fornier, Ogden, better get onto that first thing."

The governor spoke. "If we don't have the resources in Kentucky to solve this, I'm sure the president will declare it a disaster area.

"We'll want military and Public Health Service field units for doing cultures and studies of organs. This town will have to remain cordoned off. We have no idea how communicable this is. It *seems* highly infectious—but if so, why haven't the doctors caught it?"

"Bob Barrett did," said Fisher dully, glancing at Jess. "He died this morning. We may all come down with it yet. I've wondered why we haven't."

40

Mandelbaum said, "It looks like a massive viral infection. I think I'll proceed on that hypothesis."

Gustofson looked skeptical. "Doctor, you *do* intend to interview and examine the survivors?" he drawled. "Seems important to know the reasons why some of these people *didn't* get sick."

Mandelbaum stiffened. "I understand that you're interested in immunology, Doctor. Why don't *you* take care of that? Meanwhile, we'll study those who are sick and find out what made them that way."

When the sun rose, uneasy quiet had settled on the little town. Here and there an ambulance still flashed its red lights, but the sirens were stilled. The young guardsmen woke from their sleep to see buzzards circling overhead.

Even newsmen fell silent on their deathwatch, staring down into the Bensonville valley through mounted telescopes and high-powered binoculars. The smells of death and human excreta wafted to them, thin, nauseating. One reporter said, "I've only seen one ambulance in the last twenty minutes. Do you suppose that means—" Nobody answered.

Below, a few doctors and nurses could be seen walking about; otherwise the streets were empty. Cars were parked at odd angles in the middle of streets and on sidewalks.

A reporter from New York whispered, "I don't mind telling you I'm scared as hell. My home office says they know of over a hundred deaths outside Bensonville, people who'd been here recently. They think the whole senior class of Shiloh College has died—everyone who graduated last Saturday. Those kids were scattered all over the country, as far as California. Godalmighty!"

At the hospital, Nyland looked up from a patient. He was a young factory worker who had labored all night, setting up beds and carrying patients too weak to walk. In the early morning hours, he had become faint and within minutes had sunk to his knees, his

41

face a white and clammy mask. Now he, too, was gone. He was the last. Bensonville was dead.

The doctors and attendants walked outside into the brilliant sunshine of a June morning. Nobody could speak. Down the street a loose screen door banged in the breeze. A doctor went over and shut it firmly and quietly.

The handful of survivors began to avoid one another's eyes, as if they were embarrassed to be alive. The quiet had deepened to almost absolute silence. No birds were singing; their bodies peppered the ground under the telephone wires and trees. No cats chased mice; no dog barked at another.

Jim McDonald staggered from the hardware store. He was either so drunk or so exhausted that he could not walk steadily. He held a shotgun in his hand and screamed at the black buzzards circling overhead, casting their shadows across the town.

"You goddamn bastards! You're not gonna eat my people!"

He pointed the shotgun and fired. A big bird dipped and flapped its wings frantically. He fired again, and it dropped like a stone, hit a telephone wire, spun around violently, then fell to the street.

From a hill above the town, a rifle shot whanged out, then another and another, as the guardsmen, too, released their fright and anger by killing the buzzards. One by one the birds were hit and dropped, until at last silence settled again over the dead town.

4

UNTIL THURSDAY EVENING, the helicopters dropped into Bensonville at irregular intervals from all over the state, bringing pathologists, bacteriologists, technicians, officials, and soldiers. More truck caravans brought army medical field equipment into town, and doctors set up several centers to begin the grisly work of performing over 1,000 autopsies. Graves Registration troops searched the streets and homes for bodies and took them to the centers.

By Friday morning the horror felt by the newsmen had eroded to frustration and anger over not being permitted to enter Bensonville for a firsthand account. The army had very early set up emergency tents and field telephones for them, and the communications center was flooded constantly with calls from their home offices asking for details of the disaster. Special reporters from the *New York Times,* the *Chicago Tribune,* UPI, AP and even Reuters and Tass were there, as well as a number from medical journals, *Scientific American,* and *Science News.*

Television crews with their vans of equipment had nothing to show except telephoto shots of the town and commentators trying to elaborate on the little they knew about the catastrophe.

However fearful they had been at first for their own safety, the newspeople grew more and more anxious to see, film, and report the year's biggest story. The announcement that Governor Cartwright would hold a news conference at 11:00 that morning brought boos and catcalls; they didn't want secondhand information, though they'd accept it in lieu of anything better.

About 9:00, two olive-drab trucks pulled into a large field overlooking Bensonville, and as the reporters watched, soldiers began to build a platform. They brought in a generator and hooked up loudspeakers and microphones. More trucks arrived with hundreds of chairs for the press, most of which were filled as soon as they were unfolded. Four microphones on stands were distributed throughout the audience for questions. Television crews set up cameras. Technicians clicked their fingernails against the mikes, testing them, while others grimaced at the sound.

It had rained in the night, and fields and trees still soggy from the downpour steamed as the sun rose higher in the clear June sky.

At 11:00 the roar of reporters subsided into whispers and then silence as two limousines arrived carrying the governor, Dr. Mandelbaum, and their associates.

Walter Cartwright was sopping wet and gray with fatigue. His famous smile had given way to grimness. Cameras began to grind when he walked to the lectern.

"Ladies and gentlemen of the press, I've called this conference to report to you the terrible events of the last two days and to explain the steps taken by the Commonwealth of Kentucky and the United States Public Health Service."

The governor paused as his voice faltered. He shook his white head sadly, and his hand trembled as he reached for a glass of water. When he began again, the old resonance had returned.

"The moment I heard of the calamity, I sent a team of doctors from the medical school in Louisville, I notified the Center for Disease Control in Atlanta, and I ordered the National Guard to quarantine the city. As most of you already know, the guardsmen were replaced by the regular army yesterday afternoon.

"You also know that the president has declared this a disaster area.

"There are facts I know you're anxious to learn.

We'll try to provide some of them now, and then we'll open the meeting to questions.

"First, most important, apparently the epidemic has passed. There've been no new deaths, not even illnesses, since yesterday morning. But the quarantine will have to continue for another two weeks.

"Dr. Mandelbaum, the head of the CDC team, will speak to you now. Then the army's Colonel Wellers will explain the security measures and outline the plans for a funeral service."

As Mandelbaum walked to the lectern, Jess turned to Dr. Gustofson and said under his breath, "Tell me, Gus, is this Mandelbaum really good, or is he the pompous fool he sounds and looks?"

Gustofson's tired, red eyes suddenly twinkled, and he chuckled. "Jacob Mandelbaum is one of the finest virologists and microbiologists in the country, son. He's an efficient organizer, he's called in the best men in all the appropriate specialties, and he'll see to it that all the conventionally right things get done. If this turns out to be something within the scope of our usual methods, you can be sure he'll nail it. If it should be something really new and different, though, you can be just as sure he won't."

Despite the humidity, the enormous Jacob Mandelbaum was impeccably dressed. Only his eyes showed how dog-tired he must have felt after thirty sleepless hours. His voice was deep, and he spoke out of massive authority. "Ladies and gentlemen, I believe that this represents a medical disaster without precedent in the United States. During the Middle Ages, of course, it was not uncommon for towns, indeed entire provinces, to be literally wiped out by attacks of bubonic plague or smallpox. This catastrophe is nearly that bad. It is my regrettable duty to inform you that of Bensonville's 1,242 inhabitants, 1,039 have died."

A mutter of shock swept through the crowd.

"And we are not even certain that that is the full extent of the catastrophe. We know that a number of people who had been in town in the last week or so

45

died during the same twenty-four-hour period and in the same manner as the local victims.

"May I remind you, however, of Governor Cartwright's statement that there has been no new infection since yesterday morning, when the last victim expired. This is an indication that the epidemic has spent its force."

Some of the reporters frowned skeptically, but Dr. Mandelbaum swept on. "I want to pay a particular tribute to the physicians of Bensonville, Chalmers, and Bloom. I also want to commend the heroic physicians who came from the medical school in Louisville. Despite the fact that there was a mysterious, a deadly dangerous, epidemic devastating this peaceful hamlet, these men came and gave unstintingly of themselves. One of the local doctors, Dr. Robert Barrett, made the ultimate sacrifice of his own life."

Gustofson nudged Jess. "I suppose you noticed he's really reminding the press how heroic *he* is to have come into this 'peaceful hamlet.'"

Mandelbaum continued. "Now, regarding the steps we are taking to ascertain the cause of the tragedy and prevent it from happening again: Of first importance was the quarantine. Next was medical care for the victims, however futile. We have only begun the investigation. Doctors under the direction of Dr. Jordan Brown, our CDC pathologist, are conducting autopsies on each of the victims.

"In addition, Dr. Ogden and his assistants are studying food supplies and the water and sanitation systems of the town.

"Dr. Fornier is investigating the possibility that toxic chemicals were discharged into the water or air by local industries.

"We are checking to see if any train or truck going through town might have leaked some poisonous substance, and the governor has requested a report of all flights over the area. We want to be absolutely positive that no mistake was made by a military aircraft carrying bacteriological or chemical weapons.

"In addition, technicians are checking local crops

to see what insecticides and pesticides have been used. To sum up, every conceivable lead will be followed by our investigators. Now to the question period."

Virtually every reporter lifted his hand; Mandelbaum recognized science reporter Dan Holland.

"Dr. Mandelbaum, a local doctor was briefly interviewed as he passed through a checkpoint, and he said that the victims didn't exhibit any particular syndrome but seemed to die from a number of causes, even such innocuous things as colds and chicken pox. Would you comment on that, please?"

Dr. Mandelbaum's eyebrows pinched together, and his double chin quivered. "Well, now, the question you've asked is a difficult one. We have just begun the autopsies and the culture studies, so I think I must defer any precise answer until we've had a chance to receive the reports. I am sure, however, that when we have finished our thorough investigation, we will find that one agent caused the outbreak and that it exacerbated other infections from which the patients were already suffering. I am sure you realize that is not uncommon in cases of severe illness. For example, cancer patients are frequently victims of infections."

"Good old Mandelbaum," Gus muttered. "Never use ten words when a hundred and forty will do."

Again hands waved frantically, and Dr. Mandelbaum recognized William Talmadge from *Scientific American*. Talmadge was one of the most knowledgeable and respected writers on scientific subjects in the United States. He drawled, "Well, now, Doctor, if one agent caused all these different things, what the devil could it have been? Do you know of any single virus or bacterium capable of producing such a diversity of symptoms?"

Dr. Mandelbaum was perspiring now, and his white collar had wilted. He cleared his throat. "Mr. Talmadge, I am sure you know from your reporting of epidemics in other parts of the world that the stress of invasion by a particular organism can cause a variety of symptoms in the host. As the body tries to give battle to the new organism, it loses the fight to other

47

diseases already present. I am sure we will find some such happening here. Next question."

There was an immediate tumult and a sea of waving hands, but again Mandelbaum recognized a science reporter, this time Theda Gereaux of the *New York Times*. She was an older woman, squarely built, with a raspy voice. "Dr. Mandelbaum, is it possible that one of the oil companies is experimenting with some gasoline additive that might have caused this outbreak? We've heard rumors that a number of additives have been used which, when burned, create compounds in the atmosphere that are dangerous to man."

Dr. Mandelbaum was on more secure ground this time. "Thank you for that acute question, Mrs. Gereaux. I assure you that we are taking samples of gasoline from every single station in town. We are also checking fuel in automobiles and trucks to make sure that there was no additive in use a week or so ago that does not show up in the station tanks today. Next?"

This time it was a young reporter from the maverick bimonthly magazine, the *New Scientist*, who gained the attention of Mandelbaum. "Doctor, we all know the noxious effects of certain fertilizers used extensively in the past. Is it possible that rains have carried such fertilizers into the water system of Bensonville and caused this problem? For example, we know that nitrates can become harmful nitrites. Did this happen?"

Mandelbaum confidently assured the young man that the town water supply was being studied carefully and that the organs of the victims were being removed and examined for the presence of toxins.

The next to be recognized was a boisterous reporter from the *New York Daily News*, Herb Wood. His readers loved his pungent style and the sensational items he brought to them through his column. "All right, Dr. Mandelbaum, I'll ask the question that's on everybody's mind but they're too chicken to bring up. Did Russia do this to us? Did they shoot a missile full of gas or germs at this little town as an experiment—or as a threat?"

The journalist for Tass gripped a microphone and shouted, "In the name of the Soviet Union, I protest such an allegation!"

Dr. Mandelbaum spoke quickly. "We have absolutely no evidence of any artificial agent causing this disaster. Naturally, we have asked for a report from the air force on aircraft in the vicinity in the last few days, or of any indication that such an object as a missile could have been fired into the city. We also asked the Army Intelligence Corps to question the survivors about any strangers in town. All of this has been done to make sure that our investigation is thorough, but I can assure you that the preliminary reports show an absolute lack of evidence of such external activities."

"What he said," murmured Gus in Jess's ear, "was 'No.' "

A young man shouted into one of the mikes until he was finally recognized. He identified himself as Jeffrey McMasters of the *Journal of Proper Nutrition*.

"Isn't this disaster really the consequences of years of defective agricultural practices? Isn't it true that we've returned to the soil in which our food is grown only phosphates and nitrogens and none of the other elements so crucial to the formation of nutritious food? In other words, couldn't this tragedy be the result of people being overfed and undernourished?"

Mandelbaum reacted securely. "Certainly not, young man! The American people are the best-nourished people in the world. There is nothing to indicate that soil depletion could contribute to, much less *cause*, a disaster such as this. Next question!"

Rudolph Klemperer, the author of twenty-five books of science fiction, said, "Doctor, have you heard the reports of the flying saucers that were sighted in this area? And are you aware that seventeen reliable witnesses swore they saw a saucer hovering over the hills just outside of Bensonville in the early hours of Wednesday morning?"

There was a ripple of laughter, and even Dr. Mandelbaum smiled condescendingly. "Sir, our investigation will center on more probable lines of inquiry. However, we would be delighted to talk to the witnesses whom you have secured."

For almost an hour, Dr. Mandelbaum answered (or did not answer) further questions. His sentences grew noticeably shorter. At last he turned to the military man seated on the platform and said, "Ladies and gentlemen, Colonel Wellers."

Mandelbaum returned heavily to his chair, and the colonel stepped to the lectern. Wellers was a small man with a tired face that came of a lifetime of responsibility. He stood stiffly before the microphones and spoke with a surprisingly strong voice.

"The army's job here is to enforce the quarantine, protect the property of the deceased, and ensure that the medical men are free from interference.

"We're protecting the property of the victims, and when the quarantine's lifted, relatives can make their claims. Survivors aren't allowed to leave the area until the quarantine's lifted, but they've been helped to inform relatives of their own safety by phone.

"Memorial services will be held at eleven o'clock on Sunday morning. We've asked the archdiocese to take charge of the Roman Catholic ceremony, and a rabbi's coming from Louisville to conduct the Jewish rites. As for Protestant services, a Baptist will be handling them."

A florid, sweaty man tapped on a microphone for attention and, without waiting to be recognized, shouted, "Colonel, I think it's an insult to the clergy of Bensonville to call in outsiders! Why haven't you asked one of the local reverends to conduct the services?"

Colonel Wellers said quietly, "Well, sir, they're all dead, or we would have done that."

The florid man sank into his chair, his mouth hanging open.

A trim, well-dressed man moved to a mike. "I'm Clarence Schmidt of the *Southern Morticians' Monthly Journal,* and I'm deeply concerned about one item to which you have not alluded, Colonel Wellers. The services are planned, but what about the *burials?* When may relatives claim the remains to provide them with appropriate interment?"

Wellers hesitated, then said firmly, "Mr. Schmidt, for medical reasons, the victims can't be buried normally. The Public Health Service has ordered the army to prepare a large common grave and to inter all victims there as the autopsies are completed."

The man at the microphone frowned. "Do you mean, Colonel, that they will not be properly casketed? That their families will be unable to view the remains? That the bodies will not even be *embalmed?* Speaking for the morticians of the entire state, we are deeply offended by such sacrilegious treatment of the dead."

The colonel said, "Those who died in the early hours of the plague *were* taken to the two local funeral parlors but were never embalmed. You see, all the morticians and all the attendants who handled the bodies caught the disease themselves and died. All of them. Think that over. Then, if your organization insists, it may be that the medical people will reconsider. But I believe you would be well advised to reconsider your own position instead."

The mortician subsided, looking somewhat shaken.

Another microphone was taken by J. H. Humphrey of the *Washington Post.* "Colonel Wellers, I'm not a science reporter. I can't ask intelligent questions about the medical aspects of this plague, but I can ask you and Governor Cartwright something just as important. Do you have any understanding of the tremendous impact this has had on our country? People haven't just fled from this area; a lot have even left Kentucky. In other cities, where some of the residents of Bensonville died, there's been panic.

"I think that you, as the officer in charge of security here, and the governor, as chief executive of Kentucky, *must* permit us to go into Bensonville. Only candid reporting of the facts can stop the rumors and dispel the fears. I strongly urge you, sir, to allow us to enter the city!"

Wellers stiffened. "I'm acting on the directions of Dr. Mandelbaum, who feels it could be medically disastrous to do that." With this, the officer nodded curtly to the reporters and sat down.

The governor stepped to the microphone to end the conference, but before he could say anything, J. F. Loutit, reporter for the *Louisville Courier-Journal and Times,* said, "Governor Cartwright, I have a question for you. Why are you permitting federal authorities under Dr. Mandelbaum's direction to conduct this investigation, when our own Commonwealth of Kentucky has a world-famous epidemiologist within its boundaries? Why haven't you appointed Dr. William Gustofson to lead the investigation of this tragedy?"

Walter Cartwright warmly thanked the reporter for his question before he answered. "I think you all know that Gus is one of my best friends and has been my personal physician for more than thirty years. I'm well aware of his qualifications. But the resources of the Atlanta CDC are so impressive that I felt it would be wise to have Dr. Mandelbaum head the effort. Dr. Gustofson has agreed to assist.

"And now, ladies and gentlemen, this conference is ended. Believe me, as soon as we have any information from the autopsies, we'll give it to you immediately. Good day."

Dr. Gustofson leaned over to Jess. "Loutit's a good friend of mine, but I wish he'd kept his big mouth shut. Look at Mandelbaum. He's got an ego bigger than his belly, and he's so piqued that his sweat's turning to steam."

The two men watched as the speakers left the platform and walked toward the limousines.

"Let's get back to Bensonville, Jess. There's work to do, and you can help me with it, help a lot." Gustofson had dealt with great tragedies before, and he had seen grief destroy some of the survivors. He was disturbed by the blank look on Jess's face and his listless attitude.

"The other doctors will be studying the environmental factors, performing autopsies, taking cultures, making toxicological studies. What I aim to do is interview everybody who lived through this trouble and discover why they didn't die. After what they've been through, they may not want to talk to strangers, even world-famous strangers, but everybody knows you. What do you say, Jess?"

Jess nodded mechanically. "O.K., Gus, I'd be glad to."

"Good. Let's see if we can finagle a jeep."

They did. The driver, Private Curtis, was more impressed with having Jess Barrett as a passenger than he was with the doctor. He eagerly started the engine as soon as Jess had climbed in the back. Dr. Gustofson took the front seat. "Now, Jess, you'll have to tell this young fellow where to go. I don't know your town yet."

Jess leaned forward. "Straight ahead on the highway till we get into town. I'll direct you from there." He sank back, the ravaged face of Ginny Lowell forming again in his memory. He wondered if he'd ever stop seeing her.

5

Dr. William Gustofson was a character, a word applied to him by both his enemies and his friends. His yellowing moustache drooped down over his mouth and gave him a benignly skeptical look. So shaggy and disheveled was his hair that it seemed much longer than it was. He had always looked rumpled, and as he aged, he simply gave up any attempt at neatness and began to look more and more like an old beanbag, which was precisely what some spiteful colleagues called him behind his back.

The desk in his small office at the medical school was heaped with so many papers and reports that there was hardly a place for his coffee mug. Numerous ashtrays were filled with well-worn pipes; stale, half-burned tobacco; and an occasional dried apple core.

The doctor spoke in an exaggerated Southern drawl. This and the fact that he moved slowly and seemed so disorganized caused some people to consider him lazy. His wife had kept him in some kind of order, but since her death, he often seemed lost in a world of vagrant thoughts. Only those who knew him best recognized the awesome mind that burned so brightly behind his green eyes.

Gustofson had begun his career as a country doctor, but he was quickly taken into the faculty of the Louisville medical school as a part-time lecturer on preventive medicine. Students loved the iconoclast, who went his own way, and they learned to respect the ferocious temper that was easily aroused by medical inanities.

The dean of the medical school realized the unusual

creative ability of the young doctor and appointed him a professor of internal medicine.

Slowly, over the years, Gustofson shifted to the study of epidemiology. He loved to solve problems, and his new subject gave him the opportunity to travel to various parts of the world and to deal with fluid, immensely challenging situations.

His propensity for being right had driven his peers half mad. While they went their organized and meticulous ways investigating epidemics, his method was more casual. He talked with people, walked all around the problem, pondered, and more often than not came up with the answer.

His medical hunches extended beyond his own specialty. For years, most physicians had claimed that because cancer was a product of the host's own body, it did not provoke any immune response. Gustofson maintained that cancer was antigenic—that is, *did* force the body to mount an immunological defense—but that for various reasons this defense was not effective. At meeting after meeting, in cancer seminars and conferences, in article after article, he needled his peers and insisted that they would be better off spending their time in finding out how to stimulate or strengthen the immune system of the body to deal with its tumors than in surgically removing great quantities of flesh from their hapless patients.

Gustofson insisted that cancer could develop from a number of sources but that it only did so when the bodily immunological resources were for some reason already exhausted. His theory that cancers are developing all the time but that in normal people they are destroyed by the immune system before they consist of more than one or two cells gained credence. The search began in earnest for ways to assist the body to deal with its tumors. It was given new impetus by Denis Burkitt's discovery that children afflicted by the tumor bearing his name could be successfully treated by injecting them with various cancer-destructive chemicals until the malignancy was reduced in size. With the challenge to the body thus diminished, the immune system seemed to take over and destroy the rest of the cancer.

Gustofson appeared well on the way to being proved correct. But far from making him more popular, it made him more intolerable to many of his jealous peers.

In recent years his famous style of studying survivors rather than victims of medical disasters had led him to new honors. His greatest triumph had occurred just seven years before the Bensonville catastrophe. A strange plague had erupted in Bolivia and had spread from one village to another. So rapid was its progress and so devastating its effect that there was panic throughout much of South America. The U.S. State Department quickly offered medical help, and Gustofson was chosen as a member of the team.

Already an old man, he had not been pleased at the thought of another long trip, but he finally agreed to go because of the desperate situation. In South America, he had thoroughly annoyed the other members of the team by what seemed aimless walks and drives through the infested area while they labored in hospitals and sweatbox laboratories.

On one of his drives, he found a village unaffected by the plague. Gustofson noted that the Indians of this village were members of an obscure religious cult and constantly chewed a nut from a strange local tree instead of the usual coca leaves. He took a large quantity of the nuts to a laboratory, where he discovered that they had potent bactericidal qualities. After only a month, he was able to isolate a powerful drug that retarded the growth of many microorganisms.

Almicidin, as it came to be called, was soon synthesized and had become an indispensable part of every doctor's pharmacopoeia. But this brilliant discovery also led to the intensified jealousy of many of Gustofson's colleagues. The day he reached sixty-five, they tried to force him into retirement. Only his good friend the governor kept him at the medical school.

This was the man who sat, crumpled and mussed and apparently dozing, in the front seat of the commandeered jeep, riding into what had been Benson-ville.

Within minutes they had covered the short distance, and Jess sighted an old woman crossing Main Street.

"Wait," he said. "I know her."

The jeep drew up to the old lady, who was walking with her head down, and Jess called, "Mrs. Newcombe, may we talk with you just a minute?"

The old lady turned her head, and a wisp of white hair blew across her face as she squinted in the sunlight. "Why, Jess Barrett, thank God you're still alive. Have you ever seen anything *like* this? The Lord himself has struck us with a thunderbolt."

"It's terrible, Mrs. Newcombe, just terrible. I—ah—want you to meet Dr. Gustofson from Louisville."

Gus stepped out of the jeep and offered her his hand. She peered with amazement at the old doctor, who was a far cry from her idea of a physician.

Jess said, "Dr. Gustofson's trying to find out what happened here so that they can keep it from ever occurring again. Would you mind answering his questions?"

The old lady looked hard at the doctor and shook her head. "I don't think anybody could ever find out what happened. It was the hand of the Lord, that's what it was, the hand of the Lord."

Dr. Gustofson nodded sympathetically. "Mrs. Newcombe, please sit here in the front seat and rest yourself while I talk with you, ma'am." He helped her gallantly into the jeep and stood beside her. "Now, Mrs. Newcombe, have you ever been sick?"

"Sick? Huh! Been sick all my life. Always wondered why my husband married anybody as sickly as me. I had all the kid diseases you could think of, and then with every baby I had complications.

"My husband—now, he was never sick. Healthy as a horse from workin' out in the sun, construction engineer for the highway department. Since he retired, he's worked most every day on the house or the yard —now he's gone. I don't understand it. My son, Jeff, not a sick day in his life, nor his wife or little girls, and now they're all gone. Me, with arthritis and a weak heart and forty ailments, I'm still alive. Don't make no sense."

As she spoke, Gustofson scribbled in his notebook. "Mrs. Newcombe, why do you think you're alive then, when they died?"

"It was the hand of the Lord." Tears welled up in her faded eyes, and she added, "I'd been gone for three weeks. My sister died in Nashville. I went to help with the funeral and get the estate settled. Just came back last Friday. I missed three whole weeks with my family, and then—" She gestured hopelessly around her.

Gustofson made another note. "Friday. Gone for three weeks. Thank you, Mrs. Newcombe, I appreciate your talking to me."

Jess helped the old lady up the steps of her little house and came back. "When I was a boy," he said, "we usually came here for milk and cookies after our vacant-lot football games. Her son Jeff was a good friend of mine."

"Jess, why do you think *you* didn't get sick?" asked Gustofson.

"Well, probably for the same reason Mrs. Newcombe just gave you. I'd been out of town, too. I was in France for almost a month and got back the night before this thing hit. Pretty plain that there was an incubation period of at least a few days."

Again, Gustofson jotted a note, muttered to himself, and said, "O.K., let's go find someone else."

Jess turned his head. "What's that noise?"

The sound of a motor accelerating and then declining drifted from the direction of the park, two blocks away. There was also the clatter and screech of caterpillar treads.

Gustofson watched Jess closely. "Why, Jess, that's the bulldozer."

"Bulldozer?"

"Enlarging the grave, filling it in. After the autopsies, the bodies are put down in there right away to prevent the spread of infection. You know that."

58

Jess said softly, "I'd like to see it."

"Sure you want to? The bodies are in burial bags. The organs were all removed for autopsy."

"I've got to see it."

The jeep wheeled around the corner. At the edge of the town, in what had been the park, the bulldozer had gouged a trench 8 feet deep, 8 feet across, and 200 yards long. A small army semi marked Graves Registration had backed up to the trench so that the corpses could be unloaded. Each was enveloped by a dark plastic bag.

The soldiers lifted the sacks out of the truck one by one and handed them down to the men in the trench. They lined them up side by side and in three layers; then the bulldozer clanked over to heap dirt thickly on top.

Two people stood watching silently. One was Ruth Bianci, the taxi dispatcher. The other was Al Pastore, the liquor store owner who'd questioned Jess so rudely at the golf course. The pair stood next to the swing set that McDonald had installed just a year before for the town's children. Al's fists were clenched tightly. Jess climbed out and walked slowly over.

Ruth looked up. Her hardened face was swollen from crying. Her hair was frazzled, and her dress hung loosely from her body. She gazed at him a moment. "Jess," she said, "I don't have anybody left, Jess."

Then Al began to cry. "They wouldn't even let me see Phyllis. I don't know if she's in there or back on one o' them tables. If I could just see her one more time."

"It's probably best that we remember them all as we knew them," said Jess. He thought, I can't recollect Ginny healthy and laughing. I wish I'd never seen her dead.

Ruth, as though reading his thoughts, said, "Jim McDonald told me they're bringing Harvey Lowell's body from Atlanta. You won't believe it, but that son of a bitch was in a whorehouse when it hit him; before they could get a doctor, he was dead."

Jess said nothing, but his eyes narrowed. Maybe Ginny was better off; at least she never knew how her husband died. He turned and called back to Gustofson. "Gus, you want to interview two more survivors?"

The old man nodded and took out his notebook as the three came toward the jeep. The bulldozer's engine roared, and again there was the rattle and thump of dirt cascading onto the bagged bodies. The Graves Registration semi was now unloaded, and it drove away toward the hospital.

Gus said, "Ma'am, maybe you can just tell me flat out why you think you didn't get sick with all the others?"

It was a repetition of Jess's and old Mrs. Newcombe's explanation.

"I reckon it's because I was out of town for over a week. Got back Tuesday night. But, then, I've never been sick, so maybe that's all there is to it."

"Look," said Al Pastore, "that can't be it. I've *always* been sick one way or another. Any little bug goes through town, I get it, but this time—well, look at me."

Gustofson's pencil raced. "You been out of town?"

"I never go out of town. Hell, I haven't had a vacation in five years—always that damn store needs taking care of. Planned to go to Louisville with my bowling team for a tournament about three weeks ago, but even that didn't work out."

Frowning, Gustofson scratched his shaggy head. Then he thanked them and drawled, "Jess, let's see who else we can find."

As they drove away, they saw Ruth and Al walk toward another truck unloading bodies at the trench. Two zombies, watching, understanding nothing but their pain.

Ahead of them a bowlegged little woman walked down Main Street. Jess called, "Sadie, Sadie." He jumped out and took the woman's hand. She was in her middle forties and had huge owllike eyes. When Jess took her hand, she winced and tried to draw

60

away. He said, "Don't be afraid, Sadie. We only want to ask you a couple of questions."

The outsized eyes rolled weirdly. "Have you seen Laurie? Where's Laurie, Jess, where's Laurie?"

Jess had helped take Laurie's body from the hospital. He patted her hand and said, "Sadie, it's all right. Don't worry about Laurie. Dr. Gustofson wants to ask you something."

Her nose twitched nervously. "Don't know nothin', don't know *nothin'*," she chanted. "Just got back from the hospital two days ago. Don't know nothin', don't—"

Gus said gently, "When did you go to the hospital, Sadie?"

"A long ways ago, they took me back a long ways ago. Don't know when. Maybe six weeks. Or three. They're always taking me away."

"But you came back home just recently?"

"Two days ago. I know *that,*" she said, watching him with the strange eyes.

"O.K., thanks a lot. Sadie. We'll see you again. Can you get home all right?" Jess asked.

"Of course I can get home all right. Think I'm a child?"

As they drove away, Jess said, "Poor Sadie! She's been odd as long as I can remember. Her mother and father tried to treat her exactly as they did her sister; but Laurie was clever and pretty, and poor Sadie is retarded, possibly schizoid. Now and then she's excited and becomes dangerous. When her parents died, Laurie and her husband took Sadie in with them; she's been there ever since, except when she's in the hospital. Now she'll really be alone. I'd better tell someone to look after her—but who?"

All that afternoon they drove through the streets, and Jess helped Gustofson interview any survivor they could find. By evening they had talked to sixty-eight.

Finally Jess said, "Gus, where are you staying? Would you like to go out to Bob's with me? I slept there last night and told Alma I'd be back. I can guarantee she'll give you a decent meal, better than that gunk the army puts out."

Gustofson said wearily, "I'd like that. And I'd like to talk to her, too. But first, can we drop by the hospital, see how things are going there?"

The lights had already gone on at the little hospital. The old man climbed stiffly out of the jeep. "Jess, I want to check with Jordan Brown's office. Besides collating the data from the autopsies, they're marking the residences of the dead on a city map. Sometimes you find an unsuspected pattern in these things. I remember once, in Haiti, we studied an epidemic and figured out that everybody who'd died had been drinking from the same well. That gave us the answer."

When they stepped through the front door, Jess's guts tightened, and a chill took him. The dead were gone from the halls, but he could still hear their horrible screams and smell the overpowering foulness of diarrhea and vomit and blood.

They passed the cafeteria and saw many of the doctors wearily filing in. "They don't eat *here,* do they?"

"No, Jess. We're using the cafeteria for a headquarters."

Gustofson walked into an office where Jordan Brown was sitting behind a desk, his face haggard and unshaven. He smiled wanly. "Hello, Gus. Find anything that makes sense in this mess?"

"Well, it's a little early, Jordan. How about you?"

Dr. Brown shook his head. "The only thing we know is that these poor devils died of *everything.* That's a lot of progress, isn't it?" he said bitterly.

"Jord, where's that map of the victims' homes?"

"I think it's in the secretary's office. I haven't seen it yet myself." He got up, and the three men walked into the darkened room next door. Brown fumbled for the light switch. On the wall was a large map of the city, studded thickly with a legion of red pins. The moment he saw the map, Jess's blood turned cold.

Gus shouted, astonished, "My God, Jord! Look at that!"

Dr. Brown whistled. Jess Barrett stared, silent, motionless, in awe.

The original plat of the town was laid out in a grid pattern that approximated a square. A number of the newer houses were just outside. The red pins formed an almost perfect elliptical pattern superimposed upon the square map of the city.

Dr. Gustofson growled. "That sure as hell doesn't follow the shape of any water or sewage-disposal system."

"Let's not jump to any conclusion, Gus," said Dr. Brown. "Maybe the first bodies were simply those from the center of town." He stared at the map, "But that shakes me," he said. "I'm not even sure *why*—but it shakes me."

Gustofson studied the map. Abruptly he turned to Jess. "Do you know the addresses of the survivors we interviewed today?"

"Most of them."

"O.K." Gus pulled out the battered notebook. "Where does Ruth Bianci live?"

He searched the desk drawer, found a box of blue-headed pins, and as Jess pointed out the residences of the survivors, Gustofson marked each one. Within half an hour, they were all located.

"For God's sake, will you look at that!"

The red ellipse of death was almost precisely encircled by the blue pins. Only a few had been placed inside it.

Brown squinted at the map. "Something very strange is going on here," he said inadequately.

"There sure as blazes *is*," Gus agreed. "Of course we've got to wait till more data are in, but I think we've finally got a break!"

"An eerie break," said Jordan Brown. "An incomprehensible break—oh, Mandelbaum's called a meeting for Sunday night. I know he'll want you to be there, Gus."

Gus stared at the map for a full minute longer. Then

he said, "I'll be there; I wouldn't disappoint Jacob. Let's go, Jess. We have to let that soldier get back to camp; he must be as starved as I am."

"Let's have him drop us at my house, and we'll get my car. You know, I could drive us around tomorrow; there's no need to bother the army."

"Well, we'll use your car now, but I'd rather be chauffeured tomorrow. I like to be in that open jeep, so I can pounce in and out." He grinned for the first time in hours.

Brown chuckled. "Gus, your pouncing days are as far gone as mine. Could you fellows drop me at the motel?"

"Glad to," said Jess, "if you don't mind crowding into my sports car for a few blocks."

At the jeep, Gustofson spoke to the driver. "Son, I'd like you to pick us up here tomorrow morning at seven o'clock."

"Yes, sir. Where to now?"

Jess directed him through the streets of the darkened town until they arrived at his small white clapboard house with the green gingerbread trim. The three men walked to the garage. Inside was a beautiful ice-blue Porsche.

As they climbed in, Jess said quietly, "When I came home for the first time, last night, I found my Great Dane, Duke, dead."

"God*damn*," said Gus, sympathetic.

"Now, when death hits dogs, birds, squirrels, and everything, don't you think it must be caused by some gas or chemical?" He backed the Porsche out to the street, leaving the garage door open.

"It certainly looks like an artificial agent at work, especially considering that pattern on the map," Dr. Brown said. "It's no random virus, that's sure."

Gus grumbled, "But there's never been any chemical or gas—or organism—that would cause such an incredible variety of diseases." He rolled down the Porsche's window. "Hey, what's going on at the motel?"

A small group of soldiers had clustered around a man lying on the sidewalk. Jess stopped the car, and they elbowed through to the unconscious figure. It was Jim McDonald. Gus bent over him. Jess said, "Surely it isn't beginning all over?"

Then a lieutenant came running. "All right, break it up! What happened? Is this man sick?"

A young soldier with a puffy, livid eye said, "No, sir. At least I don't think he is, sir. He's just out cold. In fact, sir, I knocked him out."

"You *what?*" snapped the lieutenant. "That man's the mayor of this town."

"Sir, he acted crazy! He came up to me and kept smiling and saying he knew all about it. I said, 'All about what?' And he got mad and took a punch at me."

"He hit you?" asked Gustofson, straightening up.

"Yes, sir, he knocked me clear across the sidewalk, and then he came at me again, yelling that I was a murderer. Finally, I had to swing back. I didn't hit him very hard, but he fell like a rock. I think he's drunk."

Gustofson nodded. "You're right. He *is* drunk."

Dr. Brown said sadly, "You know, all day he helped us to identify bodies. Late this afternoon he started going out for a minute or two at a time. I knew he was taking nips. I couldn't blame him. When we quit, he was pretty well saturated."

Jess sighed. "Well, he lost his family and his town; he had a right to dull the pain. But what was he talking about, do you suppose—this boy being a murderer?"

The young soldier was frightened. He looked at Jess, the lieutenant, the doctors. "Sir, I don't know, but *I* never murdered anybody."

Dr. Mandelbaum had come out of the motel. "I think I can answer that. He came in to see me this evening, and he was, of course, drunk. He said he'd been thinking all day, and he was sure that the army had decided to use Bensonville as a test area for poison gas. He became so abusive and incoherent that I told him to go home and sleep it off."

"Let's get him to bed. He'll be all right in the morning," Brown said.

"Come on, Jess, let's go," said Gus. "See you tomorrow, Jord. And say, Lieutenant—no charges against this young fellow, right? Clear case of self-defense."

The officer smiled and agreed.

The two men got into the Porsche, and Jess aimed it toward Alma's. "Jim McDonald is no fool, Gus. Oh, hell, he's pompous at times, plays the Kentucky colonel, and thinks he owns the town, but he's as intelligent as the next man. He has every reason to come apart at the seams—I only hope he doesn't completely lose his mind."

Gus said in the darkness, his head turned away, "Can you imagine anything more likely to drive a man insane than what he's been through? You don't need to make excuses for him. Great snakes! He's looked into hell!"

Gustofson and Barrett spent all Saturday interviewing. They had the driver take them systematically from house to house. Jess knocked on each door, and if anyone answered, Gus joined him. By midafternoon Gus had stopped asking anything except their whereabouts during the three weeks prior to the disaster.

That night at Alma's, Dr. Gustofson asked Jess if he was going to the mass funeral the next morning.

"Gus, I can't do it. If I get up there, I'll be a target for the reporters, and I simply can't face that right now."

They looked at Alma, who slowly shook her head.

The three sat silently. At last Gus said, "Well, then I'm going to sleep in tomorrow. I've about run out of steam. Getting old. Everybody'll be up there on the hill anyway. Good-night, friends."

It was past 11:00 on Sunday morning before Gustofson, considerably more vigorous, joined Jess and Alma at the kitchen table. The children—nine of them now—

66

were playing outside in the June sunshine. Gus sipped coffee, spread his map on the table.

"Do you have a large piece of paper, Alma? Maybe a big sheet of accounting paper?"

"E.J. has a drawing pad that's enormous." She went out and found it for him.

Gus opened it and drew vertical, then horizontal lines on the top sheet. Down one side, he listed the names of all the survivors they'd interviewed; and at the top he wrote three weeks' worth of days. Jess watched closely as the old man consulted his book and made notations on his chart.

Alma padded noiselessly about, serving them brunch. Her face was strained, but otherwise she showed no sign of her tragedy.

Finally Gustofson looked up, and his eyes were bright. "Jess, nearly every one of the survivors who live inside that damn neat ellipse has been out of town sometime during the last couple of weeks, but there are a few exceptions. Let's see if we can work those out."

He read from his notes. "First: Al Pastore lives in the center of town, but where does he work? Where's his liquor store?"

"About two blocks from his house. Here." Jess tapped a finger on the map.

"Hmm—inside the ellipse. And he said he hadn't been away. Well, we might have to talk to him again. Maybe he's forgotten something. Next is Cliff Hague, manager of the radio station. Lives on Walnut, hasn't been out of town for months. Where's the radio station?"

"At the north end of town, near the end of the oval."

"Inside or outside of it?"

"Outside, I think. Let's see." He bent over the map. "Gus, look at that, it's right at the end."

"O.K., now—"

"Wait, Gus! The golf course! It's outside the oval, too—and Al plays there all the time, no matter how hard he claims to work. Could that be it?"

67

"It sure could, and that takes care of your doctor friends, too. Didn't you say they played every Wednesday?"

"Yes, except for Bob, who often worked straight through. He didn't play last week, did he, Alma? I think Ken Fisher mentioned that he hadn't."

"No, he had an emergency at the hospital. I remember because on his way he took Rob to work at the college, to save me a trip. Rob had to be there early, seven forty-five instead of eight thirty. Most days I dropped him after I took the little ones to school—" Her voice broke on the last words, and she looked down to hide tears.

Jess put his arm around her, then asked Gus, "Who else?"

"That does it!" Gustofson stood, stretched painfully, and rolled up the chart. "Come on, Jess. I really think I've finally managed to hatch an idea. I want to talk to the people who live on the edges of town. Then we'll go back to the clinic and find out what dope they have on the victims who died away from Bensonville. O.K.?"

6

BY 8:00 THAT NIGHT all the doctors, the governor, Jess, Mayor McDonald, and a few others had gathered in the hospital's little cafeteria. Three large chalkboards hung on one wall, the tables had been stacked against another, and the chairs were arranged in cramped rows facing a lectern.

Mandelbaum's voice rolled, thunderous and impressive. "Gentlemen, so far as I've been able to determine, this epidemic is unique in the history of the world. The crisis it has brought on is of major national importance. We *must* find the cause as quickly as possible, and we *must* prevent its recurrence. I've personally received a communication from the secretary of HEW promising any resources we need. The president has called Governor Cartwright and offered assistance. However, we don't know what further help would be useful at this point. It's really up to us. Now let's see where we stand. Dr. Fornier."

Fornier, the pollution expert, was bone-tired, and his voice showed it. "Gentlemen, I'll tell you in one word what we've found: *nothing*. We tested the chemicals used by the furniture factory and the gasoline in every pump and automobile in town. Nothing. We checked on the cargo of every train that's gone through Bensonville in the last six weeks. Nothing. We've examined earth, air, water—everything but fire, for heaven's sake!—and there's no trace of an industrial pollutant that could have caused this trouble."

He slumped into his chair. Mandelbaum licked his lips and called, "Dr. Ogden."

"Well, I'm in the same situation as Dr. Fornier. We didn't discover a damned thing either. The sewage system here is part of the county system and perfectly adequate. Oh, sure, some of the houses outside town have their own septic tanks, but there's nothing unusual about 'em—no drainage into the town's water system. And that's O.K., too, an adequate purification process and no abnormal features.

"We did find out that this hospital conducted an extensive x-ray program a week and a half ago to detect early signs of tuberculosis, but the machine they used wasn't defective and didn't give off any unusual amount of radiation. Only about sixty people were involved in that program, so there's no reason to suspect irradiation by x-rays. In short, as my friend says—nothing."

Dr. Mandelbaum grimaced. He was sweating heavily, which added to the impression of slickness from his shiny black hair to his carefully polished shoes. "As you know, I have personally been culturing organisms from the victims. It's much too early to make any definitive statement, but I'm sorry to say that so far we have drawn a blank, finding only the usual, normal flora—although in far greater quantity than one would ordinarily expect.

"We *have* collected some facts on the residents who were out of town at the time of the disaster, and those who fled in the early stages of the epidemic. Nearly all those who left hoping to escape perished on the road or in neighboring towns within the same twenty-four-hour period in which the populace here expired."

Jess thought irritably, What sort of stuffy rhetorical ass could have seen all those mutilated corpses and say they'd expired? They died, Mandelbaum; they died in agony. Stop running for office, and tell us what killed Bensonville.

"One of the most tragic and yet medically interesting facts of this case is that the entire senior class of Shiloh College died," said the fat man, as though he'd heard Jess protest. "There was a single exception. Miss

70

Joan Drake left a week before graduation to join a tour to Europe. The State Department located her this morning and found that she's perfectly healthy. However, three other graduates of Shiloh were also touring Europe after attending graduation. All three died, one in Denmark and two in Italy.

"I might add that following the deaths of these young people, when it became known they were students at Shiloh, a near panic resulted in those two countries. The bodies are being flown to us for autopsy.

"There are more strange facts. Only two students outside of the senior class died. Both of them had remained at Shiloh for the graduation ceremonies. Lamentably, the entire faculty with the exception of Dr. Jess Barrett, whom you all know, fell victim to the plague.

"In addition, the whole board of trustees, which met here for three consecutive days prior to graduation, perished. Yet none of them lived in Bensonville.

"The driver of a gasoline truck who makes deliveries in Bensonville three times a week died in his home in Chalmers, fifteen miles away. This may have been a natural death, but initial reports indicate that it was similar to those which occurred here."

As Dr. Mandelbaum spoke, Gustofson was furiously scribbling in a fresh notebook. Then he unrolled the large chart that he had been keeping, spread it on the table, and made more entries. At the rustling of paper, everyone turned to look, and Mandelbaum glared and coughed, but the old man went on scribbling.

Mandelbaum said loudly, "Let us hear now from Dr. Brown, who has been in charge of the autopsies."

As Brown walked to the front of the room, Jess saw that his hands were shaking with exhaustion and his steps flagged. He put his notes on the lectern and began, "Well, I don't have much news either—or rather I have a lot of news, but none of it's worth much. In thirty years of medical practice, I've never seen anything like it.

"You all know that well over a thousand people have died, many of them from common, ordinary illnesses that became fulminant overnight. Our studies haven't unearthed one exotic disease. Well, I'll qualify that: We did find some youngsters who died of poliomyelitis. Every one had been vaccinated within the last three weeks. The attenuated virus somehow became virulent and killed those poor kids.

"And a family of five died of smallpox. They'd been vaccinated against it shortly before. One man had contracted elephantiasis when he served in Vietnam. Though it had been in remission, within twelve hours his legs swelled till they were larger than his body. I found that the parasite had infiltrated vital organs, such as the liver, and caused massive hemorrhaging; he actually died of loss of blood.

"If that isn't enough mystery, there were victims whose teeth had decayed like—like sugar lumps under a faucet."

He shook his head, wiping his eyes. "Approximately twenty-five percent of the victims died in this manner, that is, from diseases that simply ran amok. In them, there was a sudden outbreak of some specific illness.

"The majority, however, about seventy-five percent, died of massive septicemia or bacteremia caused by a diversity of organisms. In them, the bacteria had multiplied so explosively as to cause the patient profound shock and a quick death."

Mandelbaum rose. "Gentlemen, we know that we're dealing with some entirely new organism here, probably a virus. It may be a long while before we're able to isolate it, culture it, and develop a vaccine—which of course we will certainly do in time. Meanwhile, we must make sure that it does not spread beyond Bensonville."

He spoke with assurance, but Jess noticed his eyes shift uneasily as he expressed his confidence.

"Now I suggest that we—"

But before Mandelbaum could adjourn the meeting, a tall man who sat slumped at one of the tables said, "Oh, hell, Doctor! I've been doing cultures ever since I've been here, and I haven't seen anything remotely new. There's no way to account for what happened here! You hear me?" He slammed his fist on the table. "There is *no* way!"

Dr. Gustofson looked up. "Oh," he said mildly, "there's *one* way. There's one thing that accounts for what happened."

Dr. Mandelbaum glared angrily as every man in the room turned to look at Gus.

"Mandy, you mind if I use your blackboard for a minute?"

Mandelbaum's nostrils were pinched together, but he said, "Of course, Doctor, if you have some theory to advance. I'm sure we're all anxious to hear from the distinguished epidemiologist."

Gus walked to the front of the room and stood beside the chalkboards, his rolled chart in his hand. He looked around until he saw Dr. Brown and said, "Jord, do you mind bringing me that map?" Gustofson drawled, "While we wait, I'll tell you again that there's only one way to account for what happened here, and it's perfectly clear what it is, if not what set it off."

Dr. Ogden muttered, "Well, by God, I'm glad it's clear to somebody."

"The only explanation is that the victims suffered some kind of trauma that caused a *total collapse of the immunity system* and left 'em prey to whatever bacteria or viruses were present in their bodies. If they already had an illness, it fulminated, and death came mighty fast. Where no illness was present, the bacteria normally carried in the body were able to multiply at fantastic rates and cause the massive bacteremia described by Jordan Brown."

"Gus, you're right!" It was Dr. Tull from the Louisville team. The other doctors had suddenly become more attentive, straightening in their chairs, leaning forward to listen. Dr. Tull said, "What the hell could cause the immunity system to blow all its piston heads at once? An immunity system isn't a simple thing, after all. It's antibody and skin and cellular tension and lymphocytes and—well, it's complicated."

"Right," said Gustofson, "and I think we need a

first-rate immunologist before we can make a final determination, but I tell you *I know* that those folks died because their immunity systems were paralyzed somehow."

Jordan Brown carried in a bulletin board with the map on it. In the map were the pins, red and blue, clearly showing the ellipse of death. When he set it on the tripod stand, there was an audible, universal gasp. Obviously they all realized the horror for which the red pins stood.

Mayor McDonald had been drinking again. He stood up and shouted, "It *was* an airplane, by God! That shape is a splash pattern!"

Dr. Mandelbaum hammered on the lectern. "Mayor McDonald! We must not hurl accusations. Please take your seat."

McDonald stared around piteously, then slowly sat down, as though realizing that the liquor was making a fool of him.

Mandelbaum studied the map. "What are the blue pins?"

Gus said, "The homes of the people who survived."

Mandelbaum pursed his lips. "Well, then, I don't see how it could have been any kind of chemical agent dropped on the city from the air. Some of those who survived were right in the center of the red area. And look at the precision, the perfection of that outline! No, nothing from the sky made that pattern."

"That's right," said Gustofson, "but now let me show you something else." He unrolled his chart and taped it to one of the chalkboards. "Look at this." He pointed at a column headed "Wednesday, May 26." "I interviewed all the survivors I could find, and in nearly every case they lived beyond the limits of the elliptical area or had been out of town prior to the outbreak. With the help of Jess Barrett, I narrowed that down. I can tell you now that every survivor was outside that area between seven forty-five and nine forty-five A.M. on Wednesday, May twenty-sixth, one week before the outbreak."

"Jesus," said someone reverently.

74

"I don't have any such definitive data on the victims, but so far it looks as if everyone who died was inside the ellipse during those two hours. The information we heard tonight confirms what I'm saying.

"I conclude that a trauma of unknown source occurred inside the elliptical area between seven forty-five and nine forty-five on May twenty-sixth, the Wednesday before the disaster, which caused the deterioration and eventual collapse of the immunity system of each of the victims."

McDonald growled, "I told you so."

Gustofson held up a hand. "Mayor, we don't know of any chemical, gas, or bacteriological agent that can destroy the immunity system. I know a little bit about chemical warfare—I keep up on it—and I can tell you there's nothing in our national arsenal or any other country's that's capable of doing what was done here four days ago. Oh, we'll check that out with the CIA and all, but it's my bet that nobody's even thought of such a thing till now. It could never be kept a total secret. Word of any such notion would get out. Remember, even the atom bomb wasn't a brand-new idea; the enemy was working on it, too."

McDonald shook his head emphatically. "Blast it, if it wasn't our own experimenting, then it was the damn Russians. Or maybe the Chinese. Somebody dumped something on my town that killed all my people, and I'm going to find out who it was, and I'm going to—"

"Take it easy, Jim, take it easy." Jess soothed him. "Let's just listen to what these guys have to say. I think they're getting somewhere now."

McDonald stared at him. Then, surprisingly, he smiled. "Jess, boy, I've had one too many bottles. You're right. I'll hush up." And he did.

Again Mandelbaum hammered on the lectern with his palm. "Gentlemen, Dr. Gustofson has given us some startling ideas. Whether their medical value is as great as their dramatic value remains to be seen. However, it's obvious that the pattern on the map is significant. Personally, I agree with my colleague that

75

no known chemical could have caused the Bensonville casualties; though if the immunity mechanism *is* involved, I think it must have been an attack by an invading organism, which jammed the system and prevented it from defending the body. I will continue to look for such an organism in my virological and bacteriological studies."

"Then why," drawled Gus, "haven't any of us caught this thing? Or any of the army personnel?"

Mandelbaum said, "You mean, Doctor, that none of us has caught it *yet,* don't you? I'm sure our cultures will provide the answer to your question.

"Meanwhile, to cover even the remotest possibilities, I'll arrange for interviews with top officers of the chemical corps and the air force. I'm also going to request that Public Health send an immunologist to advise us on the value of Dr. Gustofson's theory. In fact, I think I'll ask for an old friend of mine, Jack Goerke, whose credentials are peerless. If Dr. Gustofson agrees?" he added with courtesy that bordered on sarcasm.

The old man smiled. "Why sure, Mandy. Jack Goerke's as good a man as there is in the country, and it'll be fine to see him again. We might even get a poker game going."

There was an isolated chuckle or two, and the meeting broke up. The gloom had been slightly thinned; the men were more hopeful that they would eventually find an explanation of the baffling catastrophe.

Jess and Gustofson went out and climbed into the Porsche. On the highway, Jess held the wheel with both big hands and leaned forward, staring at the road as he thought aloud.

"You know, Gus, when I looked at that pattern again tonight, I realized that it couldn't have been caused by a chemical or gas—just as Mandelbaum saw, too. The extreme western edge of that ellipse follows Poplar Street for quite a way. Your notes show that all the people on the east side of Poplar died, while those on the west side lived. No cloud of gas or bacteria could make such a definite line."

Gus pulled out his old black briar. "Of course you're right, Jess. I never claimed it was anything dropped or sprayed. I never made so much as a wild guess about how it was done, not out loud, did I? Only poor McDonald did that. No, the method has me stumped." He lit the pipe, staring sideways at Jess in the flare of the match. "You have some notion in that quiet head of yours, don't you, son? Spit it out," he said.

"Gus, that ellipse looks like some kind of *dipolar electromagnetic field.*"

7

"A MAGNETIC FIELD?" said Gus at breakfast on Monday, having slept on the notion. "How could that have anything to do with an epidemic? It's a unique notion, all right, more in your line than in mine. Ideas, Jess?"

"I don't know. Maybe some sort of—I don't know. For it to have done any damage to people, it would have had to be pretty strong, yet no one we talked to mentioned that anything unusual happened—no sudden light or explosion or sensation whatever."

"How could they? Everyone who survived was out of the area."

"Wait a minute, I think I *have* got an idea," said Jess. "Remember Cliff Hague, the manager of the radio station? He lives in the middle of that ellipse and works just outside it. Since he was so close, maybe he'd know if anything happened in town. Why don't we ask him?"

"Good thought. Alma, any more coffee in that pot?"

Private Curtis drove them to the top of the hill that overlooked the north end of town, where they saw a simple station, consisting of one low, flat building with the radio tower in front. As they approached it, Jess said glumly, "I've always hated this miserable station. It broadcasts almost nothing but raucous country music, and anytime you want the news, it's so slanted it sets your teeth on edge."

"You know Hague well?"

"Pretty well. I think he could have a good station if Jim McDonald would leave him alone, but the mayor's out to make money, and this is a gold mine. It broadcasts to the farms and towns for miles around. Jim sets the editorial policy, and he's so far to the right that you wonder sometimes if he believes in democracy."

Gus chuckled, and the two of them entered the building, which looked abandoned. The reception desk was vacant, so were the broadcasting and control rooms, with their recording and reproduction equipment, shelves of tape cassettes and vinyl records, mikes, and earphones. At the end of the hall was the manager's office.

The young man behind the desk started to his feet and greeted them as they opened the door.

"How did your men here at the station make out, Cliff?" Jess asked without preamble.

"Well, there are five of us left, and strange as it seems, four of us, Ed and Jack and Allen and I, were the ones on duty the day the world fell in. The night crew and the weekend crew are all gone. All except Ziggy," he said with obvious admiration. "That tough little bastard made it."

Gustofson said, "Mr. Hague, I need to interview all survivors. How many of those boys are here now?"

"They're all here." He grimaced. "No place else to go."

"Can I talk to all of you together?"

"Sure, why not? We're not even on the air now. Jim doesn't want us doing any more broadcasting until he gives the word, so we're just sitting around overhauling equipment and shooting the breeze."

Hague got up and left the room, returning shortly with the four men. Like himself, they were young, casually dressed in vivid slacks and sport shirts. Jess introduced Dr. Gustofson. They all solemnly "howdied," brought folding chairs into the small office, sat down, and the doctor began his questions.

"First," he said to Allen, "were you out of town on Wednesday morning, the twenty-sixth, a week before the plague struck?"

"No, I was right here, working at the station. I work

from six in the morning to three in the afternoon on Wednesdays."

Gustofson glanced at Jess, who unfolded the small map he had brought with him. On it, he had drawn the mysterious ellipse. He laid it on the desk and marked the location of the radio station.

"What about you, Jack?" asked the doctor. "Where were you?"

"On duty, right here."

"Ed?"

"Same."

"You, Ziggy? I understand you're not on the Wednesday crew."

"No, I was in town."

Jess glanced at Gustofson. "You were in *town,* Ziggy? What were you doing?"

"Well, I drive the school bus to pick up the kids in the country on my day off. That's the kind of moonlighting a fellow needs when he works for Jim McDonald." Ziggy's narrow knife-edge of a face twitched with momentary displeasure. Gus noted that the sharpness of that face was mirrored in the rest of his body, which was as thin as a ribbon. He did look, as Hague had said, like a tough little bastard.

"Tell me about your bus driving. What time do you leave and get back? What's your route?"

"Well, hell," said Ziggy, "I pick up my bus—I mean I did. There's no reason for a bus anymore, is there? Probably won't be no school next year. I pick up my bus at six thirty, and then I—"

"Where did you pick it up?" interrupted Gus.

"At the garage. Let's see, I reckon I usually leave the garage about six forty-five."

"What time do you get back to town?" pressed Gus.

"Well, I'm always back by eight."

"You're back every morning by eight o'clock?"

"Have to get the kids to school on time," said Ziggy.

Gus whistled slightly under his breath. Quickly he made notations on the chart, which he unrolled and spread out on top of the map.

"Look, Jess, we've narrowed down the time to fifteen minutes! Your nephew, Rob, had to be at the college, which is inside our ellipse, by seven forty-five; and Ziggy was back in town by eight, after being outside the ellipse for over an hour. There's no question about it; the time was between seven forty-five and eight." He looked up. "Mr. Hague, what happened on Wednesday the twenty-sixth of May during that interval?"

Hague thought a minute. "Well, nothing that I can remember. It was just any old ordinary day." He flipped back through the pages of his desk calendar and said, "No, there wasn't anything."

Gustofson insisted. "*Something* happened that day; I'll swear to it! Did you hear an airplane go over? Did you hear any strange noises? Did you see a cloud over the city? Was there a peculiar light? Did you feel or smell or—or taste anything strange?"

Some of Gus's urgency communicated to him now. The manager said, "Jack, you're the news editor. Go check your files and see what happened that Wednesday."

Jack shook his bearded face. "Cliff, I don't have to go back. I know nothing happened. It was just as dead as—good Lord! I mean as quiet as every other day in this little burg—at least until the middle of last week."

The man named Ed squinted, thoughtful, and said, "Cliff, what day was it when we heard our sound? I mean, when we made our sound? You know, the *sound*. Wasn't that a Wednesday?"

"Yeah, I think it was," Jack agreed. "Cliff, you remember that noise?"

"Yes, I do." Hague frowned. "But that couldn't have anything to do with what the doctor's after."

"What sound?" Jess demanded.

"Oh, it was just a funny sound. I don't know if it was a Wednesday," said Hague, "but I do happen to remember the time. It was exactly seven forty-six in the morning. I know because we were playing a commercial. You see, we have these tapes." He gestured toward a shelf of cassettes. "They're commercials. We record them when we first get a contract;

81

then we use them over and over. Well, that day we were playing a plug for Star Used Cars, the one that always goes on at quarter of eight for one minute; and there was ol' Bill Star telling everyone how honest and wonderful he is and how every car he sells is better than the last one, and all of a sudden the damnedest sound you ever heard in your life came over. I can't describe it except that it was like the ringing you get in your ears sometimes when you feel lousy—but louder.

"Well, we stood there a second or two with our mouths open, trying to figure out what was happening. I must have looked at the clock half a dozen times in six seconds, worried as hell that there might be something wrong with the transmitter. Before we could start checking, though, the sound had stopped, and there was Star still yammering about his cars. We kept looking around half of that day, tryin' to figure out what went wrong. Finally somebody thought to play that tape over, and I'll be damned if the sound wasn't on the tape. How it got there I'll never know. We asked everybody at the station, and none of them had fiddled with the tape. There hadn't been anybody in here except our people, so who could have done it?"

Gus scratched his head. "You don't still have that tape, do you?"

Cliff pursed his lips and said, "Well, we might. One of the boys took it down to the repair shop. I'll see if I can find it."

"I'll go with you," said Jess.

The two walked down the narrow stairs to the basement. Cliff turned on the lights, and Jess found himself in a windowless, air-conditioned room with a jumble of equipment spilling off the benches onto the floor. After rummaging through the piles of material on the workbench, Cliff shook his head. "I guess we must have thrown it away, Jess. It doesn't seem to be here."

"How can you find anything in this mess? Is there anyone else we can ask?"

Cliff sighed. "Well, Bill Banks was our chief engineer, but—"

"Yes," said Jess, "oh, yes. Well, let's look around a little longer. What about the wastebasket?"

Cliff upended the tall metal waste can, and out tumbled a cassette. He read the label. "How about that? Here it is, sure enough!"

They went upstairs and shoved the cassette into a player. The pure oleo voice of Bill Star, your friendly used car dealer, came from the speaker. Suddenly there was a strange, high-pitched, throbbing sound, not precisely painful to their ears, but uncomfortable and eerie. It lasted for several seconds and then was gone, and Bill Star continued.

Hague snapped the button on the player. "That's it. Isn't it the weirdest noise you ever heard? I can't figure out how it ever got on there. I *know* nobody was in the studio but us."

"Do you mind if I take that tape with me?"

"Sure, go ahead, Jess. But what's it have to do with what you boys are looking for?"

"Danged if I know," said Jess mildly.

On the way back to the center of town, the doctor said, "Jess, what do you really think that noise is?"

"I don't know—unless someone, somehow, used the radio station to send a signal to a bomber to drop a bomb or whatever. But that's back to the sky-attack theory, which I don't believe. I just don't know, Gus."

They rounded a bend and came out on the flatland at the edge of Bensonville. The radio tower loomed above them. Jess said to the driver, "Wait a minute, will you?"

The jeep stopped, and Jess stared back up at the structure. It towered sixty feet into the blue sky, its gaunt framework painted red and white.

Jess shuddered. "I said I've always hated that thing. Now I can't help thinking that it had something to do with what happened. Why is it right at the end of the oval? Why did it broadcast that sound? That tower. It looks like an anatomical drawing of an arm with all the skin peeled off; the muscles red, the tendons white, like the arm of death." He shook his head. "Gus, let's get out of here before I crack up."

Private Curtis accelerated the jeep.

"Jess, boy, I don't think we need to hunt for any more survivors; we've covered the town. I want to go back to the hospital, talk to Jordan Brown, and look over the reports on people who died out of town. Why don't you spend the day with Alma? She's beginning to look pretty shaky again." He patted the young man's enormous shoulder. "I'll invite myself for dinner, and we'll go to the meeting together."

Gustofson was excited that evening as they drove to the hospital. But Jess, having spent the afternoon with Alma and her growing pack of orphaned children, was suffering the magnitude of the tragedy all over again, and he was annoyed at Gustofson's excitement. He said nothing, however, and as they entered the meeting room, he once again felt gratitude toward the old doctor. Jess knew that genuine concern for his grief had led Gustofson to include him in the investigation.

Mandelbaum was at the lectern, talking with an athletic-looking middle-aged man whom Jess didn't recognize. In the front were two officers, one air force and one army. Governor Cartwright sat next to them, and Jim McDonald was slouched in a chair beside the governor. The mayor, thought Jess, wasn't noticeably recovering.

Shortly Dr. Mandelbaum called the meeting to order. "Gentlemen, without preamble, because we're all anxious for news, I am going to introduce Colonel Carson of the air force."

The officer stood up and began by assuring his audience that the air force did not possess bacteriological weapons and never transported lethal chemicals or gases in its aircraft. He stated that he had personally checked the records for three weeks prior to the disaster and had accounted for every aircraft that had flown over the Bensonville area. "Oh," he said casually, "except for one small private plane that didn't file a flight plan. But we're sure there was no significance to that flight, since it was on a Wednesday morning a full week before the disaster. Naturally, we intend to track down the plane and its pilot."

Gustofson glanced at Jess.

Next, Colonel John Aherne of the Chemical Corps spoke with cheery confidence. "Gentlemen, I want to assure you, without equivocation, that the United States Army has absolutely no responsibility for the terrible tragedy that occurred here.

"As you know, when Richard Nixon was president he directed that all bacteriological weapons be destroyed. Since then, due to information that the Communists are developing new, more sophisticated germ weapons, we've begun some research and are developing a few strains of bacteria. However, they're safely locked in our research laboratories. None of them has been within five hundred miles of Bensonville, and *nothing* in our arsenal can produce the symptoms described to me."

He strode back to his chair as the physicians exchanged glum looks.

Ogden, Fornier, and Brown had nothing new, and Mandelbaum admitted that results to date on the cultures were disappointing, not a single unknown organism having appeared. For the first time even Mandelbaum sounded discouraged. He turned wearily to the stranger. "Well, Jack, there it is! Gentlemen, this is Jack Goerke of the Colorado Medical Center."

Dr. Goerke ran his hand over his crew-cut head and smiled disarmingly. "I'm flattered to be called to join this distinguished team, and I hope I'll be of some value. But after working here for only six hours, I begin to doubt that I know much about medicine.

"However, even at this early stage I can say this: I believe that Dr. Gustofson is, as usual, correct, and the disaster was caused by a collapse of the immunity system."

Mandelbaum was observed to blink several times and regard the newcomer with a little less enthusiasm.

"You all know that the immunity system is an enormously complex mechanism, composed of many virtually independent subsystems and capabilities. Discovering the cause of a woman's death from shingles wouldn't necessarily explain the fatal infection of a boy's acne. If we knew what specific mechanisms failed to stop infection, we still might not understand the explosive proliferation of intestinal flora.

"When I heard from Dr. Mandelbaum, I was pretty certain that you were dealing with some kind of acquired hypogammaglobulinemia or perhaps an unusual case of immunological paralysis caused by a toxin such as botulin.

"However, I was wrong. The diversity of infections, both viral and bacterial, and the explosive growth of malignancies indicate a paralysis of relatively unrelated immunological subsystems."

As he paused, Walter Cartwright raised a hand. "Doctor, I'm only a senile old man whose trade is politics. Will you tell me just what the hell you're talking about? I don't even know what the immunity system is."

Dr. Goerke smiled. "Sorry, Governor. We're all so accustomed to our own professional language that we often forget to translate it for laymen.

"With all our new, sophisticated medicines, basically the only thing we do is help the human body to cure itself. The body's wonderfully effective at self-defense, which is a good thing because we live in a sea of bacteria, viruses, and rickettsiae. Those are, of course, microbial agents capable of causing illness in man. We all take them into our bodies constantly: by breathing, through injuries to the skin, whatever we eat and drink. To a great extent, we live in harmony with them; we even *need* some of them, such as the bacteria that fill the intestinal tract and help us to digest our food.

"There are also many organisms, particularly viruses, that live in our tissues and are usually harmless. They only cause infection when there's a breakdown in the body's immunity system.

"All human beings carry a variety of potentially harmful microbes. But it's only when something upsets the equilibrium of this host-parasite relationship that disease develops. We don't know yet how this balance, or symbiotic relationship, is maintained. You'd think that either the body would kill off the microbial agents, or the agents would kill the host."

The governor said, "I understand you so far, Jack. You make this scientific stuff plainer than some others I could mention. But I don't understand the mechanisms by which my body defends itself."

"Governor, there are actually two systems of immunity. One's called 'innate,' or 'natural,' immunity. That's the system that operates to defend you against the organism entering the body for the first time. The second kind is called 'acquired,' or 'specific,' immunity. Once your body has fought off an infection, it produces antibodies that keep you immune to further infection from the same organism."

The governor interrupted, "I think those organisms must be what we used to call 'germs'—or plain 'bugs'! Explain to me about that innate immunity."

"Well," said Goerke, "very little is known about that; it's a complex and difficult system. We've spent much more time studying specific immunity because of the possibility of isolating an antibody for study in a test tube. Your innate immunity is vitally important and consists of a whole series of defenses.

"For example, one of the simplest is the human skin! Not only does it protect us against the invasion of most organisms, but it actually has an antibacterial agent in it. Bacteria which can easily be grown on a glass slide are killed if we try to culture them on human skin. There's something in this hide of ours, still unidentified, that kills the microbes.

"The blood contains a whole host of bactericidal substances. There seem to be 'normal antibodies,' which many scientists do *not* believe are the result of previous infections, yet which can kill various types of microbes.

"And there's the whole process of inflammation,

which is really the body's way of fighting off disease. If you cut your hand, the wound will likely become inflamed—red and swollen. That inflammation is a complex healing process.

"And, Governor, one of the most interesting of the body's ways of resisting infection is the production of interferon by many types of cells. It has tremendous power to resist viral infections.

"But let's go back to inflammation. After infective particles have invaded through, say, a wound, the body puts a wall of cells around the lesion and apparently tries to contain the microbes. However, some scientists have recently argued that the copious exudation of fluid into the wound actually sweeps many of the invading organisms into the bloodstream and lymph channels, both of which are rich in cells and substances that kill bacteria.

"The inflammation, which is occurring behind that wall of cells I mentioned, partly results from the arrival of certain cells called 'phagocytes,' or 'scavenger cells.' These seem to be strategically disposed and always ready to spring to the defense of the body. They actually attack the invading bacteria or viruses and eat them. They're able to do this because the surface of the microbe is coated with something that decreases the surface electrical potential and promotes adhesion to the surface of the very phagocytes that have come to ingest them."

"I follow so far," said Governor Cartwright. "At least, about ninety percent. Go on."

"One of the most interesting investigations of innate immunity was conducted by a man named Aschoff, who tried to identify the various cells that are actively phagocytic in the body. He used the term 'reticuloendothelial' to designate that group of cells. Aschoff discovered that the endothelial cells of the blood and lymph vessels and the fibroblasts of connective tissues themselves were capable of phagocytosing—that is, devouring—invading organisms.

"But he also discovered a far more important group of such cells. He found that certain cells of the spleen, of the medullary cords of lymph nodes, the lining cells of lymph sinuses, and of the sinusoids of the liver and bone marrow and similar cells in the suprarenal and pituitary glands were extremely active. These cells are called, collectively, the reticuloendothelial system and form a network through which invading organisms are carried, filtered out, and destroyed. This system is so efficient that it's virtually impossible to overload it, so long as the liver and spleen are intact and have normal circulation.

"So, you see, Governor, in the natural immunity system we find many capabilities relatively independent of each other, yet all contributing to an efficient overall system for destroying invading organisms."

As Goerke paused, the governor said, "You talk about 'antibody.' Would you tell me more about that? This thing begins to intrigue me. I hadn't any conception there was so much going on in here." He tapped his chest.

"The production of antibody is one of the most miraculous aspects of life," said Goerke eagerly. "It's what makes vaccination against various diseases possible. You may remember that Jenner discovered, in the eighteenth century, that milkmaids who'd had cowpox never caught smallpox. He took material from cowpox and intentionally infected subjects, who were then found to be protected against smallpox.

"What this means is that if the body is once invaded by a particular organism and successfully fights it off, it becomes hypersensitive, so that if the same organism finds its way in again, the body can quickly destroy it before the disease recurs. The mechanism by which it does this is antibody. Antibody is simply a very large protein molecule, which combines with certain sites on the surface of a bacterium or virus and either inactivates it, or punctures a hole in its membrane, or simply makes it vulnerable to phagocytosis by the large scavenger cells that I told you about.

"This, of course, brings up questions such as: How does the body *remember* what a measles virus looks like and alert the responsible cells so that they'll manufacture—in the space of minutes!—literally millions of antibodies to destroy the virus?

"The body must manufacture an entirely different antibody for each microbe or virus. That, Governor, is why we doctors are forever trying to culture—that is, grow—various types of infective organisms in test tubes. We weaken those organisms until they can't cause any real damage and inject them into human beings, who manufacture antibodies against them. That's inoculation."

Governor Cartwright said with respect, "How clever of the good Lord to have thought up such a miraculous body for us."

Dr. Goerke chuckled. "You're right, sir, it is a miracle. However, we don't know why, but that miracle sometimes turns against us. There's a phenomenon called 'autoimmunity,' in which something apparently goes awry and the body manufactures antibodies against some of its own tissue. Arthritis, endocarditis, glomerulonephritis, and systemic lupus erythematosus are diseases widely thought to be the results of the immunity system fighting its own body."

"Well, I have heard of arthritis," said Cartwright wryly.

"And then there's the phenomenon called 'allergy.' Hay fever and asthma strike us when the body has a violent immunological reaction to irritant substances like ragweed pollen.

"Also, the body's annoyingly efficient at recognizing foreign tissue. If we transplant a heart, a kidney, or skin, and the donor isn't genetically similar to the recipient—such as an identical twin—the body quickly rejects the transplant, destroys it. We think that a cell called a 'lymphocyte' is most responsible for rejection."

Governor Cartwright said, "Thank you, Dr. Goerke. I appreciate that explanation."

Goerke smiled. "Sir, I hope I haven't confused you too much. This is a complex field, and we don't completely understand it ourselves." He looked past the front row to the physicians, whose attention had wandered. "Gentlemen, I know that you realize there are many factors affecting the immunity system. Young children are far more susceptible to some diseases than adults, probably because we all ingest various organisms in minute-enough quantities to create antibodies but not to cause disease, so that the older we grow, the more immune we become—at least, until we reach advanced age and immunity falls off, so we're again more susceptible.

"Almost any kind of stress can reduce the immunity of the body to disease—emotional stress, fatigue, fright, injury. There are also hormonal influences, as in diabetes mellitus, where there is an increased incidence of surface infections, such as boils and carbuncles, as well as internal infections.

"Various drugs strongly influence immunity. Some patients being treated by glucocorticoids have experienced a dramatic exacerbation in arrested tubercular lesions. Apparently, after remission of a primary lesion in the lung, the infecting bacteria can live in an attenuated state for many years without any change until the cortisone disturbs that equilibrium, and the organisms again proliferate. Cortisone also diminishes the ability of the reticuloendothelial system to take up certain types of organisms from the blood.

"We know that various types of irradiation, particularly by x-rays, can cause dramatic suppression of the immune system. For example, after large doses of whole-body irradiation, there's an explosive bacteremia involving intestinal organisms.

"From what I've heard and seen of the outbreak here, I'd say that the most likely culprit was some sort of irradiation. However, I understand from Dr. Mandelbaum that there's no evidence of such a thing occurring in Bensonville. Frankly, gentlemen, so far, I'm stumped. I'd like to hear your thoughts."

Bill Nyland held up his hand. Jess realized that in five days Bill had lost a good deal of weight. Probably he'd eaten almost nothing. "Dr. Goerke, do you think this outbreak could be a kind of immunological paralysis, such as we find in massive infections by pneumococcus polysaccharide?"

Goerke passed his hand through his short hair and shook his head. "I don't see how it could be, Doctor, because such a paralysis is specific to the particular antigen. While the body is totally incapable—for a period of time, perhaps forever—of responding with the production of antibody to *that* antigen, it's still perfectly capable of responding to others. What happened here was apparently a breakdown in the *entire* immunity system—every aspect of it."

Dr. Hughes said, "I don't understand what this collapse of the immunity system could have to do with malignancies. We saw tumors grow explosively within a few hours. What does immunity have to do with cancer?"

Jack Goerke frowned. "Well, for many years we thought that because tumors grew within the body and were therefore part of the host, they weren't antigenic. We assumed that the body wouldn't produce either antibodies or immunologically competent cells to attack the tumors. But a number of investigators, such as Richmond Prehn, definitely established in the late sixties and early seventies that virtually all tumors —probably *all* tumors—are in some sense antigenic. In other words, the body does try to mount an attack on the tumor, but the attack fails for reasons we don't yet know. In the kind of catastrophic collapse that happened here, the tumor cells would have absolutely no inhibitor. And as we know, when there's no inhibition, tumor cells *can* grow explosively."

Ken Fisher stood. "Dr. Goerke, why didn't our massive antibiotic therapy do any good? In the bacterial cases, we did see initial improvement in the patient after antibiotic treatment; but it didn't hold for very long, and the patients eventually died."

"I suppose that's because we've never fully appreciated the tremendous power of the immunity system. Even antibiotics, potent as they are, only provide assistance for it. With immunity gone it's impossible to control infection with *any* dosage. And, of course, antibiotics are ineffective against viral infections."

Someone called out, "Dr. Goerke, cells that produce antibody have short lives, and their capability of transmitting information about the synthesis of the antibody molecules dies with them. Only the continuing presence of antigen within the body transmits that information to a new generation of cells. If there were radiation or perhaps drug damage to antibody-producing plasma cells, wouldn't all specific immunity collapse quickly with the death of the existing generation of cells? Wouldn't the death of the person then follow the first invasion of an infective microbe?"

Dr. Goerke thought for a moment. "Doctor, that is a brilliant idea. But I'm inclined to think that it wouldn't explain failures of the innate immunity system. Certainly, though, you must be correct in suggesting that there was a failure by the cells of the spleen, bone marrow, and lymph nodes to produce plasmacytes. Till we've done more precise histological studies of these cells, I can't comment on why they failed. Still, I think you'll agree with me that that wouldn't explain the failure of other parts of the system. For example, today, in the few victims still unburied, I found incredible lesions. I found hideous cases of ulcers. The victims had apparently first formed the usual granuloma, only to have those collapse. We found lesions similar to those we find in agranulocytosis."

The next question came from Gustofson, who had been listening carefully the whole time, pulling at his yellowed moustache. "Jack, antibody can sometimes be disassociated from a complex with a soluble antigen by greatly increasing the electrolyte concentration. Probably the salt ions compete for the sites of the antibody union with antigen ions. Do you suppose some massive dislocation of the electrolyte balance in these poor souls that died here could have caused them to become so immunologically incompetent?"

Dr. Goerke said admiringly, "Gus, that's a fascinating suggestion that must be explored. We have plenty of blood samples being tested. All I can say now is that I don't think that would explain all the phenomena encountered in this outbreak. But it's a creative, provocative thought, and I thank you for it." He gazed around the room. "We've got our work laid out for us. I'd like to make some suggestions now on what to look for in our investigations—yes, Dr. Mandelbaum?"

Mandelbaum strode up and took the microphone. "Sir, it is my theory that this horrendous outbreak was a result of a bacterium or virus resistant to phagocytosis, such as *Streptococcus pneumoniae*. I believe it invaded its victims and multiplied in such numbers as to cause paralysis of their systems and leave them prey to whatever other microbial agents might be present in their bodies." With that, he sat down.

Carefully, Goerke said, "Of course, we must look for such agents in the cultures. However, even if it were true, I don't quite understand how it could have caused the paralysis of the other aspects, such as those ordinarily handled by the lymphocytes or by interferon.

"Now, let me make these suggestions about the next few days of work. In the autopsies of the remaining victims, be especially careful in your histological studies of the spleen. I'd like particular attention paid to the Malpighian bodies. Also, we want reports on the condition of the various endocrine glands, such as the thyroid, adrenal, and pituitary.

"I know that in some cases blood samples were taken before the patients died, and I want full reports on their analyses. I want dissections of the lymph nodes of as many patients as possible, histological studies of the Kupffer cells, the thymus gland, and the bone marrow."

Dr. Goerke paused, thinking. "May I suggest that if we have any further illness, we not only try massive antibiotic therapy in case of bacterial infections and, of course, gamma globulin but also experiment with BCG to stimulate the immunity system. We might also consider the use of Freund's incomplete adjuvant. I think you're all aware that these have been used on some occasions, particularly in conjunction with in-

jected antigen, to heighten the immunity response."
He gave a polite nod and sat down.

Dr. Mandelbaum stepped forward again. "Thank you, Dr. Goerke. Now, gentlemen, if there's no other business, we'll adjourn."

There was an immediate stirring as the doctors rose stiffly to their feet. Gustofson's voice cut through the noise. "There's one more important thing to consider before we do that, Mandy."

Everyone sat down. Jess later swore that he could hear Mandelbaum's teeth grinding as he said, "Well, Dr. Gustofson, what do you have for us this time?"

Gus ambled to the front of the room with his handmade chart rolled up under his arm. He asked two of the younger men for the chalkboard, which had been turned against the wall. On it was the map of the city with the oval of death.

"Gentlemen, last night we looked at this map pretty thoughtfully. Jack, this is Bensonville, with the homes of the victims marked by red pins and those of the survivors by blue ones. I found out that every person who lived inside this neatly defined oval and survived had been beyond its boundaries during a certain two-hour period, exactly a week before the outbreak. Anybody who lived outside that area but happened to be in it during that two-hour period died.

"Today I narrowed the time down to a quarter of an hour: the fifteen minutes between seven forty-five and eight A.M. on Wednesday the twenty-sixth of May.

"When you add this to the results of our studies of the victims and to the fact that even animals and birds died, it seems about as obvious as can be that some kind of short-lived trauma occurred during those fifteen minutes, causing the collapse of the immunity system of every living creature in the ellipse.

"Now, gentlemen, I want you to hear something." He glared at them for a moment. "Something terrifying, I warn you, in its implications." He walked to his chair, picked up a small tape recorder, brought it to the front of the room, and laid it on the podium. He described the trip he and Jess had made to the radio station and told of the sound that had been emitted at exactly 7:46 A.M. Then he started the machine, and the crowd listened in hypnotized silence. There was the commercial, then the high-pitched whining noise, then the commercial again, cut off by the Stop button.

Gustofson said quietly, "Every single person who was within this ellipse at the time that signal was broadcast died. Gentlemen, I suggest that we call the FBI."

For a moment there was no sound, no movement. Then Mandelbaum stood up. "Dr. Gustofson, I know your love of drama, and I hate to deprive you of this moment." He was white with rage, and his hand trembled as he shook his finger at Gus. "But I can tell you, sir, that I'm very tired of your histrionics. This epidemic is a medical problem, not a game of cops and robbers. I have no intention of committing any such stupidity as calling the FBI."

Slowly Walter Cartwright stood up. Despite his age, in this moment he was straight as a post. He said quietly, "Doctor, if you don't call the FBI, I will. And while I'm at it, the CIA, too, because this may have been a foreign plot. The meeting is adjourned."

8

JESS LAY IN HIS BED at Alma's house and tried to relax. His body cried for sleep, but his emotions would
not relent nor his mind slow down. He thought of the
day, of the visit to the radio station, of that red-and-
white arm reaching into the sky above Bensonville.
He thought of the oval on the map and of the few
blue spots in the sea of red. Memories of the youngsters
who had graduated from Shiloh and died hundreds of
miles away came back to him. He thought of Bob, of
squirrels dead under the trees. And he thought of
Ginny.

A doze finally softened the pain. His mind went
hazily to thoughts of the strange sound as he drifted in
and out of sleep. Could it have been signaling a
bomber to drop its lethal load? Gas would not leave a
pattern so precise. What could possibly account for
that?

Vague memories of other patterns eased themselves
into his half-conscious mind. He saw a physics book
lying open, with drawings of various types of electric
fields. Again there was the radio tower, a dreadful
flayed arm shadowing Bensonville.

Suddenly into his nightmare came the high-pitched
whine, and Jess saw lines of electric force leap from
the radio antenna and encircle the town of Bensonville.
Like spears, the lines impaled screaming women and
children until they glowed like colored lights. Their
very screams were transformed into garish patterns
that merged gaudily with the lights dancing through
and around them.

Jess came upright. He was sweating coldly. For a

few moments he sat there, dazed, trying to recover the nightmare that had awakened him. He shook his head, rolled out of bed, put on a robe.

In the kitchen he got out a bottle of milk and a box of crackers and sat down at the table. Again he tried to recapture the exact picture from his nightmare. Something about it nagged at him.

Electric sparks impaling the people of Bensonville, illuminating the pathetic town. Abruptly he stopped chewing. A dim thought had surfaced long enough for him to identify it: Sparks flew from one terminal *to another!*

That was what he'd forgotten about his dream: At the opposite end of the oval was *another antenna!*

With the rush of that memory into his consciousness came another. On the day of terror, when he'd chased the ambulance to force it back to Bensonville, he had stopped the driver beside Stover's Woods.

Had he seen something that day? A light flashing from just inside the woods? A reflection from a mirror or piece of metal?

He finished a cracker and washed it down with milk, went into Bob's study. There he rummaged in the desk until he found a map of the city. He took it to the kitchen and spread it out on the table. With one finger he located the tower of the radio station. As nearly as he could recollect it, he traced the outline of the oval. At the other end was Stover's Woods. Slowly he folded the map, put it back in the desk, and went upstairs to bed.

On Tuesday, Dr. Gustofson awoke with the realization that it was already late. He hurriedly showered, dressed, and went downstairs, where he found Jess and Alma at the kitchen table.

Jess looked up and smiled at the old doctor. "We didn't wake you because we figured that after the past few days you must be absolutely exhausted. How about a couple of eggs with your bacon?"

Gustofson agreed he'd needed the rest, said he would like some eggs. Alma went to the stove. As

Gustofson sat down, he looked carefully at Jess. Something about the young fellow was different. The grief had released its hold, and his face was not so lined. No, he thought, not exactly relaxed. Confident? Determined? Assured?

Jess saw the doctor eyeing him. "Gus, today you and I are going to take a ride. I've got an idea." He offered no further information, and Gustofson asked for none.

The old man ate a leisurely breakfast while Jess and Alma talked. The children were screaming in delight as they ran through the sprinkler in the yard; Gustofson marveled at how quickly they could adjust.

It was almost noon by the time Jess brought his Porsche to the front of the house and picked up Gustofson. "Gus," he said, "about that oval shape: You remember that I said it looked like some kind of dipolar electric field—which is preposterous on the face of it. But there's that signal from the radio station.

"Well, I had a dream last night, and it stirred a memory that I wasn't even sure *was* a memory; but the longer I think about it, the more certain I am. Here we are now."

Jess had been driving along a country road that ran parallel to the southern edge of Bensonville. Off to the right was a new subdivision of houses. It was within the oval, and all the residents had died. On the left of the road were only two houses. They were just inside the end of the ellipse. Jess pulled into the driveway of the second house, now empty, and stopped the car. "Let's go for a walk. I don't think we'll have to go far."

As they tramped into the woods in the back of the house, Jess told Gus how he had chased the ambulance and caught a glimpse of something glinting in the sun as the driver ran.

"Watch out for that sinkhole, Gus," warned Jess. "Let's cut back this way. I want to take a look at that clump of trees over there."

Even as he spoke, they saw it, hidden behind the trees.

Gus's voice was barely a whisper. "My God!"

9

LOOMING IN FRONT OF THEM stood an antenna. It was fourteen or fifteen feet tall and made of aluminum pipes. The center pipe had been driven securely into the ground. At the top, a cup-shaped piece of aluminum faced across the town directly toward the radio station. Below it were a series of curving arms. The uppermost half ring was not more than eighteen inches across; there were seven more, which increased in size until the bottom arm was at least six feet from tip to tip.

Jess walked around the structure, testing its arms, inspecting each detail. Then he walked away and looked at it from a distance.

Gustofson watched him for a moment more, then spoke. "Jess, this is the other end of the ellipse, isn't it?"

Jess nodded silently and continued to stare at the antenna.

"Is there a chance this is only for TV?" asked Gus.

Still Jess said nothing as he squinted up at the shining framework. Finally Gustofson offered, "I have my Polaroid camera in the car; I'll get it." He went back and rummaged among charts and jackets and notebooks until he found the camera. Then he returned to the antenna.

Jess said, "Gus, this is it. This has got to be it. I don't know how, but whoever put this up killed Bensonville. And, Gus, I'm going to find out how they did it and who they are, and I'm going to—"

"Take it easy, Jess. We don't know for sure that this object had anything to do with it. Have you any idea how, or for what, it could be used?"

Jess shook his head. "No, I haven't. But look, here's a hole drilled into the tubing, so something was plugged into the damned thing. My guess is that a signal was broadcast from here that erased the tape in the radio station and recorded that sound. Somehow, a field of some sort was established between here and the station. Gus, I think that field was what paralyzed the immunity systems and killed everyone."

"Jess," said Gus, his voice trembling, "this is your special domain. Do you know of anything that could produce such an effect?"

Jess shook his head again. "I don't know how it was done, but I know that's what happened. And I'm going to find out who did it."

"Let's get some pictures." The doctor lifted his Polaroid and took several shots from different angles. As he pulled each one out of the camera, he handed it to Jess.

When they were satisfied that they had enough, Jess said, "Gus, I want the army to tear this thing down and take it to the radio station; I'll use their workshop to make some tests and see what kind of field can be created by using it as an antenna. I admit I don't have much of an idea at this point, but if I tinker with it enough, I'll find out how they did it."

The old man nodded, and they looked up at the antenna once more. It glinted in the sunlight. Gustofson whispered, "God, it's a frightening thing, isn't it!"

"You know, Gus, years ago, after my mother died, my father took Bob and me to New York. We visited a museum to see a special exhibit on armor. I remember one suit that had been made for a giant of a man. It was mounted on a stuffed horse. When I commented about how brave the man who wore it must have been, my father snorted. He told me that most of the knights were bullies. He described a cavalry charge against infantry, who were always peasants. He said it was considered great fun for the cavalry to slaughter the helpless men on foot.

"I remember gazing up at that helmet, with the slit through which the knight had looked, and thinking

101

how cruel it seemed. In this antenna, I see the same sort of pitiless stare."

"Horrible," nodded Gus, "I see exactly what you mean. How did they do it? How can you use electronics to paralyze the immunity system of human beings?"

"I don't know, Gus. But I know this is it. Let's go."

It was a group of exhausted doctors who gathered for the meeting on Wednesday morning the ninth. Mandelbaum's face had a gray cast as he took the floor and rapped for attention. "Gentlemen, I'd like Jack Goerke to give us his observations after another day of studying our reports and supervising the histological studies."

The figure who came to the podium was hardly recognizable as the natty, athletic man of Monday night. He had looked at pictures of victims, read reports, participated in the last of the autopsies, talked, and listened for thirty-six of the past forty-two hours. The sheer magnitude of the disaster had stunned him, and his mood was subdued.

"I don't have much to say. I was confused Monday after a preliminary examination of the data, and I'm more confused after a thorough investigation.

"I do support Dr. Gustofson's theory that the cause of death, of all those deaths, was the total collapse of the immunity system. The reticuloendothelial systems of the victims we examined were undamaged, yet they failed to strain out and kill the invading organisms. The phagocytic cells simply lay there while hordes of bacteria swept past.

"I've looked at the reports on the spleen and found no severe damage. The Malpighian bodies are intact, but the bacteria poured through the spleen itself. They did no damage to the organ, but the spleen did nothing to the organisms either!

"The bone marrow and lymphocytes suffered no damage that would have brought about immunological tolerance. The electrolyte balance: normal in almost every case. Vitamin B levels in the blood and tissues: normal. The thymus glands: no damage. Toxicological

102

studies gave us no evidence of corticoids or of immunosuppressive drugs.

"We've studied the arteries and arterioles, even capillaries, to see if they failed to develop the permeability that lets the phagocytic cells pass through. We drew a blank. The Kupffer cells of the liver should have been engorged with antigen; instead, they showed no sign of having registered the diseases at all.

"We found a few medical curiosities. I believe the immunity system of each victim at first mounted a defense, at least in the case of local infections. It later collapsed, and the person died.

"Apparently antibodies never did develop, and those antibodies already present perished early, permitting the ordinary diseases against which the victims had been immunized to reassert themselves and cause death. The immunologically competent cells—for example, small lymphocytes—also failed to function."

Goerke sighed loudly. "It'll take many, many weeks before we can reach any final conclusions."

He slumped into his chair. Mandelbaum rose wearily to dismiss the meeting, but when Gus stood up, he looked resigned, waved his hand, and sat down to listen.

Gustofson summarized his and Jess's findings and passed around the photographs. There were numerous questions, the one most often repeated being unanswerable: "How the hell could a radio signal do anything to the immunity system?"

Dr. Gustofson said, "Gentlemen, I don't know how or who or why, but I know we've absolutely got to get those answers because somewhere out there is somebody who knows how to wipe out a whole town at a time."

The telephone rang. The soldier who answered it stiffened, and his eyes widened. He held his hand over the mouthpiece and said to Mandelbaum, "Sir, it's the president."

The fat doctor blinked. "The president?"

"The president of the United States, sir. He wants you."

Mandelbaum took the telephone. "Yes, sir? . . . Yes, yes, sir." A long pause. "Incredible! . . . Yes, Mr. President, of course, immediately. . . . Good-bye, sir."

Mandelbaum put the telephone down. "That *was* the president." He was staring blankly over their heads. "Three hours ago a town in Minnesota called Bridgeton was stricken with the same kind of outbreak. Several hundred have died already, and more are dying. The town's population is over seven thousand."

"Oh, dear *God!*" It was Ken Fisher.

Mandelbaum continued. "President Weaver is sending his personal assistant, Micah Maruyama, to lead a team to investigate. The president feels that this second disaster may indicate a conspiracy. He asked me to choose a team from among you to go to Bridgeton immediately. Helicopters are on their way to take us to Louisville, where we'll board an air force jet."

There was a stillness.

Mandelbaum looked around at the group. "Of course, I want all the men from CDC and you, Jack. And—" There was a pause, as all the doctors looked at Gustofson. "I guess you'd better come, too, Gus. We'll leave immediately."

10

IT WAS ALREADY DARK when Jess Barrett left the radio station. Since early that morning he had been struggling with the antenna, studying the insolent thing; and from what he had learned, he could deduce only how little he knew. Between the radio tower and the monstrosity facing him, some sort of electromagnetic field had formed. There had been a power drain across that field which had flowed into the earth through the antenna's base, where Jess had found burn marks.

In the horizontal plane, the field was elliptical in shape and had lasted exactly 5.8 seconds. Apparently there had been no noticeable effect at the time of the signal.

Jess had carefully examined the harmonics of the sound on the radio station's tape. There was nothing acoustically outstanding about it: a simple pulsating rhythm with an unusual number of undertones. It could not possibly have had any effect on human physiology; probably the noise was only the side effect of another phenomenon. Jess had tried to recreate the sound on the tape recorder by feeding signals to the antenna, but he had been unsuccessful.

Finally evening came, and Jess put away his equipment, turned off the lights, and left the building. The astonishingly heavy June heat was gone, and in its place a cold rain misted down. Pulling up the collar of his sports jacket, he dashed to the Porsche. The powerful little engine started immediately, and Jess swung the car around in a tight arc and headed down the hill toward the heart of Bensonville.

Barrett was a man who occasionally enjoyed solitude. Lost in his work today, he had forgotten for a few hours the loneliness that had descended upon him when the team left Bensonville for Minnesota. Mutely he had watched old Dr. Gustofson and the others climb into the helicopters, which flapped toward their rendezvous with the jet in Louisville. He had not realized until that moment how much the sheer intellectual stimulation of working to find the answer to the tragedy had eased his grief.

Bensonville quickly became even more of a ghost town. The few mourning survivors stayed inside their homes. Several doctors stayed on at the motel, waiting for the quarantine to be lifted so they could return to their families. Their work was finished, the autopsies completed, the bodies buried. The Public Health Service mobile units had packed up and moved out in a caravan for Minnesota, following the departure of the CDC team.

Jess Barrett had long been Bensonville's most famous resident. In high school he was an All-State fullback and led his team to the state championship. When he entered Northwestern, the people of the whole commonwealth followed his progress eagerly. But in three years of watching Big Ten safeties chase the tall young man across the goal line, they did not see the change that occurred in him.

At the beginning of his freshman year, he was eager to be drafted by the pros as soon as he'd graduated, but he soon changed his mind. He had a new love: electronics. His teammates accused him of calculating wind direction, local gravitational perturbation, and the strength of the solar wind to know where a pass would come down.

Blessed with great size, remarkable speed, and consummate coordination, he led the Big Ten in rushing and total offense three years in a row. In fulfillment of his early dream, the pros were ready to snap him up. But abruptly he announced that he would not play professional football. Instead, he accepted the Rhodes scholarship offered him and then, after returning to the United States, quickly earned his Ph.D.

For some time he worked for NASA on the effects of interplanetary environment on instrumentation. Recently he had gone out on his own. With a professorship at Shiloh and a lucrative consulting business, he kept busy.

Now, as he drove down the hill into town, loneliness swept over him. For the first time in his life, Jess Barrett felt utter panic. He felt as if the world had dug a grave and dropped Bensonville into it—both the living and the dead. At the edge of town a light flashed red at him. The traffic lights in town were still working automatically. Automatically, too, Jess stopped, though he had no reason to do so, for there were no other cars on the street.

The road sloped evenly down and then up in a gentle grade at the other end. Ahead he could see the half-dozen rain-blurred stoplights along the silent street. Synchronized to ensure a smooth flow of traffic, they changed from red to green. But there was no traffic. Only the rain swept along the street, veiling the town. Jess sat hypnotized as the lights continued to change, signaling to people no longer there.

Finally he shifted into low and moved through the intersection. He drove through the rectangle of light illuminating the street in front of Harper's Real Estate office, which was being used by the army as a command post. An officer behind the desk was reading, and a soldier stood at the door, staring out at the rain. No one else was in sight.

On the steps of his own home, Jess paused and stared at the tree in his front yard. Its wet branches caught the streetlight. Cardinals, called redbirds by Kentuckians, frequently came to its feeder. A week ago, after the epidemic had finally spent its force, Jess had found a cardinal dead under the tree, like a great drop of blood staining the ground.

Jess shook himself, entered the house, and snapped on the light. Quickly he went to the bedroom and rummaged through a dresser, looking for a turtleneck sweater. Taking off his coat, he pulled on the sweater. The clamminess he had felt yielded to the pleasant

107

warmth of wool around his body. Quickly he put on his sports jacket and went to the closet for a raincoat. As he walked through the hall, he glimpsed himself in the mirror and stopped, turned, studied his reflection. The face that stared at him was hardly recognizable as the relaxed, handsome young man who had left to play golf the week before. It was drawn and creased, and the gray of pain had crept into the creases. Jess smiled wryly, flipped off the lights, and went outside to his car.

As he turned the key, it occurred to him that thinking was the way out of his depression. As a little boy, after his mother's death, he had learned quickly that keeping his mind occupied was the best answer to grief. He switched on the radio and pushed one button after the other until the country rock music gave way to a well-known news commentator.

"Reports from Bridgeton, Minnesota, indicate that there have been no more cases of illness or death since early this morning. As at Bensonville, Kentucky, this tragedy has been unspeakable, the horror indescribable. And yet it has passed, again within twenty-four hours.

"Newsmen are not permitted to enter Bridgeton, but because there are so many survivors in this much-larger town, the information reaching the press is more extensive. It tells of children dying of such common diseases as tonsillitis, of people collapsing in the streets to die of whooping cough.

"This morning the president announced that he has asked his personal assistant, Dr. Micah Maruyama—theologian, politician, and troubleshooter—to head up the investigation. One wonders why the president would send a man whose doctorate is in philosophy, not medicine. However, it seems clear that the medical teams have been thrown into a bewilderment approaching panic. Aides believe that Dr. Maruyama will bring organization, iron discipline, and a new, clearer focus to the problem."

Jess turned off the radio. "Micah Maruyama," he mused.

When Dr. Mandelbaum first announced that Maruyama was going to meet them in Bridgeton to take charge of the investigation, Jess had applauded the president's wisdom. He had good reason. He had known Micah at Northwestern. At that time Maruyama was a pretheological student preparing to follow his father into the Presbyterian ministry. Jess had won first honors in his class, but Maruyama had been number two, with a grade average hardly distinguishable from Jess's. While Jess was at Oxford, Maruyama received his theological degree at Union Seminary in New York. While Jess studied for his doctorate in physics, Maruyama received his in philosophy.

It was during Governor Weaver's campaign for senator that Jess and Maruyama met again. At the request of Weaver's headquarters, Jess made a television spot commercial affirming his belief in Weaver's honesty and competence. Jess was surprised to find that the governor's campaign manager was Micah Maruyama.

Jess had followed Micah's subsequent dynamic rise with interest. When Weaver was elected to the Senate, Micah became his aide. When Weaver ran for the presidency, Maruyama again conducted his campaign; and when he was elected, Micah was named his senior assistant. Shortly thereafter Maruyama headed a commission appointed by the president to study the armed forces, and there were violent objections. But the military forces that emerged from their encounter with the brilliant, soft-spoken young aide were slimmer, cheaper, and unquestionably tougher and more effective. Jess smiled thinly, remembering all this. If anyone could bring order out of the confusion of Bensonville and Bridgeton, it would be Micah Maruyama.

As Jess's car swung round the circular driveway in front of Alma's, his headlights caught the magnolia tree, with its huge, fragrant blossoms. For a moment he forgot even his grief in wonder at the beauty of this countryside, his favorite spot on earth. Just beyond the house, in the woods, he could see in the powerful beams giant mountain laurel and magnificent rhododendron. Quickly he closed the car door and walked through the slackening rain to the house.

Apologizing to Alma for returning so late, he went upstairs to say good-night to the children. Alma's two were already asleep; he bent and gently kissed first one, then the other. They were freshly bathed, and for a moment he held his face close, marveling at the smell of their innocence.

He walked across the hall to the room where the Lowell boys were. John was asleep, but Tommy watched him as he entered the room. As he pulled the covers up around John, Tommy sat up in bed, and Jess, startled by the action, turned and sat down beside him. Silently the thin child put his arms around Jess and leaned his head against the big man's chest. For a moment the two of them sat together, and a wave of loneliness and grief rose up in Jess until it seemed that he would drown in it. He cupped a huge hand around the child's head and held him close.

"Tommy, it's time for you to go to sleep. I'm sorry I got home so late tonight, but tomorrow we'll play catch." He tucked the child under the covers, kissed him, and went downstairs.

Alma had taken his dinner from the oven, and they visited while Jess ate. The conversation was mostly trivial. She told him about the activities of the children during the day. He did report to her the work he had done with the antenna and his failure to come up with a clear concept of how it had been used. She watched Jess closely; as he talked, he stared out the window at the moon coming from behind the rain clouds.

Jess and Alma rarely talked deeply about any subject, not from any hesitation, but because they didn't need to. Over the years they had developed a solid friendship and mutual respect. Alma had learned the secret to the young man who was such an enigma to others. She saw that behind the keen intelligence and the immense talent was a man of simple desires who was unpretentious because he was not impressed by the glitter of life. He was an innocent in the best sense: a man who saw the world clearly and yet, far from turning cynical, retained his—there was, she thought, no other word for it—his purity. And she understood that because of the difference between the impression that he made and the inner man that he was, he would always be lonely.

That night she sensed his deepening loneliness, his feeling of rejection because the team had left. He stared vacantly out the window, and she knew he was thinking of the people in Bridgeton, wondering what horrors had overtaken them and if their ordeal was as terrible as that of Bensonville.

As he drank a second cup of coffee, Jess said, "Alma, I don't think I'll go back to the lab tomorrow. I'll just work around here, tidy things up, spend a little time with the kids."

She put her thin hand on his shoulder. "Jess, you've got to go back tomorrow and work with that antenna. If anyone can find the answer, you can. *That's* your job, not staying here."

Jess fingered the cup and continued to stare out the window. "I don't know, Alma. It seems so hopeless."

Alma's face drew tighter as she watched him. The telephone rang. They both jumped.

It rang again before Alma picked it up. She listened, then said, "Jess, it's for you: President Weaver's assistant, Dr. Maruyama, calling from Bridgeton."

For a second Jess hesitated, then took the receiver. "Hello, Mike," he said.

As the helicopter flapped its way blindly through the cool Minnesota darkness, the words of President Weaver rang in Micah Maruyama's ears.

"Mike, I can always count on you. Our country's never faced a worse crisis than it's facing now, and I'm probably giving you the biggest responsibility you'll ever have. I think you can handle it. Go to Bridgeton, and take over that medical team. Report to me every day exactly what's going on, what progress those doctors are making, if any.

"I've asked Morrison from Public Health Service to give you a briefing on what they know so far." He'd stared at his assistant. "Mike, if you succeed, the world's your oyster. If you don't within a reasonable length of time, I'll put someone else in charge."

Since receiving that commission, Micah had had little sleep. He read the reports, received the briefing from Morrison, and talked with doctors from the National Institute of Health, agents of the FBI and the CIA, and men from the army's chemical corps and the air force. He quickly decided after those conferences that the military forces had no responsibility in the matter. He also knew that for the time being he didn't want to involve the FBI or the CIA. He wanted time, first, to talk with Gustofson about his theory that radio antennae were involved in the disasters.

That night as he stared down from the helicopter, he saw long lines of red and white lights: automobiles jamming the freeway, fleeing the stricken area around Bridgeton. Micah knew that up ahead a town was in its death throes. Although the twenty-four hours of horror had ended, bodies were still being collected, and doctors were beginning the grisly work of autopsies.

As the rotor blades of the helicopter sliced up the distance, a cluster of lights rose on the horizon, and Micah knew they were approaching Bridgeton. He took off his heavy horn-rimmed glasses and settled back to wait.

Micah was a small man, somewhat thin, with rather bushy black hair, high, wide cheekbones, and typically Japanese features. He was the first Japanese American to hold so high a position in the government of the United States. Although he had intended to enter the ministry, his strong belief in the relevance of religion to life had led him to work for the election of Governor John Henderson Weaver to the Senate and later to join his staff.

The senator noted that Maruyama was the most efficient of all his assistants. His division worked faster and better than the others. The little Japanese man spoke so softly that his voice could scarcely be heard, but he had a knack for keeping the jobs flowing and for motivating others to work efficiently.

Maruyama discovered that the field of efficiency in Washington was a great wasteland. Nothing could be done without devious maneuvering through circuitous channels. He was stupefied by the unwillingness of anyone to decide anything. He did not operate that way; he *would* not. And Weaver found Micah to be the proverbial breath of fresh air. When he became president, he named him his senior assistant and gave him enormous authority. Micah used it wisely.

Within a year he became known as the man who singlehandedly repealed Parkinson's law. His method was simple. He used as few people as possible, made sure that they had all the authority and tools they needed to do the job.

His complete honesty soon earned him a large group of loyal supporters and an equal number of enemies.

The news media loved Micah Maruyama. Particularly they admired his complete candor. They soon realized that he would never lie and that he rarely dodged an issue. They also knew that wherever he was, things would happen. Before long they were comparing him with Kissinger, of previous administrations, and wryly dubbed him "Super Jap."

Naturally, people soon began to speak of him as a possible presidential candidate. When such suggestions were made to him, he never changed his impassive expression. Only once did he wistfully state that there was no real future in American politics for people of Japanese ancestry. It may have been his actual lack of hope that he himself could attain high elective office which made him so completely objective and efficient. He pandered to no special interests, yielded to no pressures.

Ahead, a floodlit building loomed out of the darkness. It rested gleaming white in a spider web of light. The helicopter circled to land beside it: a large warehouse near the railroad station, in the very heart of the city. It was a new building, its purpose expressed in featureless white walls and stark geometric lines. Micah had arrived, and a chill came over him.

It was early evening, and the town should have been alive with traffic. Instead he saw only a few ambulances. Nobody was there to greet him. Micah shrugged and started toward the main entrance. The door was unlocked, and he walked into the building, finding himself in a foyer. There was no one in sight. Hearing noises behind one of the large doors, he pushed it open and entered. What he saw wrenched a gasp even from his disciplined lips.

The huge room had been used to store furniture. Now scores of tables, no more than a few feet apart, filled the center of the room. On each lay a naked corpse.

But the room was alive with activity. Orderlies pushed body-bearing gurneys back and forth, and doctors worked at each table, eventually consigning the bodies to shelves to await burial. The murky combination of blood and other body fluids was collected in a bucket beside each table, then poured down a drain in the center of the floor. Stretching across the room, rows and rows and rows of feet stuck into the air, identification tags tied to their toes. Dozens of faces—old, middle-aged, young, even babies—were frozen, staring upward, often mutilated by the abominable deaths that had come to them.

Shelves reaching to the ceiling had once held furniture. Now they held the dead. On one side were bodies tagged and still clothed, that had been brought in by the army's Graves Registration soldiers. On the other side were bodies that had been autopsied, now naked and mutilated.

Micah stood beside one of the shelves. The skull of each corpse had been sawed open and the brain removed, and the emptied heads hung over the edge of the shelf. One of the bodies was that of a little girl about six years old whose blue eyes still registered terror and, Micah thought, accusation. As he stared at the child, an orderly trundled a gurney down the aisle of tables toward him; on it were five more bodies.

Micah backed out of the room into the foyer and stood there for a moment to collect himself, clenching

114

his teeth to keep them from chattering. A soldier walked toward him.

"Sir, are you Dr. Maruyama? Dr. Mandelbaum heard that you'd arrived, and he's looking for you."

Before Micah could answer, a third voice interrupted. "I'm Dr. Mandelbaum. I'm sorry we didn't have anybody meet you, but I'm sure you can understand the confusion here. Most of us have been working for almost ten straight days and nights." Mandelbaum's face was pasty, and his terrible fatigue robbed him of whatever dignity he had once enjoyed.

Micah offered his hand. "No apologies, Dr. Mandelbaum. I see that you have things—uh—under control."

Mandelbaum frowned. "You've been inside, then? An unpleasant sight. I hadn't intended you to see that without warning. At least we doctors are accustomed to death. Why don't you come with me, Mr. Maruyama? We've taken over some offices in the back; we can talk more easily there." He walked down the hall, talking over his shoulder. "I understand the president wants you to take charge of this investigation. Well, you're welcome to it. So far it's been nothing but a nightmare. I imagine the press is after my blood."

He turned into an office, and Micah followed. The fat man collapsed into a chair behind the desk. Micah seated himself carefully across the room. "Dr. Mandelbaum, the president is aware of the tremendous problems your team has faced. I'm here to represent him and his concern, to organize the effort, and to be sure that your team has all the facilities and resources it needs for its investigation. The president specifically asked that I handle all interviews with the press and political leaders so that you'll be free to carry on your medical work."

Mandelbaum nodded. He understood perfectly well the implications of Maruyama's words. He sighed. "We've commandeered a row of houses just across the street, Mr. Maruyama. It may make you feel queasy at first, staying in a house whose owners are newly dead, but at least it's close."

Maruyama laid his attaché case on the desk in front

of Mandelbaum. "I'm anxious to meet the other members of the team as soon as possible. I've read the report you sent to the Public Health Service. It sounds simply incredible."

"It is incredible, as you've seen." He waved his hand toward the autopsy room. "But what you'll see tomorrow and hear when the reports come in will be even more unbelievable. It's all impossible, and yet it's happened. *Twice.*"

"After reading your report and talking to the men in Washington, I decided not to call in the FBI or CIA yet," said Micah.

Mandelbaum roused a little. "That was sensible. This is a medical problem, which is also why I can't understand the president—"

"Sending me? Well, there are other things involved such as organization and dealing with the press and politicians. Doctor, you're exhausted. Why don't you show me my room?"

"That is your house, Mr. Maruyama, and this one and the one across the street are where the rest of us are staying. Would you like to meet the team? I see they're still up."

Micah nodded and followed Mandelbaum up the few steps to the front door of the nearest home. Inside, Micah saw a number of men sitting in the modest living room, plainly too tired even to go to bed.

Mandelbaum nodded grimly to them. "Gentlemen, this is Mr. Maruyama, President Weaver's assistant, who'll be chairman of this group from now on. Mr. Maruyama, this is Dr. Jordan Brown, our head pathologist, and this is Dr. Ogden, sanitation expert."

Brown wearily shook hands; Ogden merely nodded.

"Dr. Fornier, our specialist in pollutants; Dr. Goerke, our consultant on immunology. And this," he waved his hand, "is Dr. Gustofson. Epidemiologist. If you'll excuse me, I am now going to bed."

Maruyama stood watching as Mandelbaum ponderously descended the steps. Then he turned back to the exhausted doctors slouching in their chairs and couches. He eyed them one by one and reflected that he had not seen men look so tired and discouraged since the war in Vietnam.

He said, "Gentlemen, I'm sorry to meet you under these circumstances, but I count it a privilege to be a member of such a distinguished team."

Only the oldest member, Dr. Gustofson, had enough energy left to nod in appreciation.

"I've been in the warehouse," said Micah, "so I have an idea of what you've been through. I don't know how you've maintained your sanity."

Dr. Jordan Brown, whose face was gray and blotched, shook his head, mute.

"I also want you to know that the president will send anything you need to deal with this epidemic. You certainly realize that we are now facing one of the worst crises in the history of our nation. Today the stock market went insane. People are heading for Canada and Mexico by the thousands, although both of those countries have sealed their borders against us. The Mexican air force even shot down a light plane that was trying to escape our country—and we don't blame those gunners. England has demanded that all American ships tie up outside the ports for a two-week quarantine before landing passengers or cargo. Believe me, we've got to nail this damn thing double-quick. Have you any ideas at all?"

Dr. Fornier's face rippled nervously and his long, narrow nose twitched. His voice had a whining quality that Micah sensed was foreign to it. "All I know is that these poor devils keep dying, and nothing we do helps them."

Micah studied Fornier and said, "When I was briefed by the Public Health Service, they wanted me to ask if you had tried using gamma globulin or Freund's incomplete adjuvant?"

Jack Goerke, who had been leaning back in a rocking chair, opened his eyes slowly. "We used gamma globulin by the quart, and it did nothing. Does PHS think we're amateurs, for God's sake?"

Jordan Brown shook his head. "This plague is un-

117

precedented in the annals of medical history. My God, Dr. Maruyama, we've done toxicological, hemotological, and histological studies of everything—the liver, the spleen, the bone marrow, the arteries, every single part of the body. Do you know what we discovered? What clues we found to the cause of this horror? *Nothing.* All we know is that these people's bodies simply put up no resistance at all."

Micah had read the reports and knew that in Bensonville they had been unable to discover significant medical clues, but he had not expected such a complete blank. "I noticed from the report that there was a great deal of discussion about a plane having dropped gas or perhaps bacteriological substances or chemicals. Do you think it could have been something like that?"

Dr. Brown sighed. His gray hair was dirty and matted around his bald pate, and it shook as he wagged his head from one side to the other.

"No, Dr. Maruyama, I think Gus—Dr. Gustofson here—proved conclusively that it couldn't have been a chemical, a gas, or even a bacteriological substance."

There was silence for a few seconds, and then Micah said, "In Washington I was approached by a doctor from HEW who actually maintained that the cause had to be some kind of death ray. At first he suggested an extraterrestrial source, like a flying saucer. Then he backed off and said it was probably a laser from a Russian satellite orbiting the earth. What do you think of that?"

Fornier said querulously, "One more of these disasters, and I'll believe it's a witch on a broomstick."

Only Dr. Gustofson seemed to have listened with all his faculties to what Micah had said. He reached inside his coat and pulled out a penlight. Slanting it slightly, he flashed the beam on the floor and observed it thoughtfully.

Dr. Goerke said, "Well, Gus, are you giving up your idea about the antennae?"

"Oh, yes, Dr. Gustofson," said Micah, "I read that

118

you have a theory about a radio station. It sounds, I have to be frank, rather farfetched."

The old man looked at him from under bushy eyebrows. "What's happened in these two towns *is* pretty farfetched, youngster. Sit down, and I'll show you something." He picked up a roll of papers from a corner of the room. "One of the first things we epidemiologists do is locate the homes of the victims. When we did that in Bensonville, we found one hell of a mind-boggling pattern. We stuck red pins in a map to represent the victims, and blue pins for the survivors. I took a picture of that map. Let me show you."

He unrolled an enlargement on which the red oval of death gleamed, inimical. Micah gasped. "It *does* look as if someone had trained a death ray on that town!"

Gustofson fished a pipe out of his coat pocket, after some difficulty in finding it among papers, matchbooks, and a cold, half-eaten hamburger. Stuffing tobacco into the bowl of the pipe, he growled, "My colleagues here aren't completely in accord with my theory, and I don't claim that what I've discovered really explains much. But I think you'll find the facts are striking. Look."

He tapped the stem of his pipe on one end of the ellipse. "Right here is the antenna of the radio station. Here, hidden in a grove of trees, we found another antenna. We've got a picture of it." He laid before Micah Maruyama one of his photographs. "Now, that bowl-shaped convexity with its weird arms is pointed exactly at the radio station."

As Micah studied the picture, Gustofson found a match, lit his pipe, and puffed out a huge cloud of heavy smoke.

Dr. Ogden roused himself to throw open a window. "Gus, can't you take up pot, or become an alcoholic, and give up that damn pipe?"

The old man paid no attention. "Now look," he said, "see the blue dots inside the ellipse? All those survivors had been out of town during a certain fifteen-minute period exactly one week before the disaster. On the other hand, the red dots *outside* the ellipse represent people we know were *inside* it during those fifteen minutes—although they were out of it when the disaster struck. Even the students who died in Europe, thousands of miles from Bensonville, were inside that oval during that quarter hour. Now listen to this."

He went back to the corner where his things were piled, picked up a small recorder, set it on the table, and started it. First there was the used-car dealer, then the high-pitched whine, then the rest of the commercial.

Gustofson explained how they'd found the tape and when the sound had been broadcast. "Now, Dr. Maruyama," he said, "my theory is that some vile, crazy, brilliant son of a bitch plugged a kind of infernal device into this antenna and beamed something to the radio station, and the two of them formed, for a few seconds, a dipolar electric field. I think that impulse dealt a death blow to the immunity systems of the victims, that in a week they lost all immunological capability and died. Now if you ask me how the hell any kind of radio wave or electric field can cause such damage to the immunity system, I admit that I haven't the slightest idea. But the coincidences involved in this whole pattern are just too thick to be shrugged off."

Maruyama continued to stare at the map. "Remarkable—do you have any data on Bridgeton yet?"

The doctor sucked on his pipe and exhaled more smoke. "Well, I've got a little something."

Again he went to the corner and returned with a small bulletin board on which was a map of Bridgeton.

"I think you can understand, Dr. Maruyama, why we have only some scraps of data so far; we've spent most of our time treating patients. However, I anticipate we'll eventually have exactly the same kind of pattern. I managed to interview a few dozen survivors, and every single one was out of town a week before the disaster here."

Micah was stunned. "Dr. Gustofson, this is unbelievable. There's a radio station here, too, I assume?"

The doctor took the pipe out of his mouth and

pointed to one end of the elliptical area. "The radio station is here."

"My God, it's the same thing!" said Micah. "You haven't been there yet, have you, Doctor?"

Dr. Ogden did not open his eyes, but said dryly, "Surely, Dr. Maruyama, you didn't need to ask *that*. While the rest of us were treating patients, Dr. Gustofson was naturally off in a jeep at the radio station."

Gustofson, unruffled, pulled the first cassette out of the recorder, put in a second one. Again there was part of a commercial, and again a high whining noise, the same kind of sound. "This was played exactly one week before the havoc hit—at two minutes after eight in the morning—and up to now every survivor I've talked with says he was out of town at that time."

Micah whistled. "That coincidence stretches my credulity too far. When I read the report about this oval and the radio signal—well, frankly, gentlemen, I thought you were all crazy. I told the FBI and the CIA to keep their men in Washington. Now I'm going to have them here by tomorrow. This is more than coincidence. Like you, Dr. Gustofson, I don't know how the devil radio waves can cause such damage. But they obviously did. Can anyone explain it?"

Gustofson scratched his head. "I think it's a lot less likely," he growled, "that any of us *medical* men could explain it than that an electronics man could. And I'd like to make a suggestion."

He pulled on his pipe, found it had gone dead, sighed, and knocked the ashes into a huge, cigarette-filled tray. "I know a man who'd be an ideal consultant on electronics. By a damn lucky chance, he lives in what's left of Bensonville, and he's a brilliant guy. He came up with the idea that this pattern was a dipolar field, and then one morning he led me right to that second antenna. He's doing experiments with it now, tryin' to figure out how it could have been used to produce these effects."

"Who is he?"

"Well," said Gustofson, "his name is Jess Barrett.

At one time he was quite a football player; you may have heard of him. He lost his brother in Bensonville, but he was certainly valuable to us there. He worked with NASA on the effect of various types of radiation and electromagnetism on instruments. And he's studied exotic forms of electronics. He's a sort of international troubleshooter in that field. I'd like to suggest that you have him join us here."

Maruyama nodded. "I know him well! Jess and I were in school together. He won the Heisman Trophy and became a Rhodes scholar."

"Yes, down Kentucky way we're mighty proud of Jess Barrett. He's not only very bright, he's also an outstanding citizen."

Maruyama smiled as he thought about Jess. "Yes, I knew him, and I think he'd be just the man for us. I'll call him right away." He dialed the phone. "Operator, this is Micah Maruyama. I want to call Bensonville, Kentucky—Jess Barrett, please." Gus hissed a few words, and Micah added quickly, "He's staying in the home of his brother, Robert Barrett. . . . Yes, I'll hold."

Micah glanced around at the group. "Apparently all the sickness has stopped, following the Bensonville pattern; but if you need more medical supplies, they can be here within hours."

Gustofson shook his head. "They won't do a damned bit of good anyway. What we need is to discover a way to make people immune to this bane."

Ogden snorted, "Oh, Gus, that's like making people immune to arsenic."

"Which *can* be done with time enough," Gus reminded him.

"Now, dammit, Gus, you're dreaming. This thing is hopeless!"

Maruyama's voice was so low that they were barely able to hear him. "Well, Dr. Ogden, if you feel that way, why don't you just go home, and we'll find a replacement for you."

There was a long silence. Finally Ogden looked at

the Japanese with a new respect. "I'm only tired. Of course we'll find the answer if it's possible."

Again Micah spoke, the others straining to hear him. "We cannot afford that attitude. *We are going to find the answer to this.* If it's an organism, we'll isolate it. If it's a chemical, we'll discover it. If it's a plot, we'll solve it. And if some foreign power is responsible, we'll punish them. But we *will* find the answer."

Under half-lowered lids Dr. Gustofson's eyes twinkled as they slid toward his colleagues. He sighed contentedly, folded his hands on his stomach, and leaned back in his chair.

Jess Barrett's voice came on the line. Maruyama greeted him cordially but briefly, then told him of what Gus had found at one end of this second ellipse. Jess whistled. "Any luck with your own work on that sixteen-armed antenna? . . . Well, never mind. Drop it. I need you here. A helicopter will pick you up tomorrow morning and take you to Louisville. Make it seven A.M. I'll see you in the afternoon, Jess. Any questions? . . . Fine. Good-night."

In quick succession he called the directors of the FBI and the CIA, and the chief of staff of the air force. From the first of these, he asked for a quick, thorough check on the possibilities of a plot; from the second, the same, plus a particular agent, Brad Adams, who was out of the country but who could be jetted to Minnesota by midafternoon the next day. From the air force general, he requested—his request, after meeting an objection, became a purred demand—that the unidentified plane which had flown over Bensonville on May 27 be located and that every flight over Bridgeton for the past three weeks be checked out. He made arrangements for Jess Barrett's transportation and hung up. Then he dialed a fifth number: that of the White House.

"Good evening, Mr. President. I'm sorry to disturb you so late, but I have something to report." Briskly he summarized Gus's findings. "Yes, sir, I'm receiving excellent cooperation from everyone. . . . Oh, yes, they're both sending men tomorrow. . . . Thank you, sir. I'll call you tomorrow. . . . Good-night, sir." He put down the phone, frowning in concentration.

At last Ogden spoke. "Well, Dr. Maruyama, if that was meant to impress us, it did. We realize now that you *really* are the boss." His voice was tinged with sarcasm.

Micah looked steadily at him. Then he said slowly, in a voice barely over a whisper, "Dr. Ogden, I have neither the desire nor the need nor the time to impress you. The only purpose in that would be to ensure your utmost effort and cooperation. I have those already— or if I don't, I will replace you."

He paused until the silence was unbearable, then spoke again, cheerfully. "Gentlemen, I think we should all get a good night's sleep. I know you're exhausted and your nerves are frayed. Would one of you direct me to my house, please?"

Jordan Brown opened his eyes and stood up. "Mr. Chairman, it would be a pleasure to show you to your quarters."

11

Jess put down the telephone. For several moments there was silence as he sat looking morose. Alma went to him, caught his chin in her hand, and lifted it. "You wanted to turn him down, didn't you? I saw it in your face, heard your hesitation."

Jess said, "I have a responsibility to you and the children, Alma—yes, even to Bensonville. I hate turning my back on—"

"As soon as quarantine is lifted," she said forcefully, "I'll move back to Richmond. I'll take Ginny's boys with me, since they're alone now. The other kids will go to their relatives. Jess, you were never meant to stay here. You belong out there, doing your own job. Get out, Jess! Get out and be what you were meant to be!"

A wry, respectful smile came to Jess's face as he looked up at her. He had once told Bob that she was 105 pounds of barbed wire.

"Alma, this town is a shambles. It needs someone to stay and help and—"

"Jess Barrett, you be still. Bensonville is *dead*. It'll never recover. You've got to cut the umbilical cord between you and this town. Jess, your mother's dead, your father's dead, Bob's dead, Ginny's dead. If you stay here, you'll die, too, your spirit will die. You were never meant to stay here. Ginny knew it. That's why she would never marry you. You kept coming back to Bensonville because you thought it was home, but it's time you admitted that home will never again be a place—only something or someone inside you.

"I've watched you since that team left. You've been like a dead man. Maruyama ordered you to join

125

them, and you couldn't refuse. That's a godsend. Get upstairs and get packed!"

He was silent. Then he said, "Alma, I'll see you in Richmond when the problem's solved."

Jess hardly slept that night, and by 5:00 he was fully awake. Already the sun's rays were slanting down from the eastern hills, piercing the curtains billowing in the June breeze. The air was fresh after the rain, and Jess breathed great draughts of it. He lay in bed thinking about Alma and the children, about Bob, Ginny, Bensonville, the antennae, the signal, Bridgeton, old Dr. Gustofson—and about Micah Maruyama and the excitement of being part of the team again. Jess realized that he was smiling for the first time since that black Wednesday.

He stretched and began to count off in his mind the clothes he'd take to Bridgeton. Suddenly he sat bolt upright. From the woods just beyond the house came a sound, one he had not heard for more than a week, one that had once been so common he'd taken it for granted. It was a mockingbird singing. Jess jumped out of bed, went to the window, and stood listening. For a full five minutes he hardly moved, drinking in the glorious sound of the bird that had tipped back its head and was singing as if the world were normal again. Abruptly he turned and began to throw clothes into a suitcase.

Alma was already frying bacon when he came down. In silence the two of them ate, and then Jess went back upstairs to peek in at Alma's children and Ginny's boys. He stayed there, watching them, until he heard the army staff car stop in the gravel driveway.

Downstairs he looked at Alma. Soon she would be closing her house and taking the four children to Richmond to start a new life. She would do it alone, never complain and never cry. Wordless, he hugged her hard. For a moment they stood together before she said, "Better go, Jess."

He went out to the waiting car.

Bridgeton's airport was three miles from the center

126

of town. The jeep carrying Dr. Gustofson to meet Jess neared the city limits and was stopped by army sentries at the checkpoint. A half mile farther was a second checkpoint, then a third before they reached the airport. Gustofson had never seen so thorough a quarantine. There were three belts of soldiers around the town, keeping people in. None of the belts connected with another, and none let anyone through to the outside world without special permission. The airport itself was under tight security. Only military aircraft were permitted in and out of the tiny field, and few helicopters were permitted to penetrate into the heart of the town itself.

Gustofson went into the airport terminal, now a command post for the army. He clicked his tongue at Mandelbaum's efficiency. Acting on his conviction that an organism was the cause of it all, Mandelbaum had concluded that the only way the disease could have leaped the thousand miles from Bensonville to Bridgeton was through an infected person traveling by aircraft. Among many other precautions, he'd asked the Public Health Service to ground every aircraft that had been at Bridgeton Airport in the past week.

Soon an officer notified Gus that Jess's plane was arriving. The jet—a STOL, designed for military use in jungle areas—circled the field twice and then, flaps down, lowered its landing gear and came in to the tiny strip. The pilot touched down on the very edge of the concrete runway, and a cloud of smoke went up from the rubber wheels. The engines roared as the pilot reversed them to slow his speed. The plane taxied to the terminal and stopped, rocking back on its gear. The canopy snapped upward, revealing two men. The one in the rear lifted himself smoothly out of the cockpit. Gustofson recognized Jess Barrett. The pilot got out, opened a compartment in the belly of the plane and took out a bag; Barrett thanked him and turned toward the terminal.

When he found Gustofson, he greeted him warmly,

and they walked together to the jeep. "How are things, Gus?"

Gustofson pulled a large map out of the jeep and unrolled it on the hood. A crayoned ellipse covered the central part of the town. Gustofson pointed to one end. "There's your radio station. Location of opposite end, uncertain so far, but apparently just beyond this golf course. Let's see if we can find it. There'll be a general meeting of the team tonight, and I want a report for them."

"How's Dr. Mandelbaum? Is he surviving since he isn't chairman of the group?"

"He's pouting like a girl who's just lost her beau. And Jess, in all honesty, I have to admit that he's done a good job of organizing all the usual things."

"How's Micah doing?"

"Maruyama? He's quite a fellow, isn't he? He speaks very softly, but that's one hell of a big stick he carries."

Now their driver headed for town, turning at Gustofson's directions toward the area covered by the upper end of the ellipse. The pattern of death had not annihilated Bridgeton as totally as it had Bensonville; this town was much larger. The ellipse extended obliquely across town; its major axis aligned approximately northwest, southeast. It spanned the business district and included the most heavily populated parts of the city. Eventually they would discover that the death toll was over 4,800, but 2,200 people had survived, principally those who lived and worked in the outlying areas.

They saw a number of people walking aimlessly along the streets and sidewalks or dully watching army vehicles come and go. Jess looked at the ambulances and trucks grimly.

"Are they still hunting for bodies, Gus?"

The old man nodded his shaggy head. "They're still finding some in homes or apartments." He said a few words to the driver, and shortly they entered a residential neighborhood of small white houses. Everywhere the smell of death lingered. Doors were

128

ajar, windows open, clothes hanging on lines in back-yards, and empty cars parked at crazy angles. Then the scene changed. The houses were the same, but this area was alive. Cars stood neatly in driveways. People moved beyond windows. Children were playing in yards.

"All right," Gus said, "let's turn around." With a crayon he noted on the map the exact spot where the area of death had ended. "Down that street, driver; I think it outlines the area we're looking for."

For some distance the street curved almost exactly with the ellipse. On one side houses were empty; on the other side, inhabited. Often people stared at them from windows or front porches.

"Pull up a minute," said Gustofson.

They stopped in front of a small house where a man was watering his lawn. Gus got out, spread the map on the hood, and began to draw a precise line along this street. Jess looked around, then spoke to the man on the lawn. His face had the blankness of lingering shock. To questions about the death line he only stared, speechless, moving the hose mechanically back and forth. Jess climbed into the jeep again, and they moved on.

They were nearing the golf course, and the houses were larger, more expensive. Back and forth they crisscrossed, in and out of the death area. But there was no sign of an antenna. Bit by bit the precise line of death on Gustofson's map progressed across the top of the page. At last it led them to an apartment building near the golf course.

The two scientists walked around the building, checking each tree and telephone pole, even squinting at the television antenna on the roof.

"Dammit, Jess, it's got to be here. This is the end of the field." Gus lit his pipe and puffed for a few minutes while Jess chewed his lip, looking around the area.

A young man came out of the apartment house with a sack of garbage. He dumped it in a bin, saw the scientists, and walked toward them. His face wore an expression of permanent anxiety.

"Howdy, friend," said Gustofson. "How's it going? We're with the investigating team. Had anybody sick around here?"

"You from the doctors? Have you found out what the hell's going on?"

"We're still trying to trace how wide a path the sickness cut. Anybody in your building get it?"

"Yeah, they sure did. Joe Turner and his whole family died. It was awful."

"Anybody else?"

"Grandma Thompson, the old lady on the second floor, died of pneumonia. Two girls that roomed together on the third floor. Hell, come to think about it, everybody who lived on that side of the building."

Gustofson's eyes lit up; glancing at Jess, he asked, "Well, young man, if you wouldn't mind, we'd like to see the whole building."

The man led them around to the front door and into the lobby. He pushed the elevator button and squinted at the indicator. "Oh, hell, the car's stuck on the fourth floor again. Let's take the stairs."

They went to the back of the shaft, where a stairwell had been built into the same center structure. They began to climb. Soon Gus was wheezing, but their guide bounded up ahead of them with vigor. When he realized that the old man was falling behind, he paused. "I didn't mean to go so fast, but I get plenty of practice; so many old folks here jam the elevator. Hey, where's your big friend?"

Gustofson looked down the well. Jess was staring at the wall. Now he called up. "On which side of the building did the people die?"

The young man gestured. "Why, that side right there."

"O.K. Now, which way is downtown?"

"Right there." He pointed the same way.

Jess shook his head. "Those sons of bitches! We don't need to look any farther, Gus. Come here."

The doctor, frowning until his eyes all but disappeared under his brows, descended. "What is it, Jess?"

"Look." He pointed to a three-inch-wide strip of aluminum tape that ran down the wall and disappeared through the crack that separated the landing from the elevator shaft. At the floor level another strip could just be seen in the wide crack, running parallel to the floor and crossing the vertical strip.

"You don't mean they put their goddamned antenna right here in this building?" Gus shouted. "But would tape work?"

"Why not? Any good conductor would. I first saw that there was a long strip running along the crack on the ground floor, and as we came up, the strips grew shorter, like that Christmas-tree thing in Kentucky. Let's see what's up above."

Their guide looked in amazement from one to the other, then at the strip of tape. "What are you talking about? This ground? The guy who put it up told Mrs. Webster it was a new kind of ground for better TV reception. He's coming back to hook up all of our sets."

Jess almost shouted, "Did you see him, talk to him?"

The man blinked in alarm. "Take it easy, mister. I didn't do neither. Mrs. Webster told me about it."

"Did she describe him, say anything about him?"

"No, she just said what I told you, that she saw a man puttin' up those strips and asked what he was doing."

"Well, goddamnit, was he young or old, black or white, big or small? What did he look like? Was he alone?"

"I told you, I don't *know*. She just said she saw a man working when she came up from doing her laundry and had to take the stairs because someone had the elevator and—"

"O.K., which is her apartment? I want to talk to her."

"It'll be kinda hard, mister. She died on Wednesday. She had this sore, and—" He spread out his hands.

"Dammit, somebody else must have seen him."

Gustofson put a gentle hand on Jess's arm. "Easy, easy."

"Mister, I don't know why that little strip's so all-fired important, but I can tell you that nobody else saw that man. He was working at night, and Mrs. Webster only happened to see him. It was quite a topic of conversation around here for a day or two, so I know."

Jess was urgent, his eyes afire. "But someone else might remember more of what she said. Let's talk to everyone in the building."

"Well—I—O.K., mister, if you want to tackle it, we'll start at the top."

As he turned to climb the remaining stairs, Gustofson whispered to Jess, "Better leave this to the FBI. We're only going to spook everyone and start rumors. We know we've found it. Let's go back to headquarters and have Maruyama get his men on this."

Jess snarled in frustration. "O.K., but let's look at the top and the bottom. It's some sort of new system. The antenna's been refined, and I want to see how they did it."

At the top of the stairs the strip of tape ran up the side of the shaft, along the ceiling to a skylight, and out to the roof. Jess clambered up the ladder to the skylight, opened it, and saw a saucer-shaped piece of metal nailed to the plaster wall of the shaft and pointed toward the downtown area. It was no more than fourteen inches in diameter.

In a rage, Jess reached over and tore it off the wall, ripping the tape attached to it. He raised it above his head to hurl it to earth far below, caught himself in time, glared at the thing in his hand. Torn from its wall and from the deadly tape, it looked ridiculously like a metal Frisbee. He sighed, climbed back down the ladder to show the saucer to Gustofson.

"My God, Jess, you don't mean that little thing could—"

"Say, what's going on here? Are you guys saying

that this had something to do with all those people dying?"

The doctor glanced warningly at Jess. "No, of course not. But we saw some tape like this in Kentucky and thought it might be infected."

The man jumped backward, his eyes huge.

Gus reassured him. "But now that we've seen it closer, it's not the same stuff at all. And this thing, which is part of the grounding apparatus, is completely different. Sorry to have alarmed you, mister. Just a false alarm, right, Jess?"

"That's right." He grinned easily, and the man relaxed. "Why don't you go on back to your apartment? We'll find our way out."

Immediately the man disappeared. Gus and Jess went down the stairs, carrying the saucer with them.

"God, I *am* sorry, Gus. I got so excited that I lost my head."

In the basement they found that the tape ended in a common outlet box. There were two holes in it for the prongs of a plug.

"Jess, I don't know anything about electronics, but wouldn't it take some power source to make this thing work?"

"Sure, but I don't believe it would need much power. Probably it could be plugged into a wall outlet, and he could send out his signal."

"He?"

"They. Whoever did it."

"But, Jess, this is a *lot* different from the one in Kentucky. Could it do the same thing?"

"He's refining his system. This seems more primitive, but it's actually quite an advance. It's many times larger and presumably would have a greater range. It's also simpler and would be easier to transport and construct. He's more dangerous now than when he had the other antenna," said Jess somberly. "Let's get back to headquarters. I want to see Micah and talk to him about this." Then Jess paused. "Our enemy's progress is incredible, Gus."

12

THE UNITED STATES was now in the grip of an unexpected nightmare. The destruction, by unknown agents, of two towns separated by nearly 1,000 miles brought panic to a nation long accustomed to reasonable security and prosperity.

By Friday morning, June 11, the president had prohibited all trips that were not of emergency nature or necessary to business. Yet every flight out of the country was booked solid, despite the fact that most nations had by then denied entry to Americans.

The stock market, America's most sensitive barometer, had plummeted after the first outbreak and recovered by the beginning of the following week. With the second catastrophe and the lurid stories that came out of Bridgeton on the ninth, the market merely shut its doors Wednesday afternoon and did not open at all Thursday. The president affirmed the decision of the board.

People were urged not to gather in crowds until the crisis had passed. Baseball games and races were canceled, Broadway closed its doors; Times Square was almost deserted by eight thirty at night.

The transportation of perishables within the country slowed so drastically that food supplies dwindled and people panicked and began to hoard. The massive, incredibly complex American economic system slowed, shuddered, and seemed destined to grind to a halt.

Cut off from the rest of the world, with their supplies in danger of rotting in fields and warehouses, prosperously soft Americans found within days—within hours—the hickory toughness that had saved them again and again in times of emergency. Truckers who had parked their rigs, refusing to move until they had assurance that the epidemics were over, looked at each other in shame and said, "Oh, hell. People gotta eat! Let's go." Farmers squinted at the sky and the fields and went out to care for their crops. Cities began to move again; trains ran, and offices filled. By the beginning of the following week, the country had warily returned to something approximating normality.

The moment the little white Lear jet touched the ground, soldiers moved; and when it taxied to a stop in front of the small terminal building at Bridgeton Airport, they surrounded it. Mayor James McDonald stepped confidently onto the runway. From the terminal strode Dr. Mandelbaum. "What are you doing here?" he asked sharply.

"Mayor McDonald is here on special orders from President Weaver," Micah Maruyama said, behind the doctor.

Mandelbaum stared, drew Micah aside. "We've had trouble with him already. He's a drunkard, and he carries a gun."

"The president thought there ought to be a representative of the grieving survivors on the team. He chose the mayor."

"Representative of the—my God! This is *politics,* isn't it?" said Mandelbaum under his breath.

Maruyama looked at the huge doctor speculatively. "Yes, of course it's politics. McDonald's a very small politician, but he's contributed large sums to state and national campaigns, and he's influential. The president wants him on the team."

"Well, as a scientist I resent it and deplore it, but I don't suppose that matters," said Mandelbaum bitterly. "Just keep an eye on him."

Micah said, "Thanks, I'll give him an honor guard of one alert soldier. What are you doing out here, by the way?"

"I'm meeting a distinguished biochemist from New

York, who'll bring crucial information to bear on this *medical* problem."

"I see. Next time check with me beforehand," murmured Micah gently.

"Surely you said we could have any help we needed?"

"You may have every resource, Dr. Mandelbaum, but first ask me for it." He turned to the mayor. "Well, sir," he said politely, "please excuse our medical conference. We're extremely busy, you understand. Now I'll take you into the town and show you the quarters they've prepared for you."

McDonald spoke for the first time. "Right," he said crisply. Micah noted that he did not sound like a drunk.

For days Gustofson had driven through the city in an army jeep, interviewing every survivor he could find and plotting their homes and places of work, their times in and out of the death oval. Jess had accompanied him once more; then a mass of electronic equipment had arrived, and Jess was absorbed in his own work.

Even today, Tuesday, six days after the disaster, semitrailers were still coming and going with their grim cargoes as Gus slammed to a halt at the house where Jess was staying. He walked in without knocking and found Jess watching an instrument on which a needle flickered, jumped to a vertical position, shuddered, flipped all the way over to the right. Jess swore, turned off the machine. "Hello, Gus."

The dining room table was covered with various instruments. Piles of documents took up several chairs. In the kitchen, on the counter, Gus could see a computer teletype. He asked, "Gettin' anyplace?"

"No, but at least I'm eliminating possibilities. You?"

"Same thing, Jess. No doubt about it any longer. Same as Bensonville to the last detail. Now if you can tear yourself away from the shiny machines and equations, we'll eat something before Maruyama's meeting."

The meeting was held in the town library, one of those small-town libraries that seem to have been stamped out with a die and put up all over the United States. Low, faded, soundproof ceiling, fluorescent lighting over Formica-covered tables, pervasive smell of books. Tonight the stacks had been pushed to the walls and extra chairs brought in. At the front of the room were a microphone and lectern and more seats, facing the others.

Jess saw several men he hadn't met, some of whom looked so fresh that he knew they'd only recently arrived. He and Gustofson found a place near the front. Quickly the room filled up behind them.

At 7:00, Maruyama took the microphone and began. "I want to commend you all for your very hard work. You never faltered, never considered your own welfare or safety."

He paused. "But it's thirteen days since the first outbreak, nearly a week since the second, and we don't have the answer yet. We have to improve our efficiency and performance. Drastically.

"When the president put me in charge of this investigation, I intended to be largely an observer and coordinator. Now I realize I must take a more active role. The president agrees.

"We have almost three hundred people here, and our meetings are often chaotic, so I'm going to reorganize. I'll appoint eight leaders who will, in turn, pick their own teams of assistants and be responsible for their work. Our meetings will consist of only myself, my secretary, and those eight men; after I've named them, the rest of you may leave for the evening. Your team leaders will brief you later.

"The leaders are Dr. Mandelbaum, general medical chief; Dr. Brown, head of pathological studies; Dr. Ogden, of sanitation investigations; Dr. Fornier, of pollutant studies; Dr. Goerke, of immunological studies. Dr. Gustofson is general consultant; Dr. Barrett, electronics adviser; and Mayor McDonald, representative of the survivors.

"Except for those government officials expressly invited tonight, everyone else is excused. Thank you."

Chairs scraped, and most of the people in the room began to file out, some relieved, others furious. Micah quietly studied his notes as he waited. Finally only a handful remained. He looked up.

"One reason for narrowing the team is security. You are all officially notified that anything discussed tonight and later by this group is not to be shared with any other person except at my instruction. To do so will be a federal offense."

Maruyama paused. Some of the others glanced nervously at one another. But Mandelbaum, only a moment before relieved to learn that he was still on the team and in charge of the medical investigation, looked annoyed.

"Dr. Maruyama, I suppose this means that you're taking seriously Dr. Gustofson's dramatic theory about a human cause. I want to go on record as being convinced that a virological or bacterial agent is responsible."

"Thank you, Dr. Mandelbaum. I'm aware of your opinion."

"I have something I want to say." It was Dr. Ogden. "I resent the intrusion into this group of Mr. McDonald. He's purely and simply a politician in a highly scientific investigation. I see no good reason—"

"There is no *good* reason for his presence, Dr. Ogden. There's a superficial reason—public relations —for the sake of which President Weaver insists that he remain."

"Are you aware that he attacked a young soldier in Bensonville? That he's carrying a gun right now?"

"Well, Ogden, you damn snob, I got a permit for my gun, and I'm going to show you how to carry on an investigation. I was in the Criminal Investigation Division in the army."

Micah said, "Mayor McDonald, you keep that gun in its holster and stay out of the way of the medical men. When you have any ideas, I'll talk them over with you. Now let's get cracking." He gestured to two

138

men in the front row, who stood up. "Gentlemen, Bill Petersen, FBI."

Petersen was in his middle fifties, with a thick chest and huge shoulders. His deeply seamed face was set in an expression of perpetual pain at the follies of the world. A smile was difficult for him, but he did manage to nod pleasantly to the group.

"Bradford Adams of the CIA," said Micah.

Adams nodded easily. About forty, he was nattily dressed in a pin-striped suit and vest. His confident eyes moved from one face to another. Jess felt that they were all being filed away in a photographic memory.

"Now, let's get on with the reports. Dr. Mandelbaum?"

"Uh, in general, our studies, the cultures we are completing, have shown—uh—the same pattern as in Bensonville. We've found the usual microbial agents, but in quantities unheard of before these outbreaks.

"However, we've only begun. The electron microscope arrived just two days ago, and already we're finding suspicious-looking particles in tissue slides from diseased organs, indicating the possibility of mutated strains of viruses." He sat down. Micah slid his black eyes to Fornier.

"Nothing. Zero."

"Dr. Ogden?"

Ogden shook his head.

"Dr. Brown? Anything new from pathology?"

"The same damned thing. Every kind of disease known to man, some not seen in this country for fifty years, killed them. It's just like Bensonville—except that here nobody died of a fractured skull."

"Fractured skull?" snapped Micah, alert.

"Yes, I just read the last of the Bensonville reports. One autopsy showed a fractured skull."

"Who was it?"

"Let's see—I've got it here somewhere. Richard Joffee."

"Mayor? Know him?"

"Joffee? Never heard of him."

Brown waved a hand. "Oh, it says here: 'place of residence, Chalmers. Body picked up in woods. Approximate date of death, June second.' "

"Petersen, that's your baby; check it out, will you? Find me all you can," said Micah. "Dr. Goerke?"

"I don't know one iota more than I did nine days ago."

Maruyama gestured at a wall map of Bridgeton, overlaid by the familiar red oval. "As you see, the pattern here is the same as Bensonville's. Doctors Barrett and Gustofson have again discovered a second antenna, somewhat different, hidden in an apartment house at the exact end of the oval opposite the radio station. This makes a case too strong to be ignored. Jess, tell us about your research with the antenna."

"Mike, I've used a harmonics analyzer to find out what kind of wave it's giving off, but it's so complicated I don't know much yet. I think it all depends on what he used to make the broadcast."

"Then we know nothing except that a signal was broadcast, probably similar to that in Bensonville. Bill, do you have anything for us?" he asked Petersen.

The FBI agent stood. Only the corners of his lips moved slightly as he said, a little stiff and formal, "Dr. Maruyama asked the bureau to investigate the possibility that these epidemics were caused by a subversive group. I checked our undercover agents and informers. Frankly, gentlemen, we successfully infiltrated every radical and alien organization in the United States quite a while ago. I doubt that a foreign power could be operating inside our borders without our knowledge. We haven't had a whiff of any conspiracy that could have caused this."

Micah said, "I asked Brad Adams to check his foreign contacts for information of any plot against this country. Brad?"

In contrast with Petersen, Adams was urbane, confident, and thoroughly accustomed to speaking before an audience. He was one of the men the CIA used to testify before Congress.

"Mike, I came up with nothing, too. As you know,

after our meeting at the airport I flew right back to Washington and checked all our contacts, at least all that could be reached in such a short time. There's no indication of any new hostile action against us."

"What about research? Are the Russians or Chinese carrying on bacteriological or toxicological research that could have led to this?"

"No, Mike. I swear we'd know of it if they were. Frankly, with the advent of atomic warfare most bacteriological weapons became obsolete. Nobody today is doing research on any agent that could cause anything remotely comparable to these damned elliptical blasts."

Micah nodded. "O.K., let's hear from the air force. Will you bring in the colonel, please?" A soldier left the room. Micah continued. "You remember that a light plane flew over Bensonville seven days before the disaster. I asked that it be checked."

A tall, blond air force officer came in. Micah saw the urgency in his stride and asked quickly, "Something significant, Colonel?"

"Yes, sir. The plane you asked about was a Bonanza owned by Joseph Bowman, a food salesman from Cincinnati. He buzzed Bensonville at exactly seven forty-six A.M. on Wednesday, May twenty-sixth."

"Seven forty-six?" Jess shouted. "Are you certain, Colonel?"

"Absolutely. We found a farmer who was on the way to town that morning in his pickup and saw the plane. He said it flew so low over him that it almost touched the trees. It dove down into the Bensonville valley, buzzed the town, and disappeared to the south."

"But the *time,* Colonel. How do you know the time so exactly?"

"Well, that's a funny one. He was listening as he drove to the Bensonville station. When the plane flew over, he suddenly heard a weird noise over the radio. He thought it was from the plane, but later he was talking to one of the station's men whom he knew

—called, ah, 'Ziggy'—who said it was due to some sort of malfunction of their equipment. I checked the station and found that the malfunction happened at seven forty-six. They said you already knew about it."

Jess whistled, Gus stared at him, and Maruyama asked in a careful, quiet voice, "Have you interrogated that pilot, Colonel?"

"No, sir. He's dead. One of his children had the mumps a couple of weeks ago. It didn't bother the child too much, but the Wednesday when everyone died in Bensonville, Mr. Bowman died of the mumps. The odd thing is that he'd had them as a child and shouldn't have contracted them again. Of course, when adults get mumps, it's much worse, isn't that right?"

He looked inquiringly at the stunned doctors before him. Nobody responded to his question, and he stood there, obviously astonished at the effect of his report.

Maruyama said, "Thank you, Colonel. You may go now."

When the man had left, Micah's eyebrows arched quizzically. "Well, what's the significance of that? Was Bowman an agent who dumped something on Bensonville, got careless, and died of it himself?"

Gustofson frowned fiercely. "Dumped what, Mike? We've already proved it can't be anything dropped from an airplane."

"Not only that, but if he was the Bensonville murderer, who killed Bridgeton?" asked Jess.

"Maybe Bowman was an innocent party, paid to drop something he thought was harmless, and then it killed him, too. Neat way to get rid of an embarrassing witness," Fornier mused.

Mandelbaum looked at him scathingly. "Come now, Doctor, don't tell me *you* are beginning to think this epidemic was a plot?"

"I don't know what I think, Mandy. About the time I decide it's all hogwash, along comes something like this to make me believe it's the only explanation."

Ogden said, "Every disaster is full of odd coincidences. You know that."

Micah interrupted. "Well, we need more information on this one. Petersen, get everything you can on that pilot. *Everything.*"

"We'll know more about him than his wife knows, but it'll take a few days."

Maruyama looked at him steadily. "Bill, I want that information in no more than two days. Put the whole bureau on it if you must, but get it to me within forty-eight hours."

Petersen stared at him and then nodded his head.

"There's another item of business: several tons of mail. Personal letters have been given to you already. But we also have hate mail and warnings from preachers that the epidemics will continue unless the country repents of its sins. We have reports of sixty-seven flying saucers over Bensonville and three hundred and eight over Bridgeton. We've also received letters from responsible scientists making suggestions. The disposition of these is important. They all receive a preliminary reading. Crackpot letters are disposed of. Borderline suggestions are being considered by army medical personnel. Those from people who claim they caused the epidemic—and there are about a hundred so far—go immediately to the FBI. But that leaves many, many others.

"My secretary is supervising the staff that's sifting them. I'll give each of you those letters that deal with subjects falling within your specialty. For example: Dr. Mandelbaum, here are eighty-one letters containing suggestions for you. Since some of them run to many pages, you'll have your hands full."

He gave the doctor a thick file. Jess felt that if he'd been anyone else but Micah Maruyama, he'd have worn a broad, mischievous grin.

One by one he gave files of letters to the others. Finally, he came to the packet dealing with the general subject of epidemiology and started to hand them to Gustofson, but the old man objected.

"Dr. Maruyama, if you don't mind, I'd rather spend my time studyin' the survivors. I'm not much for reading mail anyway."

Micah paused a moment, till Mandelbaum settled the issue.

"If Dr. Gustofson can't consider the suggestions of men of science who've taken their valuable time to write to us, I'll be glad to accept his share of the burden." He took the file from Micah.

"Why, Mandy, that's mighty kind of you. My eyes are so old and weak, I can hardly read anything anymore. Thank you."

Maruyama was frowning at the remaining file. He opened it, took out a registered letter addressed to him, and looked questioningly at his secretary. She smiled feebly.

"It came just before the meeting. I didn't have time to tell you," she glared at the others, on the defensive. "It's from Vera Norman, the famous astrologer, and I'm sure none of you believe in it, but—"

"Good God! Astrology! Flying saucers, sin, electronics, and now astrology." Ogden put his heels on the rung of his chair and tipped back.

Mandelbaum said, "Why not open it, Dr. Maruyama? I imagine her suggestions will concern electrical antennae and—"

"Sure, open it, Mike," drawled Gustofson. "Maybe it'll identify the virus that interferes with the entire immunity system."

Micah, unsmiling, opened the envelope and read the letter to himself.

Dear Dr. Maruyama,

Perhaps you may remember that we once met. At that time I told you about a branch of astrology called mundane, which is the study of groups: corporations, cities, states, and nations.

In the last two years I have specialized in this study, collecting astrological data on most of the towns of the United States. When the disasters occurred in Bensonville and Bridgeton, I studied their natal charts, did progressions for them, and made an event chart for each catastrophe.

I found that common astrological conditions

144

existed over each of the two towns. I discovered a baffling thing. Something appears to have happened one week *before* each of the epidemics. Using what I learned, I searched through my computerized files and found that identical conditions prevailed for the city of San Salino, California, last Wednesday, June 9th.

Therefore, reluctantly, I predict that another disaster will occur on Wednesday, June 16, in San Salino.

Perhaps my warning will enable your medical team to take steps to blunt the force of the epidemic.

Yours truly,
Vera Norman

Micah folded the letter and returned it to the envelope. But Ogden said, "Come on, Dr. Maruyama, let us in on the fun."

Micah looked at the sneering doctor, realized that he disliked him intensely, opened the letter, and read it aloud.

Brown gave a low whistle. Gustofson's green eyes narrowed to slits.

Ogden grinned malevolently. "Well, Mr. Chairman, tomorrow's the sixteenth. Aren't you going to put us all on a plane and ship us out to California? We might actually—"

But Goerke interrupted him roughly, "Shut up, you blasted fool, for God's sake shut up! Didn't you catch it?"

"Oh, come on, are we going to take the ravings of a stargazing witch seriously?"

"Dammit," snapped Brown, "didn't you hear what Dr. Maruyama read? She knows that something happened a week before the event. Nobody knew that except this group."

Mandelbaum, outraged, roared at him. "Jordan, don't tell me you're following this rumpled pied piper with his chatter about antennae? That drivel means nothing!"

145

"Then how did she know something happened a week before each disaster?" Goerke had stood up in his agitation.

Mandelbaum put out his hands in protest. "Oh, Jack, this is preposterous; nothing *did* happen a week before the epidemics."

Jess Barrett exploded in frustration. "Dammit, Doctor, when are you going to open your eyes? Two signals, two radio stations, two antennae, two elliptical areas of death. My God, what more evidence do you want?"

Ogden jeered. "Mr. Barrett, when you've been involved in as many investigations of epidemics as we have, you'll know that coincidences are a dime a dozen."

"There's a lot of coincidences this time, Doctor," drawled Gustofson. "One hell of a lot!"

Petersen turned to Adams but spoke to them all. "It's too many. In nearly every criminal investigation we find coincidences. But this is too many. There's only one answer."

Adams looked at him thoughtfully.

"You think she's in on it?"

Petersen nodded vigorously. "She has to be."

Jess scowled. "Then why would she write to us, give herself away?"

"Who can tell why? I've known a number of criminals to tell people in one way or another what they're doing. Even Jack the Ripper wrote to the newspapers and bragged."

Micah said, "Well, Bill, there's another assignment for you. It's domestic, so Brad can't touch it. Find out about that girl; find out everything about her."

With that he gathered his papers, put them into his attaché case. "That's enough for tonight. I'm going to bed."

He snapped the case shut and walked outside. The driver was waiting for him; the jeep swept round in a circle and headed for Micah's house. As he rode, the cool night air whipped his face and cleared his mind. He thought of the letter and the woman who had

146

written it. Images of her came back, even the smell of her perfume. He was surprised at the vividness of his memory and the hunger it awakened in him.

For Micah knew Vera Norman. He had met her at a cocktail party in Washington. He knew that she did work for several heads of nations and for important financial and governmental figures in the United States, whom Micah had privately branded superstitious.

She was a beautiful woman, younger than Micah himself. They had struck up a conversation, and he was surprised to find that she was brilliantly knowledgeable about a variety of subjects. He had no interest in astrology; indeed, he was one of the few persons in the United States who didn't even know his own Sun sign. He had always assumed that astrology was on a level with witchcraft and idol worship. But she not only impressed him with her intelligence, she also gave him a demonstration of the value and power of her ancient art.

During their conversation she suddenly asked, "Were you by any chance born in mid-November?"

He stammered, admitting that he was, and asked how she knew. She smiled, told him he was a perfect Scorpio, adding that she was almost certain he had to be of the Cancer decanate of his sign.

From there the conversation had gone deeper into her subject. She told him of the difference between mundane, natal, and horary astrology. He listened in fascination until she told him that horary astrology dealt with answering questions by casting a chart for the time the question was propounded to the astrologer. Then he smiled wryly.

"Well, Miss Norman, I wish you could use your horary astrology to tell me what to do about Mustafa Karim, who is about to plunge the world into war."

To his astonishment, she glanced at her watch, opened her handbag, pulled out a blank astrological form and a book full of figures, and cast a horary chart for the question. When she had studied the chart for a few minutes, she informed him, seriously, that there was nothing more to worry about: The dictator was going to die soon!

"In fact," she said, "I think he's going to be assassinated, but so cleverly that nobody will know he was poisoned. His death will be called natural, and murder won't be suspected until years from now, when the deed will come partially to light."

Micah had not laughed, and ten days afterward the dictator had fallen dead of an apparent heart attack.

Now Micah thought of that remarkably accurate prediction, and of the fantastic letter in his attaché case. He tried to focus his mind on San Salino, which, if Vera was right, had been doomed last Wednesday. Yet his thoughts returned stubbornly to that evening in Washington.

Micah had never had a serious romance. There had always been the need for work—hard, unremitting work. Even with his sudden fame, he found no time for involvements. Sometimes loneliness came over him like a wet fog, and he'd see a girl occasionally. But Micah found no one exciting. They were either too flighty or too slow-witted for him.

Then he had met Vera and for an evening was caught up in the intellectual excitement of someone as brilliant and hardworking as he.

It was only after they had been talking for some time that he fully realized he was looking at an astonishingly beautiful young woman. Her hair was dark and thick; her skin, smooth and unlined. Her most startling feature was her clear gray eyes, accentuated that evening by the floor-length, blue-gray dress she wore. She was tall, elegant, and poised. Her bare shoulders and arms were without blemish. She smiled easily, and when she did, her eyes lit up, and her whole face cooperated in giving an impression of complete openness. She was easily the most striking woman at the party; yet as he watched other women warmly greet Vera, he knew they were not jealous of her. He found himself wondering why they were not—and why anyone so lovely, cheerful, and intelligent should still be single.

But Micah could not solve the mystery because to do so he would have had to understand some of the same traits that made him so unfathomable to others. Vera provoked no jealousy because she was not a huntress, and other women sensed it. They also intuitively knew that for all her sophistication, she was essentially without guile. They had little fear for their husbands around her because they knew that she was almost hopelessly idealistic, and her idealism protected her innocence and kept men from being too interested. But most of all they had no fear of her because she was so unself-consciously intelligent. Women knew that while men might be drawn to her, they would soon be turned away by her threatening brilliance, which she took no pains to hide.

Micah had come to know Vera instinctually and without working out all these answers. He had, without trying, stumbled across the only way one could ever reach her. He had met her on the level of mutual mental respect.

Afterward, when he thought of her and yearned to see her again, it was too late. He was in Washington, trapped in his work; she had returned to New York. He could have arranged a meeting, but somehow he had done nothing. For so many years he had suppressed personal feelings in order to be completely rational that it was easier just to continue as he was.

Now the letter. He shook his head. What would his friends, his professors in theological school, his associates in the White House think of his taking an *astrologer* seriously?

The jeep passed the warehouse, drove up beside the row of houses, stopped. He thanked the driver and went inside. A hot shower refreshed him and at the same time drained him of energy. He quickly put on his maroon pajamas and went to bed.

More than 1,000 miles away Vera Norman lay awake. It was a hot, humid night in Manhattan, and even with the window open, the air was close. Finally she got up, closed the window, and turned on the air-conditioning unit that she so disliked. With its help, she fell asleep, only to toss and turn and wake often.

Vera lived in her own large brownstone on West Seventy-fifth Street. Visitors admitted through the glass-and-iron-grille door found themselves in a hallway richly carpeted with an Oriental rug. Immediately to the right was the reception room, where deep-cushioned chairs surrounded a large, circular coffee table. Joanie, her secretary and assistant, had an office directly behind that. Vera's own consultation room was across the hall.

The second floor was done in black-and-white vinyl tile and held her computer terminal and, at the other end, a comfortable sunny study looking out on the small backyard.

On the third floor was the living room, carpeted in soft beige rugs and filled with three couches grouped around a marble fireplace. Adjoining was a small, elegant dining room where a crystal chandelier hung over a polished mahogany table. The kitchen to the left was also small, but modern and cheerful.

Vera's bedroom and the guest room were on the fourth floor. She had enlarged the windows so that those rooms were airy and full of light. She loved to be awakened by the sun streaming across her bed.

On Wednesday morning, after her shower, she switched on the television and listened to the news as she dressed. There was nothing spectacular. Her digital clock said 7:00; she mentally noted that it was only 4:00 in San Salino.

Downstairs she brewed a cup of coffee, frowned over the headlines in the *Times,* turned on the radio, paced the floor.

By 7:30 she was in her office at the manual of her computer terminal, which was connected with an IBM computer downtown. Although she was often dismayed when the monthly bill arrived, she loved the convenience. It shortened the time for horoscopes or progressions to a fraction of the hours ordinarily required. In addition she was engaged in research on a massive scale and fed great amounts of information into the computer for correlations.

This morning she shaded her eyes from the bright sun shining through the window so that she could see the figures of her client's horoscope. It was easier to read from the terminal screen when the shades were closed and the lights on, but she disliked artificial light as much as artificial air and at every opportunity dispensed with it.

As she read, she turned to a microphone attached to a large, sophisticated tape recorder. It was voice-activated and responded instantly to her words, the spools of tape slowly turning. She had developed a method of using the recorder in the way a pianist uses his instrument to produce music. As her fingers fed information from the keyboard into the computer, it sent figures back to her, and she gave an instant interpretation to the recorder.

She paused in her study of the chart before her on the specially made terminal screen, reached for the playback button. Her words flowed out to her; dissatisfied, she ran the tape back to the beginning, dictated a corrected interpretation. After some minutes of this, she played the entire cartridge. Satisfied now, she pushed a button, and the cartridge slid out into her hand. She slipped it into an envelope, already addressed, which she laid on her secretary's desk.

Vera did very few such horoscopes or progressions for clients anymore. Demands for her work had increased with her fame until she had no time for personal life or to do research; so in the past few years she had reduced her clientele to a fraction of what it had been.

Increasingly she turned to research, frustrating admirers who wanted her to write her astrological column for the newspapers again or at least to accept more individual clients. But she had tired of the endless telephone calls in the middle of the night from clients wanting to know if they should accept this or that offer or marry this or that girl.

At 7:55 her petite, dark-haired secretary let herself in and ran upstairs. Vera was standing by the window, pensively looking out on the little flower garden in her backyard.

"Vera? Are you all right?"

"I couldn't sleep last night. I kept thinking about all those people. It's so horrible."

"Don't you think Dr. Maruyama got your letter in time to do something?"

"Well, the crucial event had already happened last Wednesday, before I knew anything about it. I have a strong feeling that the damage was already done." She shuddered, recalling the newspaper reports from Bensonville. "The doctors could do nothing. I doubt that they'll be able to now, either."

Joanie glanced at the clock. "Do your figures indicate that it'll start soon?"

"Yes, very soon. Damn. I'm hoping, praying that it never will, that I'm wrong about this."

"You know you're not."

"Yes. I know I'm not wrong. Well, there's nothing I can do about it now. Let's go to work."

The two of them were busy dictating letters to clients when the bell rang. Vera looked over with an ironic smile and sighed. "Joanie, the full moon is exactly conjunct the progressed ruler of my twelfth house, which is already under a heavy progressed aspect. It's the end of my freedom; I enter a time of restricted movement. See who it is."

In a few seconds, Joanie stood at the door of the private office. "Vera? It's the FBI. Two of them. They have a warrant."

The men appeared silently at her shoulder, staring at Vera. "Miss Norman? We've come—"

"I know. My bag is packed. Let's go."

13

GUSTOFSON'S EYES were so red that the green in the corneas stood out in bright contrast. His hair looked like a slovenly bird's nest. He slouched in a deep chair in the meeting room of the motel.

In front of him was a huge map of San Salino. Two young women, medical assistants from the army, were thrusting in red pins for every reported death. Three others were taking phone calls from the Graves Registration office. Slowly the number of pins grew, here and there becoming clusters, as whole families were reported dead.

The old man hardly moved except to sip a cup of cold coffee, almost white with the cream he had added. Now and then he sighed, lit his pipe, and smoked in silence, watching as the picture of death was painted in red.

On the plane that brought the team from Bridgeton, Micah had given strict orders for their operating procedures. None of the team was to engage in therapeutic efforts. He had seen their fatigue and the paralysis of their minds in Minnesota. He wanted them alert and able to think.

But he also wanted order in the chaos, in the efforts to contain the disease and treat patients. If these already exhausted men plunged into the care of the sick, they would lose all effectiveness at control and coordination. So on his strict orders, the physicians returned to the motel after setting up treatment procedures.

Micah's instructions concerning Gustofson were particularly clear. He was worried about the old man, whose energy was greater than his strength. Micah was afraid he would kill himself working. He told Gustofson he was to sit quietly in the motel and supervise the plotting of the victims' homes.

Jess also was ordered to stay out of the town, so now he paced the floor, watching the ugly splotch spread over the map like blood, covering more and more of the city. Finally he stepped outside and stood in the cool night air.

The highway in front of the motel was choked with traffic, and every vehicle was an ambulance. Ambulances bumper to bumper were winding down the valley and over the hill into and out of San Salino. None of them had a siren wailing; none had a red light flashing. "Why should they," he said aloud, "when they're all going to the same place at the same speed?"

On and on the ghostly procession went, silent except for the sound of engines and the hiss of tires on the pavement. No driver called angrily to another; no car radio played; no horns honked. Just hundreds of ambulances, civilian and military, moving silently past the motel, returning later with patients for the hospitals designated to receive them. Worries of contagion had declined when it became apparent that in the other two cities no one had been stricken after the first virulent outbreak.

Jess watched the ambulances for an hour and saw no end, not even a thinning, of the procession. At least, he reflected, this time the authorities were prepared and had moved quickly. He doubted, however, that their efforts would save any of the sick. He went back inside.

Gustofson fell asleep in his chair about 3:00 in the morning. At 6:00 he awoke and grimaced at the arthritic pangs in his stiff body. Blinking painfully at the light, he slowly regained his vision. What he saw made him jerk awake instantly.

The map was almost totally covered with red pins, and more were being added by the moment. But there were few blue pins, and most startling of all, there was no oval shape. Instead, the red pins followed the city limits, spilling over in places into the countryside.

The epidemic had annihilated the entire city with a brutal efficiency not seen in either of the two earlier towns. Almost 15,000 souls had died in twenty-four hours. But there was no pattern. The old man struggled to his feet, swore violently, looked around to find Micah, Jess, Mandelbaum, and Petersen sitting behind him, watching the development of the picture of death.

Jess looked at him, shook his head. "Well, Gus, there's no ellipse this time. No pattern of any kind."

"Where's the radio station, Jess? Is the ellipse so enormous that we can't spot the pattern?"

Jess went to the map, pointed to a green pin. The station was near one end of town, but surrounded by red pins. "I looked up the address in the *Yellow Pages*. The nearest other stations are in Sacramento."

"Goddamnit! What happened? Is this different from the others?" The old man banged his fist on the back of the sofa.

It was Mandelbaum who answered. "No, Dr. Gustofson, it's the same syndrome, a collapsed immunity system, and death from a hundred diverse microbial agents. But this time there is no ellipse. You almost had me persuaded with your antennae! But this time it's clear that we're really dealing with a medical problem." Mandelbaum turned on his heel and walked away.

Jess frowned. "I don't know what we *are* dealing with here, Gus, but so far I know that your reasoning's been sound."

"This is a fairly well populated area, Jess. There must be other towns, other radio stations. Where are they? Maybe—"

"There are the stations in Sacramento, but people around them are fine. It's only in this area that anyone died."

"Goddamnit, look at that! Lines of red meandering off in every direction."

"Yes," said Micah, "but they represent people liv-

155

ing along the roads going in and out of town. For a considerable distance, people living on those roads died. A pattern is clear this time, too, but it's different. Here in San Salino virtually everyone died. Whatever they did to San Salino is far more efficient than what was done the first two times."

"Mike, I'm telling you, somewhere in this mess there's an antenna, maybe two homemade antennae, and between them is an ellipse so big that it takes in a lot of open country. I'll bet those bastards put up two this time, and we'll find them when we go out!" Gustofson was shouting.

Micah shook his head sadly. "No, Gus. Look here." He pointed to a place above the red mass and yet well within reach of the thin bloody arms stretching out along the highways. "There's a whole cluster of houses here, a group of ranches. These people are in good health. I've tried. There's no way you can fit an ellipse into this pattern."

"Well, I know one thing. As soon as you let us inside San Salino, Jess and I are hying ourselves over to that radio station. And I guarantee you that, pattern or no pattern, we'll find out a signal was broadcast!"

It was noon before Micah let Jess and Gus go off on their exploration. Hundreds of trucks and hearses were still trundling along their grim rounds, and Gus impatiently sent the jeep rocketing past first one and then another. His famous bad temper had at last surfaced, and fury burned in his eyes. The apparent evaporation of the only lead they had and Mandelbaum's aura of vindication had combined to provoke him. He slowed at a corner, hesitated, finally stopped.

"We must be lost, Jess. This is where the damned thing is supposed to be."

Jess went over to a sign standing in the lot, read it, came back, and said quietly, "Gus, this *is* it. The new state highway's coming through here. There was a radio station, but it's been razed."

"Well, dammit, somebody might have told us! Where's the new one?"

156

"There isn't any, Gus."

"Well, then, where the hell is the antenna that broadcast the signal? There's gotta be one! Must be homemade, like I said—both of 'em! Yes, sir, *two!*"

Jess put his hand on the old man's shoulder. "Easy, Gus. I have a hunch they pulled something new here. In Bridgeton they refined their system, and I'll bet now they've refined it even further. We'll find it, but it's going to take time."

"We don't have time, Jess. Look what they did already—killed more than twenty thousand people. There's *got* to be an antenna!"

"But no radio station was involved, Gus. There isn't any—and there isn't any ellipse this time."

The two men sat for several minutes. Neither spoke.

Finally Gustofson said, "Jess, we've gotten this far by investigating the survivors. Let's go back to that method."

For hours they drove around town, looking for survivors. It was hard because there were so few, but by late afternoon it was clear that they had not lost the scent. Every survivor had been out of town a week before the outbreak from about 7:00 to 9:00 in the morning.

Gustofson's excitement and confidence returned.

Although it was time for dinner, he refused to return to the motel. He pushed on in his search, taking careful notes.

They were at the edge of town, on a road that disappeared into a canyon, when they saw a tumble-down house and barn. A forlorn dog barked loudly at them, and little children playing in the yard came to stare as they braked to a halt.

It was early evening, and smoke curled up from the tin chimney at the top of the house. The children were Chicano. Gustofson waved and said hello, wondering if they spoke English. Their father appeared at the door.

"Hello, *señores,* welcome."

Gustofson smiled. "We're with the team of doctors

investigating the epidemic in town. Wonder if we might ask you all some questions?"

"*Sí*, but what can we say? God has been kind to us, and none of us is sick."

Gustofson got out of the jeep and stretched. He rubbed his tired eyes. "Senyore, this here is Dr. Jess Barrett, and I'm Dr. Bill Gustofson. Tell me, if you don't mind, have you or any of your family been out of town lately, say a week ago?"

"No, *señor* doctor, we must stay here to tend to our farm and care for the animals. We have not moved from this place for months."

Gustofson's eyebrows raised, and he said, "Really? Well, this is mighty pretty country, and I can see how you'd want to stay right here, but don't you ever drive into Sacramento? Mightn't you have been away even for a few minutes a week ago, say on Wednesday morning?"

"Oh, no, *señor,* in the morning I milk the cow and feed the chickens." He smiled. *"Señor* doctor, we eat now. Will you join us?"

"That's mighty kind of you, senyore. O.K., Jess?"

Jess agreed that he could stand a bite. Inside they sat in hardbacked chairs while a tired woman in a ragged dress dished out beans and salad and the little children watched from the other room. As they ate, Gustofson, clinging to his subject, heard from the woman, too, that the entire family had been home during the fatal moments. They also learned that other families farther out on the same road had died.

Finally, Gus began to write in his notebook. He squinted to see in the darkening house. Absent-mindedly, he flipped the switch on the lamp beside him. Nothing happened.

Their host was apologetic. "Oh, *señor,* I am so sorry, but there is no light. Two weeks ago the man came and shut it off. He said I did not pay the bill. A foolish man. I would have paid it someday! He made me so mad, I decided to let him keep his light and use *la kerosena.*"

With that he brought a kerosene lamp. Gus wrote

for a few minutes, then thanked their host for the meal, unobtrusively dropped a five-dollar bill in a dark corner, and left with Jess.

They turned onto the highway and headed for the road that reached out into the next canyon. Shortly they saw lights ahead, heard singing, and drove into a circle of little tar-paper shanties. It was a commune of what had once been called hippies. Around a huge campfire a dozen adults and eight or nine children were cooking meat and toasting bread. They all looked up cheerfully as Jess and Gustofson approached.

"Howdy, folks. We're with the Public Health Service. Mind if we join you?"

A bearded man in a leather vest and dirty jeans, evidently the leader, motioned them to a bench beside the fire.

"Sit down, man, sit down."

"Anybody around here been sick?"

"No, we're all healthy as oak trees. We don't weaken our bodies with frantic living. We take life easy, do a little farming, a lot of loving, and more sleeping."

"Well, now, that's mighty sound thinkin', I'd say. Do you move around much? Been away lately?"

"Man, who wants to move around when you got a place like this? We never go anywhere—'cept maybe into town to rip off something we need." A bray of laughter erupted from the group.

"Well, let me ask you right out, were any of you away last Wednesday—a week ago yesterday—in the morning?"

The young people looked at one another thoughtfully for a moment and agreed that they'd all been right there on Wednesday.

The old doctor scratched his head in consternation. Finally, he asked if he might go inside one of their houses to make some notes in the light.

The leader laughed; in the fire's bright glow his white teeth flashed against his black beard. "Man, you think the company would give *us* lights? We got no electricity."

159

"I'll use the flash in the jeep. Thanks for the information, folks. Let's go, Jess."

They drove to the road and then paused while Gus wrote in his notebook, muttering to himself about people who lived like that, rejected by a whole city, without even electricity.

While he waited, Jess stood on the side of the road looking at the city below, lost in thought. The night was clear and dry, and the stars seemed as close as the lights below.

Gus wearily put his notebook in his pocket, clicked off the flash. Then Jess turned excitedly, shouting as though they were thirty yards apart. "Gus, I've *got* it! Those dirty bastards! Do you know what they've done? They're refining their system again—horribly!"

"What are you talking about? Spit it out, son!"

"Gus, I know *something* about how they did it! Look, in Bensonville, in Bridgeton, they used a huge antenna, broadcast something over it that interfered with the radio station's transmission, forced it to join in the broadcast, making a dipolar field. Right?"

"Well, that's what we think, anyway. But there's no station here, no antenna that we know of, and people survived inside the area of death. I'm beginning to doubt—"

"No, Gus, don't doubt anything. I know how they did it. I just realized where the antenna is. It's right under our feet!"

Gus looked down instinctively. "How could it be?"

"It's the *power lines,* Gus. They're using the power lines as their antenna."

He came over beside the jeep, laid a hand on the old man's shoulder. "The first two times, they set up their rig in the broadcast area of the radio station. There's a lot of energy carried by radio waves, of course, and somehow—I still don't know how—they were able to suck the station's energy into their antenna. This created an elliptical field between the two, which apparently destroyed the immunity systems of everybody caught in it.

"It was this sucking of energy that caused the squeal

of the radio stations! It was like a squeal of pain at anything so unnatural.

"Here, though, they invented a much more effective method. The power lines act as their antenna. They connect something to the power lines. Then they cause the energy to be drawn off into the ground and surrounding atmosphere. The people served by the power system are caught in the field so created, and their immunity systems are destroyed."

"I still don't see how they did it," Gus said.

"Neither do I. They've found a way to make the power drain do the damage. I don't know of any mechanism by which this could be done, but obviously it can."

Gus puffed on his pipe. "Wouldn't we have something here like the sound? Another squeal of pain, except this time from the power system? What should we look for?"

Jess thought. "Probably a drop in the line voltage for a few moments. But Gus, these murderers are using the power system, I'm sure of that. The commune kids and Chicanos lived because they aren't plugged into the system, so no field developed around here.

"I'll bet that when we're through, we'll find that the pattern of death is the pattern of the power system. People out there in the hills who survived either had no electricity, weren't in the area when the interference occurred, or are using electricity from another system."

"My God, Jess," said Gus softly, "I may not know much about electronics, but that makes sense to me. How can we check it out?"

"Let's get to the power station. I happened to find out that San Salino has its own power system, which is fairly unusual for a town of its size. The plant's about three miles from here. Let's go take a look at their log, see if anything happened to their transmission last Wednesday morning. I bet we'll find something."

The jeep sped off down the highway with the cool, dry air blowing in their faces. But they had gone

161

hardly a mile before they saw, off to their right in another of the canyons, a cluster of lights. Gustofson turned the jeep toward it, and within minutes they shot into the driveway and halfway around the parking circle of a luxurious ranch-style house. Almost immediately curtains parted; a man looked out, then opened the door.

After formalities, Gus and Jess were invited inside; they established that the owner, a banker, had not been absent during the critical period a week before. Gus was crestfallen and Jess stunned at this apparent refutation of their theory.

Jess persisted in his queries. Finally he asked almost angrily, "Well, how can you be so *sure* you were here that day? You've said that you often go for walks in the hills early in the morning."

The man's eyes bulged. "I don't know who you think you are, coming up here and acting like policemen! I told you I was here, and my wife and daughter, on that Wednesday morning, and we were. I remember because of what happened that day."

Jess stared, and Gustofson turned from the window. *"What* happened that day?"

"It had nothing to do with this plague, I can assure you. You see, they're building a new house, or rather they were. I doubt they'll finish it now that—"

"Dammit, man, tell us what happened that day! We don't have forever. What happened?" Gustofson's temper had snapped.

The banker pouted. "If you'll give me a minute, I'll tell you. Every morning they started work on that house early—right down there, see the outline against the sky? They'd start at all hours, and that morning they must have begun at six o'clock.

"I woke up to the sound of a bulldozer digging out the basement. I was furious, since I work quite late at night on Tuesdays and like to sleep till eight on Wednesdays. But after lying there, trying to go back to sleep, I finally decided it was no use.

"I got up and was making myself a cup of coffee when suddenly the coffee maker just gurgled and went off. I couldn't believe it. What a morning! I tried to flip on the lights—sure enough, no power! Then I figured it out. That damnable dozer had cut the power line."

Gustofson, who had been listening with rapt attention, began to laugh. Jess laughed with him; it was inappropriate, but their relief had to find expression. The banker watched them apprehensively. Finally Gus said, "Mister, you'll go down in history. I wish I could buy you a drink. You're the perfect example of the exception that proves the rule. I want to thank you for your cooperation." He turned to leave.

Jess asked one more question. "Just tell me this, sir. Do you know the exact time your power went off, and for how long?"

"Yes," said the fellow proudly, "I have a perfect memory for figures, and all our clocks are electric. The power went off at seven thirty-eight. And it was almost nine before the company got the cable repaired."

Jess was bone-tired, but the night air cleared his mind as they drove toward the power plant. Gus had abruptly recovered from his weariness, and Jess marveled at the fountain of youth that bubbled away in that ancient body.

"I guess it's silly at my age to get so excited about something like this, Jess, but I am. For a while there it looked as if all our ideas were wrong. This shows we're on the right track. We'll catch 'em now, for sure."

"We're a long way from catching anybody, Gus. And we still don't know much of how they did it. All we know is that they're working some kind of electronic wizardry."

"Yeah, I do wonder how they can alter the frequency in a whole power system."

"I'm not sure, but it might be pretty simple. At first I believed they'd have to tap into a main line, but the more I think about it, the greater the possibility seems that all they'd have to do is plug their infernal machine into an ordinary wall outlet."

"That's as frightening an idea as you've had yet, Jess."

"It is. You see, most cities aren't on an independent system like this, but are part of a grid system, involving whole geographical areas. You certainly remember the power blackout in the Northeast in 1965."

"Yeah. They never did quite figure out what caused it, did they?"

"No, frankly, they didn't. And it showed just how sensitive those systems are."

The jeep skidded to a halt, and Gustofson stared at Jess. It was a moment before he could speak. "My God, Jess, you don't mean to tell me that they could plug into an ordinary wall outlet and alter the current in a whole power grid? Kill everybody in—?"

Jess's voice was husky with emotion. "I don't *know* much of anything about this yet. But that's exactly what I'm *thinking*—that when this idea came to them they decided to try it out first on a city with a little independent system."

"And then?"

"Exactly. And then? Will they use it on some huge metropolitan center?"

"With hundreds of thousands of people?"

"Maybe millions, Gus. Millions of people."

They sat there in the silent jeep, with the city below them, a city brightly lighted by men searching for the dead.

"We've got to find those maniacs, Jess—soon!"

"Well," said Jess, his voice hollow and unconvincing in his own ears, "maybe the whole idea is wrong; maybe we'll find that there was no interference in the power output that day."

"A few minutes ago, I was afraid we wouldn't find that. Now I'm terrified that we will. Let's go see."

14

VERA NORMAN tried to sleep in the air force jet carrying her to Sacramento. She was exhausted after her twenty-four hours in the custody of the FBI. They had questioned her, going over every part of her life, repeating the same questions in different contexts, on and on. They recorded everything, and she knew they were checking all her statements even as they questioned her further. Nobody had been discourteous or mistreated her. But when they were through, she felt as though she had been undressed and examined by a succession of curious people.

Then, after only a few hours of sleep, she was wakened by a courteous, typically efficient agent who asked if she'd be willing to go to California to talk with the president's assistant, Dr. Maruyama. She had, of course, expected that invitation. She signed a statement that she was going of her own free will and soon was boarding a supersonic jet transport. To her surprise, she and the FBI agent were the only passengers. He carried an attaché case, and she knew it contained a full report of her character, history, associations, and work. She slept through part of the flight, waking as the jet began its descent and craning to see the city below. It was late, yet Sacramento was alive with lights. The plane circled the city in a landing pattern, and she saw, off to the north, a stream of traffic flowing out of the capital. She suspected it was heading toward San Salino.

A limousine was waiting for the plane; the agent handed his attaché case to the man who stood beside it, nodded to Vera, and disappeared into the jet, which took off at once. They got in the car and drove away from the airport.

"Miss Norman, I'm Bill Petersen, FBI. Dr. Maruyama asked me to thank you for your willingness to come."

She smiled, wondering what would have happened if she'd objected. "Is it terrible out there, Mr. Petersen?"

The stocky man didn't answer for so long that she began to wonder if he'd heard her. When he finally spoke, his voice was flat, like that of a man hypnotized. "Miss Norman, I've been through a war, and I've seen murder victims by the dozen. But I have never—" He paused, searched for words, found none, gave up, merely shook his head. Then he added quietly, wearily, "We've got to catch them."

"Then you do think it's a human agent causing this?"

"We're not supposed to talk about it, but I guess I personally think somebody is doing it to us, yes."

Vera said confidently, "I *know* there's somebody doing it."

Petersen glanced sharply at her, then out the window at the traffic. Nearly every vehicle was a military truck or an ambulance going toward San Salino. At last he said, "What makes you so sure? Unofficially, off the record, how could you predict that the sickness would strike here next?"

"I thought you knew. I'm an astrologer, and I find signs in the stars that tell me what's likely to happen."

"How could stars make any difference in our lives?" he asked. "I think we make our own lives, and when something goes wrong, it's our own fault or nature's, but not the stars'."

Vera was used to this attitude. "The fault, dear Brutus, is not in our stars"—that had been quoted to her more times than she could count. She said, "I could explain some of the facts of astrology to you, but I have a feeling that I'll be asked to do it again when we arrive."

Petersen nodded. "You're right. I'll sit on my curiosity." He drove on in silence.

The motel that served as team headquarters was surrounded by a circle of green military vehicles. As Vera got out, Petersen took her arm. "This way, Miss Norman." They went through a lobby filled with doctors and officials, back to the banquet room, on into the reception room Micah used for an office. Inside, several people were busy on telephones, while others stood in front of a huge map, still plotting victims and survivors. Doctors in long white coats stood talking or slouched in chairs. The overall impression was of unutterable weariness.

As they paused in the doorway, a small man talking to a group saw her and detached himself. It was Micah.

A memory of the evening they had spent together came to her. Vera had been courted by dozens of rich, talented young men, but none of them had really interested her. They were too slow mentally, or bigoted, or unpleasantly eccentric, or staid, or self-centered, or calculating—always some flaw turned her off.

The sort of mind a man possessed was of vital importance to Vera, and Micah's brilliance appealed to her. Her only real reservation would have surprised him. It was not his race but his apparently emotionless personality that bothered her. However much she valued a keen mind, it was equally important to her to find warmth and sensitivity, perhaps all the more so because she herself was sensitive to the point of being terribly vulnerable. Micah had not shown any romantic interest in her, yet she found herself delighted as she watched him walk toward her. She wondered if this was to be the man she had seen coming into her life in her progressions. She smiled back at Micah.

"Miss Norman, it's good to see you again, though I'm sorry it's under these circumstances. I hope you haven't been too inconvenienced; you realize we had to check every possibility. Won't you sit down?"

He indicated a comfortable chair, and she sank into

it with relief. Across the room a huge man with a fat face and thin moustache stopped talking and glared at her.

Micah had already seated himself and was reading the papers from the attaché case Petersen had given him. She knew it was the FBI report on her; in fact, she knew she'd been picked up, questioned, investigated, and brought to California on Micah's order. But she felt no anger. It was the intelligent thing to do, and she was never annoyed by intelligence.

Micah scanned the report with the speed of one accustomed to much reading. It was about what he had expected, although he was surprised to learn of her prominent social background.

Vera Norman, the subject, was the only child of Arthur P. Norman, former chairman of the board of Norman Oil Corporation. Family prominent and respected internationally, both socially and industrially. Subject educated at best private schools until college level, which she attained at age fifteen.

Subject attended Radcliffe College and majored in psychology, achieving top honors. During this period she became interested in astrology and studied extracurricularly under some of the leading astrologers of the time. Despite the objections and ridicule of her professors, she announced her intention to make that her profession.

She went on to take a Ph.D. in psychology at Harvard.

Since then, subject has performed astrological services for prominent citizens of Washington, New York, and Boston. Subject has also published works on numerous astrological subjects, including one that received international acclaim, *The Transits of Neptune.*

In recent years has confined herself mainly to research, using computers to record and correlate data. The few customers she still accepts claim that she is a greater astrologer than Evangeline

Adams. The wealth she recently inherited permits her to spend her time as she wishes.

Subject achieved wide recognition through television appearances and writings. She has made spectacular predictions which have been featured in the press, and it is reputed that certain heads of state make no major decisions without consulting her.

Subject lives quietly in a brownstone house on the West Side of New York. In the first few years of her fame, she dated regularly and was often seen in the night clubs of Manhattan and Washington. During the past two years she has rarely dated and is known to have no current romantic interest.

Micah realized that he had paused at that sentence and reread it. He frowned and read on.

Subject is not known to be a member of any politically active organizations and is thought by all her friends to be moderate in social attitudes. Subject is well known in foreign circles, but all who know her insist she has no friendships or associations with people inimical to the interests of the United States.

This year subject has worked with the New York City Police Department. Inspector Joseph Ryan states that subject has contributed to the solution of several difficult crimes.

At the time of the Anthony Rossi kidnapping, subject wrote Inspector Ryan insisting that the victim was already dead and that the kidnappers had buried the body near water. She also stated that the kidnappers were employees of the victim.

Rossi's body was found near his home on the Hudson River. Police carefully investigated the employees and found incriminating evidence against the chauffeur. He eventually confessed and implicated the victim's male secretary.

Ryan maintains that the subject contributed to

other cases. Most spectacular was the Roland Wilson murder. Victim had died from what appeared to be a heart attack. Detective John Mendez of the homicide squad believed that foul play might be involved and asked this question of the subject: "What were the circumstances surrounding the death of Mr. Wilson?" Mendez reports that he supplied the subject with the date and exact time of death and the date of the deceased's birth.

Subject, allegedly on the basis of that data alone, insisted that the victim had been murdered with a drug or medicine, that he had been involved in some way with transportation at the time of his death, and that he had been in poor health. She speculated that the victim might have been given a lethal overdose of his own medicine.

Subject also insisted that there were two significant documents involved, one public and the other secret and unknown; that inheritances were the reason for the murder; and that the murder was committed by two people, a partner (or wife) and an employee.

Subject predicted that careful questioning of a sister or brother would provide the break needed in the case. Mendez reports he questioned a sister intensively and in that conversation mentioned that the victim had been found without his false teeth. The sister then blurted out that Wilson's wife had probably driven him out of the house in a hurry, as she often did in one of her rages.

Mendez questioned sister further, found that she suspected murder but was too timid to mention it for fear people would think she was bitter over having received nothing in the will.

When Mendez mentioned the possibility of a secret document, the sister speculated that reference might be to a letter the deceased had said he was writing shortly before his death.

A search of the deceased's office brought to

light this letter, which contained information leading to the arrest of the wife and lawyer.

Wilson's body was exhumed, and a post-mortem showed subject to be correct in saying the victim was poisoned with lethal overdose of his own medicine. He had died while driving his auto.

When Special Agent Franks questioned Mendez and Ryan on possible disloyalty of subject to the United States, both became abusive of the FBI for doubting subject's integrity.

Attached is a study of subject's daily activities during the past six weeks. All are innocuous and normal.

Conclusion: Subject has nothing in her background to cause suspicion of her loyalty to the United States.

Micah looked up, smiled at Vera. "Well, Miss Norman, you've had an eventful life and made some faithful friends."

She smiled back, said nothing.

Just then Micah saw a very tired and grubby Gustofson come into the room, followed by Jess Barrett. He stood up and said, "The last two men we've been waiting for have arrived. Come and meet the team."

She accepted his hand. Together they walked into an adjoining room, where a dozen chairs circled a table. Other members of the team followed them into the meeting room, and Micah introduced Vera.

Dr. Brown looked at her with a twinkle, as if glad she was there. Goerke was friendly and trim; Ogden, handsome but sour and anxious that she know of his contempt for astrologers. Then came Mandelbaum, the huge man she had noticed earlier; Fornier, thin and tired and seeming to care little about anything; a big, tanned, black-haired, unshaven, half-drunk man in expensive clothes, carrying a revolver under his coat, whom Micah introduced with not-quite-concealed distaste as Mayor McDonald; Petersen, the FBI agent;

and a sophisticated man named Adams, of the CIA.

Last into the room came a bent old man with incredibly crumpled clothes and a drooping moustache, and a tall, broad-shouldered man who looked at her as if unable to believe his eyes. She smiled warmly at him. He was not exactly handsome, but he was nice-looking, and she liked him on sight. Ordinarily, she was not attracted to big men. She prized sensitivity and warmth, and it seemed to her that many big men tended to be brutal or overbearing. But this man had a sensitive look about him.

"Miss Norman, this is Dr. Gustofson of the Louisville medical center, and this is Jess Barrett, our electronics expert."

Jess's eyes held hers for a moment before Micah said, "Miss Norman? Will you sit here?" Then he turned to the others and began, his soft voice remote, lacking the warmth she had felt earlier. She looked at Barrett and found him staring at her. Uncharacteristically flustered, Vera returned her attention to Micah as he told of having her exhaustively questioned. He concluded by saying that the FBI report had given her a clean bill of health, that her credentials were so good that he had no hesitation in including her in their top-level conference.

"Miss Norman," he said, "let me ask you the question in everybody's mind. How did you predict this catastrophe?"

She looked around the big table. "Well, you see, I'm an astrologer. I know many of you may not believe in astrology, but—"

"Miss Norman, you already show psychic abilities. Many of us do *not* believe in astrology." Ogden was at his sarcastic worst.

Micah waved his hand in annoyance, and Vera continued. "When I heard of the disaster in Bensonville, I did an event chart for the moment of death, that is, the moment the plague began. Then I looked up the date and time of the founding of the town, did a mundane chart, and progressed the chart to the present. I was astonished at what it revealed.

"It confirmed what I'd seen in the event chart. You see, two years ago I began research in mundane astrology. I noted then in the progressed chart of the United States that we would have disasters involving widespread loss of life. So I used my computer to do charts for thousands of towns and cities. I tagged every town with an afflicted eighth house—that is, every one in danger of loss of life.

"After I saw the charts for Bensonville, I asked the computer to kick out the charts of all cities with active eighth houses; I read through hundreds. One was Bridgeton, which was destroyed the day I found the chart. I discovered that the same conditions existed over it as had existed over Bensonville.

"I then searched through the danger charts again and saw that San Salino would fall under the same conditions this past Wednesday. So I wrote the letter to Dr. Maruyama."

McDonald suddenly jumped to his feet. His face was red and sweating, and his body swayed as he spoke. "Lady, there's only one way you could know what was going to happen—and that's by being in on the conspiracy that did this."

"Is that the reason she wrote to warn us about San Salino, Mayor McDonald? Please sit down." Micah spoke softly but firmly.

Jess put his hand on the drunken man's shoulder and pulled him down. "Get hold of yourself, Jim," he murmured.

"But, Miss Norman, will you explain, please?" Micah whispered politely. "We don't understand astrology. What are an 'event chart' and 'mundane chart' and 'progressions'?"

"Well, it's all very complicated, and I don't quite know where to begin. Astrology has many branches. One is genethliac or natal, the study of the effects of the stars on individual lives. We cast a chart of the heavens as they were at the moment a child was born. That tells us the kind of person he will be: his character, his intelligence, his likely vocation, and to a great extent, the sort of things that will happen to him.

"To get more exact knowledge of the time the events of his life will occur, we progress the chart—which is to say, we move the planets ahead one day for each year, and from that we can tell what may happen to him."

"What are you talking about? This is all mumbo jumbo."

Vera looked at Dr. Ogden and nearly said something sharp, but caught herself; she had heard the same reaction so many times before. She knew that these men were exhausted. And also, she reflected impishly, the sarcastic doctor was probably an Aquarian with his Mars squared by Mercury—

Micah interrupted her thoughts. "Miss Norman, I apologize for our short tempers and bad manners. Will you please try to explain more slowly and simply?"

"As to a bunch of little boys," Gus added.

"May I use the blackboard?" Without waiting for an answer, she went to it and picked up a piece of chalk. "When I first heard about astrology, I considered it the craziest thing in the world. I was a psychology major at Radcliffe and thought I knew everything." She smiled sweetly, but the eyes that slid from face to face challenged them.

"The reason I grew interested in astrology and became a professional is *not* because I understand how planets can influence us but because *it works*. I think you'll admit that it has worked again." Again she smiled innocently, but nobody missed the taunt, and nobody took up the challenge. She noted that both Jess and the old doctor grinned.

"Astrology deals with the influence of the ten planets on the lives of human beings."

"Uh, Miss Norman, did you say *ten* planets?" Jess was frowning, and she smiled brightly at him. She liked his attentiveness, the respect in his voice.

"Yes, ten. I'm aware that there are nine in orbit around the sun. In astrology, we don't count the earth because it's the center of our interest—our residence, if you will. But for convenience' sake, we call the sun and the moon 'planets.' I realize that is astronomically incorrect, of course."

Barrett nodded. She noted how pleasant his smile was.

"Also for the sake of convenience, we consider that these planets circle the earth. We know they do not, but the relationship between the planets and earth makes it *seem* that they're circling us. And since we live on the earth, it is for us the center of the universe." She drew a circle to represent the earth. Then she began to draw a wide ribbon around the circle.

"When astrologers speak of the zodiac, we're referring to this band, which is in reality a number of fixed constellations surrounding the entire solar system. This band, these constellations, the signs, form a great backdrop before which the planets move. There are twelve signs, each composing thirty degrees, covering the ecliptic, which is the path of the planets across the sky. The first, Aries, is marked by the vernal equinox, the position of the sun on the first day of spring. The others follow around the sky to Pisces, the twelfth sign, which ends where Aries begins."

"So far, even I'm with you," said Gus, "pooped as I am."

"The planets circling around the earth appear to go *through* the signs. So when we say that the sun is in Virgo, what we mean is that from our vantage point here on earth, the sun seems to be moving through the area of the sky measured by that sign. When we say that a person is a Virgo, we mean that he was born during the time when the sun was in that section of the sky.

"But there are other things for an astrologer to consider. The position of the sun when a person was born tells us much about him, but the positions of the other planets in the signs are also important.

"For example, a man with his sun in Leo is likely to be proud and yet magnanimous. And the chances are he won't bother much about details. But if his Mercury is in Virgo when he's born, he probably *will* have a proficiency for details not typical of a Leo.

Likewise, the positions of the other planets in the various signs tell us more about him.

"You certainly are justified in wondering why we're so positive that each person is influenced by the signs in which the planets reside at the time of his birth. Frankly, we don't know why! We only know it works. When I first became acquainted with the art, I was so dumbfounded at the unaccountable accuracy of it that I made some studies. I had psychologists draw up descriptions of people on the basis of batteries of tests, while astrologers did the same on the basis of birth date and birth time alone. Neither the psychologists nor the astrologers knew the subjects personally.

"I gave the descriptions to friends and acquaintances of the subjects and asked them to find the one that best described the person in question. I found that those drawn by astrologers were most often chosen by the friends and that the psychological descriptions were often mixed and confused."

"By descriptions, Miss Norman, do you mean of personality?"

"Yes, Dr. Maruyama, and *character*. Astrologers became aware over the centuries that something more than merely the signs in which the planets are found at birth influences a person's character. They found that the position of the planets relative to each other makes a difference. If they are at ninety degrees to each other—what astrologers call a square—it seems to have one influence, generally malefic or difficult; and if the planets are trine, or one hundred twenty degrees from each other relative to the earth, a different influence is exerted, largely beneficial."

"Oh, come now, Miss Norman! The sun is the center of this solar system, and if you want to talk about signs and position, then you must relate them to the sun."

"You're correct that the sun is the center of the solar system, of course, Dr. Mandelbaum. But we don't live on the sun. The earth is the center *for us*. I admit that some people have suggested to me and other astrologers that we should move to the sun or some

176

other comparably warm place, but—" A ripple of laughter relaxed the tension, and Mandelbaum rolled up his eyes. Vera went on.

"The relationships between the planets we call 'aspects.' We list a number of them, such as conjunctions, when the planets are lined up exactly or very nearly so; sextiles, when the aspect is sixty degrees; squares and trines; and oppositions, when the planets are opposite to each other with the earth in between.

"Those aspects are said by us to have a beneficial or harmful effect, according to the nature of the planets themselves."

Barrett interrupted again. She was pleased that he was listening so carefully. "What do you mean, 'the nature of the planets themselves,' Miss Norman?"

"Mr. Barrett, we've concluded that certain planets exert a stressful influence; we call those planets 'malefic.' Other planets seem to exert a beneficial influence, and we call them 'benefics.' Mars, Saturn, Pluto, Neptune, and Uranus are negative in their effects. Jupiter is the great benefic and Venus the lesser. And the sun, the moon, and Mercury are beneficent. Now, if you ask me *why* one planet out there in space should be good and another bad, I don't know."

"Well, then, Miss Norman," demanded Dr. Mandelbaum, "why do you practice this occult and cabalistic art if you don't even know why it works? As you say it does," he added heavily.

Vera looked at him ingenuously. Her words were measured and her voice without expression. "I suppose for the same reason that science used aspirin and penicillin and other drugs for years before anyone knew why they worked."

Gustofson swallowed a cloud of smoke and began to cough loudly. Mandelbaum scowled at the old man but said nothing.

Vera went on. "We also say that in certain signs, planets seem to lose some of their power; and in others, they seem very powerful. Thus, we say that in Aries, Venus is not so strong, and so forth.

"Then there's the matter of the houses. The earth

travels around the sun, making the route once a year. But it also turns on its axis, so that it seems that the sun is moving around the earth, and in a sense travels through the entire zodiac once a day.

"That is important, and astrologers have discovered that the very time of the day we were born influences the kind of person we are, and what happens to us in our lives. So if a person is born when the sign of Libra is just coming up over the horizon, we say he has Libra rising or that his ascendant is Libra.

"The signs and the planets in aspect tell us the type of person he is, but the houses tell us the kind of experiences he'll have. For example, if he has Jupiter unafflicted in his second house, it's likely that he'll be financially lucky. But—"

"Please, Miss Norman, what is a 'house' in your profession?" Gustofson, listening raptly, won a smile from her.

"I'll explain that. Long ago, astrologers discovered that certain parts of a person's life are influenced in direct relationship to the part of the skies the planets occupy when he's born. If the moon, say, is directly overhead, regardless of what sign occupies that part of the sky, he's likely to have a public life—sometimes evil, sometimes good, but public.

"Planets rising about two to four hours after his birth affect his financial prospects. For instance, if Jupiter is in that position, the person is likely to be rich.

"Or planets rising about six to eight hours after birth influence his home life. If Saturn's in that area, the person will likely have heavy family responsibilities.

"So, out of all these empirical observations, astrologers over the centuries decided that the heavens are divided into twelve segments, like slices of a pie. It takes about two hours for each of these to rise over the horizon. We call the segments, or spatial divisions, 'houses,' and they refer to the compartments of one's life. The first house, which is the part rising during the first two hours after his birth, rules his appearance and personality. The second rules his personal possessions;

the third, his brothers and sisters; the fourth, his home; and so on."

Vera drew a chart of the heavens on the chalkboard as she talked. When she finished, she heard someone, either Ogden or McDonald, say, "Baloney!" She winced, turned, and brushed back a wisp of hair, leaving a spot of chalk on her forehead.

"Well, now, while there's much more to astrology, those are the basics. But there are many kinds of occasions for charts. The most common is natal astrology —when we draw a chart for the moment of birth and predict a person's character, personality, and many of his life's events.

"The most accurate predictions are made by doing what we call 'progressions.' That's a process by which we draw a chart for as many days as there are years in the person's life. We find that we can make very accurate predictions from that.

"But there are other kinds of astrology that often make headlines. Mundane astrology is the study of groups: nations, corporations, cities, states. We take the time of incorporation as the birth time. We can then treat a group like an individual, predict its character, even the events of its life. That's the way some astrologers have been able to make stunning predictions, such as the assassination of President Kennedy, radical changes in the stock market, and so forth.

"Some astrologers do charts for things like the launching of ships, and one predicted accurately the fate of the *Thresher* long before the accident that destroyed her.

"Another kind of astrology is the horary branch: the art of interpreting events by casting a chart for the event itself or of answering questions by casting a chart for the time the question was asked. This is the most difficult of the branches. It's been a specialty of mine."

As she paused, Micah said, "Thank you, Miss Norman; we have at least some idea of what astrology is now. Will you tell us how you used these techniques to make your remarkable prediction this week?"

She brushed at the wisp of hair again and left another chalk mark on her forehead. Jess smiled fleetingly.

"Well, as soon as I heard of the disaster at Bensonville, I did an event chart for it. I found some difficult aspects but not enough to cause the calamity.

"I found that Saturn was precisely squared by the moon at the exact moment Mars was coming over the horizon in opposition to Uranus. Some of the usual portents of disaster were there: Part of Fortune in Pisces, making it the Part of Misfortune, moon in the degree of the nodes, Caput Algol in the degree of—"

"Goddamnit, lady, will you speak English?" snapped McDonald.

"But the most amazing thing was that quite obviously the real precipitating event occurred *one week before the outbreak*. I could tell that from the fact that the moon had last passed over Neptune a week before."

"She couldn't know that unless she was in on this thing!" McDonald was getting worse by the minute. Vera suspected that the water glass from which he took constant sips did not contain water after all.

Micah never looked at the mayor, but murmured, "Be quiet, McDonald. Miss Norman, your letter said that, too—that the plague was caused a week before it struck. Can you elaborate?"

"Well, when I saw that fact, I turned to mundane astrology. I got the date for the town's incorporation and did a natal chart, then progressed it to this year. There were some very dangerous indications, particularly eighth-house dangers, which mean the danger ought to be from taxes, death, or some other eighth-house matter.

"Then I made an even more precise calculation, found not only the month of danger but the week, and began to do daily charts. Using my computer, I found the critical moment for Bensonville: seven forty-seven A.M., Wednesday, May twenty-sixth, one week before the town died."

Micah's face was motionless; his eyes never left

Vera. He said, through the muttering of the others, "Tell us how you determined that precise time."

"Well, I found the moon in opposition, to the minute, to Saturn; and for some time now, Mars has been in opposition to Uranus. At precisely seven forty-seven A.M., Mars was coming over the horizon."

Ogden snapped, "Oh, for God's sake, Miss Norman, if I know anything about astronomy, Mars and Uranus will hold their position for some time now. And there are lots of towns on the same longitude as Bensonville, which means Mars was rising for them, too, and they didn't suffer anything extraordinary."

"I'm afraid you don't understand. I'm not saying that the planetary alignments *caused* the disaster. They mirrored it. Those aspects would mean nothing to a town whose natal charts didn't show a susceptibility to disaster by afflicted eighth and twelfth houses."

Micah said carefully, "I'm not sure I follow you, Miss Norman. Are you saying that two conditions had to exist before the disaster could happen? A condition in the progressed mundane chart of the town to make it susceptible and at the same time a certain formation in the heavens?"

"Good for you, Dr. Maruyama. You're getting it. That's exactly what I'm saying."

"How did you predict this third catastrophe?" It was the old doctor, Gustofson, leaning across the table eagerly.

"Well, when the second disaster occurred, I quickly did another event chart and found conditions similar to those at Bensonville the day of the outbreak. Then I did a mundane chart for Bridgeton, progressed it forward, and found conditions almost identical to Bensonville's—except that on the week before the outbreak, the moon-Saturn aspect was an opposition, not a square. But in the case of aspects from the great malefic, Saturn, squares, oppositions, and conjunctions are all difficult."

"What were the similar conditions?"

"Well, the mundane chart had dangers to the eighth

and twelfth houses, and the event chart showed similar conditions the week before the outbreak."

"But what about the *third* time?" Gus insisted.

"When I saw the similarity of the conditions, I realized it could happen every week if there were a city on the right longitude with eighth- and twelfth-house dangers in the progressed chart. So I followed the longitude that would be affected by the rising Mars at the precise moment Saturn and the moon were in aspect. I checked the mundane charts of all the towns on the longitude until I found one with similar dangers in the mundane progressed chart. It was San Salino."

"That must have taken an enormous amount of time." Micah watched her intently.

"Oh, it would have been impossible except for two things. I have access to a computer and can do hours of calculations in seconds. And I've studied mundane astrology for two years and had already placed masses of data in the computer regarding towns, cities, and states in our country."

"When you could predict this disaster so accurately, why didn't you warn us in time to prevent it?" Goerke was showing some interest at last.

"Well, remember I said that something happened to each of these towns a week before the actual outbreak. So by the time I learned about San Salino, it was too late to stop the event. Whatever it was, it happened the same day that Bridgeton became ill, just as the trauma that caused the Bridgeton disaster occurred the day Bensonville was actually stricken."

Micah spoke slowly, precisely. "Miss Norman, you speak of trauma. What kind of trauma? Have you some idea what is causing these disasters?"

Vera's eyes widened. The men sat frozen, watching her closely, even McDonald. Her voice was deliberately soft, her words carefully articulated. "Why, of course, Dr. Maruyama. It's quite clear from the charts I've done that these disasters are of human origin."

"What do you mean, 'of human origin'?"

"It's my opinion, based on the involvement of Uranus and certain aspects to the eleventh house, that

182

all this has been caused by a human being—by one man. An insane genius, I'd say, a religious fanatic, is causing these horrible slaughters."

"A religious fanatic?"

"Yes, his significator is Neptune aspected by Jupiter."

"What makes you think it's only one man?"

"Partly common sense. Strangers, even only two or three, would have been noticed in a town the size of Bensonville, and you'd already be looking for them. I surmise it's one man working alone."

Petersen's nerves had been stretched too far. He snapped at her in frustration, "How could one man do this?"

Ogden shouted, "Ridiculous!" and McDonald howled.

Micah held up his hand again, never taking his eyes off Vera. When silence had returned, he went on, his voice now deadly soft, others straining to hear. "Miss Norman, if one man did this, *how* did he do it?"

The violent response to her last statement had frightened Vera. She gathered herself and said slowly, "Dr. Maruyama, I can tell you that, in principle at least. He is using electronics in some way to capture and amplify the malefic emanations from Saturn, Mars, Neptune, and Uranus to paralyze the immunity system. Victims are unable to resist infection of any sort, and they die of whatever germs happen to be in their bodies."

15

PANDEMONIUM BROKE LOOSE. Above it Jack Goerke shouted, "Young lady! How did you know about the collapse of the immunity system? We've had tight security on that fact!"

Fornier asked loudly, "How does she know about the electronics, too? Not a word's been given to the press about that."

Micah rapped his hand on the table for attention. But when he'd quieted everyone and begun to speak, Mandelbaum overrode him, his great voice quivering with rage. "Well, now, I'm very glad for this little act. I'll admit that I was almost beginning to believe the electronics rubbish. But it's clear now what's happening. Our Shakespearean actor, Dr. Gustofson, and his friend the football player have given this female charlatan their theories, and she's supporting the nonsense with her astrology. 'Malefic emanations'!"

Dr. Gustofson drew calmly on his pipe. Mandelbaum swept on. "But, Gustofson, this time your stupid coincidences, your antennae and ellipses, are totally absent. So you—"

Micah interrupted wearily. "Dr. Mandelbaum, have you forgotten that she predicted San Salino? How could she have gotten *that* from Dr. Gustofson or Dr. Barrett?"

He had never raised his voice, but Vera was amazed at how he dominated the bellowing Mandelbaum.

Micah turned to her again. "Miss Norman, there have been certain circumstances in these disasters which have been, ah, difficult to understand or explain. The symptoms do indicate a complete collapse of the immunity system. Because of the devastating effect of

184

these events on our country, and because we aren't sure of much of anything, we haven't released that news to the press. How do you know about it?"

Vera was tired from her long interrogation, the trip, this meeting. But she was excited at the chance to show what astrology could do. "Well, frankly, I read a good many domestic and foreign newspapers, and scientists here and abroad are speculating that the epidemics were the result of such a collapse. There was the relationship among Mars, Uranus, Saturn, and the moon—and Neptune was active. It would have been difficult for me to conclude the effect of such complicated aspects with certainty; however, they *could* cause paralysis of the immunity system, which I determined, after reading so much about it, to be the logical explanation."

Vera turned and chalked a diagram like a spoked wheel. Around the border, at each spoke, she drew a symbol for a zodiac sign. Inside the wheel she placed the planet symbols, talking rapidly.

"Here are the classic signs of a catastrophe: the placement of Caput Algol, the afflicted moon, a malefic in the fourth, the moon in the degree of the nodes, lack of benefics angular to give protection—each bad in itself, and so many of them indicate large-scale disaster. But Uranus, having to do with electronics, is strongly related to the third house of communications and—"

"And Jupiter is in the outhouse," said Ogden loudly.

"Shut up," rumbled a voice warningly.

Without looking round, she identified it as Jess Barrett's and warmed with gratitude to him.

"How'd you ever catch on to the fact that these catastrophes were caused electronically?" asked Gustofson.

"Again, it's complicated, but it has to do with the relationship between Uranus, which rules electronics, Mars, which rules accidents, murder, and particularly massacres, and Mercury, which rules communications. A strange fact, however, is that Mercury was *not* involved in San Salino."

Jess raised a hand, like a boy in school, a little skeptical but polite. "Miss Norman, you amaze me when you suggest that he used electronics to—what was it, amplify emanations coming from the planets? Would you elaborate?"

She said, "The aspects here don't account for the magnitude of the disasters. The more I wondered what he might be doing, the more I realized that he had to be an astrologer. He's chosen his towns carefully. Now, mind you, I'm a professional astrologer with access to a computer, and it's taken me hours to find a town that fits the requirements in its progressed chart. This man must have done it first.

"That made me wonder if he wasn't using astrology to do more than pick out a susceptible town. He knew that harmful emanations can come from these stellar configurations and that if those could be amplified, their effect on susceptible people would be devastating. I think that he's a genius not only in astrology but also in electronics and in medicine, since certainly he's aware of his machine's effects on immunity."

"Goddamnit, young lady, you tryin' to tell me that them little stars up there are giving off some kind of —of power that one man can magnify? Hell! I still think the damn Commies flew an airplane over and dropped gas or germs on my town."

"Jim, we've proved that no cloud of gas or bacteria could form the precise pattern of an ellipse." Jess tried to soothe the mayor.

"But, Jess," Brown said, "there isn't any such pattern here, is there? I still hope to hear that the investigation of that pilot who flew over Bensonville will prove somebody paid him to drop something and that we'll catch them."

Petersen sat up quickly. "Oh, Dr. Maruyama, in the attaché case there's a report from the director on that investigation."

Micah found the letter and opened it, the others watching in silence. He read it, shook his head. "Nothing! They did an exhaustive study of the man's life. He was a salesman with a mistress in Bensonville, and on his weekly route he'd buzz the town, and she'd wave at him. Why he died is beyond me."

Mandelbaum stood. "To medical men, Mr. Maruyama, it's obvious. He flew through viable organisms in the air, scooped them up, and became infected, then died later."

Micah was too tired, too disappointed to argue. He only muttered, "What organism, mumps virus?"

Jess said, "I think what happened to that pilot, poor devil, is quite clear. He flew down just as the signal was sounded. The field reached out from the axis hundreds of yards on each side and upward as well. When he flew through the field, *his* immunity system was ruined, too. He didn't unload anything, didn't ingest any organism."

Micah, reading further in the FBI report, said, "Remember that Dr. Brown reported one of the autopsied bodies hadn't died like the others, but of a fractured skull. Well, here's his report. Richard Joffee of Chalmers. He was the ambulance driver that day."

"What?" Jess exclaimed. "Why, that's the fellow who ran away! I stopped the coward and tried to reason with him, but he ran. I took the Chalmers ambulance and drove it the rest of the day."

The others looked at him, startled. He said, "I didn't hurt him; I only slapped his face. Then he ran away."

Micah smiled. "Jess, take it easy. We know you wouldn't hurt him. But it's odd that he should be killed. I suppose somebody who was sick or trying to help the sick saw him running and bashed his head in. I can't blame the killer—or poor, scared Joffee. I'm afraid it has no relevance to our problems." He pushed the report back into the attaché case.

Adams said to Petersen, "Bill, if this young lady is right—and Lord knows I don't understand anything about astrology—but if she is, then we should look for a man who's remarkably educated in three fields: electronics, medicine, astrology. You check out the universities here in the States; I'll have my men contact those in Europe and Japan. China and Russia will be harder, but we'll try. O.K.?"

Petersen nodded emphatically and scrawled notes on a pad. Micah agreed absently.

Mandelbaum rose. "Mr. Chairman, I object to all this. For us men of science to be taking an astrologer seriously is utterly absurd!"

"I remind you again that Miss Norman predicted this disaster."

"Coincidences keep astrologers alive. But this time there are fewer coincidences. There's no radio station, no signal, no ovals which—"

He was interrupted by Gustofson knocking out his pipe on a glass ashtray. He hammered and hammered, as though with a gavel, then picked at the remaining ashes with a pocketknife. Mandelbaum having subsided, Gustofson said, "Uh, well, Mandy, you're *partly* right. Fact is, come to think of it, you're most always partly right, but this time you're also partly dead wrong."

He groped for tobacco, and while the others waited and Jess smiled at the old ham, he filled his pipe, leisurely lit it, and puffed out clouds of smoke, to the annoyance of Ogden, who said, "Dammit, Gus, couldn't you turn to cigarettes and take a chance on lung cancer? With that foul old engine, you'll give it to all of us."

Micah watched, silent, amused. They had all been living in a nightmare for days, and the old man provided the only relief.

"Well, now, Jess—this big jock here—and I went for a ride this afternoon. We drove to where the radio station had been and found that it was gone—physically, literally gone."

"Stolen?" asked Ogden innocently. "Or just strayed?"

With equal innocence Gustofson answered, "Damn thing had been sold and razed. We found out later it's been out of business for four months. Couldn't compete with those slick stations in Sacramento. I don't know why. Never did like these big-town stations with their smart-aleck disk jockeys—but I'm wandering from my point. Happens when you get old, you know. Where was I? Oh, yes, no radio station.

"So Jess and I drove around, talking to some of those good folks, though there were blessed few of 'em survived. Anyhow, we began to find the same pattern we found before. Everyone was out of town the week before between seven and nine in the morning. The more we talked, the more we saw we were on the right track. But we kept askin' each other about that radio signal. Why wasn't it there?"

"Oh, God, Gus, spare us the histrionics, the innocent good-old-country-boy bit, and tell us what you found." Dr. Ogden was literally grinding his teeth.

Gus seemed not to hear. He puffed hard until his pipe fired up again. "Well, we discovered a few people who were home during the critical period. First there were some Chicanos up there aways in a canyon. Nicest folks you ever met. And cook? Man, that little brown woman can cook. I never tasted better—"

"Oh, Lord!" Ogden buried his head in his arms.

"Yeah, straying again. Hmm. At first I wondered if maybe they were just so tough, they couldn't be hurt by a radio signal or whatever it was. Decided no. They weren't particularly healthy; in fact, they're so poor, they're undernourished. Don't even have electricity; use kerosene lamps. Mighty sad for such nice people.

"Well, the jock and I drove on and found a friendly bunch of hippie folks, living out there with none of the modern conveniences—like sanitation, Dr. Ogden. Think of that. All these folks down here with their running water and nice shiny toilet bowls are dead. But the hippie people, dirty, diggin' a hole anytime they want to relieve themselves, they're alive. Funny thing."

"Dr. Maruyama, I see no reason why we should be subjected to this inane twaddle!" spluttered Mandelbaum. Micah only waved his hand, and Dr. Brown smiled outright.

"Those hippie people didn't have electricity either. Well, now, for a senile old man like me, that didn't mean a thing. But the big jock, he had an idea. He decided maybe this murderous bastard we're huntin' had stumbled across a new method, that he doesn't need a radio station anymore to amplify those celestial emanations Miss Norman talks about—though, of course, we hadn't heard about them yet. Jess, son, why don't you tell these *medical* men your idea? Make it simple, now!"

Jess heard a sigh of relief from Ogden, who straightened up slowly and looked at him as he began to speak.

"It occurred to me, after we found that second pocket of survivors, that our killer, or killers, might not need radio waves, only some form of electrical energy. The fact that the survivors didn't have electricity made me think that perhaps the power system was used to create the electric field instead of a radio signal.

"We talked to one other family and found that at the critical time, they'd been without power, too.

"Then we drove to the power station, checked their log. There was a six-second drop in the power output on Wednesday, June ninth, at seven fifty-two A.M. I think that everyone within the boundaries of that system was affected by the electric field that he, or they, created, and died a week later.

"I obtained a map of the power system to compare with our map showing deaths. While you men were coming in, I checked them and confirmed my guess. The pattern of death exactly coincides with the power system."

"Well, I'll be darned! They did it again, Batman and Robin." Fornier was open with his admiration.

"That's the change I thought I saw him making," said Vera.

"You mean this murderer can use the power system of a town to trap and amplify lethal radiation from outer space? That certainly makes him far more dangerous than he was before, when he had to rely on radio stations." Micah pondered the new bombshell.

Jess said somberly, "Mike, this means he can use an entire power grid. Do you remember some time ago when the whole Northeast was blacked out because something trivial went wrong with the grid? Well, that shows how interrelated these systems are. My guess is that this skunk has learned how to plug his little machine into any wall socket, turn it on, and alter the current in the whole system so as to make it lethal. Now he can—well—"

"Good God, Jess, some of these cities are tied together in grids for hundreds of miles, involving millions of people. Are you saying that he can kill whole metropolitan areas, whole states, whole regions?"

Jess nodded slowly. The others sat absolutely motionless; the magnitude of what they heard made the previous horrors mild by comparison. Brown tried to speak, but his mouth was too dry. He shook his head.

Finally Adams said, "Maybe he's going to extort money, ask for a billion dollars or something like that. Maybe he's just been showing what he can do, and now he'll make his demands."

Petersen agreed. "Sure, Brad, you have to be right. We'll hear from him any day now. And then we'll nab him."

Micah said, "No, I don't think so. He'd already have made his move if that were his motive. It's something else."

"But what? What possible motive could drive any human being to kill twenty thousand of his fellows? What sane man—" Jack Goerke stopped in midsentence.

Jess nodded. "That's just it, isn't it? What sane man?"

"Miss Norman already said he's a religious fanatic."

"Some religion!" said Ogden, appalled.

"Mr. Maruyama, you're our theologian-in-residence. What religion would lead a man to do this?" Mandelbaum was still sarcastic, but muted.

"Sick religion. More crimes have been committed in the name of religion than for any other cause."

The next voice was so vehement, so filled with hatred that everyone turned in amazement. It was McDonald. His eyes seemed to be fixed on something inside his own memory. "I'll get him, so help me God, I'll get him! He killed my Marilu and my children. All my friends. My town. I'll find him, and when I do, he'll suffer the way Marilu did. I *have* to get him!" The half-drunken man dropped his head in his hands and began to sob. Most of the others had become so accustomed to thinking of him as a fool and a boor that they had forgotten the reality of his overpowering grief. As he sobbed uncontrollably, they watched in embarrassment. But somehow, seeing the mayor, not as an offensive dolt, but as a deeply suffering human being shook them out of their paralysis.

Petersen stood up. "Wait! I have an idea. Miss Norman predicted this disaster. Apparently there's something to astrology. Well, let's ask her where it's likely to happen again. And we'll alert every cop and soldier in the state and catch him red-handed!"

They all turned to stare at the elegant, slender young woman whom they had treated so badly half an hour before. They were asking for help when they didn't even believe in astrology. She started to speak, then shut her mouth. There was a long silence, and Fornier whispered, "Oh, God, I know why you're hesitating. He fires his signal a week before the outbreak. If a town's going to die next week, he's already fired the signal, flipped the switch, or whatever."

Micah looked intently at Vera. "You already know, don't you, Miss Norman? You know which city is under sentence of death. Which one is it?"

In the long silence that followed, every man looked at her in dread, silently begging her not to name the city where a daughter was in college; where a wife was hanging out the wash in the clean, warm June air; where an old mother lived in a nursing home. Disbelief was suspended, and tension mounted until it was hard even to breathe.

"Damn you, woman, where is it? Is it Atlanta? Tell me!" It was Ogden screaming at her.

Vera shook her head. "No, it's not Atlanta."

"Which city is it?"

Vera licked her lips nervously. "Well, I don't think

192

he's going to do any more of this for a while. I haven't had time to make all the studies I want to, but I think he had this new idea, and now he's going to develop it. None of the cities on the longitude look quite right; the only one close doesn't have as afflicted an eighth house, and its twelfth house is not—"

Micah insisted softly, *"Which city,* Miss Norman?"

"Denver."

"Denver! A million, maybe two million people on that power system."

In the faces of the men around her, Vera read relief that their own families were not involved, mixed with the horror they saw ahead for others. But on Goerke's face there was no relief, only dread. "Why did you have to choose Denver? My God, my wife and children are there!"

"Please, Doctor, I didn't choose Denver, I only read the charts. *He* chose Denver—or rather, I don't think he *did* choose it."

"I'm sorry, of course you didn't choose it, Miss Norman." Goerke spread his hands, distracted. "But couldn't you have warned us in time, so we could get people out, so we could catch him?"

"I just found out myself, and I don't think he's going to destroy Denver! Besides, none of you would have believed me."

"What city comes after Denver, Miss Norman?" It was Micah, quietly.

"I can't find any place for the next week that fits the requirements astrologically, and I haven't had time to study the following week."

"But he can do this thing; he can murder a city every week?"

"Yes."

Micah acted quickly. "All right, gentlemen, we're not going to sit here and do nothing. Petersen, start that search for a man who's a genius in three fields; use the whole FBI if necessary. Brad, get all your men, every agent we have in the world, checking foreign universities. Mandelbaum, is there any reason we should stay here? Let's go to Denver, organize every

193

medical facility there to deal with the sickness if it comes."

Mandelbaum sighed. "Why not? We have men here who can handle this investigation." Then he added, "Won't the press suspect that we—"

"Right, but let's get moving. Maybe if we're there early enough, we can save those people. I'll have a jet ready. The trip will be made under the utmost secrecy. My secretary will give a cover story to the press. Now, how many of you want to go to Denver?" He looked around.

Almost every hand went up. Vera knew they'd abandoned the hope of finding anything new in San Salino. The mere thought of leaving the scene of horror and doing something that might result in success excited them, even to the point of forgetting that they were accepting the advice of an astrologer whose discipline they despised.

She smiled ruefully to herself as the doctors talked, organizing their efforts and actions. They were acting on her words but ignoring her remonstrance that Denver didn't fulfill the conditions needed for disaster. So she interrupted their preparations. "Gentlemen, I want to remind you that the situation in Denver, astrologically speaking, is not the same as it was in the other towns, just similar."

"Yes, Miss Norman, I understand that," said Micah. "But I think we must go for two reasons. The first is that there are a million, perhaps two million, people involved, and we might be able to save at least some of them if we're ready. I can't risk overlooking their welfare. The second is that if we were on the very spot at the time of an outbreak, we might learn something new about the epidemic."

Goerke asked, "Dr. Maruyama, may I call my wife, tell her I'm coming home?"

"You may call and tell her you're coming home for rest and study. You may not share any of the things we've discussed here with your wife or anyone else. If word of this possibility gets out, it will only panic the nation further."

Jess had been brooding as the others talked. "Mike, instead of going to Denver, I'd like to go to Evanston, to Northwestern. Several years ago they had men researching the effects of celestial bodies on living organisms. As I recall from my student days, a biologist named Brown discovered that clams responded to the motion of the moon even when they were in tanks with no tides. That certainly indicates that the planets do influence living creatures. Brown's work caused quite a furor at the time. I'd like to talk to the men in the department there, O.K.?"

"Good idea, Jess, with the same restrictions."

Vera said, "And may I return to New York? I'd be of no earthly use in Denver and I *don't* believe anything's going to happen there. If I can use my computer, I can make calculations and find out something about this man. We know a good deal astrologically about these events, and perhaps I can parlay our knowledge into some firm information about the killer."

Micah was instantly interested. "What kind of information?"

"Well, I hate to be specific till I've worked on it, but what can be done is often amazing. This man, the killer, must be most remarkable. Such men are born under unusual stellar configurations. Sometimes they can be identified—"

Her voice was drowned by the exclamations and questions of half a dozen men. She held up both hands in protest. "I can't make promises! I don't know what I can do till I've gotten into it! But I may be able to help."

"We'll get you to New York tomorrow morning." Micah looked at his watch. "More precisely, this morning." He walked out. They all knew that while they slept, he would be talking with public health officials, military leaders, probably the president.

One by one the men got up and drifted from the room. Ogden was first to leave, followed by the grim-faced Goerke. Brown and Fornier paused to congratulate Gus on his and Jess's work.

Vera was talking to Petersen, who had discarded his

195

earlier notion that she was in league with the murderer. Jess joined them, towering over the stocky FBI man. He saw Gustofson leave the room, glancing at Vera and giving him a thumb's-up signal as he vanished; Jess chose to ignore the implication.

Adams put his arm around the other agent's shoulders. "Bill, we've had quite a day, but Miss Norman's had a worse one. Let her go to bed." They made her polite little half bows and left. Jess cleared his throat.

"I know you're tired," he said, "but since you'll be going home in a few hours, could you spare me a couple of questions' worth of time?"

She smiled and laid her hand on his arm. "Mr. Barrett, let's have a drink in my room. I'm worn out, but so keyed up I know I won't be able to sleep."

In the elevator he studied her face, feeling rather like a freshman on his first date; it had been a long time since he'd seen such a beautiful woman, even longer since he'd felt an attraction to both a face and a mind. The hell of the past weeks receded as he watched her. She appeared to be memorizing the pattern of the elevator door. Neither spoke.

They walked down the hall to her room. Jess said, "What would you like to drink, Miss Norman?"

"Please call me Vera. Gin and tonic, thanks."

He called for room service. She took off her jacket and shoes; her figure was as flawless as her face. She sank into an enormous chair, sighing with relief. He ordered the drinks.

"I don't want to impose, but I'd like to absorb a little more astrology before I talk to the Northwestern people."

"You're not imposing. I'm glad you came. What can I tell you?"

He began to walk up and down restlessly, thinking it out. "You said that the killer's amplifying emanations. That word gives me my first hint of what he's doing with his electronic devices, whatever they are. But what emanations? Do you imply that Saturn or Uranus is radiating some type of energy to earth?"

"I told you, I don't know the first thing about your field, Dr. Barrett—"

"Jess."

"Jess, of course. I do know that some planets exert an influence on the earth that can cause disasters."

"I'm not doubting you with these questions," he assured her, "but I don't understand. How could energy from one planet be different from, in fact quite opposite to, the energy from another? I think we understand fairly well the various ways of transmitting energy across space and what kind of energy is involved. How can there be *evil* energy from Saturn and *good* from Jupiter?"

Vera watched him as he paced back and forth. She heard him, the technical aspect of her brain took in his query and delighted in formulating an answer, while the Vera Norman who hadn't had a date in so long that she couldn't recollect the last one was asking herself, Is this the man my progressions told me was coming into my life? I thought it might be Micah, but—

Aloud she said, "Sagittarius, I imagine, and probably Jupiter in your first house."

"What?"

She laughed. It was a fine, open, honest, ingenuous face he showed her. "I think in astrological terms, Jess. I make a game of trying to guess what sort of chart a person has—a foolish game, almost impossible to win when you realize that any given trait can come from a number of sources."

"How did you know I'm a Sagittarian?"

"Many reasons. Your athletic interest, your amusement at the mental rigidity of others—common traits with Sagittarians. But you must have Jupiter in the first house to make you so big. And you don't talk nearly as much as most Sagittarians, so Saturn must trine your Jupiter. All that energy means a strong Mars."

Their drinks arrived. As the door closed behind the bellman, she said, "Dr. Mandelbaum, now: I felt he was a Leo at once because he likes to be the boss. But if he is, he must have an afflicted sun."

"He's afflicted with jealousy of Gus, you may have noticed."

"Now, *there's* a fascinating man," said Vera. "I said 'Sagittarius' at first, but now I doubt it. Pisces rising is obvious, but he's wily, and that makes me think he's Scorpio. But what a Mars! It must be beautifully aspected to give him such energy." She was sketching rapidly on her napkin. Then she stopped, and her eyes filmed slightly as she stared past Jess at something only she could see. She turned the napkin over, scribbled, studied what she'd done.

Jess kept silence, letting her think. He knew how maddening it is to get an inspiration and have a companion insist on chattering. At last she smiled apologetically, coming back to him. Her eyes were shining, and the fatigue in her face had given way to excitement.

"Sorry! I started thinking about the killer. Wondering what sort of chart *he* must have. A fascinating astrological puzzle. But I shouldn't let it interrupt my helping you, Jess."

"I imagine that Mike Maruyama is astrologically interesting," he said suddenly.

"Very. A strong Libra placement—or perhaps Libra rising—to have the ability to get all of you working in harmony. And his power! That must come from Mars strength in the chart. I know he's a Scorpio, maybe Libra rising, Mars in Aries."

"You talk in symbols constantly," he said, smiling. "Worse than a scientist!"

"I *am* a scientist, after all. Hey! I'll put a dollar on the line that he has a sun-Pluto conjunction!"

"Who?" said Jess a little bleakly. "Mike?"

"Heavens, no! The killer. That's it for sure: a sun-Pluto conjunction!" She was triumphant, and Jess had not the least idea why.

He said, "How are you going to find out about him? All you know is what he's done."

"But that tells a lot, don't you see? He's invented something that no one else ever thought of, and he's controlling vast forces. He's an incredible genius. And he's using his invention to kill people, which likely means he has an obsession—which is sun-Pluto—about the control of masses of human beings." She reached for a pad on the desk and began to write again, paying no attention to Jess. He watched her with a painful mixture of admiration and exasperation.

At last she said, in a thoughtful mumble, "This man not only does these things; he's clever at covering his tracks. Amazing man. Must have been born under a remarkable configuration of planets. Maybe with a comet conjunct his sun at the moment of birth. Or maybe—"

Jess watched her for a few minutes longer. Then, standing in front of her, he said quietly, "Vera Norman, you are the most beautiful woman I've ever seen, and you could drive me to drink with your Pluto-conjunct-rising-Libras." He took a long swallow of his whiskey.

She looked up at him, and her lips parted in astonishment. She said huskily, "I am?" Then, with a mischievous grin, "I have Libra on the ascendant and Venus in the first house. That does it every time."

He laughed. He had not laughed so easily and happily in many weeks. He pulled her to her feet and held her close and kissed her. Momentarily she was limp with surprise; then she moved against him, kissed him back, tightened her own arms around him. They bent backward slightly, holding hard; stared at each other in startled pleasure. Then she leaned against his great chest.

Someone knocked on the door. Neither of them moved. The knock insisted. Jess swore in a whisper, released her, and went to jerk the door wide.

Micah looked at him blankly. "Jess," he said, for once at a loss. Then, "Jess, you two ought to know that I phoned Denver, the power company there. At seven fifty-eight yesterday, Wednesday morning, the sixteenth of June, they had a power failure. Miss Norman, was that the critical moment? The time when Mars was rising and the moon squared Saturn?"

She nodded, her eyes wide, her voice lost.

Micah turned and left the room.

16

THE SUN FILTERED THROUGH the Venetian blinds and striped the desk with light. The branches of the maple moved in the early morning breeze, and the rustle of its leaves brought Micah to full consciousness. He had fallen asleep at his desk.

He stirred, stood up painfully, stretched, walked stiffly to the window. It faced one of the residence quadrangles. Reflecting that the sirens of arriving ambulances must constantly awaken the people living there, he grimaced at the thought of more sirens. He was in an office of the giant Fitzsimons Army Medical Center in Denver. He looked at his watch: 6:00. Three more hours yet, or less. Jess had established that the three previous epidemics had begun exactly seven days, or seven days plus an hour at most, after the signal had been fired.

Later, children would come to play under the window. Micah had watched them each day since he'd arrived in Denver. They laughed happily, skittered about on the grass, played on the slides and swings, climbed on the Junglegym. They were healthy children, and this morning, as Micah stared down at the empty enclosure, he wondered if he would shortly see them brought into the emergency room pale and in shock or burning with fever.

If it hadn't begun by 9:00, they'd be safe.

He wondered, too, if the doctors, by being on the scene before the epidemic began and knowing what to expect, might be able to save some. He doubted it, though he was impressed with Mandelbaum's preparations. However much he disliked the man, Micah admitted that Mandelbaum knew his job and had worked as hard as anyone could.

Mountains of supplies had been shipped quietly into the huge hospital, where the team was staying. Ambulances from all over the West had entered the base at night so as not to alarm the populace. They were now concealed at Fitzsimons, Lowry Air Force Base, Buckley Field, and Fort Logan Mental Health Center. More were at Fort Carson, their drivers awaiting the summons to duty.

Physicians from the Public Health Service were flown in under strict security and, assigned to different neighborhoods, walked the streets, carrying their instruments and emergency medications in briefcases, toolboxes, and grocery bags. When nurses accompanied the doctors, they posed as couples. Others were stationed in the major hospitals.

Micah had alerted the directors of all hospitals in the Denver area without telling them the whole story. They were informed that a San Salino victim had visited Denver just before his death and that they must take precautions; that the incubation period of the virus believed responsible for the disasters was seven days, and so if there was trouble, it would come on Wednesday, June 23. They had grimly, quietly prepared for a possible emergency.

Not that Micah expected much help from them or any of the doctors and nurses in Denver. If the killer had already administered his lethal blow to the city, they, too, were doomed.

Micah shuddered and turned away from the window. The brilliant sunshine and bright blue sky were too painfully lovely, contrasted with the horror he feared would soon strike.

He glanced at his watch again: 6:30, time to leave. He walked down the hall to Mandelbaum's office. The huge doctor sat behind an equally huge desk giving sharp orders to some Public Health Service physicians.

"Dr. Mandelbaum, I'm going to meet Barrett and Petersen, then go on to the Colorado Medical Center. If anything—Well, I may be back later."

201

From there he went to Gus's room, and despite his gloom he smiled. There were books piled on the desk and papers strewn on the floor. A pair of dusty shoes sat on top of the books, and stockinged feet were propped on the desk. The doctor was sound asleep.

"Gus?"

The old man snorted and jerked, opened his bleary eyes, looked at Micah from under craggy eyebrows. He ran his tongue over cracked lips and growled, "Ummph. Gotta stop smoking."

"Gus, I'm going to the airport now. Want to come along?"

"Rmmphpf." His feet slapped down, and he reached for his shoes. He blew some of the dust off them, slid them on without tying them, and walked out into the sunshine with Micah, wriggling to ease aching joints.

The limousine took them to Stapleton International Airport. Micah asked the driver to wait, and they walked into the terminal, down the concourse. Even this early it was bustling. Neither spoke, but each had the same thought: How many of these people would within a few hours turn feverish, vomit, collapse?

Micah almost bumped into a young mother and daughter hurrying to a plane. He looked at the child and blinked. She was so much like the little girl who had stared at him in death at the Bridgeton warehouse. That must have been years ago.

The big jet came over the city, swung toward the mountains, then into the landing approach. Jess looked down at Denver. The sun was still low in the east, and the sky had not yet filled with the day's smog, so he could see the city clearly. He had always liked Denver. It was small compared with Chicago, Los Angeles, and New York, but it had some of the advantages of a larger city. It was the center for the entire Rocky Mountain area and therefore had a disproportionate number of cultural opportunities. The medical facilities were among the finest in the world.

It had problems: some poverty and some prejudice, some slums and some rising traffic congestion.

But it had none of the air of desperation that older cities so often wore. It was a lovely place, and this was a magnificent June day. And if their fears came true, it was also the day the city would die.

Jess thought of the day when his own little town had died, of trying to find the cardiac kit for Bob, of working vainly to save lives, of Ginny dying in his arms. He remembered the stench of the three towns he had seen prostrate. What would it be like for a city this size? He glanced at his watch: 7:30. One hundred minutes before Denver became hell?

Gus was surprised to find how glad he was to see the big athlete. He frowned fiercely, shook hands, and said, "Ain't you picking up a little weight, Jock? I never noticed you had a spare tire before."

Jess grinned. "Any news yet?"

"Thank God, no. Not a sign of anything unusual. Of course, it's early yet—" Micah let his sentence hang.

Gus asked, "Jess, did you find anything at Northwestern? Any ideas?"

"A few."

Micah said, "We've got to get over to Gate 16; Bill Petersen's coming in on a government jet. He was in Washington coordinating the university search for Vera's maniac-genius. Let's hope he has something. Brad phoned last night; the first reports from other countries are utterly without a lead."

The moment Petersen walked through the gate, they knew the answer. There was no good news in that sagging frame.

Outside, Petersen took a cab to Fitzsimons. The others got into the limousine, and Micah told the driver to go to the Colorado Medical Center.

"I promised Dr. DuBay I'd join him in the emergency room," he said. "He's been a prince, cooperating in every way. He and Goerke have been friends for years."

The driver turned onto Colorado Boulevard, one of the busiest of the city's arteries, thick with traffic.

"It's rush hour, I guess. What do you figure's the

203

danger hour, Mike?" Gustofson was staring moodily out at the heartbreakingly normal panorama of life.

"Nine, Gus; I've told you that twice. Get past nine and we're home free. Driver, turn down Seventeenth. I want to go past the midtown hospitals, then to the medical center."

At Mercy Hospital, only a few cars were parked near the emergency entrance, and two nuns were just disappearing into the building. Everything was normal.

"Now check Presbyterian Medical Center."

Again they found a quiet, peaceful area outside the emergency room.

"Saint Joseph."

From the street next to the hospital, they could see the entrance to the emergency room: no activity.

"Children's Hospital, then Saint Luke's."

Normal activity everywhere. Micah said, "O.K., driver, now the medical center."

When they arrived, Micah got out. "I'll be here till ten at least. What will you two do?"

"Well, I'd just like to drive around a bit and see what—"

Jess's words were cut short by the scream of an ambulance as it came around the corner and pulled up in front of them.

Micah snapped, "Wait a minute; I'll see what this is." He raced into the room where attendants had wheeled a stretcher.

Jess and Gus waited in silence. The driver kept the motor running, and the *thum, thum, thum* of the engine sounded like the roll of funeral drums. Jess was too apprehensive to speak, and Gus leaned forward, watching for Micah. Within a few minutes he returned, walking at his normal pace.

"Automobile accident. It's eight fifteen. Will you pick me up back here at ten if—?" They nodded.

Jess asked the driver to go downtown.

Life in Denver was in full swing. The hot sun had already raised the temperature into the eighties, and lawn sprinklers were on everywhere. They drove down Eighth Avenue, past the governor's mansion, across

Broadway, past Denver General Hospital, then left and left again onto Sixth, past the hospital again. 8:25.

On Lincoln the baffled driver turned downtown. The fatal time was near, and neither Gus nor Jess spoke. They searched the faces moving past them, looking for some sign of sickness. The enormous potential of death hypnotized Jess, and he stared at people in horrified fascination.

The driver turned down Sixteenth, into the downtown section. Ahead they could see the mountains, looking deceptively close under a sapphire sky.

The river of faces rolled past them, occasionally casting up a familiar one, one that might have come from Bensonville. It would bob into view, be swept along for a moment, then disappear into the crowd, the face of a stranger after all. Jess gritted his teeth, trying to shake off memories, to stay alert. Mothers with small children smiling in the warm sunshine, young girls hurrying to work, old men watching the crowd, all streamed by them.

Gus nudged him, said in a whisper, "Look, Jess."

A crowd had gathered at the intersection ahead, craning their necks. Someone was lying on the street.

Jess reached for the door handle as they came to a stop. But the crowd parted, dispersed. A black boy was dusting himself off with one hand and holding onto a bicycle with the other.

The driver of a car stopped in the middle of the intersection was saying, "You gotta obey the laws, too, kid. You come across an intersection through a red light like that and whatta you expect?"

The boy glared, mounted his bike, said, "Shove it, man," and was gone. Jess breathed again. The incident had relieved some tension, shaken him out of his memories.

The driver circled again through the area, then headed south.

Micah stared at the emergency room clock, watching the second hand sweep in circle after circle. He was unable to look away. Dr. DuBay sat beside him and watched it with the same fascination.

A faint sound disturbed the silence. At the desk a nurse was nervously tapping a pencil. When she saw them looking at her, she smiled shakily, and the noise stopped. The clock's hands continued their silent movement.

The telephone rang at 8:50.

"Yes?" The nurse listened. "Bring her in right away. Do you want an ambulance? . . . All right, I'll get one there." She hung up the phone. Both men stared at her, waiting.

"A woman, very sick. Husband says she woke up sweating, skin clammy, very weak. It sounds like—"

"Like a serious bacteremia," said Dr. DuBay. His own face was damp with perspiration.

Gus looked at his watch. It was 8:58. "Well, Jess, I think we're going to make it. It was a false alarm. And I haven't had my coffee! Driver, pull into that shopping center. I want to get some good strong—Jess, look!"

The driver had pulled into the parking lot as a middle-aged, heavyset woman came out of a market carrying a bag of groceries. She seemed to hesitate for a second, took another step, and collapsed, groceries spilling out of the torn bag. Jess ran toward her, Gus stumbling behind.

When the ambulance backed up to the door, Micah and DuBay were waiting outside. On the stretcher lay a young woman, her eyes closed. Dr. DuBay stopped the young resident who got out of the ambulance. "Doctor, what's wrong with her?" His voice was so urgent that the resident looked at him with surprise.

"Ruptured appendix," he said, and shrugged and walked past them into the hospital.

The emergency room clock said 9:02. Micah smiled. "Doctor, let's have that coffee you offered me earlier."

The woman sat up shakily, looked at her groceries,

then at Gustofson and Jess. She pressed her lips together in anger. "Darn it! I broke the heel off my shoe. Will you help me up, or are you just going to stand there?"

Gustofson found his voice first. "Yes, ma'am, we'll be glad to help you."

The two men picked her up, gathered her groceries, and supported her to her car. They looked at their watches simultaneously. It was 9:06.

Jess swallowed. "Driver, I think we'll get that cup of coffee at the medical center."

As they walked into the coffee shop, Jess saw DuBay and Maruyama at a table in the far corner. Beside them sat Jack Goerke, laughing too loudly. Gustofson raised his eyebrows questioningly to Micah as they entered, and the little man smiled and made a circle with his thumb and forefinger. "All serene," he said, "here and at Fitzsimons. And it's nine thirty. What about you?"

"Not a whiff of trouble."

"What I want to know is what you're doin' here, Goerke," said Gustofson. "You should be home with your family."

Micah smiled. "He was here at six. The old warhorse couldn't stay away."

Goerke was so incredibly relieved that he laughed again. "Well, I got to thinking that the Bensonville doctors didn't leave their posts to find their families, and I—well, I *am* a doctor."

They drank their coffee in silence for a few minutes, ate Danish pastries, and watched people come and go through the lobby. Never, Jess thought, had human beings looked so beautiful. He asked, "Mike, have you checked to see if any city's been hit today?"

"Yes, I called the president's office at nine fifteen. He's set up a special group to monitor all cities. There's no report of any outbreak."

"Then you told the president the whole story? About Vera and her prediction?"

Micah nodded. "I never withhold anything from the president."

"What did he think about his assistant packing up the team and coming to Denver on the advice of an astrologer?" Jess realized how hard that decision must have been for Micah, how it could affect his career.

"Well, he didn't say much."

"Are you in trouble, Mike?"

Micah said carefully, "It's important that I get some results soon. Whether I do it with astrology or witch doctors or orthodox methods doesn't matter to the president. He'll be pleased, of course, that there was no outbreak here. It's the first Wednesday morning in four weeks that hasn't brought a calamity."

Gus patted his shoulder paternally. "Mike, you did the right thing to bring us all here. I know that, even if the president doesn't."

"I'm glad to hear you say that. Right now, I'm feeling ridiculous. Here we are, hundreds of doctors walking the city streets in civilian clothes, hundreds of ambulances lined up waiting for hell to erupt, all on the word of an astrologer."

"Who predicted the last outbreak! And then you call here and find there was a power failure at the critical moment."

"That blasted power failure!" Mike exclaimed. "Do you suppose this murdering genius tried to use his machine and failed, Jess? Shorted out, bit off too big a territory to chew? There's hope there if that's what happened."

"I don't know. But the coincidence is too much— the same moment that the lethal blow had to be dealt."

Micah whispered, "I keep thinking about Vera. She predicted the last disaster, but she missed on this one. Why? If her astrology works, why didn't it work this time?"

Gustofson had tamped his pipe full. He lit it, talking as he did. "Well, Mike, you keep ignoring something. She insisted that conditions weren't quite right at this time. She said something about the eighth house and the twelfth. *We* wanted to come to Denver. *She* objected."

"You're right, Gus."

"Now, I admit that the power failure shook her pretty badly, too, and she finally stopped objecting. But she never did predict a disaster here. She only said that Denver was the only city approximating the conditions on this longitude." Gustofson pointed to the clock. "It's almost ten. What do you say we try to get a newscast?"

"We can go to my office," offered DuBay.

He led them upstairs, and soon the voice of a local announcer was booming at them as DuBay motioned them to chairs.

"In announcing the results of the special election yesterday, the mayor reminded citizens of Denver that the decision of the voters to go ahead with the purchase of the utilities company carries with it the provision for increased taxes. He congratulated voters on their action and promised that the city will immediately replace the outmoded, overloaded machinery at the main plant—to which, the mayor reported, last week's power outage had definitely been traced."

"Damnation!" Micah exploded. "They were to notify me the second they found the cause of that outage." He clicked off the radio.

"She did it again!" Jess chuckled. "Do you remember, Vera said it was Denver's eighth house that had dangerous aspects? Well, the eighth house in astrology rules not only death but also *taxes!* That tax increase satisfies her prediction."

"How can the same house have to do with death and taxes?"

"Well," Gustofson offered wryly, "people always have associated those two."

"How could she predict a raise in taxes by looking at the stars! Will you explain *that* to me, Jess?" Micah was exasperated.

"Don't ask me, Mike. I'm having enough trouble rearranging my own ideas about the universe. I heard and read things in Evanston these past few days that I'd never have believed without the proof."

"Tell us about them." There was a tinge of eagerness in Micah's cool voice.

"I did research for NASA a few years ago. We were surprised at some of the effects different areas in space could have on our instruments. In one place the most sensitive interplanetary probe often gave very different results from those of its duplicate in another place. We found a way to make allowance for the difference, so NASA ended the project. I wonder, if we'd stayed with it, if we might not have traced some of those disturbances to the planets.

"When I went to Evanston, I wanted to see what I could find about the influences of any celestial or cosmic events on earthly organisms. By a lucky coincidence my alma mater, Northwestern, has been the site of some of the most interesting work done in the field. Dr. Brown, of the biology department, has done work of great significance. Unfortunately, he's out of the country right now, and considering the state of things, it may be some time before he gets back. But I did talk to some of his assistants, and they gave me a great deal of information.

"Dr. Brown pioneered research into the influence of the planets on living things. He found that potatoes, algae, carrots, earthworms, and salamanders kept in sealed rooms carried on activity which showed they were responding to the position of the moon and sun. You see, somehow, they *knew* when the moon rose and when it set."

"Fantastic," Micah breathed. "Go on!"

"Some of the men working with Brown discovered that chick embryos appeared to be aware of the rising and setting of the sun, although they were in a controlled environment with uniform lighting and temperature.

"But the most interesting of Brown's experiments was one in which he had oysters brought to Evanston from Long Island Sound in sealed containers. He observed them in his laboratory a thousand miles from the ocean. At first those damned oysters continued to open and close to the rhythm of the tides washing Long Island. Then, slowly, their rhythm changed, became tuned to the tide which would wash Evanston if it were on the ocean. In other words, those oysters were opening when the moon passed over the local meridian. But how did they know when that was?

"Brown studied rats and found them to be more active when the moon was above the horizon. But how did they know? They were in sealed cages."

Dr. Goerke leaned forward. "Do you mean those rats and oysters were sensitive to the gravitational pull of the moon, as the tides are?"

"Well, it's more likely that they reacted to changes in the geomagnetic field caused by the movement of the sun and the moon."

"But how can the moon affect the magnetic field of the earth? It has almost no field of its own."

"I don't know. But there's evidence that it does. Satellites have proved that the solar wind is stopped and deflected when the moon is in a certain position with respect to the sun. The charged particles from the sun hit the earth at a different angle from what we'd always thought. And there's little doubt now that lunar phases partially regulate the amount of meteoric dust that falls continuously into our atmosphere."

Dr. DuBay said, "Jess, if what you learned about those animals is true, that they're reacting to the movement of the moon that affects the geomagnetic field, then animals must be extremely sensitive living magnetometers."

"Right. Homing pigeons probably guide themselves by being sensitive to the magnetic field. Someday that may explain migrations of birds and fish.

"But it isn't only the moon that affects the magnetic field. Biggs suggested that Venus and Mercury have an effect on the magnetic storms blowing on the earth. Atkinson believed that Mars does, too."

"Well," said Goerke thoughtfully, "I remember reading that an RCA scientist insisted that the positions of the planets make a difference in the static we get over the radio."

"Yes," chimed in DuBay, "but didn't he think they disturbed the atmosphere of the sun itself, causing sunspots and that sort of thing?"

"That was John Nelson," said Jess. "He thought at first that sunspot activity could explain it all, but later he came to believe that the position of the planets themselves in relation to the sun caused certain types of radio interference. He thought that when planets were in conjunction, at right angles with each other, or in opposition to each other, the interference was greater."

"But none of this proves anything about astrology, Jess. It's a long way from radio interference to predicting an increase in taxes," said Micah.

"Right. But all this does prove the one thing we refused to believe at all until recently: that the planets exert an influence on the earth. We know that in some ways they do, and we know that animals can sense it."

"Well, I can believe that," said Micah. "But to have half the effect on humans that astrologers claim, the energy from the planets would have to be enormous."

"I don't think so, Mike. Have you ever heard of the alpha waves in the brain that are measured by electroencephalograms?"

"Of course."

"We know now that the atmosphere contains waves of very low frequency but great length. It's thought they affect the sprouting of wheat, bacteria growth, and the activity of certain insects. Those waves are of very low energy. Oddly, they're almost indistinguishable from the electroencephalogram wave patterns of the human brain."

"That could just be one of the coincidences in nature," said Goerke.

"Sure, but the human organism is very sensitive to waves of extremely low frequency. There's a scientist at Yale who maintains that the human brain and the central nervous system are the most elaborate stations for the reception of electromagnetic waves known to exist.

"Almost certainly, we're influenced by the magnetic field around us, and *that* is influenced by the planets."

"Jess, I can conceive how we might pick up some psychic impressions through those waves or others," said Micah, "but I don't see how they could be so low in energy and still harm us."

Gustofson interrupted before Jess could answer. He waved his pipe. "I've been doin' a little reading myself this past week. What I learned—how do they say it?—blew my mind. Couple of French doctors wondered if solar storms could affect their patients; they checked and discovered that twenty-five transitions of sunspots were followed twenty-one times by an increase in sickness and death. Since then, others found the same kind of thing. Professor Tchijewsky of Moscow claimed that wars and revolutions coincide with solar eruptions more times than not. He also claimed—and this is fascinating in the light of our own case—that the great plagues, the fatal diphtheria and cholera epidemics of Europe, and the smallpox outbreaks in Chicago all seemed to follow the sun's eleven-year periodicity."

"Eleven-year what?" asked Micah.

"Gus is referring to the fact that the sun's activity, its spots or eruptions, appears to follow an eleven-year cycle. This has interested scientists for a long time."

"If Professor Tchijewsky's right," Gus said, "great epidemics occur during years of maximum activity on the sun.

"Solar eruptions seem to result in an increase in cardiovascular patients; in fact, Soviet scientists claim a *threefold* increase! Deaths from tuberculosis are much higher on days of solar eruptions; same's true for eclampsia and mining and traffic accidents. And we know for sure that admissions to psychiatric hospitals increase during those magnetic disturbances."

"Gus, in your research this week, did you run across the work of Dr. Takata?" asked Jess.

"Sure did."

"What did he do?" asked Micah.

"He was a Japanese scientist who noticed that the flocculation index, which has to do with a property of blood serum, changed on days of solar activity. He took people up in airplanes and down into mines to study the effect. He found that solar activity strongly affected the index except when there was an eclipse; then, somehow, the moon shielded people from the radiation causing the effect in the blood. So, indirectly, the moon affects our blood."

DuBay said, "That's interesting because just the other day I was talking to a dentist who swears, after a lot of research, that hemorrhages are much more frequent near the time of the full moon and rather rare at the time of the new moon. I don't see how the devil that could be, but—" DuBay shook his head.

"And there's a Russian doctor who claims that lymphocytic counts drop with sunspot activity. That's critically important because lymphocytes are prominent in immunological activity."

"Right. But, Gus, are you and Jess agreeing with Vera—without reservation—that planets have a direct effect on us?"

Gus waggled his head. "I'm only saying that evidence is piling up damn impressively that the planets *do* influence our health."

"I can understand solar radiation affecting us," said Goerke. "But the moon? The planets? The moon has almost no magnetic field, so far as I know."

Jess said, "Well, Jack, remember, we already said the moon *does* affect the geomagnetic field, so it could be affecting us that way. But it may be by gravity alone. After all, we are mainly water, in one form or another. And water's far less stable than we'd thought. We know it'll change in its conductivity when exposed to a small magnet. The body, made up of so much water, must be sensitive to waves, particles, and magnetic changes.

"But I also think there's a chance our bodies respond in some way to the gravity of the moon. If the moon can affect the tides and the atmosphere, isn't it also affecting us—perhaps through the water molecules in our bodies?"

Goerke smiled. "Oh, now, I find that rather far-fetched."

"I admit I'm guessing. But a biologist in Zurich had a hunch that animals might be reacting to the gravity of the moon. So he put a lot of beetles into a container with opaque sides. Then he brought an eighty-pound hunk of lead near the container, and the insects clearly responded to the advance of the lead. Now, since the moon and sun exert far more gravitational pull on earthly creatures than a hunk of lead did on the beetles, it's certainly logical to assume that we're influenced by gravity alone."

Micah said, "Jess, I *can* imagine that sort of influence. But all the things astrologers believe—about personalities being determined by the nature of planets and their position in the sky?"

"That, too, has been scientifically studied, in part at least." Jess suddenly grinned. "I've been reading about astrology ever since we listened to Vera Norman the other night," he admitted. "A French statistician named Michel Gauquelin and his wife did a study of famous people and found, surprisingly, that some of the old assertions of astrologers were correct. For example, they found that surgeons, military leaders, and athletes had a tendency to be born when Mars was rising or in the midheaven. They found that writers tended to be born when the moon was in a comparable position, actors and politicians when Jupiter was rising or at the meridian, and scientists under similar influences of Saturn. The Gauquelins had no satisfactory explanation why that should be so, but their results have been confirmed by others."

"That's still hard to believe! How could a planet millions of miles out in space cause a person to become a politician or writer?"

"Damned if I know, Mike. But the Gauquelins even found a significant correlation between the planets prominent in the sky when a person was born and his personality. For example, if Mars was rising, he was likely to have a bad temper, be energetic, bold, and daring. But if Jupiter was rising, he was likely to be egotistical, good-humored, and power-loving—in other words, to have exactly the personality traits astrologers have associated with those planets for centuries."

"It seems so preposterous," said Micah, frowning. "Death and taxes and personality—"

"It does. The only thing I can figure out is that we're all sensitive to the magnetic fields in which we live and that those fields are influenced by the planets. Our bodies could have been set to certain frequencies, rhythms that determine our dispositions, our mental qualities."

Micah glanced at his watch. It was 11:00. "I've got to talk to Mandelbaum, and then we'd better get back to Fitzsimons."

He called Mandelbaum, scheduled a meeting for 7:30 that evening, listened a moment, and hung up.

"Vera just phoned. Wants me to get in touch with her immediately." He dialed New York, got her at once, and listened for a long time, his face registering first anxiety and then hope. "All right, we'll see you tonight. . . . Flight 562. Good." He hung up. "She says she has some distressing astrological news, but also that she may be able to help us."

"Did she say what the distressing news is?"

"She wouldn't tell me over the phone. But remember, she wanted to go home to use her computer and find the city likely to be the next target of this madman."

Gustofson sighed. "Mike, I didn't get any sleep last night, and if I'm going to be fresh for your meeting, I've got to sack out for a while. But one piece of advice: Don't ignore that young woman. She's smarter'n hell."

"I can assure you, Gus," said Micah, "that I'm taking her as seriously as I ever took anyone in my life."

When the team members began to file into the

conference room, Micah consulted his watch. Vera was late. He wondered if she'd been delayed, missed the plane. With everyone else assembled, he opened the meeting.

"Gentlemen, I've just finished talking with the president. There was no outbreak anywhere in the nation today. Brad and Bill haven't found a trace of anyone who's a genius in astrology, electronics, and medicine. Therefore, as of right now, we have nothing at all to go on—unless you've found something in the San Salino data."

No one spoke.

Micah turned to Jess. "Will you give us a report?"

Jess was summarizing what he had learned at Northwestern when Vera walked in, stunning in a trimly tailored blue suit. Her face was tense, and she looked tired.

Micah greeted her warmly. "What do you have, Vera?"

She glanced nervously around, took the seat he pulled out for her, leaned forward, and spoke, her voice tight. "I have another prediction to make that is frightening—no, it's too terrible for such a weak word. It's truly *beyond* words. I searched my files for cities coming under the same dangerous aspects as Bensonville, Bridgeton, and San Salino. I found no city susceptible this coming week; but two weeks from today, July seventh, at seven thirty—well, first let me tell you the problem I ran into.

"I told you the nation had difficult aspects in its progressed chart. That made me aware that there'd be a serious loss of life in our country this year. That aspect becomes exact in two weeks. When I looked through my records to find the city most likely to fall under the fatal influence in two weeks, I had trouble. Many of the cities in the critical area are so old it's impossible to determine the exact date of their incorporation.

"Then I heard Dr. Barrett's theory about the power system being used as the weapon. With that system, all those cities are tied together on a grid, and their

217

fates are tied together, too. I decided to consider entire states. But *that* was difficult because I had to ask myself if their original charters were valid, or if—You see, the problem is that the states in question are the original thirteen colonies. Under the circumstances, the only valid date to use for their incorporation is the same as that of the nation, since the Declaration of Independence in a sense gave birth to new states."

Vera drew a long breath. "My calculations indicate that the entire East Coast will fall under the fatal aspect in two weeks. Therefore, I predict that the killer is preparing for the big moment of his life. I think he is going to plug his machine into the power grid that now reaches from Montreal to Georgia and try to wipe out about eighty million people."

17

SHE SAT DOWN as they reacted to the horrifying impact of her words.

Micah turned to Jess. "Can he do it? Is his machine capable of upsetting a whole grid, covering hundreds of miles?"

"Mike, I think he can. He's learned how to use the power system. There's no reason why he can't go all the way."

Micah shook his head in disbelief. "Eighty million people. My God, *why* would he? Because he's insane, of course, but—" He shook his head again.

Brown said helplessly, "What are we going to do? We've got to stop him, and we don't have a single clue."

Mayor McDonald stood up. He had stopped drinking in San Salino, but tonight he was intoxicated again. "I'll tell you what we're gonna do. We'll catch the son of a bitch, and then—"

"You're going to kill him. Yes, we know, Mayor McDonald. But first we have to catch him."

The mayor stood unsteadily. "Well, if you'd get off your tails and go after him instead of sitting in these damn fool meetings, you might just do that!" He stumbled to the door and left.

Jess sighed.

The silence grew. Even Mandelbaum was quiet. The more they thought, the more hopeless it looked.

"Maybe we can get the president to turn off the power grid during the critical period," Jess offered. Micah sadly warned them that the president would not do it. What evidence did they have? Two, but not three, odd-looking antennae; two, but not three, ovals of death; the advice of an astrologer. "The president is a rational man, and he will adopt any reasonable line of action. But"—he gestured hopelessly—"when I suggested just such an action to him, in case this possibility did come up, he gave me a flat *no*."

Again the silence descended like a black curtain.

When Vera spoke, her voice was soft, but everyone heard her, and everyone listened.

"Perhaps I can help."

She had waited till exactly the right moment. They had looked into the pit of hell and recoiled. The eyes that turned to her were filled, not with contempt, but with hope.

"You remember I said that if I could get back to my computer, I thought I could help to find out something about this man? Well, I did a study on him using what we know already.

"You see, in astrology there are rigid laws, just as there are in other sciences." She looked defiantly around the room. "When a remarkable man like this killer appears, he has to have been born under an equally remarkable configuration in the skies. He's a genius. He has incredible hatred, and he's mentally unstable. He's brilliant in astrology, electronics, and medicine. That tells us a lot about him.

"I decided to see if I could reconstruct his natal chart to find out when he was born. There are, after all, a finite number of possibilities. In addition, his fantastic genius must result from more than aspects alone. His chart must get its power from some other source. The possibilities of that are even fewer.

"I decided to check comets first. Visible comets appear every few years. I checked over what I believed to be a reasonable period but became convinced that it couldn't have been a comet that gave the power to his chart.

"Then I tried multiple conjunctions. The greatest one in many years occurred in 1962. But that was too recent.

"Using my computer, I went back for seventy years,

220

seeking another multiple conjunction or a great stellium—that is, planets close together in a bunch—but found nothing that would quite fit the case.

"Then I turned to eclipses. No lunar eclipse could give that kind of power unless combined with a really remarkable stellium, but I decided to check them out, as well as solar eclipses, to be sure. Since there can be as many as seven eclipses a year, at least two and as many as five of them solar, I had my work cut out for me.

"Because it seemed to me it would have to be a total eclipse, I concentrated on those. I ran hundreds through my computer, checking to see what other aspects existed at the time. That was difficult, for there are many possibilities to explain a given trait.

"But I had some ideas of what aspects to look for. I expected to find a negative aspect between Mars and the sun at the exact moment of the eclipse. This would give him his violent nature, also eccentricity and deep emotions. I searched for a strong Uranian influence because it would make him a genius in electronics. Aspects with Neptune under certain conditions can cause insanity, and a strong relationship between the sun and Pluto gives obsessional traits and the ability to manipulate large numbers of people.

"In addition, I knew I would find large numbers of squares, oppositions, and conjunctions with malefics, which would give him power and also make his life difficult. I suspected I would find a grand square, a rather unusual formation of the planets, when four or more are in opposition and at right angles to each other, forming the corners of a square.

"Finally I found a solar eclipse that occurred at the same time there was a formation of planets capable of producing the man I was seeking."

She paused and picked up the water glass before her, took a drink, then another. Nobody spoke.

"The eclipse was total for exactly seven minutes. The man had to have been born during those seven minutes. But that wasn't accurate enough. I needed to know the exact time.

"We astrologers frequently have a client who doesn't know and can't find out the exact moment of his birth. When this happens we can pursue a course called 'rectification,' in which we try astrologically to recover the exact moment of birth.

"In that process, from the major known events in his life, such as the death of a parent, we can tell exactly when he was born. For when great events happen, the planets must have progressed into sensitive aspects with each other and with the cusps of the houses.

"Now, we know only three events in the life of this man: the murders of three cities. However, by using rectification, I was able to determine that he was, indeed, born during the solar eclipse, and also the precise time of birth: seven thirty-two A.M. When I had the exact minute of birth, it was a relatively simple matter to cast a chart, interpret it, and do progressions for each year." She picked up one of the sheaves of paper from the table. "Here's the interpretation of his chart. The sun gives a person his basic personality center or structure. This man is a Leo."

Vera suppressed a smile as she saw Mandelbaum stiffen at the mention of Leo. So he does know his Sun sign, she thought.

"This position of the sun indicates tremendous pride. In this case the effect of the sun's position is doubled because of the eclipse with the moon, and two other planets, Venus and Pluto, are also conjuncted with the luminaries. This gives him tremendous power as well.

"Now, in this man's chart, all these planets fall into the twelfth house, which is like locking up these characteristics. He will be introverted and frustrated all his life, and his tremendous power can only work its way out as hatred.

"Now, that's not usually true of Leos. Leos are not evil, only occasionally pompous.

"The fact that Pluto conjuncts the eclipsed sun indicates a paranoid personality and a great desire for power, a desire which will be frustrated and make him mad for recognition, since both planets are in the twelfth house."

Vera went to the chalkboard and began to draw the chart, marking planets and cusps of houses.

"You'll be better able to understand what I'm saying if I show you as I go along.

"Pluto indicates the man's connection with large masses of people and with mass destruction. His Mars falls in his fourth house, squaring all the planets in Leo, and forms a grand square by squaring Jupiter in his sixth house and opposing the Saturn-Uranus conjunction in his tenth house.

"The square, or ninety-degree aspect, is the most stressful in astrology. This grand square makes violence a fundamental part of his personality. But since the square, except for Mars, falls in what we call 'cadent houses,' the violence would not be immediately noticeable.

"Mars is in Scorpio, the most emotional of the signs, which gives great depth and strength to his hatred. He has outbursts of violence, but in general, his nature is internally expressed. All his life, he's been like a time bomb waiting to go off.

"Jupiter squares his ninth-house planets. That means he also goes to extremes in the area of his life ruled by that house, which are his religious beliefs.

"This man wants reform, but he goes to extremes to get it. He is willing, even eager—because of his poorly suppressed hatred—to use force. Erratic and eccentric elements are strong in his chart. The Saturn-Uranus conjunction which squares the eclipse intensifies his erratic nature into something close to insanity.

"But our man has some good aspects, too, aspects which grant talent and opportunity. He has trines and sextiles which are considered fortunate. His trines give him a tremendous mind." She pointed to the board. "Look. Mercury trines Saturn here, as you can see, giving him discipline and the ability to work hard. The sextile with Mars gives mental energy and the ability to go right to the heart of the matter.

"But Mercury also conjuncts Neptune, giving him an underhanded, scheming, plotting side.

"But note that the planets signifying the most important influence in his life are in Leo, the proudest of the signs, demanding recognition. Yet, they all fall in the twelfth house, which denies recognition and pride.

"There are even more frustrations for this man. The ascendant, which is the cusp of the first house, rules, among other things, appearance. In this case, the ascendant falls in Virgo, and the planets in that sign are Mercury and Neptune conjuncted. This makes him a meticulous person anxious to be neat. He's the kind of man who carefully buttons his jacket and has creased trousers, but it does no good. He is nondescript and wishy-washy in appearance.

"He has an elusive nature. People don't remember him because he fades from their memory even as they turn away from him. His brilliance and frightening strength are not seen on the surface.

"You've heard of people described as charismatic, full of personality, and dynamic in appearance. This man is the opposite. He sees himself as a great man, the greatest in all human history, and others don't even notice him.

"He's so restless that I doubt he ever stays long in one place or remains in a job for any time at all.

"Not surprisingly, he's never had a real friend. He's so cold and aloof that few are attracted to him in the first place. Anyone who befriends him is soon driven away by the man's sick ego and his violent outbursts.

"There's a worse factor. The moon and sun are in conjunction, perfectly so, since there's an eclipse. That means that the men and women in his life, which those planets represent, are caught in the twelfth house and in the grand square. They also represent his parents, and that conjunction squares Mars, which means violence. Further, the eclipse is in Leo, and Mars is in Scorpio, the two signs most associated with sex, a rape.

"Not only that, but Saturn crossed the midheaven of his chart a few weeks after his birth, indicating the disappearance of his father from his life. In this way, his father was very important to him, not by his presence, but by his absence.

"Now, when we have the natal chart, we can progress it or move it forward a day for a year, as I explained to you last week. This tells us the kind of events that happen to the person as he moves through life.

"I haven't had time to do an exhaustive study of his life, to ascertain the events exactly. But some things are obvious to any astrologer. I'll tell you about them shortly. It's vital that you know this: In a few days he's coming to the great moment in his life. His progressed moon is returning to its original position on the chart. Already it has activated that conjunction, since it has passed over one of the planets involved. He began his murders when that happened.

"Astronomically, the return of the progressed moon is not even an event. But astrologically, the moon makes a cycle every thirty years or so. In this case, because of the eclipse with the sun and the conjunction with the other planets, it's the supreme event of this man's life. He must be stopped now, or he'll succeed in that mad plan of his."

"Can you predict if he will succeed?" Micah whispered.

"No. I can only tell you that it's the climax of his life. Whether that means success or death, I cannot tell."

Vera went back to her seat and took another drink of water. They were listening, really listening. Still, as she thought of her next statement, she dreaded the reaction she knew would follow. She decided to prepare them for it.

"I've told you how I discovered the day and time when he was born. Of much greater help to you is the fact that I know the *place* where he was born. That might sound difficult. Oddly enough, it wasn't as hard as finding the date. It turns out that the eclipse under which he was born was a very famous one.

"You know that eclipses can be seen at many points over the earth. People both north and south of the path it takes can see it, but not fully. Also, as the moon overtakes the sun in their seeming rotation around the earth, it will begin to cover the sun and then continue for a long time. That means that it can be seen rather well for many, many miles, even thousands of miles along the east-west path. The path itself is never more than one hundred and sixty miles wide.

"But despite all that, an eclipse is precise, exact, over only a much smaller spot, and that spot can be pinpointed easily by astronomers.

"Because this eclipse blotted out not only the sun but also the other planets in conjunction at the time, and because of the spot where it was exact, it received a great deal of interest. Some of the Eastern astrologers declared that it meant the end of the world or at least great wars. Others predicted equally direful things.

"Frankly, I'd forgotten all about it, since I was a small child when it occurred and knew of it only through literature. Also, when nothing of great significance happened during the days succeeding the eclipse, people lost interest in it.

"Now, though, we know the true significance of that astrological event.

"For you see, this man, the killer, was born on August eighteenth, at seven thirty-two in the morning, thirty years ago, during the solar eclipse—in Bethlehem of Palestine."

There was a crash as Dr. Ogden brought his fist down furiously on the table. "What kind of nonsense is this? This is nothing but goddamn superstition, and we're sitting here listening to it!"

"Dr. Maruyama, I have tried to be patient, but—" Mandelbaum was winding up for an oration.

"Are you trying to tell us that this man is the Christ, that he represents the Second Coming?" Fornier was jolted out of his gloom.

Vera glanced around, noticing that even Jess looked skeptical—no, more like a man betrayed.

Adams smiled and said sarcastically, "Apparently, Dr. Fornier, it's not Christ, but Antichrist."

When they had quieted under Micah's level gaze, she went on. "Due to the unusual conditions surrounding his birth, and because of its location, this man has delusions of grandeur. He thinks he is the new Messiah. He is, of course, completely human.

"Also, because of the circumstances of his birth, astrologers in the area must have made some unusual predictions about him. The child grew up knowing those predictions, and he undoubtedly thinks, in his madness, that he is the new Christ."

Micah frowned slightly, raised a hand to speak. But Vera didn't want to be interrupted to defend her method until she'd finished what she had to say. She continued in a rush.

"I told you this man was the product of a rape, and his father disappeared from his life immediately. He was reared in deprivation, often going hungry. More important, he was emotionally deprived. His mother was important in his life, but because of the rape, she hated him. Only the predictions of the astrologers kept her from abandoning him in an orphanage. Then when he was eight, she died, and he was brought up by others.

"He was brilliant from the start but received almost no formal education. That's why your intelligence agencies found no trace of him in the universities.

"He was brought to this country when he was fourteen, probably by the people who'd been taking care of him since his mother's death. He was used and exploited by them. They were almost certainly Americans who'd been living in Bethlehem.

"Because of their exploitation and his emotional deprivation, he grew up consumed with hatred. He particularly hates the United States and wants to destroy it.

"My guess is that his madness led him to believe he is the new Adam, the third Adam, who is to destroy the human race and begin another. He sees himself as the progenitor of a race of supermen.

"He probably plans to keep a few individuals to serve him but to destroy everyone else.

227

"So here you have a man who sees himself as the new Christ, king of the human race, while everyone overlooks him or treats him with contempt. That feeds his natural tendency to violence. When he turns to violence, he escapes because he's clever but also because he has a face no one can remember.

"He is unusually strong for his size, even though during his childhood he was ill a good deal of the time. Imagine the sickly child of a working mother who despised him. Then, later, the servant of people who exploited him and cared nothing for him.

"Soon after he arrived in the United States, he ran away from home. He's never had any money, despite his ability. He's lived alone, moving constantly, spending most of his waking hours in libraries. He reads voraciously and has a facility for languages.

"I think that's about all the factual information I have for you at this point." With that Vera began to put her notes back into her briefcase, and Dr. Mandelbaum stood up, trembling with anger.

"Mr. Chairman, you have ignored the words of the men of science in this room today and, for that matter, ever since you were foisted off on us as chairman. Now I demand that you listen! This—this *woman*—" His voice had risen to just short of a roar. "This woman led us on a wild-goose chase to Denver, where we made fools of ourselves. We'll be the laughingstock of the nation."

He was panting for breath in his rage, and Vera started to interrupt, to say that she hadn't wanted them to come to Denver; but a glance at Micah, listening with complete calm, dissuaded her. Mandelbaum got his breath.

"Sir, I demand that this puerile talk of spies and stars and maniacs and electronic death rays cease and that we start to treat this matter as the medical problem it is. We're wasting valuable time. Look at us. Men faced with a series of epidemics—and whom do we have on our team?" His finger stabbed accusingly at Jess Barrett. "A superstitious, football-playing electron-pusher." He waggled a finger at Gus. "A

228

dried-up, senile, half-baked has-been of a frustrated thespian. And two"—he sputtered in his fury—"*two gumshoes!* And as if that weren't enough, a broken-down, drunken, unstable, pistol-toting redneck whose only contribution is to stay so inebriated that what advice he does give is mercifully brief. Now, sir, I demand that you dismiss these people and let us scientists get to work on the worst medical disaster in the history of this country."

Ogden said firmly, "I agree!"

Fornier exclaimed, "Mr. Chairman, I was impressed when Miss Norman made her prediction about San Salino, but this—"

Micah sat motionless as the tumult swelled and subsided. He made no attempt to restore order. Instead, he looked thoughtfully at Vera. Her eyes asked a question, pleaded to be taken seriously. Slowly, briefly, an amused smile lit up his face. His black eyes sparkled, then became opaque again. They showed no malice, no scorn. She sighed with relief.

Micah cleared his throat slightly and said very softly, so that everyone in the room strained to hear him, "Dr. Fornier, you are one of the finest authorities in your field. But have you produced one single thought as to how these tragedies could be caused? Have you been able to treat one single patient successfully?"

The thin man perspired, his nose twitched, and he stared at the pad of paper in front of him.

Micah let the silence mount. He turned to Ogden. "Sir, you are justly respected for your expertise in the field of public health. You also have demanded that I remove these other people from our team. Now, sir, tell me what suggestions you have on how to treat the patients, how to prevent a recurrence of the disasters, what you think is the cause—and then please cite some evidence to support your views." The silence became agonizing.

At last Micah turned to Mandelbaum. Nobody breathed. "Dr. Mandelbaum, you are a world-renowned epidemiologist. Your work in the specialty of virology has been brilliant and earned you a fine reputation. You have worked indefatigably, efficiently, and faithfully to find a solution to these disasters. You have advanced a theory that this syndrome is due to a microorganism which invaded the immunity system and caused it to collapse. That is a logical and intelligent theory. I honor you for it.

"But have you uncovered a single thread of evidence to indicate that it is correct?"

He waited for an answer, but Mandelbaum said nothing, only looked desperately, pleadingly at Brown, who was puffing detachedly on a cigarette.

Micah continued slowly, precisely, softly talking to Mandelbaum.

"Have you been able to save one single patient from this disease?"

Silence.

"Have you been able to predict where this epidemic would appear again?"

Mandelbaum's pain was so great that Vera wanted Micah to let him off the skewer of his relentless line of questions, but she didn't dare speak.

"Doctor?" Micah wanted an answer, a capitulation.

Mandelbaum was staring at the table. He twitched, his face turned a deeper shade, and finally, almost imperceptibly, he shook his head.

Micah ignored Brown and Goerke, who had already admitted their ignorance. He spoke again, hardly whispering. "Gentlemen, Miss Norman has been able to make such a prediction. Furthermore, her suggestions dovetailed perfectly with what we already suspected.

"She did not suggest that we come to Denver. Indeed, she continued to maintain that the killer would not strike here.

"Now, Miss Norman has made more assertions. Her suggestions are admittedly astonishing, even incredible. But so far, she is the only one of us who has been correct in her predictions."

Vera stared at the pencil in her hand, then glanced around the room. It seemed that no one had breathed in the last twenty seconds. Ogden, Fornier, Goerke, Mandelbaum, all were motionless. Barrett, Brown, and Gustofson were more relaxed, but also silent. Adams looked amused, detached.

"Gentlemen"—Micah leaned forward slightly now—"I would like to suggest that the appropriate responses from all of us might be, first, open minds and, second, *humility*."

Dr. Brown blew a large smoke ring toward the ceiling, and Vera could have sworn that he winked at her.

18

MICAH TURNED TO VERA. "Now, Miss Norman, you've made some remarkable predictions and statements. But we must know more of how you came to these conclusions. First, I would like to hear how you concluded that he was born in Palestine, even in Bethlehem. Doesn't a solar eclipse cover a large area?"

"I realize that the birth in Bethlehem tries everyone's credulity, but that *is* where he was born," she said. "The eclipse did indeed cover a large area, but the path of its totality fell across Bethehem. Presumably the man we're hunting could have been born at some other spot along that path or in the one-hundred-sixty-seven-mile width of the path. But the eclipse was precisely over Bethlehem, and since I already knew he was a religious fanatic, it made sense to think he was born there. That's partly astrology and partly a guess, but one dictated by common sense."

Jess spoke softly to himself,

"And what rough beast, its hour come round at last,
Slouches towards Bethlehem to be born?"

When he saw the others looking at him curiously, he said with embarrassment, "All this reminds me of William Butler Yeats's poem, 'The Second Coming.' He speculated that the Second Coming might not be Jesus, the good Messiah, but an evil one."

Vera smiled at him. "Well, I don't want anybody to think that this *is* the Second Coming. *He* thinks he's the Christ, and he's unusually gifted, but he's quite human. His madness is human, too."

Dr. Ogden said, "Then, Miss Norman, you believe that genetics means nothing, that the only significant thing is the time a person was born?"

"I'm inclined to think that they're two ways of saying the same thing. One certainly cannot deny genetics. But neither can one deny astrology if he's studied it in any depth."

Vera leaned over the table, excitement rising in her as it always did when she believed she could prove something to a doubter. "I've personally seen several cases of astrological twins, and there are some famous examples. These are children born at almost the same moment in the same area, although not related. Take King Umberto the First of Italy. He met a man who looked almost exactly like him. He learned that they'd been born on the same day and at the same time. They'd married wives with the same name, and each had a son named Vittorio. The man had gone into business on the same day that Umberto had become king. Both were killed by gunshot wounds on the same day."

"Good Lord," said Brown, *that* makes you wonder, doesn't it!"

"My guess is that currents of electromagnetic energy flow through the world and people are influenced by them. For example, people born when Jupiter is prominent tend to be of a certain definite type. Their children, in turn, are likely to be born when a planet with which the fetus is in sympathetic vibration is in a prominent position. There is some evidence that the infant in utero does 'decide' when it 'wants' to be born. So you see, it may be that genetics and astrology are saying the same thing."

Dr. Fornier said irritably, "But, Miss Norman, that's deterministic. I believe in free will."

"I believe in free will, too, but I'm certainly *not* free to be born a man or to be born English or to have brown eyes. All that was determined before I was born. Is astrology any more deterministic than genetics?"

The thin doctor was still dissatisfied. He sniffed and his moustache seemed to jump sideways. "But, Miss

Norman, you went further when you said that because of the aspect between Saturn and Mars, our mystery man is likely to be cruel. That is sheer determinism."

"Well, yes and no. In the first place, many of us have a cruel or violent streak which we must resist. Indeed, all of us have some such weakness: laziness, sensuality, bad temper, what have you. But what we *do* with our innate gifts and weaknesses is up to us. Astrologers know that the great men of history tend to have difficult charts; that is, they have a difficult life. But their greatness—their strength and understanding—comes out of the struggle against their own bad tendencies or in overcoming obstacles.

"We accept the fact that sometimes a man is born with a glandular deficiency which causes him to be sexually disturbed. And some people in prisons seem to have different chromosomes from law-abiding people. The stars would mirror that kind of thing."

Goerke held up a hand in protest. "Miss Norman, you went far beyond that. I am a Christian—admittedly not as good a one as I ought to be, but still a believer, even if the flesh is weak. I find it dreadful to think of God letting some planets cause a person to be this or that, to have good or bad fortune. It's utterly unlike my concept of God."

Vera felt lifted by this turn in the conversation. "Dr. Goerke, I, too, am a Christian. But there's no conflict between my faith and my astrology, any more than there is between, say, genetics and religion.

"For reasons we've never fathomed, God permits some to be born crippled, poor, or retarded and others to be given every gift. If he chooses to use the planets to cause those conditions or simply to mirror them, does that make any difference in the problem of human suffering? Why God chooses to let suffering go on is a mystery we humans will never solve. But the situation is not really changed by whatever method he uses to control his universe."

Gus said gently, "This discussion's all very well, but we Baptists would like to get on with the problem of finding our killer, huh, Jess?"

Jess grinned at him, and Micah said, "Brad, we need a check on the suggestions Miss Norman's made."

"Right. One of our men will get to Bethlehem and check the records to see if such a person was born there. If there was, we'll trace him to the States and find him."

Micah nodded. "Bill, you'll give Brad any assistance he needs, and I'll want a report—well, immediately! I'm going to see the president tomorrow morning." He gestured at the others. "There's no sense in your staying here or going back to San Salino. I suggest, Dr. Mandelbaum, that you take the CDC team to Atlanta, study your data, and be ready to report to me next week. Jack, you can either stay here or go to Atlanta, whichever you prefer."

Goerke said with relief, "Since our problem's developing into a manhunt, I'd rather stay in Denver with my family. Of course, any time you need me, I'll come immediately."

Micah looked questioningly at Jess, who said, "I'd like to go to the Gorman laboratories on Long Island. I know the staff there. They have the equipment I need, and they're used to handling classified projects. Gus, how about coming with me? We can work together, you on the biology and me on the electronics."

Gus grinned under his drooping moustache.

Micah said, "Fine. Since our killer's probably in the East, I'm calling a meeting for this time next week in New York City. All of you plan to be there. I'll let you know the exact time and place. And I'll see to it that Mayor McDonald is notified."

Gus got up, yawned, stretched, and declared his intention of dragging his arthritic old body to bed. One by one the others followed. Petersen and Adams said good-night, gathered their things, and walked out together. Goerke watched them go. "I hope they get this skunk."

Micah took off his glasses and rubbed his eyes. "If what Miss Norman has done is correct, at least we

235

have a chance to get him. How about a drink, you three? The officers' club is still open."

Jack said, "I have a better idea, Mike; let's go to my house. Only twenty minutes from here, and I'd like my wife to meet you."

Jess and Vera readily agreed, and soon they were on their way into Denver, to Goerke's house on Eudora Street, not far from the medical center.

Sally Goerke was a charming blonde woman in her middle forties. She greeted her guests cheerfully and fixed a plate of sandwiches to go with their drinks.

When they were settled, Goerke said, "Vera, I've never read much about astrology, but I've always assumed it was nonsense. I used to see the nurses' aides reading their horoscopes for the day, and a couple of times I read mine. It made me laugh—so vague and general anybody could fit into it.

"And once I picked up a paperback written by some astrologer making all kinds of wild predictions. Most of them, as I recall, didn't even come close to being fulfilled. So when you appeared"—he shook his head—"I was, shall we say, dubious?"

Before Vera could answer, Jess put in, "I must admit, Vera, that when you sprang that born-in-Bethlehem bit, I had a few seconds of doubt myself."

Vera's laughter was like music to Jess. Her eyes sparkled and mirrored the blue of her suit. They no longer seemed gray at all.

"I can sympathize with both of you. I used to think the same thing. And let's face it, astrology has its share of nuts, probably a bigger share than the established sciences.

"But the other day I was talking with a friend, the director of a hospital. He told me about a small-town doctor who decided he could get some of the big money surgeons charge, so he operated on one of his patients for varicose veins. He put her under anesthesia and then gently lifted out, tied off, and cut *an artery*. Of course, the woman lost her leg. So even medicine has its incompetents.

"Astrology has quacks and nuts in greater proportion

because we haven't been able to set up firm standards. And although our art is well-enough proven in general principles to merit a really scientific, statistical study, the kind of data that have made medicine so dependable are lacking. The Gauquelins verified some astrological assertions and contradicted others.

"We need more studies, but it's very hard to validate an art as complex as astrology with ordinary statistical techniques. For example, when researchers try to correlate something as elementary as Sun signs and vocations, they're trying something so simple it's bound to fail.

"Take the fact that Venus is associated with the arts, and therefore Taureans and Librans, both signs ruled by Venus, are likely to be interested in the arts. That's true. But there's so much more to be considered.

"Hitler was a Taurean with Libra rising *and* many planets in the seventh house, which would intensify his interest. He *was* interested in the arts, in painting and architecture. But his Venus was conjuncted with Mars, and both were squared by Saturn, which totally changed the expectation.

"How can that complex a matter be studied statistically?"

"But it must be if you're ever to have general scientific respect for your art, Vera."

Jack Goerke was ready for a long conversation, and Vera was up to it. She had yearned to discuss astrology with open-minded scientists.

"Oh, I agree. I've been doing a good deal on my own the past four years. The reason I'm able to go beyond most astrologers in making predictions of physical descriptions is that I've made a careful statistical study of the subject. I believe we'll be able to call astrology a science within a few years."

"Do you really?" asked Sally. "I've thought for a long time that there's truth in it, but I never felt it could be called anything but an art."

"It *is* an art, just as medicine is. But it's also based on rigid rules, laws, and principles which any decent astrologer knows and can interpret."

237

Jack Goerke looked skeptical. "Now, Vera, you said it's like medicine. But medicine is a strict science, not an art."

"Jack! Medicine is both. Look, a patient comes in with a dozen confusing symptoms. They can be due to many things, including psychosomatic problems. Making a diagnosis isn't a strictly scientific process. Medicine is based on scientific facts, rules, and laws, but its practice is also an art." Vera looked at him quizzically.

He nodded in partial agreement.

Micah had been eating silently, listening, thinking. Now he joined the discussion. "Vera, the thing that stops me is the conflict with theology. I studied for the ministry before getting sidetracked into politics. I'd always assumed that astrology was nonsense until the night we met at that cocktail party. You opened my mind then, and it's stayed open—but it hurts a little. My mind was so comfortable with its roots wrapped around solid old Presbyterian beliefs."

Vera asked, "What conflict with theology, Mike?"

"Well, to think of ten planets up there ordaining our characters, our personalities, our minds—that does seem terribly deterministic. The one thing we fight hardest for in theology is the freedom for man to love and obey God or to hate and disobey him. But you make it sound as if we don't *have* that freedom."

"Oh, Mike, I didn't mean to imply that. God had to use some method to create us, to shape our lives. We accept the fact that God used evolution as the method to create his creatures. Why can't he use the stars to shape us?

"We already believe that one person is born with athletic talent and another with artistic talent. Why not believe that God uses the planets to so endow people? It's like the notes on a musical scale: Out of those eight notes comes an endless proliferation of symphonies, operas, concertos. And out of the endless combinations of ten planets, those big magnets up there, come people of all kinds."

"Well, yes, Vera, but you told us about the king of

238

Italy being assassinated at the same moment as his 'twin'—as if it were fate. And you spoke of this killer's character as if the combinations of the stars *made* him a killer."

"Yes, Mike. But if stellar configurations did cause them to die of gunshot wounds, is that so different from what Presbyterians, for instance, believe about predestination? The stars only establish certain limits within which we live out our lives.

"Look, one child is born with no arms and must deal with that tragic handicap. Another child is born a prince and must deal with staggering temptations and opportunities. And if we're given only so many years to live—some thirty, some sixty, some ninety— is that different from Jesus' parable about the men given different numbers of talents? We have to live the lives given to us."

"Vera, you haven't answered my objection. I believe that for life to have any meaning *and* for my faith to be true, men must be free to decide what they'll do with their lives. You imply that a man *must* become a criminal."

"No, no, no! But some are born with *tendencies* they must fight." She stood, walked up and down, gesturing. "You admit that many thousands of people are born into such sociological circumstances that for them *not* to be criminals is almost impossible. Is it any more unchristian an idea that the planets predispose some people to be criminals?"

"Yes, it is, Vera. It's *our* fault if we let society deteriorate so that some men are sociologically predestined to be criminals. But if the stars do it, it would be God's fault. That God would so arrange the planets as to *cause* a person to be a criminal—that's unthinkable. The notion that God would deliberately put planets in the heavens to exert evil influence on the earth is more than I can swallow theologically."

The others were saying nothing, listening raptly.

Vera sat down. "Well, Mike, astrologers talk of the malefics, but probably we shouldn't call them that. After all, without the strains and stresses they cause, we might never be worth anything. Saturn causes us to grow. So do the other malefics. We *need* them. Astrologers find that without difficult aspects from the malefics, people don't develop the strength they need. Things come too easily for them. I once cast a chart for a man in prison and was astonished to find that it was an *easy* one. Things always fell into his lap, and he was a weak man who gave in to temptation and ended up in jail."

"I can understand that. Jesus said in a number of ways that riches are dangers to the soul. That agrees with some of what you're saying. But I can't buy it *all*."

"What can't you accept, Mike?"

"I can't accept your astrological treatment of evil, of malefics, if you will. You act as if it weren't really evil, but just a prod that we need. Now, admittedly we sometimes grow spiritually from suffering. But that doesn't quite deal with evil. We've just seen twenty thousand Americans die from those malefic emanations—amplified, if your theory's correct. And they didn't grow a damn bit from dying. The Jews who died in Hitler's gas chambers didn't have much chance to grow from their experience." Micah drew a deep breath. "They just died!" he said quickly.

Jack and Jess both nodded in agreement.

"I think evil is *evil*, even if good does sometimes come from it," said Micah, more calmly. "For a child to be born without arms or legs due to thalidomide may provoke that child to rise to spiritual heights denied to us healthy ones, but I think it was evil. We must do everything we can to overcome such tragedies. There's an awful fatalism in your astrology which I can't accept."

"You're right, Mike. I was being Pollyanna. Evil is evil."

"Which leaves me where I've always been theologically, I guess: asking why God permits, even intentionally places, evil in his world. Whether we say that it's genetics that causes a child to be born retarded or that it's the planets doesn't change the basic question. God made evil. It's one of the impossible problems of life. Whether you call it magnetic storms or genetics or whatever, it seems that *God* causes the birth of someone so defective he becomes a murderer."

"Mike," Vera said gently, "maybe the old Presbyterians who spoke of double predestination weren't so stupid as our generation thinks."

"Theologically it's an intolerable doctrine, but realistically it makes sense." He frowned. "It's odd. Without that real, genuine, malevolent, destructive evil for us to fight against, we'd be shallow, mindless, soulless nincompoops. Which makes life a kind of arena in which we all struggle to become authentic *persons* who are truthful, brave, kind, and all the things that make people—well, divine. And I guess I've just argued myself into the position that there's no real conflict between astrology and my faith. But if there were, I'd certainly choose my faith."

"I would, too, Mike. But they're different things. They only come into conflict when one tries to be the other. It's like the old war between science and religion. There's no conflict there either—*if* the scientists don't think they've explained the spiritual, and *if* the religious people don't try to use faith to explain the material—such as saying that the world can't be round because if it were, people on the other side of the earth wouldn't see Christ coming at the time of the Last Judgment."

Micah laughed. "Yes, I remember that one. I also remember a Russian cosmonaut saying that while he was in space, he looked around for God and didn't see him. That was just as shallow an argument."

"It's the same with astrology. It can give some data to help us live our lives. But it doesn't fill the place of faith. I've known people who tried to guide their lives entirely by it. They made dismal failures of themselves—like the man who learned he had Venus and Mercury in the second house. That meant he could make money writing for entertainment. So he began to write pornographic books and made lots of money.

But he also became a cheap, shallow man without a soul. Christianity would have saved him from that because it deals with values, while astrology does not. Astrology doesn't pretend to answer all the questions of the world. It's only one of many intellectual resources people can use in finding guidance for their lives."

"Wow!" Sally Goerke's eyes were bright. "This is heavy conversation, but I have an idea you've all done as much as human beings can do in the past few weeks. How about getting away from it all? Jack and I have a fishing cabin on the western slope. Let's pack up early tomorrow and go there for a day or two. You'll be able to deal with your mystery far better after some unwinding."

Micah, who had to fly to Washington, declined, but Jess readily agreed, questioning Vera with his eyes.

"Oh, I'd love to, but I didn't come prepared. I only have one other dress with me."

"No excuse," said Sally. "We're about the same size."

Vera smiled, nodded, and accepted an invitation to stay the night with the Goerkes. Jess and Micah drove back together to Fitzsimons.

By the time the Wagoneer bumped over the narrow trail to the cabin, it was already early afternoon. For the last hour and a half, they had crawled in four-wheel drive through a forest, where giant Engelmann spruce held up the clear blue sky.

Now and then the Wagoneer came to a bog made by the melting snows and had to winch its way through the mire to the other side. Once they rounded a bend and found the road flooded by a pond behind a beaver dam. Again the winch pulled them through.

It was a hot day for the high country. By the time they arrived at the cabin, huge thunderheads were piling up over the peaks, and in the distance they could see a shower falling. The wind brought them the smell, dense and heavy, of summer rain on evergreens.

The area was so isolated that not even a trail bike had disturbed it. They clumped into the cabin, which was left open all year for hunters and fishermen.

It was a simple log cabin with two rooms. In one were three iron cots and a small fireplace, and in the other an old table and some chairs, a wood stove, and a counter for washbasins and pots and pans. The windows were covered with cobwebs, and the floor was dusty.

Jack took kindling from the woodbox and built a fire in the stove to expel the dampness and lingering chill from the cabin. Jess started one in the fireplace, and soon both fires were crackling.

They unloaded the jeep. The women swept out the winter's accumulation of dust, then put lunch together while the men took turns splitting firewood. They would need it tomorrow morning, when there would be ice on the water bucket; it was a rule at the cabin that the men always fixed breakfast and started a fire before the ladies were allowed out of bed.

Now they sat on the porch and ate sandwiches of cucumber on pumpernickel, washed down with ice-cold Coors. After the horrors of the last weeks, the contrast was so great that they said little, lounging and letting their souls recover. At last Jack grinned and said they'd starve that night if they didn't get moving.

Thirty minutes later they were tramping uphill with their fishing gear into denser and denser forest. Finally they came to a meadow where another stream joined the one they had followed. Here they parted, Jess and Vera taking one stream and Sally and Jack the other, after promises to be back at the fork before night, which came abruptly in the mountains.

As Jess followed Vera up the stream he realized that he was already thinking of her as his. He knew almost nothing about her beyond what he sensed: her intelligence, her beauty, an indefinable pureness of spirit that he saw in those lovely eyes. On the strength of a few bright smiles, a brief talk in her room that first night, an embrace, a spontaneous kiss, and the long discussion last night—no more—he knew he loved her and would always love her.

She turned and found him gazing at her and stared back in return, the generous lips curving into a smile and then an outright laugh. For a breath of time he continued to admire her, beautiful even in old fishing clothes, with her hair gathered and pinned on top of her head, and the pink cheeks of a growing sunburn diluting her cool elegance to make her more human, less unapproachable. Then he laughed loudly himself, out of clean, clear happiness, and in a rush she came to him and they kissed wildly, so suddenly that the first kiss all but missed and they laughed again. They stood there in each other's arms until she shook herself all over and said, "Come on! We have to put meat on the table." She picked up her gear. "You do look at home in jeans and a flannel shirt," she told him. "It's a pity you ever have to wear a tie."

"I hate 'em," he said.

He led the way up the meadow to the place where the gulch rose above them. They climbed the little trail beside the stream, pushing through willows until the water was no longer a flowing, singing body, but a series of calm pools connected by little falls and cascades that plunged and leaped down the mountainside.

There Jess stopped and put a fly on each of their lines. He went to the stream first to show her how, for she was a novice. Gently he cast his fly just in front of a shelf of rock at the edge of a pool. For a second it lay there, and then from the depths a speckled form flashed, the water broke into a sheet of diamonds, and the line came taut. Jess played the fish for a minute before he reeled it in and held it up for her to admire. "Brookie," he said.

"On the first try," she breathed.

"It's a good stream. Now you."

Vera tried to imitate his movements with the rod and made a mess of it; again she tried, this time too short a cast. The third attempt dropped her fly on the water, and it floated swiftly downstream. There was a virile flare of brown; the line snapped straight; the rod bent. "Got him!" she exclaimed.

"Not yet."

The wily trout tried to pull the line under a log. Jess shouted, and she obediently held the rod's tip sharply up. Soon the fish was out of his element and at her feet, fighting, twisting, flopping; it was all Jess could do to grab and retain him. He was a big German brown.

Holding hands, they moved upstream, in the current now, slipping and almost falling on logs, slogging through the leaping water to another pool. Ferns hung over the water, and banks of willow swayed in the light wind.

From pool to pool they went, filling their creels.

Above, the sky was a faintly dusty azure, and the trees seemed to narrow to a point that would catch the clouds that were traveling toward them. They had come to a little meadow, a flat place in the gulch, and here for a space the stream stopped its joyous ballet down the mountain and flowed broad and gentle. There was warm sunlight on the softness of the meadow grass, and Vera and Jess sat down together, not speaking, intensely aware of each other.

They were still sitting there, simply existing in this unforeseen happiness, when the thunder rolled across the gulch with the rain at its heels. He grasped her hand, and they dashed for the cover of a fir. They stood watching until the shower had passed and stepped out into a new aspect of the world; every pine needle had been washed and was gleaming in its momentary coat of crystal. Jess and Vera were thoroughly soaked and perfectly contented. They picked up her tan fishing jacket, the fly rods, and the two canvas creels, and started down to join the Goerkes.

This time they walked along the bank, avoiding the slippery rocks, pushing through masses of soppy willows, holding tree trunks to swing around them and move downward. Soon they found a little foot trail, perhaps made by Indians many generations before, and they traveled more quickly. Their clothing steamed in the sun, and water sloshed out of their tennis shoes. It was nearly an hour before they reached the big meadow where the streams came together.

Sally and Jack were there, lying in the sunlight on a large rock. They compared catches, whistling in admiration, took the trout to the water, and cleaned them. They gathered dry old broken branches and chunks of wood and built a fire. Jack had brought sourdough for biscuits and some butter for frying the fish. Before lighting the fire, they all paused to watch the sunset. There was a haze, and here and there steam still rose from the earth as it dried after the thunderstorm. The clouds were lit with silver; rays of light slanted out from them. The mountains slowly reddened as the sun dipped; the clouds became faint orange, then a brilliant red. Shadows lengthened, every bush and tree caught by the light of the evening changed to deep red.

Vera whispered, "Look—" They turned to see a doe drinking at the stream. In that monumental silence, even her hushed voice carried to the doe, who lifted her head, enormous ears quivering. She saw them and was gone, bounding over logs and up the steep hillside to the forest, her fragile legs as supple as springs of steel. "Oh, Jess!" Vera breathed.

The clouds had held their grandeur long enough. They seemed to relax, softening to a light pink, while the bright blue sky deepened to dark velvet. Then, in a brief shift to magnificence, they turned color again, magenta and lavender and at last a thick, profound purple.

Jack lit the kindling with a kitchen match and filled the frying pan with fish while Sally put out plates. A great sizzling and scent filled the air; for the first time all four became aware that they were ravenous. Then the sourdough biscuits were brown and the fish ready, and they heaped their plates.

When they had eaten, they sat together gazing into the sinking fire, their faces lit by the flames. It was time to start for the cabin, so they added no wood; but for the moment they did not move. The pure simplicity of the day, of the evening especially, had washed them free of the sorrow, pain, horror, and dread that had clung to them like grime. They lingered, half conscious of a vast reluctance to go back to the two weeks that waited for them beyond the mountains.

It must have been close to 10:00 when they heard it, down in the valley where the cabin sat. At first they could not even place the sound, alien here; but it came closer, and they knew it was a helicopter.

It came toward them, outboard lights blinking, spotlight playing along the ground, a rude and unbearable shaft of civilization stabbing down through the soft darkness.

Whap, whap, whap, whap, whap.

Nearer and nearer, and the mountains shielding the valley echoed the ugly noise, amplified it till it was all around them, intolerably loud. Like a live thing, an enormous predatory insect, it turned and headed for them as though the machine itself, not the pilot, had spotted their dying campfire. Rage mounted in Jess. It was invading the rare peace, shredding the still beauty of the night. The light swung round to catch them in its beam. They hid their eyes. Jess stood up, tense and angry. He had an impulse to run into the brush, haul Vera to the forest's shelter.

The voice from the loudspeaker was grotesque, inhuman in its volume. "This is Captain Mercer of the United States Army." The wind of the rotors was so strong that the fire flamed up, turned to smoke. Vera began to cough. "We're looking for Dr. Jess Barrett and Miss Vera Norman. If they're among you, please wave your arms above your heads."

Jess had an urge to hurl a stone into the flapping blades of the hanging, bobbing thing above them. He lifted his arms and moved them slowly back and forth.

"Dr. Maruyama wants you two in New York immediately," said the booming mechanical voice. "A jet is waiting for you in Grand Junction. Please proceed there at once. This is an emergency."

A knot of emotions seemed to form in Jess's throat, terror and impotent rage predominant. "What's hap-

247

pened?" he called desperately. "Has another city been hit?"

The four looked upward in sick dread, knowing their voices couldn't be heard.

"Please verify that you've heard by waving your arms." Jess did so. "We can't land in this terrain. Sorry! You'll have to drive to Grand Junction. Please verify that you'll do so." Jess waved. The helicopter sprang upward and swung clumsily around, and its lights disappeared down the valley. As the racket and its echoes at last died away, the four people stamped out the remains of their campfire and picked up their gear.

19

When Vera and Jess stepped off the military jet transport that had flown them to New York's Kennedy International Airport, a black Cadillac moved to meet them. Micah got out. He said nothing until they were all inside and the car was speeding toward the gate. "You know Bill Petersen. Our driver is Special Agent Thorpe of the FBI."

They muttered greetings, and Micah continued. "Sorry to have interrupted your vacation. God knows you needed and deserved it. But something broke, and we need you."

"Mike, has another city been hit?"

"No, thank heaven, nothing like that. Petersen, tell them."

Petersen held an attaché case on his lap, and he looked at it accusingly, as if it were to blame for the obvious discomfort he felt. "Miss Norman predicted that the killer was born in Bethlehem. Brad telephoned the Israeli police in Jerusalem and asked for their help. They were very cooperative." He flicked the brass clasps of the briefcase and opened it, took out some papers.

Vera couldn't wait. "I was right, wasn't I?"

Petersen said, "No, ma'am. There's no record of a child being born in Bethlehem at seven thirty-two A.M., August eighteenth, thirty years ago."

Vera's face fell, but she said with determination, "Well, then he was born without a doctor, and no record was kept, because—"

Petersen doggedly interrupted her. "Miss Norman, the man we're looking for was born in Bethlehem on

August eighteenth, thirty years ago, at seven thirty-six A.M. You were wrong by four minutes."

Vera frowned. "Oh, no, Mr. Petersen! That's not possible. If he'd been born at seven thirty-six, the cusp of the tenth house would have progressed to—"

Jess took her hand. "Vera, darling, that's close enough. What more do you want?"

"Jess, you don't understand! Doctors are forever criticizing astrologers, and they don't even keep careful records. They look at a clock and say, 'Let's see, that baby was born about fifteen minutes ago.'"

"Mike," said Jess, "after what we've seen Vera do, I think we'll agree that she's more likely to be right than the doctor. What do you say?"

Micah nodded and told Petersen to go on.

The agent looked at the report in his hands. "The Israeli officer stated that the subject was the son of an English servant girl who was raped by a tourist thought to be a European. Subject was born during a full eclipse. The mother was told by astrologers that the child would be one of the great men of history. Their prediction, according to the report, was—" He paused, looked for the exact words. "'This child shall cause the death of many and the birth of a new and stronger race.'"

"You see, that'd be enough to lead the poor unstable child to think he was the new Adam!" said Vera.

"The child's alleged father was never traced. The mother reared the boy, remained in Israel as the servant of an American couple named Hoffman. She gave him very little attention or direction. After her death, the Hoffmans took the eight-year-old child and trained him as a houseboy. Neighbors say he was unusually intelligent but subject to fits of violence. The couple seems to have treated him brutally to make him behave. Even during his frequent illnesses, they made him work. When he was fourteen, the Hoffmans returned to the United States and brought the child with them."

Jess whistled. "Vera, that's incredible! Mike, this

gives you the lead you need, right? Why did you send for us?"

"This is a good start, Jess, but where is he now? We traced the Hoffmans. The husband is dead; the widow lives in Larchmont. We're on our way there now. We hope she'll have a picture of him. I want you two at the interview. Jess, you may learn something about what he read that'll suggest to you how he's doing this. Vera, we want you along for the same reason. Find out what he read in astrology; perhaps you can pick up helpful hints."

Jess said, "Incidentally, Mike, what's the man's name?"

"An odd one—Jephthah Smith. But it is appropriate. Jephthah in the Bible was a bastard—"

"—who made a rash vow that led to the sacrifice of his own daughter!" finished Jess.

The Hoffman house was a stone giant set back on an almost obscenely green lawn and partly hidden by dense, carefully manicured hedges and ornamental bushes.

The door was opened by a maid who looked condescendingly at them. "Yes?"

Petersen spoke. "We'd like to speak to Mrs. Hoffman."

"Is she expecting you?"

"No."

"Then you'll have to call for an appointment. Mrs. Hoffman doesn't see anyone without an appointment."

"I'm Special Agent William Petersen of the Federal Bureau of Investigation."

"Oh." She grudgingly admitted them to the anteroom, and shortly Mrs. Hoffman appeared. She was in her middle sixties. Her hair was bouffant and had been dyed and curled expensively. Her eyes were heavily made-up. Brightly lacquered nails showed that she did no manual work.

"I'm Linda Hoffman. Which of you is the FBI agent?" she asked in a whiskey voice.

Petersen introduced himself and presented the others

251

as his associates. She ushered them into a spacious, exquisitely furnished living room. The large Oriental rug showed no sign of ever having been walked on. Mrs. Hoffman motioned toward a plush sofa, and they sat down. She herself perched on a carved white chair so fragile and uncomfortable-looking that Jess wondered if perhaps her bent legs were still supporting her weight and she was not resting on the chair at all.

"Now?" she said.

"Mrs. Hoffman, some years ago you lived in Palestine, is that correct?"

She raised one eyebrow. "Yes, Mr. Hoffman was superintendent of the company's plant there."

"You employed an English girl as a maid. At the time you hired her, she had a child, Jephthah, who was three years old."

"Yes, poor dear, she needed work, and I've always had a weakness for such people."

"Later, when she died, you kept her child as a houseboy, and when you returned to this country, you brought him with you."

Her eyes wavered, then fixed again on the agent. "Well, Mr. Petersen, you seem to know a good deal. We did employ poor Jeffie when he was left an orphan, yes. And we brought him to this country. It was all perfectly legal."

"Do you know where he is now?"

"Oh, no, he ran away less than a year after we arrived. He only used us to get here." She sighed artificially. "From very bad stock, I'm afraid. His mother always let him have his way. When she died, my husband and I tried to teach him something, but he was impossible. You've no idea how hard my husband, who was a gentle man, tried to teach that boy discipline. Sometimes I thought he was learning; he'd be good, do his work, and treat guests correctly. Then his terrible temper would explode, and he'd call us names you wouldn't believe."

"Didn't he begin working for you when he was quite young? He must have been a clever boy," said Vera.

Mrs. Hoffman looked at her with curiosity. "Yes, he

was very clever. He could fix anything. You only had to tell him something once, and he remembered—when he wanted to."

"He could have had almost no opportunity for school. Where did he learn?"

"He could read when he came to us—at three. I would have sent him to the local school, but he was so bad-tempered, he'd never have been able to stay."

"Yet he stayed with you for some time?"

"Well, yes, I wanted to help him if I could. But a few months after we got back here, Mr. Hoffman tried to correct him, and the ungrateful child *struck* him! By that time Jeffie was almost grown, and he knocked my husband down. Then he ran away, and we never saw him again."

"Did he read much when he was with you, Mrs. Hoffman?" Jess leaned forward in his urgency.

"Read! That's all he ever did," she said scornfully. "Before we left Palestine, he'd read every book in my husband's library. We tried to stop him; it's bad for a boy to read so much, and besides, we wanted him to do his work."

"What kind of books did he read, Mrs. Hoffman?"

"Well, everything! He was fascinated by medicine. He went to the library here in Larchmont and checked out every medical book he could find. I *told* him he'd never make a doctor because he was so bad-tempered. He read a lot about electricity and atomic energy, too. And a lot of trash."

"Trash? Such as what?"

"Well, in Bethlehem he was forever reading science fiction and such crackpot things, strange religions like Zen Buddhism and Rosicrucianism, the whole Koran. And he had his nose in astrology books all the time. He spent hours with a scruffy pack of Arab astrologers! And I swear he *believed* that nonsense! I remember one day he refused to ride his bicycle because he said he'd have an accident. The stars told him. I needed some things from the store, and naturally I sent him anyway. Sure enough, he was hit by a car. Not hurt much, but I always wondered if he did it on purpose—such a spiteful child!"

Vera asked quietly, "Do you know what he read on astrology?"

"Oh, everything! He read Arabic, and some of the books were in that horrible language.

"But he didn't just read; he was the world's busiest tinkerer. He could take a television set apart and put it back together. Really an amazing child, he could have amounted to something if he'd just—but I did everything I could. I taught him to cook and clean and—well, I taught him everything he knew. But all he wanted to do was read and tinker."

"Mrs. Hoffman, does he have any scars or other identifying marks?"

"I know one scar he has!" she said, the viciousness slipping out. "He gave me some of his filthy lip once, and I had to throw a hand mirror at him. It's on his forehead, just above his right eye."

"Do you have a picture of him?"

She thought for a minute. "Well, I might have one. Wait here."

In a few minutes she returned with a passport photo of a dark-haired, undistinguished-looking boy.

Petersen thanked her, asked her to notify the FBI immediately if she heard from or saw Smith, and they went to the door.

She asked suddenly, "Mr. Petersen, just who are these other people?"

"Sorry, ma'am, classified information. Good day."

Anger flared in her eyes. "Well, what's Jeffie done? Is it serious?"

"Yes, ma'am, it's serious." Petersen followed the others to the car.

"Back to the city," Micah said. "We have twelve days to catch this man. If we catch him, we'll probably have to kill him. But will we kill the guilty one?"

Vera said sadly, "A little boy in Bethlehem, with no father and a working mother who didn't want him, running loose in the streets, and then at eight, a houseboy for that woman!"

Petersen said, "He was practically programmed to commit murder."

The car raced along the interstate toward the city, Thorpe weaving it in and out of the heavy traffic. Highway noises were shut out by the closed windows, and the thickly cushioned interior remained silent except for an occasional sputter from the police or federal band radios.

Finally Jess spoke. "Where do we go from here, Mike?"

"The FBI will start a manhunt, and this picture will go out on every police teletype in the country. Bill, what do you think? Can you find him?"

"At least we have a name and a picture, even if it's out of date. It's something to go on."

Vera offered brightly, "I can tell you where he is. You see, the moon—"

Micah held up a hand in protest. "Vera! Don't bother telling us *how* you know these things. I heard your entire explanation of how you learned the man's birth date, and I didn't understand a tenth of it. But if you do have some ideas, you know they're welcome. Right, Bill?"

Petersen nodded solemnly.

"On the plane coming here, I studied Smith's chart and found two things that should help. I feel certain he's come home, and from what Mrs. Hoffman said, New York is likely to be home for him now. The other fact is that he's in a period of study. If he'd ever had anything to do with a university, I'd say that's where he was; but for him, study would mean something more private."

Jess ran his hand through his hair. "There's something about the photo that nags me. I know I've seen him someplace."

"He looks just like Mister Common Man," said Vera. "Oh, Mike, we're near my house. Would you mind dropping me there?"

As the car pulled away from Vera's, Jess said thoughtfully, "Mike, if Smith is studying, he must be planning how to pull off his job in twelve days. That's why he's back here and why he skipped Denver. He must be reading up on the power grid."

"That's a great deal more than we knew a day ago, but New York's a big place, and Smith could be anybody out there—the milkman, the clerk, the wino in the alley. It still seems hopeless."

"Mike, I'm slow today! What did Mrs. Hoffman say about him? That he was at the library all the time. O.K., so if he's studying up on the grid system, where would he be? He'd be in the Science and Technology Division of the New York Public Library."

"But, Jess, aren't there a dozen libraries with the information he needs?"

"No, he's got to go *there*. He could be there right this minute. Most of the books he needs are reference books that he can't check out. I know because I've spent a lot of time in that building. Let's see if he's there or if any of the librarians know him."

"Thorpe, the main library at Fifth and Forty-second. Bill, what do you think?"

Petersen said, "Well, Dr. Maruyama, I doubt that any librarian will remember one man out of all the thousands who go in there daily. But we can try."

The library is a magnificent structure. Majestic lions of stone guard the Fifth Avenue entrance. The main reading room is gigantic, and a reader must give a slip to the attendant at the desk, receive a number, then wait until the number is flashed on a large board, announcing that the book has been taken from the stacks and is ready for him.

Other floors hold the specialized collections of books. On each of the marble staircases are landings where people loiter, some of the aged merely watching the younger ones study. Couples sit on the benches holding hands, and children wander big-eyed through the grandeur of it all.

Through the doors of the venerable institution have passed many thousands of serious scholars who can find books here that are available nowhere else. Millions of casual readers and visitors pour in and out. Because of the high incidence of theft, guards inspect each bag and briefcase as patrons leave.

It was at the side entrance on Forty-second Street that the car stopped. Micah, Jess, and Petersen got out immediately. Off to their left, close to Fifth Avenue, was one subway station entrance, with another to their right, near the park that stretches out behind the library. Newsstands clustered around each entrance.

Pigeons waddled and hopped out of their path. The three men pushed through the swinging doors and then the revolving door into the building. A turnstile made them pause, but then they were inside, where they turned down the dark, monastery-like hall to the stairs.

They hurried up one flight and passed a derelict sitting on a bench. The hallway was old and high-ceilinged, with panels of once-white marble adding elegance. When they reached the Science and Technology Division, they pushed their way through the leather-covered doors.

The desk was on the right; they stopped behind a queue of four men and a woman. The young man at the head of the line turned and walked past Petersen to the door. While waiting for the librarian, Jess looked around, carefully checking out each reader. Smith was not in the room.

About twenty-five people were at the tables or using the card catalog. The light came from the windows, from old-fashioned green lamps on each table, and from even older chandeliers with naked bulbs. The roar of traffic outside and the hum of an old fan made the room noisy. It was a hot day, and many of the readers were in shirt sleeves.

Jess turned back to the desk, where a tired librarian was answering a patron's query. When he'd satisfied that one, the librarian turned to Petersen, who was drumming his fingers on the desk. A middle-aged man, he looked annoyed at Petersen's impatience but said civilly, "Yes?"

The agent flipped open his wallet, showing his shield. "FBI. I have a question for you."

The librarian waited.

"Ever seen this man before?" He showed the librarian the picture given them by Mrs. Hoffman.

The man looked at it. His lips widened; it was more a smirk than a smile. "Is this a joke?"

Petersen snapped, "It's no joke. Have you seen this man?"

"Sure. Didn't you? He walked out as you came in."

"What? Where'd he go? Quickly, goddamnit!"

The librarian recoiled from the shouting agent and said, "How do I know? He just walked out."

Micah and Jess dashed out the door, Petersen paused just long enough to ask what Smith had been wearing.

"Uh—a brown shirt and tan pants."

The agent ran down the hall as Jess took the stairs five at a time, whirled on the landing, took the next flight in jumps, hit the floor, and started for the door at a run. Petersen, with Micah behind, caught up with him at the turnstile.

Petersen, shouldering ahead, shouted, "FBI—let us through!"

The security officer looked at him cynically. "Yeah? Let me see in that attaché case."

"You son of a bitch, let me by!" He shoved his shield under the man's nose and bulled through, into the revolving door and out to the street.

Jess, with Micah behind him, vaulted the turnstile; and before the security officer could object, they leaped for the revolving door through which Petersen had disappeared. But a little old woman bent with arthritis was inching her way through. Jess waited until she was safely inside. Then he sprang through the outer doors to the landing and down the steps. Pigeons exploded in a burst of feathers and angry squawks.

Petersen ran toward the Fifth Avenue subway, waving for Jess to go to the other entrance. But it was rush hour, and the sidewalks were jammed. Jess had to fight his way. People cursed as he shoved them aside, rammed a path through.

Micah followed in his wake. Close to the subway

258

entrance, they passed some phone booths just as a woman stepped out. Jess crashed into her and knocked her flat. Packages flew in every direction, people shouted, but Jess kept going.

He turned down the steps to the subway. Sweat was pouring from his face as he shoved and fought his way through, yelling for people to let him pass, but they only turned and glared at him.

At the foot of the stairs, the crowd spread out, and Jess and Micah smashed through. The floor and walls shook as trains thundered and roared through the station below. To the left were the change booth and gates leading to the trains. Micah stepped into line and inched his way toward the front for tokens. Streams of people walked in every direction, and Jess looked desperately around, searching for Smith.

Off to the right was a landing that overlooked a ramp leading to trains on the lower level. Jess rushed to the railing and searched the broad river of faces flowing under him.

And there, in the middle of the current, he saw him. It was undeniably Jephthah Smith. And it was also the ambulance driver who had escaped from him in Bensonville.

20

FOR A SECOND JESS FROZE, watching the killer pass below him. Smith was carrying a black attaché case. Was it the infernal device? Jess whirled and ran to the turnstiles, calling over his shoulder to Micah, who had tokens and was heading for the entrance, "Mike! I see him!"

He shoved a woman aside and vaulted over the turnstile. A policeman shouted and came running through the crowd, but Micah stopped him with a few words and a flash of government credentials.

Jess fought his way down the ramp, made a turn, dashed, shoved, shouted, cursed, rammed his way through the crowd. When he reached the lower level two trains were loading passengers, one for the West Side, the other for the East. Hundreds of people poured on and off the trains.

He looked frantically here and there in the mob; he was tall enough to see over most of the heads around him. He ran along the train headed east, peering through the windows. He reached the last car as the doors closed, and the train moved out.

He fought his way across to the westbound train. Blocked at the verge of the platform, he watched helplessly while this one, too, began to move. And as the train carried its passengers by him, he stared into the face of Smith, no more than three feet away. For a tenth of a second, an eternity, their eyes met. Then Smith was gone.

Jess ran desperately beside the train, bumping into people, who reeled away from him in surprise. But the train was picking up speed and almost instantly became a blur of windows and faces and then red lights disappearing into the tunnel ahead.

Jess stumbled to a halt and watched the train carry the murderer of 20,000 Americans into the darkness.

He shook his fists over his head and roared in frustration. People around him had recoiled, and he was suddenly alone at the end of the platform, with everyone staring. A frightened voice said, "Mister, you can get killed acting like that!"

Jess turned away and walked back to the ramp. His jacket was torn and smudged. Micah met him at the turn where the ramps joined.

"Mike, goddamnit, he got away, and I think he saw me!"

Micah put his hand on the big man's shoulder. "Take it easy, Jess. That fellow wouldn't know you from Adam. He'll come back to the library, and we'll have a stakeout waiting."

"Oh, no, Mike, that bastard knows me. I remembered where I met him. He was the ambulance driver I slapped in Bensonville."

"What? Why, Jess, he couldn't be. That man is dead."

"The real one, maybe, but not the one I slapped. That one was Smith!"

"Then he must have killed the real one. But why—and how—was he in Bensonville that Wednesday?"

"Probably to see if his damn device worked and to gloat. He must have set off his signal in Bridgeton in the morning, flown to Louisville, hitchhiked to Bensonville or nearby, flagged down the ambulance, and killed the driver. Then when he saw the National Guard cordoning off the town, he was afraid he'd get stuck. No wonder he panicked when I chased him! Can't we find the stationmaster and have him stop the train in the tunnel, then have cops ready for him when they reach the next station?"

Micah gestured at the horde around them. "In this mess? By the time we find the stationmaster, the train will be three stations away. And if he recognized you, he's getting off at Times Square right now. We've lost him."

At the top of the stairs, they headed back, dejected, toward the library. Petersen saw them and gestured excitedly. They broke into a run, and he opened the car door. They jumped in, and the limousine lurched ahead. "What is it, Bill?"

Petersen was in the front seat with Thorpe. "I couldn't spot Smith, so I went back to the librarian for his address. They got it from his card. He lives at an old, run-down residential hotel on West Sixty-ninth, the Galaxy, Room three twelve, under the name of James Robinson. We'll get him there!"

They were near the corner of Forty-second and Fifth, headed east, away from the Galaxy, and traffic was bumper to bumper; it was now the very middle of the rush hour.

Petersen fumed as they waited. "Use your siren, Thorpe."

The driver said in despair, "Sir, you told me not to bring the siren on this limousine."

The light changed, and they inched ahead to the corner. The light changed again just as they reached it, and Petersen groaned.

A sign at the corner read No Right Turn, 4 P.M.– 6 P.M.; but when the light changed, Thorpe started to turn, then saw that the avenue to their right was completely jammed with traffic. He made a quick decision and gunned the limousine across the intersection, heading toward Park. They found the street clear until they reached Park, where the light was red and cars clogged the intersection. They waited, waited, waited.

Petersen suddenly relaxed. "Why are we in such a hurry? He doesn't know we're after him. He'll settle down for a nice little dinner, and we'll nab him."

Micah moved to the edge of the seat. "I'm afraid he may know we're after him. Tell him, Jess."

Petersen jerked around as Jess told him the story of the ambulance driver. "Then we have to get there fast. Thorpe, move this car!"

Even as he said it, he could see the absurdity of his

words. Traffic was crawling down Park Avenue. A light changed, and they got a break and shot ahead all the way to Thirty-ninth, where Thorpe snapped a right turn. As far as they could see, cars were jammed into the narrow street.

"If he's alerted, he'll go home, gather his things, and beat it." He looked at his watch.

Traffic thinned as people turned off Thirty-ninth, and the limousine lunged forward. A cab stopped in the middle of the street. An elderly couple dragged themselves slowly out of the cab. The limousine waited; the motor throbbed; Petersen swore. Suddenly all his FBI training in courtesy deserted him; he rolled down the window and shouted, "Goddamnit, move out of the center of the street! You're supposed to unload at the *curb!*"

The old couple paid no attention, but the cabbie looked at them wrathfully. He was a big man with a broad, flat face. He got out and stormed back to the limousine. "What'sa matter with ya, ya bum? Can't ya see those poor old folks? Ain't ya got no heart?"

"Goddamnit, we're FBI! Move!"

"Sure you are, and I'm J. Edgar Hoover."

Jess stepped out. "Mister, move your cab immediately."

The cabbie looked up at 230 pounds of muscle. "Uh, sorry," he said, trotting for his cab. When it rocketed off down the street, the limousine followed.

They shot across the Avenue of the Americas and headed for Eighth Avenue. The road was clear until a truck that had pulled up parallel to the curb jackknifed and began to back into a loading platform. The agent leaned on the horn as the limousine rocked to a halt.

Jess jumped out and ran to the truck driver. Then the truck was pulling out, and Jess was back in the car.

Micah asked, "What were the magic words?"

"I told him I'd break his neck if he didn't move it in ten seconds."

"Sir," said Petersen, "there's no way we can make it. We have to get help. I'm going to radio Captain

263

O'Reilly of the NYPD and asked him to rush some men over to the hotel. I should have done it before," he said miserably. "That's in his precinct."

He fiddled with the radio, and there was a crackling noise.

"Emergency! This is Special Agent Petersen of the FBI. Get me Captain Terrence O'Reilly. Top-priority emergency."

Thorpe continued to fight his way through traffic, honking, cutting ruthlessly in front of other cars. Finally he reached Eighth Avenue and turned north. He was just streaking across the Forty-second Street intersection when the radio squawked and O'Reilly came on.

Petersen quickly outlined the situation, leaving out only the crime of which Smith was suspected. His voice was close to a shout.

Up ahead a car stalled. A traffic officer walked over to it. Behind, on Eighth Avenue, dozens of cars sounded their horns. The FBI limousine was caught in the middle. The blare of the horns almost shut out the captain's reply.

"Sure, Petersen, *all* your cases are more important than ours. What d'ya want us to do?"

Twelve minutes had passed since they left the library. Jess's palms were sweaty. He hoped Smith had paused for a blintz or a hot dog at the Forty-second Street interchange.

"Captain, we need a stakeout around that hotel. When the suspect enters, button it up. We'll take him when we get there."

Up ahead the officer had traffic moving in one lane.

"Look, Petersen, the FBI always wants us to drop everything and hold a guy till you get here for the glory. But right now every spare man's on traffic duty. Call your own office, and have 'em do the stakeout."

The limousine was crawling ahead two or three feet at a time. Jess grabbed the door handle. "I can *run* there faster than this!" Micah put his hand on Jess's arm, and he sat back.

"O'Reilly, this is an emergency of the utmost urgency. The man in that hotel is a mass murderer."

The limousine shot through a break in the traffic and was immediately caught between a line of cars on one side and the curb on the other. Ahead was a mound of earth and some blinking yellow lights. A sign read Sorry for the Inconvenience, but Dig We Must. Con Ed.

"Oh, yeah? What kind of warrant do you have?"

"We don't have a warrant! And we're going to miss him unless you get moving!"

Thorpe took the big car perilously close to the hole and over the mound of dirt, crushing the Con Ed sign. A driver on the left honked frantically as the limousine cut in front of him.

"If you don't have a warrant, dammit, on what authority am I supposed to pull forty men off traffic duty to surround that hotel?"

A huge bus tried to make it across Eighth Avenue on the signal, but cars were backed up ahead of it. They sat there while their green light was used up, and then the bus edged away.

Petersen, drenched in perspiration, red-faced, gripped the microphone and bawled, "On the authority of the president of the United States!"

"Oh, bullshit, Petersen! You FBI guys always claim everything you want to do is on the president's authority. If you want me to do a stakeout in my precinct, you'll have to have your boss call my boss and give authority."

The limousine lurched ahead, then slammed to a halt again at the intersection, which was clogged with cars and trucks.

"O'Reilly, you thick Mick, you get that hotel surrounded!"

"If you don't even have a warrant, how come you know the creep is a mass murderer?" demanded O'Reilly stubbornly.

Petersen looked at his watch, ground his teeth together, and lost his head entirely in his terrible frustration. "Because Vera Norman says so!"

There was a pause. This time the captain sounded downright respectful. "Vera Norman? The star girl? You wouldn't be kidding me, Petersen?"

Micah reached over the back of the seat and tapped Petersen. "Give me the microphone," he said. The agent passed it to him thankfully. "Captain O'Reilly, this is Micah Maruyama. Do you recognize my name?"

There was a crackling pause, and then, faint but distinct, they all heard someone on the police-frequency radio exclaim, "Holy saints, it's Super Jap!"

Then O'Reilly said loudly, "Indeed I do, Dr. Maruyama."

"Please consider Petersen's request as a presidential order," said Micah gently.

"Yes, sir, I'll have the Galaxy buttoned up tighter'n an Englishman's dinner jacket. Could I have a description of the suspect, sir?"

Micah handed the instrument back to Petersen and sank into the thick cushions.

Every inch of their progress was still a battle, but the tension in the car lessened with the knowledge that the police were in action.

Jess waited in agony for the sight of the hotel where Smith was living. It was hard to believe they were so close to success.

Most painful was the thought that he had once held the killer in his hands and only slapped his face and let him go. One squeeze of his hands and the man would have died, and thousands of people would still be alive.

Jess remembered the moment when Micah had announced that the body with the fractured skull was that of the ambulance driver. Jess had blurted out that he'd slapped the man. All eyes had turned on him, and he'd felt a surge of panic: Had he hit him too hard and killed him? A ridiculous idea, quickly discarded. And now he wished he *had* killed him.

Thorpe had turned off Eighth Avenue onto Sixty-ninth Street. They were moving a little faster. Thousands passed them, some hurrying home, some sitting in doorways, some running to catch cabs. And many swore at the big black limousine as it broke law after law in its fight through traffic.

In the short time since they'd left the library, Jess had

seen more people than Smith had already killed. The magnitude of the disaster that would occur if they failed to catch him made Jess shudder.

He came out of his reverie as they approached the hotel and Petersen began to swear. His language was often rough, but now it was a river of profane eloquence.

They slowed down, and Jess saw the reason for the agent's fury. The Galaxy was surrounded. Police vans were everywhere, cars with flashing red lights blocked the road, and crowds were held back by police barricades and heavily armed officers. Other policemen were stationed at the door of the old hotel.

Petersen jumped out, and Thorpe, Micah, and Jess followed.

"FBI! FBI! Let us through! FBI!"

The crowd split grudgingly, and they shoved their way to the police barricade, where Petersen showed his shield. Then they were inside the cordoned area.

O'Reilly saw them coming. He smiled in satisfaction. "Petersen? Dr. Maruyama! Well, you see we got here."

"What the hell are you doing, O'Reilly? I said to keep your men hidden. Look at the dumb bastards! Our man'll spot this circus twenty miles away."

Petersen was shaking both fists, looking more Irish than O'Reilly, who retreated before the shouting agent and held up his hands in mock defense. "Take it easy, Petersen, take it easy! That's the trouble with you Feds; you think nobody knows their business but you!"

Micah stopped the agent with a hand on his elbow and asked the captain quietly, "Why are your men in the open?"

"Because your guy went in right after we got here," O'Reilly said, "and he's still there. We got a key to his room and we got this place so sealed that nobody could get out through a water pipe."

Jess felt the load of three weeks of horror lighten.

"Good work, Captain," Micah whispered.

Petersen wiped his face. "O'Reilly, you Irish angel! Who saw him go into the hotel?"

"Sergeant di Gregorio and his partner. Hey, Greg, come here, the both of you!"

Petersen questioned them; the descriptions of Smith and the man who had entered the hotel tallied perfectly. "Has anybody been inside yet?"

"No, you said just to keep him there."

They stared at the old building. It was like so many others of its period: a once-respectable low-cost hotel that had deteriorated until it became a refuge for the poor. The brick was chipped and worn by the elements and carried an accumulation of stains from standing in New York's befouled air for seventy years and more. The windows were high and narrow. The men looked up, wondering which was Smith's room, whether he would fire at them or come hurtling, screaming, down.

Petersen cracked out orders. "Thorpe, you and I lead the search party. O'Reilly, give us a couple of men with shotguns and bulletproof vests, who're used to this kind of thing. And I want di Gregorio with me."

They gathered at the door while frightened residents stared out the lobby window. There the officers were issued flak jackets, and Petersen told them that the suspect was almost certainly armed and extremely dangerous.

Then, in a lull, they heard a shout. "Hey, Jess! Tell 'em to let me through!"

Micah said, "That's McDonald! How did *he* get here? O'Reilly, that man behind the barricade shouting at us is armed and unstable. Have your men restrain him."

Several officers grabbed McDonald as a squad of police entered the hotel. The residents, mostly old men and women, watched with a mixture of curiosity and fright. Petersen turned to Jess and Micah. "I'd feel better if you two got behind a squad car. You get hit by a stray bullet, it's my neck."

"I'm going with you, Bill," Jess told him.

"You stay out of it! This guy's already killed a lot of people, and he'll sure as hell fight arrest."

Micah said softly, "Bill, I'll stay here if you insist. But let Jess go. He won't get in your way."

"O.K.," said Petersen dubiously. Quietly they climbed the creaky stairs, swearing to themselves at the noise. When they reached the second floor, they glanced down the hall. It was empty.

At the third floor, they cautiously stepped into another vacant hall and walked to Room 312. Petersen and Thorpe stood on one side of the door, di Gregorio and an officer on the other. Jess stayed back.

"Robinson, this is the FBI! Come out slow and easy with your hands up! You're under arrest!"

There was no response.

"Cover me. If he so much as breathes, kill him." Standing clear of the door, he inserted the key. It turned, and they heard the lock slide back. Petersen held his service revolver steady. With his left hand, he turned the knob, threw open the door, leaped inside.

The room was empty.

"Dammit, he's hiding somewhere else in the building! Sergeant, take the others, and search every room. I want every person lined up outside. Jess, go through his things; see if you can find anything."

Jess entered Smith's room. It wasn't much: a single room, closet, sink, and hot plate; the bathroom would be down the hall. The bed was neatly made, but the cover was worn. A dresser occupied a whole wall, and there was a small table and one chair.

He went first to the closet. Pathetically few clothes hung inside. Three shirts, neat but worn. A sport jacket, a dark wool V-neck sweater, a plastic raincoat. Two pairs of cheap cotton pants and one pair of light wool trousers of better quality. On the shelf was a box. Inside, Jess found a pair of shoes, newly shined.

He moved to the dresser and opened the top drawer. Four pairs of socks, some underwear, and two handkerchiefs.

Jess fingered the handkerchiefs. He had never been much at hating anyone, and slowly over the last week, his furious anger at the murderer had ebbed. This morning at Mrs. Hoffman's, Jess had actually felt pity for Smith.

Now he looked at the handkerchiefs. The murderer of 20,000 people, the new Messiah, the greatest genius since Einstein—had only two handkerchiefs! He looked around the room. Not a picture of anyone, not a flower or a friendly personal object.

And up from his own memories swarmed a cloud of feelings he had thought were long since buried. When his mother died, Jess was still a little boy. Bob was a teen-ager, and his life was already launched; he survived the blow well. Their father, a judge, was so devastated he withdrew into his work.

But for Jess it was the disappearance from his life of something that never quite returned. He would not discuss his loneliness with his father, for when he tried, it always hurt the man so much that the little boy came to avoid the subject.

Day after day the child went home from school to a house filled with memories of his sick mother. Then one afternoon Jess went to a friend's after school. The moment they walked into the front room, Jess almost cried. It was like a fairyland, clean and sunny. There were pictures on the wall. A mother lived there and kept the house. Jess trailed around with his friend, staring, touching, savoring it all.

The boy's mother gave them a plate of cookies and two glasses of milk. As Jess ate he looked from one symbol of warmth, love, and normalcy to another. And then, while his friend called after him and the mother stared in astonishment, Jess ran out the door and down the street. The warmth of the home he had fled made his own life seem bleak and intolerable.

When he reached home, he threw open the windows to sweep out the mustiness of a house shut up most of the day, but it was no use. In panic—the only time since his mother's death—Jess called his father at the courthouse and begged him to come home. The judge had never known his quiet younger son to weep; he raced home to find a child hysterical with loneliness.

All his life Jess had yearned for a home full of sunlight and the smell of cookies, but it eluded him. His had been a life of fame, of as much money as he wanted. But it had also been a life of loneliness, an endless succession of restaurants and hotels, with interludes at his small house in Bensonville that were always ended too abruptly.

Now, as he looked around, Smith's loneliness became his own. But Jess knew that even he could not really appreciate how utterly empty of love and friendship this man's life had been—and how that loneliness had been turned into such towering hatred.

He tossed the handkerchiefs back and pulled out the second drawer. There he found a cassette tape recorder.

He picked it up, pushed the Play button. Nothing. He looked more closely, saw that only half the tape had been used. So he pressed the Rewind button and, when he had the tape all on one spool, started it again.

What he heard chilled him to the heart.

A flat unemotional voice read figures and facts about the great eastern power grid. Jess listened for a few minutes, hoping for some personal comment, some contact with the soul of the killer. But there was only the flat recitation of figures and quotes.

The noise of policemen shouting shook him out of his thoughts. As he walked down the stairs, he tried again through deliberately forced intuition to make spiritual contact with the mind of the assassin. What kind of man *was* he? Could they somehow reach that twisted mind?

Jess recognized that it was hopeless. The genius was as inaccessible psychologically as he was spatially. The soul of man, like nature, abhors a vacuum. When there is no love, the soul either crumples under the weight of its loneliness or fills with hatred.

Jess found the lobby empty. Everyone had been herded into the street. He went out and quickly surveyed the ranks of old and middle-aged men, some angry, some trembling in fear. Smith was not among them.

He stood with Micah in silence and disappointment

as the police who had searched the hotel emerged empty-handed. Petersen hailed the officer who had seen Smith enter the building.

"All right, Sergeant di Gregorio, where is he?"

The sergeant looked at the group. "There! That one in the brown shirt and tan pants."

For an instant Jess felt a surge of unutterable relief; then chagrin took its place. The man resembled Smith but was not the killer.

"Vera *said* he looks like everyone else," Micah said. "The sergeant made an honest mistake. Look, Jess, there are at least four men in that line-up who'd fit the description we gave O'Reilly. But now Smith knows we're after him; he'll use all his intelligence to evade us."

Petersen showed the picture of Smith to the police. Not one had seen him. They questioned the hotel residents and then let them return to their rooms. The crowd that had gathered hoping for some excitement dispersed.

Suddenly a familiar voice spoke at Jess's elbow, and he and Micah turned to face Mayor James McDonald, too plainly liquored up again.

"Maruyama, you had no right to keep me out. I'd of caught the son of a bitch; I got incentive! How come you let him get away?"

"We didn't let him get away. He wasn't inside after all."

"I heard you and Petersen talk to the captain, and you said that for sure you had this mass killer in the Galaxy—"

"We were wrong. How could you have heard that conversation?"

"How? Hell, I got a radio that takes police calls; picked you up while I was cruising."

"Well, we thought we had him. Now I suppose he'll go into hiding."

"How'd you find out who he is? From Norman, really?"

"How? Dammit," said Micah, losing his patience for once, "you were there when Miss Norman told us

272

all about that man! Oh, no, that's right, you, uh, left before she spoke. But when she gave us her ideas, we checked them out and traced him this far. We also have a picture of him as a boy."

"You got a picture? Let me see it. Who is he?"

Micah fished in his attaché case. "His name is Jephthah Smith, alias James Robinson. Here he is."

He handed the mayor the picture Mrs. Hoffman had given them. The scar over the right eye showed clearly. As he stared at the photo, McDonald began to tremble, and his mouth sagged open.

Jess said, "What is it, Jim?"

The brash mayor stared at them, and for a moment they thought he would weep. His chin trembled, and he looked sick. "I—I just talked to this man five minutes ago. He's older, but that scar gives him away."

"You *what?*" Petersen grabbed McDonald by the lapels, jerking him around.

"I talked with him in the crowd a minute ago."

"Why didn't you grab him—or call us?"

"How in hell was I supposed to know who he was?"

Jess pushed Petersen back, and Micah asked quickly, "Where did you talk to him? Quick!"

"Well, you birds wouldn't let me inside, and I was standing at the barricade when this little weasel comes up and says, 'What's going on here?' And I told him, 'They got a mass murderer holed up in there, and they're gonna root him out.'

"Then he says, 'I do hope they catch him. This city's dangerous enough! There must have been some good police work to locate him.' And I said, 'Way I heard it, wasn't the police at all. It was that astrologer, Vera Norman.' And he says, 'Vera Norman? She must be a superwoman to catch a mass murderer.' Next thing I knew, he was gone."

Micah frowned, muttered, "Oh, God. Now how will we ever get him?" His face was gray. "At least we know without a doubt that he exists. If only I had something more definite for the president. He's under pressure to remove me and let the scientists handle the investigation."

Jess perked up. "Mike, we *do* have something tangible to give the president. Look!" He held up the tape recorder he'd found in Smith's room, explaining what he'd heard. Micah whistled and asked to hear the tape. So Jess laid the little recorder on the hood of the limousine, and Petersen, Maruyama, Thorpe, and McDonald crowded around. Jess ran the tape back to the beginning, pushed the Play button. Almost immediately there was the flat voice, reading into the tape statistics about the power grid, estimates of the amount of power being delivered to various cities, the location of plants, the interconnections. They played the tape all the way through.

"It's his voice," said McDonald.

"That's tangible, all right. I'll play that to the president over the phone tonight." Micah thought for a few minutes. "You know, Jess, I've believed that this devil existed and that he was going to try to commit this massacre, but somehow it wasn't real until I heard that voice. He's so—"

Jess supplied the words. "He's so inhuman. He's almost a machine."

"A machine made in hell," said Micah somberly.

"Will you give me a lift to my car?" said McDonald. "I couldn't get anywhere near this place."

They slid into the limousine. Around them police were taking down the barricades, and the vans and cars were beginning to leave.

Micah said, "Bill, I presume you've taken care of having his room thoroughly searched, fingerprinted, and so forth?"

"Yes, sir. I've asked the police to put a seal on the room, and the office is sending one of our own crews to go through it tonight."

The road ahead was still cluttered with police and milling spectators. They waited while the police worked to clear the area. Micah glanced at his watch impatiently. "Jess, let's hear that tape again while we wait."

In the car the voice sounded louder, clearer, and more frightening. It droned on emotionlessly. Then abruptly the words were replaced by a sound that sent terror into the listening men. It was a high-pitched wail, as if the very machine were crying out. They had heard that sound before, twice before, on the cassettes from Bensonville and Bridgeton. It went on and on, and McDonald held his hands to his ears, gasping.

Thorpe turned from the wheel. "What the hell is that?"

The normally fearless Petersen asked in a voice that quivered, "Was it the death signal?"

The effect of the sound was appalling. Jess turned off the machine, tried to calm his nerves so he could think. Micah and McDonald stared at him, waiting for his answer.

"No, or rather yes, it's the signal, but it can't hurt us now. It's only effective during the fatal aspects, and we still have nearly two weeks until they happen again. Mars isn't rising; the moon and Saturn aren't in aspect; the area isn't susceptible yet. So it can't be hurting anybody now. But what the hell is he trying to do? Wait! That signal couldn't be coming from the power station anyway. This thing is battery-powered. He must be using his radio transmitter. But why?"

He pushed a button and, when the machine had rewound, played the tape again. This time there was no voice, only the sound.

"That answers my question, Mike. He turned on his radio transmitter to wipe out the tape. It destroyed our evidence."

"It certainly worked! But I don't understand how he did it. There's no radio station here."

"I wish I knew for sure. Apparently he's able to create an electromagnetic field with his machine, which would of course wipe out a tape. The transmission he sends is probably highly directional. He just pulls up his portable antenna and points it and wipes out all the magnetic audio tapes in the area."

"How close would he have to be to do that?" Petersen growled.

Jess shrugged. "Probably within a few blocks, or he'd have to have a big antenna."

Petersen jumped out of the car, shouting over his shoulder, "Then he's still in the area. We've still got a chance to catch him."

He ran to Captain O'Reilly. They talked for a couple of minutes before O'Reilly called to his men. One by one they looked at the picture.

"It's a good idea to have them try, but I doubt they can catch Smith. He probably sent his signal from a few blocks away and then disappeared into the subway."

"What now, Mike?"

"I talk to the president and try to persuade him to let me start a full-scale manhunt. We've got to catch him, and we have"—he consulted the calendar on his watch—"less than twelve full days. With a picture and the kind of description we have, fliers, extensive TV coverage, we might be able to come up with him."

"Will the president buy it, Mike? You said he was getting more and more skeptical."

"I don't know, Jess, but what alternative do we have?"

"I have an alternative," McDonald said. "I'm gonna look for that murderin' bastard among the hippie-Commie types. While you guys *meet*, I'll find him."

Micah looked at the mayor, and for the first time he smiled, though wanly. "O.K., Mayor, go get him! Good luck!"

Petersen returned to the car. "Bill, I want an up-to-date version of this picture Mrs. Hoffman gave us," Micah said. "Will you take it to a police artist and let him talk to Jess about how Smith looks today? We're going to need it because if the president agrees, we're going to have the greatest manhunt in the history of the world."

21

ON SATURDAY, JUNE 26, Presidential Assistant Micah Maruyama and Special Agent William Petersen met with Charles Gebhart, director of the Federal Bureau of Investigation, and Commissioner Robert Serafin of the New York City Police Department in the commissioner's office. Micah swore both men to secrecy and told them there was evidence that Jephthah Smith had caused the three devastating epidemics. He informed them of the president's wish that the public not be told for fear of a panic as terrible as the plague.

They were not told that the source of most of the information was Vera Norman.

Before Micah and Petersen left the commissioner's office, the manhunt had begun. From all over the East, federal agents of the Treasury and Justice departments were called to join the search. Federal marshals were ordered to New York and sent into the streets dressed in civilian clothes. Every federal agent and every police officer in the city would soon have a picture of Jephthah Smith and be told that he was urgently wanted for national security reasons.

There were eleven days left.

The Sunday London *Times* printed a report that the most certain sign of the enormous difficulty in which the United States found itself as a result of the epidemics was not in the government crisis but in the change in the supermarkets. Many shelves were empty because transportation had not yet returned to normal. All stocks of goods that were ordinarily imported—food, appliances, household supplies, and other articles—were almost exhausted.

Of course, domestic foodstuffs were still in plentiful supply in most places but the restrictions imposed on transportation and the reluctance of some drivers to make cross-country runs had caused a shortage of beef in many places.

When the president informed Maruyama that he wished to see him Sunday evening, June 27, Micah flew to Washington, had dinner alone, and took a limousine to the White House.

If any man could count himself a friend of the president, it was Micah, yet he dreaded the interview. He had not found the cause of the epidemics, and he had undertaken a course of action that would prove extremely embarrassing to the chief executive if all the facts became publicly known. Micah strongly suspected that Mandelbaum and perhaps others on the CDC team had been discreetly campaigning against him through their supervisors.

It was raining as the limousine carried him through Washington to the White House. Puddles glittered with the reflection of the city lights. Buildings were so wet that they, too, threw back the lights like mirrors. Government buildings, so familiar to Micah, loomed up, their edges lost in the wet gloom as they faded behind the veils of rain. Micah wondered if Washington would be a dead city after July 14.

The interview was painful. President Weaver was cold and distant. His eyebrows, bushy in contrast with his thinning hair, were pinched together. He listened without comment, only occasionally nodding an acknowledgment. As usual his strong, angular face showed little emotion, but Micah could read the doubt in his eyes.

Micah told in detail everything that had happened since he'd left Washington. He did not withhold anything as he spoke of Vera's theories, her predictions, her accuracy. The president remarked dubiously that he knew senators and others who held her in high esteem. He agreed that the coincidences of the antennae, the signals, the ovals, and the time patterns were too great to ignore.

But for the first time since he had known the president, Micah saw skepticism on his face when he told him of the near capture of Smith and of the tape being erased even as they held the recorder in their hands.

When Micah had finished, the president sat in silence for a long time. Then he said bluntly that he was under great pressure to replace Micah. He candidly informed him that Mandelbaum had shared the whole sequence of events with his own superiors and had described Micah as a superstitious fool. Then the president sat again in silence, unconsciously drawing tight geometrical patterns on a memo pad. Finally he looked up.

"Am I correct, Mike, in understanding that the only evidence that led you to this man's identity, or even to believing in his very existence, came from an astrologer and was based solely on her work?"

Micah nodded.

"And there are only two people who think they've seen him, and both are survivors of the first town who are probably overanxious to pin this thing on somebody?"

"That could be true, though I wouldn't describe Jess Barrett in that way."

"And you have three tapes, with funny sounds, which you admit are harmless?"

"They are simply side effects of the main weapon. The sound itself is not dangerous. And five of us heard the data read on the last tape before it was erased."

Weaver nodded once, his face still unreadable. "Do you have any other promising leads?"

"No, sir."

"Mike, you're the best man I've ever had. Your mind's cool, and you're not easily stampeded. But the one thing that's always bothered me is your religious and mystical interest. Now you come to me with a tale about astrology.

"I don't care what your personal feelings are; if they help you think straight, more power to you. If astrology can assist you in finding an answer to this mess, that's all right with me, too. But we can't put the destiny of this nation in the hands of an astrologer.

"Here's my decision. For the time being, you'll remain as chairman of the team. You're free to conduct the inquiry as you see fit. But you have to bear full responsibility for your actions. If you embarrass this administration, I'll fire you on the spot. Meanwhile, I'll take steps to make sure that total security is maintained and that those damned doctors in Atlanta don't talk to anyone.

"I want you to do two things. First, keep any mention of Jephthah Smith and this Vera Norman woman and her astrological moonshine out of the press. Don't go to television for your manhunt! The public's just beginning to recover from three major disasters. *Nobody* must know you suspect that a murderer's causing the epidemics. If it leaks out that this investigation's being conducted on the advice of a psychic crystal-ball gazer, the country will suffer lack of confidence and hysteria—and they'll be right!

"Second, I want you to hold a press conference on Wednesday. That'll be exactly two weeks since San Salino, and by then the public will be calmer—if we haven't had another outbreak. You'll take full responsibility for your words at the conference. I won't tell you what to say, but I've told you some things I don't want you to say. If you lie and you're caught at it, I'll dismiss you. Meanwhile, the full resources of the federal government will continue to be at your disposal." The president's eyes were opaque as shale. "Do you have anything else to say?"

Micah shook his head humbly.

"That's all, then. Except for one thing." There was a long, harrowing pause. "Good luck, Mike."

When he left the White House, the rain had stopped. He dismissed the limousine and walked the blocks to his apartment. By the time he arrived, his plans were made. He phoned his secretary in New York and instructed her to cancel the Wednesday meeting of the team but to call another for Tuesday, July 6.

Then he telephoned FBI headquarters in New York and learned that they had found no trace of Smith.

It was 11:34 P.M. Less than nine and a half days left.

Richard Humphrey, the most popular of NBC's news team, said on his Monday broadcast, "From here, on top of the NBC building in Radio City, one cannot see the changes the epidemics have caused in many American cities. Everything appears normal, with thousands, millions going their way, to work, play, shop, attend church. One cannot see the thousands who have left the metropolitan centers for the country. But their absence is felt in offices and industries.

"Each of the three times this mysterious and devastating plague has struck, the town has been larger than the one before. It was inevitable that people would conclude that the disease will spread to the large metropolitan centers. Many have decided not to wait until that happens.

"The silence of the team investigating the disasters has provided fertile ground for rumors to grow. If this flight from the cities is to be stemmed, we must have an up-to-date and honest report from the team immediately."

Gorman Medical Electronics was a sprawling city of laboratories, workshops, and storehouses located on Long Island Sound. Basically an electronics set-up, Gorman was the largest supplier of medical technology in the United States. It was probably the only place in the country possessing the needed combination of medical and electronic facilities.

Once settled in the laboratory assigned to them, Gustofson looked around the glass-and-linoleum room at the neatly arrayed stacks of equipment. Everything was indecently organized, which made him feel terribly uncomfortable. The only familiar note was the persistent odor from the hundreds of mouse cages being installed at their request.

"Well, Jock, what do you think? Any ideas?"

"Gus, as I understand it, we have three questions to answer. First: How does Smith generate this killing field? Second: How does the field destroy immune function? Third: How can we nullify the effects of the field and treat people exposed to it? Does that sound right to you?"

"Yup. I took the liberty of ordering these mice cages you've been turning your nose up at. The lymphocytes produced in mouse spleens respond well to culturing and resemble human cells. I think we should concentrate our work on trying to incapacitate the lymphocytes. You try to do it electronically; I'll try to do it chemically. Got any ideas?"

Jess grinned. "What if you added hydrochloric acid? I'll bet that would incapacitate them!"

Gus grinned back through his moustache. "I have to stay within the limits Dr. Brown found in the autopsies."

Within a few hours, the laboratory work was in full swing. The equipment that had been so neatly stored was scattered around the benches and on the floor, and cables and wiring trailed underfoot. It was now jumbled enough to suit even Gustofson. Jess sat in the middle of one of the biggest piles of equipment, a hot soldering iron at his side, entrenched in familiar territory. Gus supervised the installation of several huge incubators needed to keep the hundreds of lymphocyte cultures alive.

The two men worked all day. Finally the lateness of the hour forced them to stop. Jess went right to his hotel; Gus scuffled his way to a phone, ordered a cot brought in, and slept in the empty lab next door, oblivious to the bustle of technicians as they set up equipment and tended the cultures. The next morning both men returned to work early.

The incubators held dozens of flasks full of amber fluid, the rich nutrient in which the lymphocytes lived. Magnetic agitators constantly stirred the cultures, and the laboratory was permeated by the soft whirring.

Once the cultures were settled in their new surroundings, Jess and Gus embarked on a course of abusing them. Gus deftly added minute quantities of chemicals. Jess erected one elaborate set-up after another around culture bottles. His first step had been to build several devices which threw a field that interfered with tape-recording equipment. He succeeded in producing tapes that sounded very much like the ones he had found in Bensonville and Bridgeton. Then he turned the same fields on the lymphocyte cultures. He tried pure electric and magnetic fields, oscillating fields, crossed fields, and every combination that he could think of. He also exposed the hapless cultures to radiation of many frequencies, hoping to produce paralysis with a nonkilling dose.

By the end of the day, things looked pretty bleak. There seemed to be nothing that could duplicate the observed effects.

Jess straightened up, feeling the stiffness in his back. He noted a sandwich by his bench, untouched since it was delivered at noon. He picked it up and bit into it. The stale bread crunched. He chewed with distaste, pangs of hunger reminding him that he'd eaten nothing since a light breakfast. He gave up on the sandwich and tossed it into a trash can. "Gus, what do you say we go get something to eat?"

He stopped. The old man was bent over his bench, eyes shut and moustache fluttering as he snored. Jess smiled. Gus couldn't have slept too soundly here last night; perhaps it was better not to wake him.

Jess was hungry. The plant's cafeteria would be closed by now, but New York, with its hundreds of restaurants, was only a few minutes' drive away. And Vera Norman lived in Manhattan. He wanted to talk

283

to her about astrology anyway; he could combine the meal with business. He grinned wryly.

There was a phone in the lobby. He left the lab, fumbling in his pocket for a dime.

Tuesday morning, Petersen and Micah had talked again with the FBI director and the police commissioner. This time they met in Micah's suite at the Plaza. The subject of the meeting was their failure to find any trace of the killer.

"Well, the problem is that the man knows we're looking for him. All he has to do is settle someplace and stay put. And there are a lot of places this rabbit can hide. The city is one big warren."

Gebhart said grimly, "Well, given some time, of course, he's got to come out, and we can get him; but it's time we don't have, from what Dr. Maruyama says." Then he added, "There's only one way we can get more people looking for him. We've got to enlist the citizens themselves, publish his picture and offer a huge reward."

"But the president won't have people panicked by the suggestion that we want him for national security reasons. He vetoed TV and the press."

"Well, Smith's got to be hiding someplace, and it's likely he's in the home of a friend who's protecting him. We could smoke him out with a huge reward." The director was insistent.

"I've got it." For the first time there was excitement in the commissioner's voice. "Last night there was a brutal ax murder on the West Side. A man and his wife and child were literally hacked to pieces. Let's put Smith's picture out and say he's being sought as the suspect in that murder."

"That's great!" said Petersen. "Say he's a suspect in other murders, and we believe he was in hiding with that family when he went berserk and killed them, too. If he's staying with someone, that'll make them mighty nervous."

"Offer a hundred-thousand-dollar reward," Micah said softly. "Now what else can we do?"

Director Gebhart said, "Well, the only additional thing I can think of is to get the military police. Let them help on the streets."

"You'll have them," Micah said quickly. "I want every borough covered, but especially Manhattan. I want every single person checked at every bridge and tunnel, even at rush hour. I'll also ask the president to mobilize the National Guard. Commissioner, they'll be under your command. Will you be ready to give them orders by tomorrow morning?"

The commissioner whistled. "You *do* want this man!"

"Won't that kind of manhunt let people know this is a national security matter?"

"It might, except for one thing. I won't appear to have anything to do with the arrangements. You, Commissioner, must request the president to give you help. Inform the public that Smith is suspected of having slain twenty-five to thirty people in other cities."

The men rose in agreement.

It was noon, June 29. There were eight days left.

On Wednesday, June 30, at 2:00 P.M. in Washington, D.C., Micah held his press conference in a large, depressingly brown room in the State Department Building. Steel chairs for the newsmen were ranked on tiers. Television crews had set up their equipment long before Micah appeared, and the lectern bristled with microphones. The lights were blinding as he strode to the front of the room. The reporters were hostile over the news blackout that had left them empty-handed for so long.

Because two weeks had passed without another disaster, Micah began by saying that the members of his team had reason to believe the epidemic had spent its force. They considered that the epidemic was caused by a mutant strain of a virus with a seven-day incubation period. The fact that fourteen days had passed since the last outbreak could mean that the quarantines had been effective.

He also stated that they were still examining mountains of data and would not reach a definite conclusion for some time. The members of the team were at various places around the country and would not be meeting together in the near future. When he had anything more definite to report, he would call another press conference.

Veteran Washington reporters knew that Micah was covering something up, and they closed in for the kill. He was asked to name the members of the team.

He named the four outstanding men from the CDC, Dr. Goerke, and Dr. Gustofson.

"Yes? And who else?"

"What do you mean?"

"Dr. Maruyama, there are persistent rumors that you're consulting with the CIA and FBI. Does that mean you suspect the epidemics were artificially induced?"

"We are checking every possibility."

"Dr. Maruyama, there was a report out of Bensonville that a soldier dismantled a strange-looking antenna and delivered it to a radio lab for study. Then from Bridgeton we learned that another antenna was found. Are you considering that—"

"As I said, we are checking *every* possibility, however remote."

"Our office has received reliable information that Dr. Jess Barrett, NASA electronics expert, was called to Bridgeton and that he's been with the team ever since. Is that true?"

"I can't comment on that."

"Why not, Dr. Maruyama?"

"For reasons of national security."

"Then you do feel that these disasters were produced by enemies of the United States?"

"We are checking every possibility, however remote."

"How remote is the possibility that this is a matter of national security?"

"I cannot say."

Someone made an audible remark about inscrutable Orientals.

"Dr. Maruyama, it's been rumored that flying saucers were sighted near each of the three cities. Is Dr. Barrett on the team to investigate that? Are visitors from outer space trying to wipe us out with death rays?"

"We are checking every possibility, however remote."

The reporters, more frustrated than ever, pressed him with further questions. Those who had admired him for his previous forthrightness with the press were alarmed; those who hated him were delighted.

"Dr. Maruyama, we've received reliable reports that you and your team were in Denver last week and that medical supplies were stockpiled and ambulances gathered from all over the area. Does that mean you expected the foreign power to strike there next?"

"We did have information which caused us to be concerned for the welfare of the people of Denver. We were delighted that our concern proved groundless."

"What kind of information led you to think Denver might be hit by the epidemic?"

"That is a matter of national security."

"Then you suspect Russia?"

"I didn't say that."

"But you don't deny it either?"

"I have no information to make me think that the Soviet Union is involved in these epidemics."

"Then it's Red China murdering our people. Is the president planning any retaliatory measures?"

"Certainly not. The People's Republic is not in any way suspected of causing these tragedies. And I will not comment further on such questions, since I have already said that it is a matter of national security."

"Dr. Maruyama, we've received persistent reports that the team is unhappy under your leadership and is petitioning the president to appoint a scientist as chairman. Will you comment on that?"

"No."

"Sir, there are also rumors that you suspect not a foreign or extraterrestrial power, but an individual assassin. Now, we've heard that New York City has launched a great manhunt for an ax murderer. You've been in New York. Is there a connection? Do you suspect that the murderer is in New York, planning to release his germs—or whatever he does—there?"

This was the question he had been expecting and dreading. It was obviously impossible to keep complete security. Leaks were inevitable.

Micah had always despised politicians and government officials who lied to the public. He had sworn that he would not lie, that he would either tell the truth or refuse to answer. But, if he told the truth now, a hideous panic would occur, he would be replaced, and the search for Smith would be called off. If he lied, the truth would eventually come out, either because they failed to catch the murderer in time or because they *did* catch him and had to explain it.

So before the meeting, Micah had made up his mind what his response to this question would be. "How could one assassin cause such tragedies? The manhunt going on in New York has nothing to do with these epidemics. Ladies and gentlemen, when I have more information, I will call another conference."

He returned to New York immediately and found a telegram waiting for him. It was from the president.

Press conference poorly handled. Hope you get hold of this thing soon. J.H.W.

It was 8:00, June 30. Six and a half days were left.

On July 1, Mayor James McDonald was picked up by the police for having threatened a bearded young man. He was charged with public drunkenness and released after ten hours. He showed his federal permit and regained his .44 Magnum pistol.

Tass announced that Russia had appointed a group of distinguished scientists to make its own study of the American epidemics. The article stated that Dr. Alexei Bykovsky and Dr. Nikolai Nikolaev, two of the Soviet Union's most respected microbiologists, would head the group. Their services would be offered to the United States. The article also reminded the Russian people that there had been no outbreak in a socialist country, which it attributed to their superior sanitation and medical facilities.

On the same day Jess, too, had moved a cot into the laboratory and made futile efforts to sleep there. The persistent smell of mouse cages and solder combined to keep him at least partly awake most of the night. Finally, with the newly rising sun still hidden by a thick bank of fog rolling in off the sound, he stumbled out of bed and dressed. Gus was still snoring peacefully, so he filled a pot with water for instant coffee, mounted it over a Bunsen burner, and sat down to try to sort out his thoughts.

The lab was typical except for a window. Gorman liked to maintain some contact with the outside world, but even this concession was blunted, for the glass was heavily tinted. Direct sunlight could not be tolerated in an electronics lab; nor could outside air, so the window was sealed. A recording thermometer on the wall showed a monotonously flat line at sixty-eight degrees. Absolute climate control was necessary for many delicate jobs.

Around Jess lay the signs of his work: benches littered with jumbled circuit boards, components, oscilloscopes, pulse generators, meters, and power supplies.

For some time he stared out the window, trying to come up with something radically new. The sun began to burn off the fog and the day to assert itself.

Perhaps, he thought, he was on the wrong track. Instead of trying to recreate the forces that had caused the disaster, he should be analyzing the forces the planets produced to determine their properties. Yet, no matter what they proved to be, he could not understand how they could be dangerous. While he was at NASA, accurate measurements had been made of the forces in space. They were not negligible, but he did not see how they could have the sort of effect he was searching for, no matter how highly they were amplified.

He found himself wondering whether the planets emitted anything at all. Perhaps, instead, they changed something already there. The word *ether* came swimming out of his memory.

The whole concept of ether was outmoded and derided by modern scientists. Yet, it had never really been disproved. In the early days of the century, physicists were baffled by light. Sound needed a medium to travel through. Did light? On the premise that it did, they invented a theoretical substance they called the *luminiferous ether,* a thin, elastic material. They theorized that it filled the vast reaches of all space, penetrating even the interstices between atoms. They believed it acted as the light-bearing medium.

Many experiments had been designed to detect the ether; all had failed. When Albert Einstein published his theory of relativity, the idea was dropped. Scientists had not proved that the ether did or did not exist. They had no more need for ether because it had been demonstrated that light did not need a medium.

But suppose that ether did exist?

Suppose it had an effect on everything: mind, matter, attitudes, health?

Suppose the planets influenced each other, not by the energy they emitted, but by their positions, by the way they affected the ether around them?

Jess knew the idea was dangerously close to lunacy, that at the very least it would be considered bizarre. Yet scientists spoke of the "fabric of space" and conjectured that space was "bent" by the presence of matter.

If such a thing *did* exist, its structure would be altered by the very presence of the stars and planets. The ether through which the planets moved would bear a pattern impressed by the fixed stars.

Jess was excited. If that were true, the effects of the planets would vary with the location because the underlying ether would be different. Well, that agreed with the astrologers. They maintained that the planets had different influences according to which sign they fell in.

But there was more. Jess felt sure that if such a space-filling fabric really did exist, he himself could devise a way to trap a dangerous influence in a specific area and amplify it. And if *he* could, *Smith* could.

He stretched and found he was stiff. He had been standing with his foot on the window ledge for an hour.

Moving abruptly to the workbench, he cleared an area, pulled out a ream of paper, and began his calculation. He started by constructing a mathematical model to describe the ether. Then he tried to develop a description of how mass might affect it and how this effect could be amplified. To his surprise, it seemed to work.

By the time Gus padded silently into the lab, Jess had sketched the outline of a mathematical proof that such a thing was possible. He had vague ideas of how to translate the theory into a solid apparatus, but that would have to wait.

"Jess, have you been fiddling with this culture?"

Jess swiveled around in surprise, not having noticed the old doctor's entrance. "No, of course not, Gus. What's wrong with it?"

"It's murky. Must be some sort of contamination. Damn."

Gustofson removed the culture from the incubator, carried it to a microscope to examine it. Jess, absorbed in his work, hardly noticed.

"Goddamnit, Jess, it's bacteria!"

"Huh? *What* is bacteria?"

"The culture, Jess. It's murky with bacteria. Something must have gotten into it."

"So it's ruined?" Jess wondered vaguely why Gus was bothering him with the news.

"Of course it's ruined. But Jess, lymphocytes *eat* bacteria. Anything that fell into the culture should have been gobbled right up. But this fluid is milky with them. Come on, take a look."

Jess did. He closed one eye and peered through the microscope. "I suppose all the white cells must be dead."

"No, Jess, they aren't. Don't you see?"

Jess searched, and then he saw a lymphocyte. It

looked perfectly healthy, but it was mobbed by much-smaller specks, bacteria. Yet the killer cell, which should have been feasting on the bacteria, just sat there doing nothing as the fluid around it filled up with the tiny parasites.

He sat back. "You're right, Gus. These lymphocytes have been deactivated. Which culture is that?" His curiosity was aroused. It was just like Bensonville. Bob's blood had filled with billions of bacteria while his lymphocytes did nothing.

"Number eighty-three. One of yours. What did you do to it?"

Jess consulted his notes. "I treated it with radiation that produced a signal like that on the Bensonville tape. Lord! I guess it worked!"

The rest of the day, Jess was unable to return to his promising theoretical work. Instead, he and Gus labored over the inactive culture, and by evening both were so tired they could hardly stand. They had determined several things. The lymphocytes had lost the ability to recognize bacteria. There were minute changes in the free-floating ion levels in the culture and in the protoplasm of the cells themselves. The deformability of the cells—that is, their ability to squeeze through tight places—had dropped noticeably, too.

Gus rubbed his eyes. "Dammit, Jess, we're on the right track, I'm sure. But I have to quit for a while. Too old, can't see straight." He sagged into a chair, looking disgusted with his frailty.

Jess gazed at him sympathetically. Gus's normally bright green eyes were so streaked with red that they looked like psychedelic marbles.

"Gus, you get some sleep. I'm going to take Vera to dinner. When I come back this evening, we'll do some more work."

Gus smiled. "That sleep bit sounds good. What are you seeing Vera about?" He suddenly realized the question was foolish.

Jess smiled. "Well, I have to learn more about these planetary forces, don't I? Especially how they act, what they do."

"Okay, Jock, have a good time."

Gus watched the big man head for the door and gave a sad thought to the years when he'd been young enough to work a twelve-hour day and then go out to dinner. He stood, feeling the age in his legs, shook his head, and started for the cafeteria.

At dinner, Vera was glum. She told Jess she'd found only one new fact about Jephthah: He was searching for something. And she was having unusual difficulty in determining what it was.

"Have you come up with anything, Jess?"

"Quite a lot, Vera. But not enough, I'm afraid. We've found a complex electromagnetic field which, when applied in great strength, prevents lymphocytes from recognizing bacteria. In other words, a few days after exposure, the cells can't function, though they're normal in all other ways. Gus will do most of the work on that; it's out of my field. He found some ion imbalances in the cell protoplasm that he thinks are significant. Tomorrow he wants to try to induce the same differences chemically. He hopes that in a few days he may be able to find a way to prevent it from happening—"

"That's wonderful!" Vera interrupted.

"—in mice!" finished Jess. "It's not as wonderful as it sounds. We have a way one signal will disrupt one type of lymphocyte. But there are many other types of immunologically competent cells in the body. Granulocytes, monocytes—"

"I see. And other things, too, if I remember my college biology. Inter—"

"Interferon. We don't know where it comes from, or why Smith's device should stop its production. What it amounts to is that we've solved a very small part of the total problem."

"Then you don't believe that Smith is using the malefic influences of the planets? They do blanket the earth. If you could only figure out the way that he amplified those forces."

"Yes, I do think that's the way he did it, Vera. I

293

have a theory, too complex to explain, that shows how the interplay of planetary forces can form the same sort of field with which I stopped the lymphocytes. You see, the power drain forms a sort of resonating cavity that acts as a giant trap—"

Vera laughed. "You're over my head. I'll take your word for it. How long before you can get something useful out of it?"

"Maybe six months. Remember, a theory just establishes that something is possible; it doesn't tell you how to do it."

"That's too long, Jess," Vera said quietly.

"I know. I'm hoping that I can come up with a way to stop it electrically at the source, but so far all I have is the outline of a theory."

Vera heard the grimness in Jess's voice; then his eyes were suddenly preoccupied. He took out a pad. "I wonder—?" He began making notations.

Vera smiled. As far as Jess was concerned, she was for the moment a million miles away.

Later, back at Vera's, they called Micah and learned that the gigantic dragnet had turned up bank robbers, drug importers, and assorted thugs, but not Smith. The police doubted he was still in New York; Vera insisted that he was.

It was late when Jess said good-bye and returned to the lab. It was just an hour short of Friday, July 2, and a little more than five days remaining.

22

FRIDAY MORNING, Micah called the president from his suite at the Plaza to inform him that the manhunt had failed so far. He asked that at the very least the government be evacuated from Washington. But he urged the president to be prepared to turn off the entire power grid between 6:30 and 8:30 A.M. on July 7.

"That's the governor's business."

"Sir, the power grid crosses state lines. It covers the entire East, from Montreal south."

Silence. Finally, "Mike, tell me again why those two hours are so important."

"Well, sir," said Micah uncomfortably, "because at that time the full moon exactly squares Saturn, and Mars is rising in opposition to Uranus."

Silence.

"Mr. President, ah, it's hard for me to explain just why those things are so dangerous, but Vera Norman says—"

"You've got to give me more reason to believe this story than the word of an astrologer. What evidence do you have—what *hard evidence?*"

"We found those ovals of death."

"Mike, we've been through all this before. The fact that the deaths form a geometric pattern means nothing. Besides, there was no oval in the third city."

"But we had the two antennae."

"There are thousands of antennae in every city. And what you allege to be the second antenna was only a lot of aluminum tape."

"But, sir, you know we have the two cassettes of that sound."

"From only two of the three cities. And when you play them, nothing happens to anyone."

"No, sir, but Uranus and Mars are not—"

"Mike, what makes you feel that this mad genius of yours is likely to try to use the power system?"

"In San Salino there was a power drop at what proved to be the critical time, and everyone inside the area covered by the power system died a week later."

"And there was a power outage in Denver at what you called a critical time, and nothing happened."

Micah was desperate. "We know he's going to use the grid because we heard the tape of his voice speculating on exactly how he was going to do it. Five of us heard him, sir, including two FBI men."

"And you no longer have the tape."

"No, sir, he erased the tape with his machine, and now we have only the sound on that tape, too."

"And when you play that sound, does anybody get sick?"

"Of course not, but the moon is not squaring Saturn, and—I *know* this sounds incredible, Mr. President."

Prolonged silence.

"Mike, keep looking for your man. I'll think about turning off the power grid. I'll talk it over with some advisers and have a decision for you by Tuesday night."

It was Friday, July 2. Five more days.

On Saturday, when Jess learned that Smith had not been found, he redoubled his efforts. But finally, aghast, he realized without a doubt that it would require years, not days, to reach any conclusions from his speculations. Thwarted by the lack of time, haunted by his impotence, he called Vera, and they made plans to go to church the next morning. Shortly after, Micah phoned Jess with the same suggestion.

It was Saturday, July 3, with four days left.

When Micah picked Jess up, Vera was already with him. They were all dejected to the point of desperation and said little. Police were everywhere in the streets.

The driver took them to the Madison Avenue Presbyterian Church, where bright July sunshine flooded through the stained-glass windows and the organ swelled. For the first time since the fifties, churches were full again; the threat of the epidemics had sent people back to their faiths in great numbers.

Jess had ambivalent feelings. He had always been comforted by the assurance he felt that God was still in control of his universe. But now memories came to him of apocalyptic biblical prophecies. Was Smith the first of the Four Horsemen? He thought of the ten lost tribes of Israel. Would the United States become one more of the lost empires of history? In silence before the service, for the first time in years, he prayed intensely.

Vera leaned over and whispered, "I can't believe God will let this thing happen."

Jess grimly thought to himself that God had let the Nazis kill six million Jews. He said nothing.

The sermon was based on the story of Jacob seeking a wife. The preacher told of how Jacob had worked seven years for Rachel, only to be given Leah in marriage instead. So he had worked seven years longer to receive Rachel. The clergyman said that on this Independence Day, the United States was still searching and working for its ideal: freedom for all. After the benediction, Jess and Micah stood up.

Jess realized that Vera was still seated, her head bent. He stood waiting for her to finish what appeared to be a prayer. Then he saw that she was scribbling furiously on the back of the bulletin; while he watched, she drew a circle and began to place symbols in it.

Jess tapped her on the shoulder. She nodded apologetically and followed them. In the limousine she said, "When Dr. Bromley began talking about Jacob seeking a wife, I suddenly knew what it was that Jephthah is seeking."

"What do you mean?"

"You remember I found in his chart the fact that right now he's hunting for something, and I couldn't figure out what it was? Well, because I've been so concerned about these terrible disasters, I haven't been treating Smith as a human being. I forgot that these progressions are having an effect on him *personally*, too. You see, not only did his moon pass over Venus a few weeks ago, but it's coming to exact conjunction with that eclipsed sun, and, Jess, *it is squaring his Mars!*" She was speaking slowly and emphatically. "But that isn't all. Mars is in Leo and slowing down to go retrograde. It will go stationary on Wednesday morning to a conjunction with Smith's natal eclipse!"

Micah said wearily, "O.K., I'll bite. What does that mean?"

"It means that he is—well, he's 'horny.' "

Micah looked at her in amazement. "Why is Jephthah Smith's love life of interest to us?"

"Micah, you don't understand. Our superman, our Messiah, our new Adam is coming to the realization that it's very hard to found a new race without an Eve. He's looking for his consort! It's a long shot, I admit, but I think it might give us a break. You see, for two people to meet and have any kind of relationship, even as friends, certainly as lovers, their charts must mesh in some way. When it comes to wives and husbands, the charts must mesh tightly, something like two gears fitting together."

Micah shook his head. "I still don't get it."

"I think I do," Jess said. "Vera took what she knew about Smith and constructed a chart that led to his birth date and our identifying him. Well, she's saying that by using *his* chart and the fact that his lady friend must have one which in some ways fits into it, she may be able to come up with the lady's chart. Right, Vera?"

"Exactly. I'm going to try to find that chart and give you her birth date. It won't be easy, but *if* I can get it, maybe you can find her and watch her until he finds her."

"Mike, you know the best way to find a needle in a haystack?"

"Yes, burn the damn thing. But we can't burn New York."

Jess smiled ruefully. "Well, you're right, that is the

best way. But the second-best way is to pass a powerful magnet over the stack, and the needle will leap right out. This woman could be the magnet that will pull our genius out of his hiding place."

"But even if I find her chart and her birth date, we still have to identify her. That could be a dreadfully time-consuming job."

"We could use the National Data Center," said Micah.

"The what?"

Micah looked chagrined that he'd let something slip out. "It's a monstrosity we inherited from the previous administration. It's an amazing thing, actually, but frightening and probably unconstitutional: a huge information-storage center in Washington, where every bit of available data on our citizens is collected. It stores all the census information and contains among other things the birth dates of everyone in the United States. If the woman we're looking for was born in this country, her birth is recorded there."

"I didn't know there was such a thing," exclaimed Jess.

"It grew out of the census at first and then was expanded to include all kinds of data. There are terminals in most large cities. There's one here, and with my security clearance, I have access to it. Get me that date, and I'll probably be able to come up with the woman's name and latest address."

"Drop me home," Vera said, "and I'll try. It'll be harder than the last time. There are so many possibilities, and I only have two more days after today."

The *Chicago Sun-Times* in its book section reported that the Apollo Publishing Company had contracted with one Alfred Pastore, a survivor of the Bensonville epidemic, to write a book on his experiences during the death of the little town. Since all information on the epidemics was still classified and vigorously suppressed, the *Sun-Times* speculated that it would be quite a while before the book could be published.

On Monday, police and military personnel were still checking every car on the highways and bridges leading into and out of Manhattan, and they began to accost anyone on the street who looked even a little like Smith. The result was a hopeless traffic tie-up. The flow across the bridges and through the tunnels, which was normally bad and at rush hour hideous, became normally hideous and at rush hour impossible. Traffic backed up all the way across the island.

All evening, drivers swore as they were caught in immobile lines, still dozens of blocks from the bridges. Only occasionally did a car inch ahead. The entire island of Manhattan—indeed, the entire New York area—was jammed like a watch dipped in molasses. In this horrible morass, Smith couldn't possibly leave the city even if he wanted to. The police came up empty-handed.

That evening the TV newscaster Jonathan Ogburn departed from his usual format and gave a bitter commentary. He reported a steadily rising tension in the mood of the American people. Recent events in New York, including a manhunt so incredibly out of proportion to its alleged purpose, had made life there impossible. This in turn affected the whole country. It was time the government let the people in on the secret.

The situation in New York grew steadily closer to mass hysteria, and Jess Barrett knew there was not enough time. His work was so intriguing, he felt hard put to ignore it, but he had to admit that with just two days remaining, he was not going to find anything.

His theoretical work had emerged from a mountain of notes and jumbled thoughts into a clear-cut and elegant theory, but he wouldn't have time to prepare it for presentation, let alone try to apply it.

The theory made a lot of sense to Jess. He had a handle on something that could be the method Smith used, but he would not know for sure until he could test it, and he could not do that until he had finished the theoretical work, and he could not do *that* for quite some time. Therefore, it was futile to continue this line of work. Frustrated, Jess went for a walk.

He strode around the Gorman grounds, his face set in thought, his long strides eating up distance. Finally he hurried back to the lab.

"Gus, this is silly. We aren't going to achieve anything."

Gustofson looked up. "I'm kind of surprised you'd say that, Jess, considering what we've discovered so far. Why, we have a clue to the workings of the entire immunity system."

"Yes, Gus, but time—how much time?"

The doctor looked embarrassed. "Two, maybe three years. Not soon enough, is it? Well, Jock, you sound like you have something in mind. Care to share it with me?"

"Gus, you remember that power failure they had here in the sixties, when the whole coast went dark? What if that happened again? Say, the day after tomorrow?"

"Aha! Do you think you can arrange it?"

"Well, the president is the only one who can order it shut down, and Mike says he won't do it. So I think we have to consider the possibility of sabotage. That big failure was the result of just one circuit breaker flipping. If I got a good look at the system, I'll bet I could figure out something. Want to come along?"

Gustofson stood up. "Where to?"

"Purcell Bay. There's a generator system there, one of the biggest in the United States. It's only a few miles down the sound. I want to talk to the head engineer."

The two drove down the seashore road through an industrial district. The plant sat among towering mountains of coal. Bulldozers grunted up and down, shaping them for consumption; conveyor belts constantly ate them away, carrying fuel to the powerful furnaces; and loaded railroad cars continually added to the supply.

Jess and Gus showed their government credentials

and were ushered inside. After some delay a heavyset man wearing neatly pressed work clothes and a yellow hard hat appeared. "I'm the chief engineer, Bill Dowles. What can I do for you?" There was a trace of suspicion in his smile.

"Mr. Dowles, we're from the Federal Power Commission. We've had reports that you people are worried about holding the power output to the city this summer. If we have a power failure with the present situation in New York, it would be bad news. Do you see any potential trouble spots?"

The engineer grinned. "Oh, we're running at full load now. Summer's always the highest load because everybody's using his air conditioner. But you Feds don't need to worry. We can handle it. All the equipment's in good shape, and with the new plant at Medford, we aren't under any particular strain. No danger of anything breaking down. Even if it did, it wouldn't matter much."

Jess felt a pang. "Why is that, Mr. Dowles?"

The engineer grinned again. "Let me give you a quick lesson on power supplies." He led them through a door into the station itself, to a catwalk above an enormous room. Below them great machines hummed with a deep, contented roar. The room vibrated with power. Huge pipes and conduits crisscrossed the floor, walls, and ceilings, and the roof contained several monitoring panels.

Jess realized he didn't know much about commercial electricity. There was a world of difference between the sophisticated electronics at which he was so adept and the huge, brute-force sort of facilities here. He followed Dowles through a door at the far end of the generator room.

"This is the master control room."

The engineer gestured at a huge, mural-like panel that covered the entire wall, a good fifteen feet across. It was a map of the eastern United States, pocked with lights and crosshatched with lines.

"This is the power grid that covers the United States from Maine to Georgia. Each of the blue lights marks a generating station. The red areas are prime consumers. These lines"—he pointed—"represent primary delivery routes. As you can see, every station is interlocked with every other. This is achieved through switching stations, marked here in green. If any one facility should fail anywhere in this system, these switching stations would immediately transfer current flow to the stricken area. It's all controlled by a computer, and it would happen so fast that the lights wouldn't even flicker. We can sustain a fairly substantial loss of generating capacity without any customer suffering more than a mild voltage loss."

"What about sabotage?" asked Gus. "It'd be just like some idiot to try it, with things as messed up as they are right now."

"Not much chance of that. For one thing, it's all pretty well guarded. But even if someone did blow up a station, we have dozens of secondary delivery routes. It would take simultaneous sabotage of a dozen plants to even produce a brownout, and I doubt that you could black out any area unless you hit every station on the grid. I assure you, gentlemen, that the system's been thoroughly revamped since the great blackout of sixty-five. It'll never happen again."

Jess looked distinctly worried. "Can you show us some of the equipment, Mr. Dowles? I imagine you're right, but we have to tell the big boys we checked it all out."

Dowles gave them a sympathetic smile. "I know how it is. Sure. Let's go take a look at the switching complex. If you men know anything about electricity, I'm sure you'll be able to see that nothing short of an atomic war can break down the grid."

After an hour of examining the machinery in the plant, Jess turned to Gus. "The man's right. The genius who designed this system made it foolproof. There is no way to sabotage it."

Tuesday the police carried on such a frantic search that New Yorkers, long inured to annoyances and delays, finally began to rebel. Everyone wanted the ax murderer caught, but no one wanted to wait an hour and a half to get across a bridge or through a tunnel.

All through the day, members of the team arrived at Kennedy Airport. Because of the congestion in the city, there was only one way to get the men to their scheduled meeting. As each arrived, he was ushered into a bubble copter and flown into Manhattan.

It was a revealing flight. They could see the nightmarish traffic jam below and sense the desperation. One by one the copters landed on the giddy strip 900 feet above the city streets.

By 8:00, when the meeting began, the full moon was rising. Perhaps it was the moon which gave the city its mood that night. Or perhaps it was the haunting fear of the epidemics or the fruitless search for the mysterious killer. But there was a restlessness. Families gathered together, locked their doors more securely. The air held a sense of expectancy, even of dread. Probably it *was* the moon, riding among the scattered clouds like a beautiful lady, on her stately way to her rendezvous with the fateful aspect.

And far out in space, now almost directly overhead, was Saturn. Slowly, sluggishly, Saturn moved on his wide sweep around the sun. Like the baleful eye of a demon, exhibiting a cold yellow malevolence, he waited for the moon to form the square that would release his fearful power.

Below the horizon, still far below, was the bright red eye of Mars. At 7:30 he would rise to glare at the city, and while New Yorkers began their day, invisible lines of force would leap across the miles to deal a painless, unperceived blow to millions of Americans. A week later they would die.

Of course, New Yorkers thought little if anything about Saturn or Mars or Uranus, that evil planet so far away that only the nonhuman eye of a telescope could see it. But the moon bore down on their consciousness. She was swollen to unreal size by illusion. And she shed her china light down on those who knew of no reason to fear her.

Yet for all her beauty, men had always feared the

moon. She had smiled on untold millions of lovers, but she unnerved others. The superstitious of the world had always associated the full moon with madness, and police statistics often seemed to confirm this theory.

The sophisticated citizens of America's largest city thought they had outgrown such fears. But in reality those moon fears were only driven into the subconscious. For many the result would be only a vague depression. For others her effect would even be a stimulation to romance. But police officers were readying themselves for a rough night. The full moon always brought a rash of rapes and murders.

Officer Manuel Chavez would have a night he would never forget.

The team was scheduled to meet in the old Plaza Hotel on Central Park South. Vera and Jess decided to have dinner there in the Oak Room before the meeting. On the way they exchanged their mutual frustrations over not having found anything of value.

Vera leaned back in the soft, cushioned chair and sighed. "It's so beautiful here. But tonight—I just can't believe that we've all failed to find Smith."

Jess nodded as the waiter came to take their order. Cocktails relaxed them, and they visited quietly, avoiding the horror they saw looming before them. After salad, they sat in silence, watching the other diners. An old man with a magnificent shock of white hair read the *Wall Street Journal* as he dined on raw steak. An elegant young black couple held hands while having their drinks, and two old dowagers frowned at them.

"Oh, Jess, it's so impossible. It can't happen. Maybe the police have picked him up by now."

Jess said nothing for a long time and then, ignoring her wistful hope, said, "Vera, I don't know what the morning will bring, but I hope you know—I'm not much at talking about feelings, but—"

She took his huge hand and held it to her face. Tears brimmed her eyes. She kissed his hand. "It's

305

the same for me, Jess. You know it's the same for me."

At 7:55 they left the Oak Room, walked through the ornate lobby to the elevators, with their gold and mirrored doors, and took a car to the second floor. There security guards checked their identification and admitted them to a meeting room. The thick carpeting, the comfortable chairs, the elegance of the room made their purpose tonight seem more unreal than ever. The other members of the team were already there. Mandelbaum's impressive figure had withered from tension and fatigue. Ogden and Fornier looked rested, and Goerke fresh but solemn. Petersen was haggard, his eyes sunken and red from lack of sleep. Adams was neat and unusually subdued. Brown was grave. Only McDonald was absent.

Micah began immediately. "You know most of the facts. We traced the disasters to the actions of one man, identified by Miss Norman and the FBI as Jephthah Smith. We came very close to apprehending him, but he escaped. Some of you aren't aware that the manhunt for the ax murderer is in reality a search for Smith. So far the police and federal officers haven't found a trace of him. We know that he's in this area, probably in Manhattan. At three minutes after seven tomorrow morning, he's going to plug his infernal device into some wall outlet and kill eighty million people.

"If he succeeds, it will be the worst tragedy in recorded history, and the United States will cease to exist as a serious world power. Smith will then go on with his plan to kill most of humanity. Our only reason for being here now is to find out if any of you have ideas on how to prevent this holocaust. You've had time to study and think. Let's pool what we've learned.

"Dr. Mandelbaum, will you speak for your CDC team?"

Mandelbaum was having a hard time. The message summoning them to the meeting had outlined the events of the week, the near capture of Smith, the story of the tape recorder, the signal that erased the evidence concerning the power system, and the fact that Vera thought the killer was searching for his consort. Mandelbaum's ego was bruised, but he had never been as impervious to Vera's performance as he pretended. He was deeply impressed by her prediction of the disaster in San Salino and by the fact that her theories regarding Smith were being validated.

"Mr. Chairman, we have uncovered no new medical facts. We have no reasonable explanation and no suggestions as to how to prevent its happening again."

Micah turned to Goerke. He shook his head sadly.

"Gus?"

The old doctor stood, and his knees creaked in the stillness. "Well, I have a lot of really exciting stuff, but as this late hour, I don't think it'll do us much good." He looked at the others somberly. "The bad news isn't mitigated by the good news, so I'll give it to you fast. Jess and I demonstrated that immunological function can be suspended by an electromagnetic field. I don't pretend to understand how Jess generated that field, but he proved mathematically that it can be done using the interplay of planetary forces.

"So we believe that our—what would Mandy call it?—our 'working hypothesis' is correct. The results of this work could mean great hope for the future. For instance, I think we'll soon be able to suspend immunological function so that organ transplants will take. We've traced the mechanism of the inactivation to the balance of mineral ions in the blood. Eventually, we might have been able to artificially strengthen this balance enough to resist the effects of Smith's device. It's just too damn bad that the experiments involve so much time. It takes one whole week to prepare a single culture.

"I guess all I can say is that we succeeded in demonstrating the practicality of our theory, and that's all. We don't have any suggestions for remedial action."

Everyone in the room was silent. Micah looked at Jess. "Anything to add?"

Jess shook his head. "I think we've uncovered a whole new field of physics, but there simply isn't enough time to exploit it. Any possible results are months away." He sighed. "Given three months, I could build the device that Jephthah Smith has. Everything I've found suggests that he can simply plug it into the grid. There's no scientific way to stop him. We *must* turn off the grid. It's the only way."

Brown said, "Can't we ask people to go into the subways for a while, like bomb shelters?"

Jess grimaced. "Jordan, the subways are run with electricity, and it's electricity he uses to create the field that amplifies those celestial energies."

"Jess," said Ogden, raising his head, "to be able to use the entire power grid, he must have a physically tremendous machine."

"I don't know for sure, Doctor, but my guess is that he doesn't need anything larger than an attaché case or at the most a small suitcase."

Goerke interrupted the conversation to say, "Mr. Chairman, I don't know anything about manhunts or electronics, but I want to say that if Jess and Gus live to develop the things they've uncovered, they'll benefit humanity to an incalculable degree. I vote to ask President Weaver to turn off the grid."

"Petersen?" Micah asked.

"Nothing."

"Vera?"

"Mike, I still hope to find the chart for Smith's 'girl friend' and give you her birth date so you can identify her. It's turned out to be very difficult. I've eliminated a lot of possibilities, and that's all. I'll keep working tonight."

"Brad?"

"Nothing."

Again the group fell into the silence of hopelessness.

Micah finally spoke. "When I asked you to come for this last meeting, I told each of you to buy a round-trip ticket so you could be out of the city before the danger period. I want you all to leave now; limousines and copters are waiting. Only two possibilities are left, and they're my responsibility. I'll need your help, Jess," he said apologetically.

"Of course, Mike."

They rose slowly and prepared to leave. There was embarrassment, and some refused to look at the others.

Dr. Gustofson remained seated with Mike and Vera and Jess. Petersen gazed out the window.

Adams stared at the FBI man's back, snapped his attaché case shut, thinking of the plane waiting to take him back to Honduras. He made up his mind. "Bill, you need another man on the street? I'm an agent, not a cop, but if any team can catch the bastard, it's you and me!"

Petersen turned to look at him. "Brad," he said huskily, "I think we have every bit as good a chance as Laurel and Hardy, but if you're crazy enough to stay, there's nobody I'd rather have with me."

"Gentlemen, I have something to say, and I believe I am entitled to say it." Mandelbaum spoke in a loud voice. He licked his lips. "Since Dr. Maruyama took over this investigation—no, even before that—from the time Dr. Gustofson and I met, I have treated him with disrespect—probably because I'm jealous of his brain power.

"From the beginning I've challenged Dr. Maruyama's leadership, and I even tried to have him removed.

"In addition, I deprecated Miss Norman's invaluable contribution and was discourteous to her.

"I cannot let this meeting end without apologizing, and since I consider that this team needs its head physician present, I am staying in New York."

"By God, Mandy, you may be a son of a bitch," Gus said, "but you are one hell of a son of a bitch!"

Fornier, Ogden, Goerke, and Brown shook hands and left, looking guilty.

"Gus, your limousine's waiting," said Micah.

"Nope, I'm too tired to travel tonight. Besides, how could you young fellas get along without my sage advice?"

"Well, there's work to be done. Let's get busy!"

Jess eyed him. "Mike, you said there were still two things to do. What are they?"

The telephone rang.

"That's probably one of them now. I asked the president to turn off the power grid. He's to give me his answer this evening."

The telephone rang again.

Vera asked, "Mike, do you think he'll do it?"

"No." Micah picked up the phone and murmured his name.

"Mike, this is Commissioner Serafin. Mike, by God, we caught him! We caught the killer!"

Micah's knees went weak, and he sat down. "You caught Smith? Where?"

Vera sank back in her chair; Jess let out a bark of disbelief; Petersen grinned at Adams; Mandelbaum wiped his damp face; and Gustofson closed his eyes as though ready now to sleep for a month.

"Mike, one of our rookies, Manuel Chavez, only on patrol for two weeks, received a complaint that a man was acting strangely in a bar. He went in and found Smith. He's taking him to the precinct station, and I'm on my way there. Have that reward ready, Mike!"

"But, Commissioner, are you sure it's Smith? It doesn't sound like him to be caught that easily."

"Of course we're sure! Chavez told the captain he has a positive ID and even a confession."

"Fantastic, Commissioner," said Micah slowly. "You've been magnificent. I'm sure the president will want to speak to you personally."

"Well, no need for that, Mike, but it does make me pretty proud of my boys."

Rookie patrolman Manuel Chavez was eager to make a name for himself. His partner in the patrol car was fifty years old and bored. He let Chavez drive while he either slumped in the front seat or slept in the back.

He'd been sound asleep when the bartender had flagged them down and told Chavez that a man in the bar was acting strangely. Chavez wakened his partner and told him he was going to investigate. The older man sat up. "O.K., kid, go ahead. I'll cover you from the door."

Inside the bar the man was slobbering drunk. He was downing another double Scotch when Chavez tapped him on the shoulder. As he turned, Chavez saw dried blood on his shirt and jacket.

"Cop, huh? Hi, cop! Siddown and have a drink. I suppose you want me, huh?"

"Should I want you, mister? Have you done something wrong?"

"Tell him about all those people you killed, Mac. Tell him what you told me," said the bartender.

"Sure, I'll tell 'im. I killed thousands'a people. Greatest killer of all time. You know why I do it? I like to wash people die."

"You're covered with blood, mister. Have you killed anybody tonight?"

"Yeah, but I din' mean to. Wasn't gonna kill anymore. But that girl laughed at me, an' I won' take that. Followed her, tol' her apologizhe; she laughs again. So I hit her with my ax—" His speech trailed off into incoherent sounds.

"Mister, why don't you show me where that girl is?"

"Sure. I din' mean to kill her. Show you."

But when the man saw the body of the girl lying outside in the alley, he seemed to sober a little and tried to get away. Officer Chavez had to subdue him alone, and since Chavez was only five feet eight, that was a problem, for the killer was over six feet tall and weighed at least 200 pounds.

The commissioner was happy as he walked up the steps into the old precinct house. He chuckled to himself and winked at the chief inspector. "You know, Tamburelli, I don't say there's anything wrong with those federal types. They do a good job; they really do. But when the chips are down, by God, it's the cop who comes through!"

The captain and several lower-grade officers were standing outside the interrogation room. They shouted in their excitement, congratulated one another, assured

311

that the whole precinct would share in the glory of this moment.

"Now, where's Chavez? Where's that great kid?"

The captain grinned proudly. "He's inside with his collar. Kid knows he's made the collar of the century, but he's going right through the regular procedure!"

The commissioner pulled the picture of Smith out of his pocket. "Well, Smith, we nailed you after all," he said to it. He never noticed the sudden silence, the shifting eyes. He went into the interrogation room.

Chavez was sitting with his back to the door, and across the desk was a hulking blond man splattered with blood.

The commissioner's smile faded into a look of perplexity, then of utter dismay. "Who is *that?*"

Chavez stood up proudly. "Sir, this is the ax murderer. He's given me a full confession. I even recovered his ax."

"But, goddamnit, that's not Smith!"

"Uh, no, sir." He consulted his notes. "His name is Hornsby, Theodore Hornsby. But he's the man we—"

The commissioner found his voice. "Goddamnit, Chavez, you stupid rookie, *you've caught the real ax murderer!*"

23

AFTER MICAH GOT THE SECOND CALL from the commissioner, he said to the others, tight-lipped, "Well, it's up to me. I have to persuade the president to turn off the grid."

He dialed and in a few seconds was talking to the chief executive. He reported that the dragnet had not produced the suspect. Then he bluntly asked the president to order the power grid turned off for two hours in the morning.

"Mike, you're the best man I've ever worked with, and I've enjoyed it. I've trusted you. You were always supremely rational. But since you've been on this plague problem, you've gone mystic and—and peculiar."

"Sir," said Micah, "Dr. Mandelbaum is here with me—"

"I'm replacing you. Tomorrow I'll announce to the press that Dr. Calder, my scientific adviser, will take over, that you've been forced to resign for health reasons. I want you to go to the Bahamas for a long rest."

Micah turned cold. It scarcely occurred to him that his own career was finished. The important fact was that he had been unable to save the United States.

"Mr. President, you've got to listen to me. I've given you a full report. You know the evidence. Sound, factual evidence!"

"Yes, Mike, I've read everything you gave me. Astrology! I'm sorry, Mike, but you're fired."

"Sir, Jess Barrett and Bill Gustofson—yes, and Dr. Mandelbaum, too—have accepted the accuracy of

313

Miss Norman's predictions!" Micah took off his glasses and stared at them as he listened. Mandelbaum stood up and offered his hand for the phone. Micah shook his head; the president would not listen. "Well, then," he said, desperate, "will *you* at least leave Washington? The entire administration, Congress, the cabinet, the whole government will be wiped out."

"You're tired, Mike, all of you are tired. You know me well enough to realize that my decision is irreversible. Good-night." The line went dead.

There was silence in the room. Then Micah muttered, "He believes that we're all too tired to think straight."

"You said there were two things for us to try. What's the other?"

"Jess, we've got to sabotage the power grid. It means we go to prison, if not an asylum, but it's better than letting millions of people die."

"Mike, I checked it out. There's no way we could do enough damage to the grid to cause a blackout. After the trouble in sixty-five, they installed a foolproof system."

"Then there's nothing. If the police don't find him, we're through."

Mandelbaum said, "Gentlemen, Miss Norman, I am a doctor, not a police officer. I'm also tired, so I'm going to bed. If I can help in any way, please call me." The huge man stood and, nodding, left the room.

Petersen said, "Brad and I are going out on the street—after one stop to investigate a bar I know that serves unwatered Scotch. You can always get us on the radio. We'll be cruising all night."

Micah waved, and they left.

"There's a third possibility."

"What is it, Vera?"

"Dr. Mandelbaum gave me an idea. I've been trying to find the chart of the woman Smith is looking for. I'm convinced he won't kill the city until he's found her.

"I've been trying combinations of aspects to his Mars, the planet of sex, and his moon, the women in his life. I've assumed he'd be searching for some sex-pot.

"But I'm still not seeing him as a real human being! Depraved as he is, he's still a Leo, like dear old Dr. Mandelbaum. He won't go for someone beautiful and dumb. He wants a woman of his intellectual caliber. I must begin all my studies from Mercury and find a chart related to his mind. And it must be one showing as much stress as his."

"Can you do it?"

"Mike, I know I can if I have time. It's so *late!* Can you take me home right away? I need my computer."

"Certainly—and Vera, we'll stay with you while you work."

"Oh, Mike, that'd just make me nervous. Give me some time and silence to concentrate. That's the way I work best. I'll call you if I get something."

They were soon on the way to her brownstone. When they pulled up, Mike took out a card and wrote a telephone number on it. "We'll be at this number. It's the local terminal for the National Data Center. If you find anything, call us immediately; we'll get her name and address from the computer and be on our way to her in seconds." He looked into her eyes. "It's up to you, Vera. No one else can stop him."

Vera nodded. Jess walked with her up the steps to the door; she opened it and entered. Lights went on in her second-floor office immediately.

The National Data Center terminal was in the forties, in the back offices of a company that ran a normal business most of the time. Tonight the street was dark and empty, with only the ghostly echoes of daytime activity to break the hush. Even with the congestion caused by the manhunt, once darkness fell, the crowds disappeared like frightened children. It was unnerving.

They rang the night bell, Micah showed his credentials, and the three men were admitted. They went directly to the console room, where Jess began at once to

315

study the operating manual. After a few minutes, he shut the thick book and put it back on the shelf.

"No trouble. The system's complicated, but the directions are clear. This machine can locate anybody in the country, and it's programmed for giving information on a tremendous number of items by many methods because it was set up for statistical purposes. By that I mean if you give it a person's name, it'll hand you all the information you want; or you can ask for all men over forty-five in New York, for example, and it can tell you their names, addresses, and so forth.

"When we get the birth date, we'll ask the machine to list all the women born on that date. And then," said Jess, "we'll just hope there aren't too many of them living in New York City."

The only sound was the humming of an electric clock and the swishing of the air conditioner that kept the computer at precisely the correct temperature. The vast number of components hidden under the hoods and machine covers produced a great deal of heat, and the air conditioning was vital to their continued operation.

The machinery here was used principally for the normal operations of the business. But with certain adjustments and the correct call numbers, the machine became a terminal with access to the huge memory units in Washington.

The machines were cool-colored silver and white and pale blue. Over the console, glittering figures in green light slid across a dark screen as Jess played with the keyboard.

Micah drifted into thinking about the murderer, picturing him out there in the darkness, peering at his watch, waiting until the moon reached her exact aspect. How had he eluded them? One little man, about to destroy a nation that had shown great promise in the world.

"I'm going to ask it about me." Jess tapped out on the keyboard, CALL NATIONAL DATA CENTER. The letters appeared above him, bright green on the dark screen. Then, without a sound, the machine wrote back. DATA

AUTHORIZATION NUMBER. Jess looked at the card Micah had given him and tapped out the number. It, too, appeared above on the screen. Then he asked it for everything on Dr. Jess Barrett.

He swore at the amount of information the machine had on him, asked Micah if it was really constitutional, yet admitted he was glad it existed for tonight. Finally he left the machine and sat down in one of the comfortable armchairs. "What time is it?"

"One thirty."

"Five and a half hours. Hard to believe, isn't it?"

"The whole thing, from the beginning to now, is all impossible to believe."

"But you believe it, Mike."

"Yes, I do."

"Do you think he's really going to try it?"

"Yes, I guess I do think so."

Gus also nodded his agreement.

Silence.

"Where's the phone? Will we hear it if it rings?"

"It's right here, Jess."

"Oh, yes, of course."

Gustofson had chosen a cushioned chair and sunk into it. Now he began to snore.

Jess smiled at him and shook his head. "Mike, do you think he can sleep because he has so much confidence in Vera, or because he's bushed?"

"Neither. I think he's sleeping because he has incredible mental control. There is nothing he can do, so he sleeps. If he thought he could help, he'd be wide awake and firing out ideas a mile a minute."

The two were silent again.

"Jess, do you believe in astrology? It's still hard for me."

"I'll tell you one thing, Mike. If she pulls us out of this crisis, I'll be the world's most confirmed believer."

"Yes."

Jess looked at the clock. It was two thirty. "Should we call her? See how she's coming along."

"It'd only interrupt her. We'll hear if she gets something."

"If?"

"Precisely, *if*."

Vera went to the open window and took a deep breath. At 2:08 the rain had begun. For an hour it had fallen, till the dirty New York air was washed and fresh.

She looked out to the east and saw that the black sky was turning purple. In the little yard behind her house, birds in the tree branches were already chirping. It was nearly morning, and she had not found the answer she sought.

The sun would soon rise over the horizon, and Mars, its escort now, would not be far behind. Despite the lethal implications, Vera could not help being glad that morning was almost here. She had never enjoyed the night. She hated artificial light and loved to rise early and throw open drapes to let the sunlight stream in.

Daylight would be especially welcome this morning, for tonight she had panicked. She had tried one thing after another, all pivoting around Mercury, because she was convinced that Smith would choose his bride because of her mind. But there were still so many possibilities, an almost endless procession of them, and she was worn out.

She stood at the open window, trying to regain her composure. It was terrifying to think that she was the last chance millions of people had for life. But somehow, seeing that the sun was rising heartened her.

She went back to her console. The faint glow of the computer terminal accentuated the lines in her face, making her look much older than her thirty-two years. Her desk was littered with signs of the battle she had fought all night. There were papers and ephemerides and coffee cups. The printer for the computer had disgorged a dozen feet of paper covered with symbols and figures, now scattered over the floor. Here and there Vera had torn off pieces, so that it looked as if a mouse had nibbled it.

She stared at the last chart she had forced out of the machine. Even as she read it, she knew her mistake, knew what prevented her from getting the chart she wanted. She had been looking for a chart of someone whom Smith would love and marry. She had applied traditional concepts to the problem, and they were not applicable. No sane person would marry Smith, and no normal person could love him.

So this was the last leg of her journey. She had the answer now, in principle at least. It was only a matter of time.

A matter of time. She looked at her watch: 5:10. Vera picked up Smith's chart and studied it. She was no longer seeking a woman with aspects of love and sexual attraction to Smith. She was looking for the one who was tied to him by destiny. Quickly now she fed more and more information into the computer, reading from the charts that appeared on the terminal screen.

As she received new information, Vera dictated into her tape recorder. She hated to take notes, preferring to dictate and play back the tape.

She had only one more step: She had to draw a relationship chart. An astrologer in Denver many years before had worked out a method of doing this by taking the charts for two people who were closely related and combining them, using the midpoint between their two Mars as the Mars in the relationship chart, the midpoint between their two moons as the moon of the combined chart, and so forth. The resulting chart revealed amazing things. When the midpoints came under stress, things happened in the marriage or friendship.

Vera had to work backward. She had to look for points of stress in a chart drawn for the moment, pin those to Smith's chart, then measure off equal distances to find the chart of the woman he was seeking. But then she needed the data she had fed into her recorder. She pushed the Playback button.

319

Her voice came to her with flawless reproduction. As she received the information from the recorder, she punched it into the keyboard of the computer.

Suddenly the recorder screamed, cried at her. The sound was like a wail of pain. It was the sound Jess and Micah and Gustofson knew so well: the sound broadcast over Bensonville, the sound that destroyed Bridgeton and erased the tape on Smith's cassette recorder. But Vera, never having heard it, didn't know its meaning.

She grimaced and pushed the Stop button. She punched the Rewind button, then the Play. This time there was no trace of her own voice, only the lonely, painful wail. She hit the recorder with her hand, played it again. The same sound. Panic swept over her.

"What a time to have *you* fail me. I need you, recorder." She knew nothing of electronics and couldn't even try to repair the machine. Quickly she hauled out the *Yellow Pages,* found the section "Tape Recorders—Repair." She hesitated. Should she call Jess? No, he was downtown in the computer room, and besides, if he came, she would be distracted. Better to call for service.

She glanced at the clock, and her heart chilled. Her fingers flew over the dial. The All-Night Repair Service answered almost immediately.

"Hello." The voice was bored and sleepy.

"Hello, my tape recorder has broken down, and I desperately need the information on the tape. Can you send someone over immediately to fix it?"

"You'll have to bring it in, lady. Our shop's open all night, but we don't make calls. Or I can have somebody come for it first thing this morning."

"No! Wait! I need it fixed now. I'll pay anything you ask, but please come right away."

"Lady, do you realize what time it is? It's only half past six, and I'm here alone. The boss would kill me if I walked out of here."

"Please, I'll explain it to him, but come and help me! It really is a matter of life and death!"

"Lady, I just can't. I—"

"Please! Listen! This is Vera Norman. Have you ever heard of me?"

"Vera Norman, the astrologer? Really?"

"Yes, and I've been up all night working on a problem I have to solve immediately. The information I need is on the tape, and there's something wrong with my recorder. Will you come?" She gave him the address.

"I'll be right there."

He hung up, and Vera breathed a sigh of relief. She snapped off all the lights, for the sunlight now flooded the room. Then she returned to the console and studied the half-made chart. The longer she looked, the more she remembered what she had put on the tape. Just a couple of items and she'd have it.

Desperately she tried to recall the data on the recorder. She knew Jess and Micah had to have the birth date soon or there wouldn't be time to find the woman, and it was late, terrifyingly late! Panic reached for her, but she fought it down. Then she remembered one of the figures she needed, put it on the machine, looked for another in the ephemeris on her desk, fed that into the computer. Now she was close. Very close. She punched the computer for the trial chart. It came on the screen.

The telephone rang. It was Petersen.

"Miss Norman, Jess told me how you're going to find that woman. It's almost time. Have you got her birth date yet?"

"No, but I'm so close! I know I can get it! I'll call Jess and Micah at the computer center in a minute. I just hope Smith hasn't found her first!"

"Well, we need that date right now—"

Vera almost screamed in her frustration and panic. "I *know*, but I can't get it while I talk to you on the phone!"

"Sorry, Miss Norman. But when you do, tell Jess to call me on the radio, and I'll move instantly."

She slammed the receiver down and rushed to the console. Her heart was pounding. It was 6:45. "There just isn't time!" Her whole body felt weak.

The doorbell rang.

"Oh *damn!*"

She dashed down the stairs to the front door, opened it. The repairman was small and young, and his long blond hair spread over his shoulders. A scarlet headband held it out of his eyes. He wore blue overalls and carried what must be his tools in a large black bag that resembled a suitcase.

He smiled at her. "Miss Norman? Where's your recorder?"

Vera pointed upstairs. "It made a terrible noise. See what you can do."

He turned to climb the stairs, and she flicked the lock off the door so Joanie could come in without disturbing her at the console.

Upstairs, the youth bent over the recorder, took off the head cover, examined the recording and erase heads.

She fed what she believed to be the last figure she needed into the computer, pushed the button for the final calculations.

The chart she had been seeking for four days and nights blinked onto the screen in bright green figures. She stared at it avidly, checking out stress points, points of contact with Smith's chart. It was the one she wanted.

Now she had only to go back through the ephemeris to the date when the planets had that position. Of course, the heavy planets, the slow-moving ones, told her immediately the approximate date. Then the position of Mars brought it nearer, the sun told her the woman was a Virgo and—

Her spine had turned to water; her breath and heartbeat seemed suspended.

The chart she was staring at was a familiar one. It was the first chart she had ever done.

It was her own.

Terror such as she had never known gripped her. Her hands flew to the piles of paper beside the console. She drew out the magazine giving the hourly planetary positions, looked at the position of the moon, at her chart, then at her watch. It was 6:50.

"Oh, thank God!" she said aloud. "Thank God! He missed me! He should have found me twenty minutes ago!"

Her heart began to beat again, and she fumbled for a tissue to wipe her damp brow. But then, inexplicably, the terror returned. Her teeth began to chatter, and her hands were cold and weak. Perhaps it was the unearthly silence. She suddenly felt that she was being watched. Her skin crawling, her hair almost literally standing on end, she turned.

The repairman was staring at her, his eyes bright, a thin-lipped smile on his face. He reached up and took off the blond wig.

"Please forgive the ridiculous hair, but it was necessary to evade the police."

24

JESS FOUGHT THE PANIC welling up within him. It was so very late. Even if Vera determined the woman's birth date, they might have hundreds of names to go through before they found the one they needed. Then they had to reach her before Smith did.

It was intolerable to sit here so helplessly while the killer was consulting his watch and eagerly anticipating the moment. Jess felt like a prisoner waiting for his jailers to come and carry him to the guillotine.

He jumped to his feet and smashed a fist into the palm of his hand. "Mike, we've got to call her. There isn't any time left."

"If she had it, she'd have called. She didn't make it."

"I can't believe it's really going to happen. It's so impossible."

"Exactly. It's beyond our capacity to believe. Here was one man pitted against the entire police force of New York, treasury agents, the FBI, federal marshals, MPs, heaven knows who else. One man—he's going to win."

"And I had him in my hand once!" Jess squeezed that hand, imagining the little man's throat snapping in the grip of his fingers. "So many 'ifs' in this thing. If only I'd known in Bensonville; if only McDonald had seen Smith's picture before he met him."

"Where is Jim? He wasn't at the meeting last night."

"The poor guy's been out on the streets, cruising around in his car trying to infiltrate radical groups. He still believes he'll find out who the 'Commie' is. You know, he wasn't always that way. But this thing unhinged him, brought out the worst."

"And now he loses his final battle."

"We all lose this one. Our country loses."

Micah said, defeated, "Our world loses." He was slumped down in his chair, his usually taut, alert figure drained by despair.

"My God, Mike, I can't stand this waiting! I'm going to Vera's, see if I can help."

"Jess, then we wouldn't have anybody to run this machine if she called. You've got to stay."

So for a while they just sat there as Gus snored.

"What time is it, Jess?"

"Six forty-nine."

"It's too late. Even if she gets us the date, it's too late. Do you suppose Smith might call off Armageddon because he can't discover his girl friend either?"

Jess rubbed his stubbled chin. "I don't think so, Mike. Vera said he *would* find her just at the time he was ready to—"

"Goddamnit, Jess, this *can't* happen! There must be something we've overlooked!" Micah paced back and forth.

"Call, Vera, call!" Jess pleaded. Suddenly his face froze. "Mike, you remember how we talked about finding the needle in the haystack by using a magnet?"

"Sure. Vera's looking for the woman who's the magnet that'll pull Smith out of the haystack."

"Right, but we didn't stop to wonder how *Smith* is going to identify her. How does he pick her out of the whole city of New York, if she's really here?"

"Yes, how's he to find *his* needle in the haystack? He has a bigger job than we have."

"Mike, how do *you* think he would find her?"

"I presume he'd use the same method Vera's using: astrology. She says he's a genius at it."

"We have this data center. If Vera locates the girl's chart and birth date, we can get her name, have something to go on. But Smith just started looking, too, in the last couple of weeks! Even if he has her chart, he can't trace her in such a short time."

"Jess, you're right! And Vera said he wouldn't plug

in his machine until he'd found her and given her some kind of protection. Maybe that means he won't commit his mass murder after all."

"No, Vera said he will discover her. But dammit, how?"

"What about the other way to learn where the needle is, Jess—burn up the haystack? Which could mean he's planning to destroy the East and look for his mate among the few survivors."

"No," said Jess doggedly, "she said positively that he'd find her *before* the destruction." Then he stood up with a roar that roused Gus out of his sleep. "Oh, no! How could I be so damn stupid? We've had it all backwards! He's not the needle; he's the magnet!"

"What?" snapped Gus, wide awake.

"Smith used his murders to pull out of the haystack the one needle—the only woman—worthy of him. The one brilliant enough to find him. McDonald innocently gave him Vera's name—"

"Merciful God," breathed Micah, his skin going sick white. "You've hit it. He called her 'a superwoman.'"

"Then why didn't he go right to her?" Gus began to argue.

"He'd be leery of venturing into the streets till he had to," said Micah. "We never even thought to give her a guard—"

Jess bolted for the door, scooping up the car keys as he ran, shouting over his shoulder. "I'll call Petersen on the radio!"

Micah raced after him. "Jess! Too late to save us —but if you catch him, *kill him,* or he'll murder the world!"

The enormous limousine screamed away from the curb, hurtled up the almost empty avenue. By the end of the second block, Jess was doing eighty and still accelerating. He groped for the unfamiliar radio switch, couldn't find it, swore, slammed both hands on the wheel and barely avoided ramming a taxi, fumbled blindly for the switch. He had a long way to go.

Micah looked at his watch.

There were less than twelve minutes left.

Jim McDonald had both radios on as he cruised the streets of Manhattan, one tuned to the federal frequency and one to the police. When he heard Jess's bellowing frantic call to Petersen, he swung his car around in a hard U-turn. He was cold sober this morning, and his nerves were steady. He took the Magnum out of its holster and laid it on the seat beside him. The big car picked up speed with ferocious disdain of all laws and obstacles. But he, too, had a long way to go, and now there were five minutes left.

Petersen and Adams were even farther away from Vera's brownstone when Jess finally came on the air. Petersen stepped heavily on the gas pedal and called the police. It was then that he learned of a vicious gang fight that had erupted in Central Park, drawing off every patrol car within thirty blocks.

"A gang fight at seven in the morning?" Petersen howled. "What kind of a crazy city are you running here? O.K., just get on the horn and yank somebody off it, down to that address on West Seventy-fifth. By order," he added hastily, "of Micah Maruyama." He looked at Brad Adams. "Can you imagine it?" he said, turning a corner on two wheels. "Seven A.M. and somebody invades somebody else's turf?"

"Maybe Smith arranged it," suggested Adams.

"No," said Petersen, "that girl's converted me. It's the full moon."

Vera was shaking, her mouth was dry, her stomach knotted. The murderer had found what he had sought.

When he dropped the wig, she wondered, even in her fear, why she hadn't recognized him. He looked exactly like the picture the artist had drawn from the Hoffman photo and Jess's recollections. The youthful appearance vanished with the wig, leaving a tired and haggard man.

"You know who I am," he said, "since you're the one who tracked me down."

He waited for a moment for her to speak, but she

327

could not. She watched him in horrified fascination. He looked so ordinary—meager and perhaps a little soft, his chin weak—but his voice strong and cold. "I knew you'd find me, of course. I saw it in my progressions. I'm an astrologer, too, but far greater than you, greater than Evangeline Adams or even William Lilly."

He walked past her to the computer console. "This is an admirable set-up, but you won't need it any longer." He pushed a button, and the console lights went out. He looked at the print-out paper with its endless charts, smiled at his own and then at hers.

"You finally discovered that you're the one I was seeking. It took you long enough. I see I have a great deal to teach you about astrology. I've known of you for months. I didn't have your name till twelve days ago, but I didn't need it. The woman with this chart would be brilliant enough to find me."

His voice rose slightly. "Why do you gape like that? Are you so confused? Because you think of me only as a murderer? Jephthah Smith, who single-handed destroyed three cities, who will in a few minutes wipe out eighty million beasts who encumber the earth! Then you don't realize who I am."

Vera was desperately trying to conceive of a way to stop him. She must not panic; she must *think*. "Who are you? I know your genius, what you plan, but I don't know why you're doing these terrible things."

He chuckled indulgently, the sound like ice in her brain. "You have so much to learn, but I'll teach you; you have the capacity to understand. You'll eventually be worthy."

"Worthy of what?"

"Worthy of the world!" he said quietly, his slim body straight. Then softer still, "The consort of the new Adam, the avenging Messiah."

"Messiah?" she repeated dully.

"Of the Aquarian Age. This time the Christ comes, not in compassion, but in wrath." He caught her by the wrist. She was aware of his fingers trembling with nervous elation. "First my father sent the Piscean Christ, gentle and self-sacrificing, and decreed that man should

328

have an age—two thousand years—in which to learn to walk the earth in love. But they failed to heed his teachings. Now my father has sent me, the Aquarian Christ, to destroy humanity as in the days of Noah. This time, though, he won't leave the establishing of a new race to a drunken fool like Noah; *I* shall be the new Man of the Aquarian Age." The voice was even softer.

Vera's thoughts raced. By feeding his diseased ego, could she lead him past the time of the fatal aspect? "What will your new age be like?"

He shook his head in a mockery of forbearance. "You, Vera Norman, an astrologer, a leader of the people, ask me what it will be like?" he said. "In the Piscean Age, God sent his gentle son to teach men to love one another and practice war and crime no more, isn't that so? And look at them. They never slew and robbed and lied and enslaved with such abandon! Talking unctuously of 'love,' they tortured and starved and degraded one another, lavished their highest intelligence on weapons. Is there a word vile enough to describe what man has become?

"So I persuaded my father that this age should be mine, and through me, his," he said obliquely. She nodded and noticed that one eye had a peculiar cast. "I am the Aquarian Christ," he said softly, "the man of technology, of invention, of reason. I do not establish my dominion on anything so flimsy and ambiguous as 'love.' But reason—" His voice trailed off as he glanced at his watch.

"But why not teach men your ideas, lead them into the new age, instead of destroying them?"

"They're unworthy," he said abruptly. "I have been treated as my brother Jesus was: despised, injured, *used*. They will be treated like the demon-possessed Gadarene swine they are." He tugged at her wrist. "We must get away from this place. Someone may come, and I can't be seen. The time is very short." He looked into her eyes; he had to tip his chin up to do it. "Why were you so *slow?*" he whispered. "With a computer,

329

all the facts, and you took so long to do it! Didn't you realize that you *had* to find me?"

"But you knew who I was twelve days ago," she said.

"But surely you read in the stars that it was *you* who must make contact with *me? I* saw that in my progressions, solunar charts, transits."

"And you were waiting at the All-Night Repair Service—"

He laughed shortly. "I tapped into your line. Whoever you called, you'd have gotten me. Come on. We don't have much time."

Perhaps she could scratch that cold, mad pride. "Where are we going?"

He dropped her arm and stared at her. "The birds of the air have their nests, the foxes of the field their holes; but I have no place to lay my head. Until I come into my kingdom, there will be hardship, persecution." He was silent for a moment, his eyes on the floor. Then he lifted them, bright with fanatic elation. "Yes, when my day arrives, and those who are left alive bow down and serve me, I'll live in a palace of gold and onyx. Till then, you'll share my sufferings; in these hard days when I'm cleansing the earth, you'll hunger and thirst, Vera Norman, but you'll have *me*." He took her hand. "You'll love and serve me and learn from me," he said quietly.

In her mind Vera saw a horrifying image of this maniac making love to her. But she had to keep him occupied until the dangerous aspect had passed. He glanced again at his watch and said, "The time's near. We have less than four minutes. Come on."

Her skin crawled, and nausea almost overcame her. Then Micah's words came back to her.

"It's up to you, Vera. No one else can stop him."

Only one stratagem might work, might jam the delicate and finely tuned instrument that was his mind. He had existed without love from his birth, and sex had never entered his life. Now, with the aspects from Mars, he would be susceptible. She must try seduction.

She was revolted, but she gripped the thin hand that held her fingers, pushed herself against the taut body

330

that repelled her, pressing her breasts against his chest, and kissed him on the mouth.

She fought off another spasm of nausea, deliberately closed her eyes. Her mind spun into a gulf of black despair, and vertigo clutched at her.

She wriggled against him. He held her for a moment, then—"No, there's no time now, we must go!"

"But—"

He threw up his head. "What's that?" he said, and thrust her off and leaped into the hall, peering down toward the front door. In that split second, Vera whirled around, saw her heavy bronze paperweight, snatched it up and held it behind her. Smith stood watching and listening; then he came back to her. "I thought I heard the door open. Come on, we must hurry."

She pushed against him again, opening her mouth to kiss him as fiercely and seductively as she knew how. She felt him relax a little, only a little. She swung the paperweight at his head with all her strength.

It didn't come within a foot of hitting him. She never felt its impact. Instead, sudden pain and darkness. His hard blow across her mouth with the back of his hand sent her sprawling into the center of the room. When she picked herself up, she saw her own blood from a split lip spattered on the computer print-out sheets that lay on the floor. How could anyone's reaction be so devastating, explosive, immediate?

"You filthy bitch," he said very quietly, watching her. "You aren't worthy." Deliberately, he placed his foot on her stomach, then quickly shifted his weight. She screamed. "You're a hypocrite," he said, "and you'll die like the others."

He went to his tool bag, keeping an eye on her, though under no circumstances could she have struggled to her feet. He reached in with both hands, heaved upward as if lifting a heavy object, and brought out a black box. Vera stared at it in horror. Jess had suggested that it might be no larger than a suitcase, but this thing was about a foot long and five inches wide. He held it up in his hands.

"Look at it. It's killed three towns. Now it's ready for its greater work."

He held it in one hand and let his fingers run over its smooth surface with fondness, tracing the contours of the sealed edges. There were no screws, no indication of how it had been put together. Vera could see a switch on one face and a double prong on another.

Jephthah Smith knelt and pushed the prongs into the electric outlet beside the door. There was an audible *thunk,* and the device seemed to become part of the wall.

He pulled a white capsule from his shirt. "This would have given you immunity," he said. "You could have watched them all dying around you." He dropped it and ground it under his heel on the black-and-white vinyl tile. Then he looked at his watch.

"Time," he said and laid his hand on the toggle switch.

She had to stop him. Surely she must be as strong as he. She was half a head taller, and he looked soft and unexercised. But the power with which he had struck her! Even so—

Gathering herself against the pain, she lunged up, fingers clawing for his eyes. He caught her wrist and disdainfully flung her across the room. She fell again.

Without even glancing at her, he repeated, "Time," and threw the switch.

"One, two, three, four, five, six," he counted slowly and turned off the machine. Then a pause and, barely audible, "Now you're all dead."

He straightened up. "Damn you," he said, now shrill. "Why couldn't you have *used* your intelligence. I *wanted* you. You should have seen my truth, realized! And now you'll go like the others, festering, rotting away. Did you see them, any of them? In Bensonville, Bridgeton, San Salino? Their faces purple, wheezing for a last breath, covered with sores?"

"Yes," said Jess from the doorway, "I saw them."

Smith whipped around, his eyes big with the shock of it. "You!" he said, taking three or four quick steps backward, shoving a hand into his jacket pocket. As

Jess came at him, Smith shifted sideways, pulled out a snub-nosed .38, and fired quickly. The first slug exploded an antique gilt mirror, the shards spraying out in a broken fan. Smith dropped to one knee and shot again, two-handed; the bullet caught Jess in the leg just under the hipbone, threw him off balance. The next one took him in the middle of the body and hurled him back, grunting at the hot pain. The room crashed with echoes of shots and the woman's screaming. Jess lunged forward again, agonized, relentless. Smith stared at him for an instant, incredulous, and then fired wildly. Jess swiped the .38 out of his hand with a flailing swing, brought his great arm back, and knocked the small man headlong.

Smith rolled into a ball and uncoiled himself instantly, nose and mouth bleeding. Seeing that the gun was too far away to retrieve, he seized a metal gooseneck lamp and came at Jess, shouting wordlessly. Jess caught the lamp, wrenched it from his hand, tossed it away. He gripped the smaller man by the throat and lifted him off his feet. Smith tore frantically at the huge hands as his eyes bulged and his face darkened. His mouth hung open and a dreadful hissing, bubbling sound came from it, like the defiance of a drowning snake.

"Kill him!"

Had Jess heard the words, or was he remembering Micah shouting them after him as he pulled away from the curb?

He stared at Smith for a moment and then, relaxing his hold, let him fall.

"Jess, kill him!" Vera had managed to gain her feet. "He'll wipe out the human race if you let him live. Kill him!"

Jess, swaying, looked down at the growing stains of red on his clothing and at the man who was fighting weakly to get up. Nothing would stay in focus. "Are you all right?" he said to her.

"Jess," she sobbed, "Jess, listen to me—*kill him now!*"

Smith went across the floor on hands and knees, a

trampled spider with life and venom still in him. He picked up the revolver. Standing, choking and spitting blood, he backed toward the door.

"You scum," he said huskily. He bent for his false tool kit, never taking his eyes off Jess, picked it up, and went backward to where the instrument of death was still plugged into the wall outlet.

Vera screamed as loudly as she could, desperate to draw his attention from Jess to herself.

In the distance, sirens wailed.

"You may live a week and die in agony," he told her. "You," he said to Jess, "you won't have the pleasure of whoring with her. I see it in her eyes. You stopped her from recognizing my truth. You die this morning at the hands of me, the Messiah." He raised the .38 as Jess, half conscious, began to stagger toward him.

The sirens were closer.

Petersen jerked open the front door of Vera's house, surprised to find it unlocked. The pistol shot halted him for a second; then the triumphant crow of laughter sent him bounding up the stairs. Brad Adams drew his gun and followed.

The room was a shambles. Jim McDonald bent over Smith's body, still laughing in nerve-racked relief and a kind of unbelieving astonishment, the .44 Magnum dangling from his hand. Vera sat on the floor, Jess's head on her lap. Her face was desolate.

"It's too late," she said to Petersen. She gestured at the black box. "He threw the switch."

McDonald, straightening, said, "I'll fix that," and lifted the big gun and fired and fired, the thing kicking savagely in his hand. The slugs burst the box open, sent wires and bits of metal flying. The noise was dreadful. Petersen reached out and took the .44 from McDonald.

Jephthah Smith writhed halfway off the floor and spat blood at them all. "Generation of vipers," he gasped, "how long must I endure you?" Then he fell on his face.

Petersen went over. "Smith's dead."

Vera was crying, cradling Jess's head. "You couldn't kill him," she said. "Oh, Jess, my dearest, you couldn't kill him."

Outside, the sirens wailed and crescendoed and whined into silence. Footsteps clattered on the stairs, and Micah came in. He looked at Smith's body, saw the scar above the eye gleaming white in the sun. Then he looked at Jess, and all the breath went out of him. Gus entered behind Micah, panting. Police followed.

Petersen's voice was hardly a whisper, but they all heard him.

"We were too late, Dr. Maruyama. He threw the switch."

"Too late," Micah repeated flatly.

Gus crossed to kneel beside Jess, seize a wrist, feel for the pulse. "Will some of you chowderheads help me get this big jock onto that couch?" he demanded angrily. "Adams, call an ambulance! He's lost a lot of blood."

"He's alive?" said Micah. "Alive?"

"For a week, anyway," said Gus. "Then we're all finished. *Come on.*"

Two policemen and Micah lifted Jess from the woman's lap. As they carried him to the enormous sofa, four small glass objects fell from his pocket to clatter and roll on the floor.

Gus picked them up. He held them out toward Micah. "Look."

They were common household fuses.

"Petersen," Micah shouted, "try the lights!"

Half a dozen men were suddenly clicking switches, moving frantically back and forth, trying the lights, the radio, the computer. Nothing worked.

"He went to the basement," said Vera, trembling, touching her face with both hands, unbelieving. "He went to the basement first and pulled the fuses. And he was up here only a few seconds after Smith turned on his machine."

Micah collapsed bonelessly on a chair. "Then the thing, Smith's gadget, didn't—couldn't—work. Without those fuses, he wasn't connected to the grid. He had no electricity." He gazed at the dead man on the floor. "His machine was harmless."

Old Gustofson sat down on the floor beside the couch and patted Jess's motionless arm. Tears streaked his face.

"Well, by God, Jock," he said, "by God!"

NOW A MAJOR MOTION PICTURE

"THE FIRST CRIME MEDICAL"
Kirkus Reviews

GERALD GREEN

THE HOSTAGE HEART

As open-heart surgery begins on millionaire Walter Tench III, armed revolutionaries burst into the operating room—demanding a ransom of ten million dollars in exchange for his life.

The hospital is paralyzed, and the police stand by helplessly as the most terrifying cardiac operation in history is performed on *the hostage heart!*

"THE READER IS TRANSFIXED IN HORRID FASCINATION . . . HYPNOTIZED . . . CARRIED ALONG PAGE BY PAGE WITH BREATHLESS URGENCY."
United Press International

"Fast-moving spine-tingler . . . well written indeed."
The New York Times

 AVON/32037/$1.95   HOST 3-77

THE BIG BESTSELLERS
ARE AVON BOOKS

☐ **Humboldt's Gift** Saul Bellow   29447 $1.95
☐ **The Auctioneer** Joan Samson   31088 $1.95
☐ **The Viking Process** Norman Hartley   31617 $1.95
☐ **The Surface of Earth** Reynolds Price   29306 $1.95
☐ **The Monkey Wrench Gang**
     Edward Abbey   30114 $1.95
☐ **Beyond the Bedroom Wall**
     Larry Woiwode   29454 $1.95
☐ **The Eye of the Storm** Patrick White   21527 $1.95
☐ **Theophilus North** Thornton Wilder   19059 $1.75
☐ **Jonathan Livingston Seagull**
     Richard Bach   14316 $1.50
☐ **The Bellamy Saga** John Pearson   30874 $1.95
☐ **Between Heaven and Earth**
     Laura Huxley   29819 $1.95
☐ **Working** Studs Terkel   22566 $2.25
☐ **Something More** Catherine Marshall   27631 $1.75
☐ **Getting Yours** Letty Cottin Pogrebin   27789 $1.75
☐ **Fletch** Gregory Mcdonald   27136 $1.75
☐ **Confess, Fletch** Gregory Mcdonald   30882 $1.75
☐ **Shardik** Richard Adams   27359 $1.95
☐ **Anya** Susan Fromberg Schaeffer   25262 $1.95
☐ **The Bermuda Triangle** Charles Berlitz   25254 $1.95
☐ **Watership Down** Richard Adams   19810 $2.25

Available at better bookstores everywhere, or order direct from the publisher.

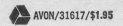 AVON/31617/$1.95

**SLOWLY, AT FIRST,
THEN WITH SHUDDERING
HORROR...YOU EXPERIENCE
THE ULTIMATE
ACT OF TERRORISM!**

THE VIKING PROCESS

NORMAN HARTLEY

"Does for terrorism what Frederick Forsyth did for assassination in THE DAY OF THE JACKAL and John Le Carre did for espionage in THE SPY WHO CAME IN FROM THE COLD. . . . There is no let up on the pace until the very last moment!"
                                                      BOSTON HERALD AMERICAN

SELECTED BY BOOK-OF-THE-MONTH CLUB AND PLAYBOY BOOK CLUB

VIKE 2-77